For Jr.

The future is yours

I believe that we are lost here in America, but I believe we shall be found. And this belief, which mounts now to the catharsis of knowledge and conviction, is for me—and I think for all of us—not only our own hope, but America's everlasting, living dream.

—Thomas Wolfe, You Can't Go Home Again

Perhaps one did not want to be loved so much as to be understood.

—George Orwell, 1984

THE
UNFOLDING

Wednesday, November 5, 2008
The Biltmore Hotel, Second-Floor Bar
Phoenix, Arizona
1:00 a.m.

This can't happen here:

He's been at the bar for ninety minutes; a dozen men have come and gone, having drowned their sorrows, done a little business, and put the whole thing to bed.

There are four whiskey glasses in front of him, each one different, none of them empty.

In one corner the television is on, volume down, the talking head post-mortem will go all night. In the other corner, by the window, there's a couple canoodling like there's no tomorrow. And in the middle of the bar a screwball with a Zippo lighter runs his thumb over the wheel again and again, scratching the flint to spark. "Windproof," he says each time the fuel ignites. "Windproof."

"It's on me as much as anyone," the Big Guy says to the bartender. "Humility if nothing else requires that a man take responsibility for his failures."

"You sound like a man pleading guilty," the bartender says.

"I am guilty."

"No prophet is accepted in his own country; no doctor heals in his own home."

"You're seriously playing that card here?"

"On Saturday nights I work at the casinos, Desert Diamond, Talking Stick. I've seen men give up the ghost right in front of me, and even on their way out, they're still feeling the high. 'Hit me. Hit me again.'"

The Big Guy shakes his head. "All men make mistakes, but making the same mistake twice is not a mistake, it's a pattern. Tonight it was like Fat Man and Little Boy got back together and planted a mushroom garden right here in Phoenix. And yet, somehow, we're surrounded by folks who have no idea what they have brought upon themselves. No idea."

A man slides into the seat next to the Big Guy, glances at the four glasses of whiskey, and signals the bartender.

"Pour me one of those," he says.

"Which one?"

"The one in the middle."

"There is no middle," the bartender says.

"The Highland Park."

The Big Guy looks up. "You can call it in the dark?"

"Slainte," the man says, knocking back the drink.

"You're not one of them, are you?"

"One of what?"

"Your hair is wet so I'm thinking you're one of the assholes who got sprayed with champagne and did a little victory dance a couple of hours ago."

"I don't think so," the man says. "I'm more like a fella who came downstairs and took a dip in the pool in order to clear my head."

"Explains the smell," the Big Guy says. "Chlorine."

The man taps his glass for the bartender. "Again."

"Were you in the room upstairs?"

"I was."

"And what did you see?" the Big Guy asks.

"A generational earthquake that split the terra firma."

The Big Guy snorts.

"I would characterize it as a heavy metal Led Zeppelin, a grim shaking of the head, the palsied all-too-knowing dip of disappointment, keening women knowing they'll have crushed male egos to deal with for break-fast. The damp, dull face of defeat. They banked on the wrong horse in the absence of a better horse while full well knowing it wasn't even a horse race but really a rat race."

"Please, tell me you're not a reporter."

"Historian, sometimes professor, occasional author, but not on the clock tonight."

"If you're not on the clock, why are you here?"

"Bearing witness?" the man suggests. "Fella traveler?"

The Big Guy flags the bartender. "Give him the Ardbeg. It's one of my favorites. I call it Santa's Paws, tastes like it crawled out of the fireplace. Smoky."

The man laughs. "Similar to Lagavulin."

"Similar. I'll tell you what I don't like, a scotch that's fruity. I don't want anything that's got raisins, cherries, or essence of Fig Newton. That's what I call a stool softener." The Big Guy belches. "Pardon me," he says. "I'm in a little deeper than I thought."

"They should just burn it down," the screwball with the Zippo says, flipping his lighter into the gun position, letting the flame go high and then slapping the lighter closed.

The bartender goes over and asks the screwball to settle his tab. "It's been a long night for everyone," he says. "Time to go home."

"There's no place like home," Zippo says, standing up. "Every dog is a lion at home." He peels twenties off a thick wad of cash, knocks back the rest of his drink, leaving the money under the empty glass.

As Zippo wobbles out of the room, the Big Guy taps his glass. "Ardbeg again for me and my friend."

The bartender pours.

"You want to know what I've been writing?" the Big Guy asks.

"Yeah," the man says.

"My memory of the dream."

"The dream?"

The Big Guy nods. "September 2, 1945, my introduction to the world."

"V-J Day?"

"I was literally born into it. The war ended and the American dream came into bloom with my name written all over it. You know what I've been saying all night? 'This can't happen here.' But it did. And it's not the first time. Happened eight years ago as well, but that time we took it back. This go-round there is no rescue plan."

The two men drink.

"What do you call that?" the Big Guy says, nodding toward the couple in the corner.

"Wound licking," the man says.

"It hasn't progressed. Two hours and they're still like that."

"They're married but not to each other," the man says. "They can get away with what they're doing now, call it grief counseling, but if they take it upstairs, it becomes something else."

"You a married man?"

"No. I would say that I am devoted to my work, but that wouldn't be true either."

"Been here before?" the Big Guy asks.

"Do you mean literally here in this bar?"

"Yes."

"I have," the man says. "As a kid, I came here with my father. There was a special knock to get in or at least that's what my father told me."

"Back in the day, the liquor used to be kept in a false bookshelf," the Big Guy says. "You see that skylight up there? If trouble was coming, they'd shine a light over the roof and the fellas would skedaddle. I'm not sure that was Mr. Wright's intention when he designed it."

"I thought it was Wrigley, like the gum."

"Frank Lloyd Wright designed it. Wrigley bought it in 1930 and put in the pool. People used to come out for the season. There was an office of the New York Stock Exchange downstairs. This was the Smoking Room. You might say I'm a bit of a history buff," the Big Guy says. "If you wanted to get in you had to know the password."

"What was the password?"

"It changed frequently."

"Was it something like 'It's raining on Mount Weather'?"

The Big Guy looks at him. Mount Weather is not a run-of-the-mill noun one simply drops into conversation. "Oh Shenandoah," the Big Guy lobs back.

"High Point," the man says, replying with another watchword.

"The squirrel got the nut," the Big Guy says.

"I left my suitcase on a train," the man says.

"You two quoting poetry to each other?" the bartender asks.

"Just singing the same song," the man says.

"Sniffing each other out to see if we're members of the same club," the Big Guy says. "I don't think I got your name?"

"I didn't give it." There's a pause. "What did you expect tonight?"

"More," the Big Guy says. "I expected more."

"Hope," the man says. "That's what he offered them and they went for it. Hope won over More."

The two men are quiet for a moment, nursing their drinks.

"I'll tell you something," the Big Guy says, looking around as if making sure it's safe to reveal a secret. "There are two cycles for political business in this country; one is eighteen months and the other is four years. We talk about the 'next go-round' like we're buying tickets on a theme-park ride. Democracy, the roller coaster. It goes up a couple of hundred feet and then plunges at a hundred miles an hour and what do people do? They get in line to go again. And again. Up and down, each time their stomachs drop; you can't escape biology; each time they feel the rush. Eighteen months. Four years. Other countries plan one hundred years out. Native Americans talk about what things will look like seven generations from now—one hundred fifty years. What do we talk about? Tax rebates. We give people three hundred bucks to blow and think that seals the deal."

"Continuity," the man says.

"The plan ensures that our government as we know it continues to stand."

"Exactly. It requires a vision."

"The last great vision was the dream."

"Bye, bye, Miss American Pie," the man says.

"It's time to get the program going. The program is the plan. You know what I'm talking about?"

"Give me another hint," the man says.

"Extraordinary circumstances," the Big Guy says. "There is a moment when you have to be ready to take action. You can't rely on others. This is the kind of story you tell your children; it's about the night you woke up, realized that things were not what they seemed, and you did something about it."

"What are we going to do?" the man asks.

"Something big," the Big Guy says, showing the pile of napkins he's been making notes on. "A forced correction."

The man finishes his drink.

"Gimme your number." The Big Guy pushes a clean napkin toward the man. "Let's stay in touch. A fella like you is a good man to have around and I suspect we have a thing or two in common."

"We've never met," the man says, preparing to leave. "But I look forward to another sing-along soon."

"Are you working on anything in particular at the moment?" the Big Guy asks.

The man shrugs. "A book. It's a brief history of the twenty-first century called *Thus Far*."

"So you're a historian but really more of a scribe."

"Till soon," the man says, leaving cash on the bar.

"Hell of a guy," the Big Guy says to the bartender. "Knows all the songs." A moment passes. "Any chance the kitchen is still open?"

"What are you looking for?"

"Soft-boiled eggs and toast soldiers?"

"Let me see what I can do."

"And pass me some more of those napkins; I've got to get it down on paper." The Big Guy scrawls in blue pen, "A patriot's plan to preserve and protect. Double Rainbows with Cherries on Top." He sketches what looks like a football play chart; two rows of players that look like red cherries in a U-shaped lineup guarding the Liberty Bell.

One by one the Big Guy finishes the drinks in front of him. It's after two a.m. when room service arrives with a dome-covered plate. Voilà. The bartender lifts the dome. "Tits up," the Big Guy says, looking at the beautiful pair of soft-boiled eggs staring up at him.

The bartender laughs. "You're more fun than you look."

"In my cups," the Big Guy says. "I am in my cups." He taps his spoon against one of the eggs; the first blow lands on the silver egg cup, sounding the alarm. He continues tap-tapping, sending the message "We are no longer safe" in Morse code. Until finally, the shell cracks.

The Day Before
Tuesday, November 4, 2008
Laramie County, Wyoming
6:08 a.m.

Earth and sky are open and endless. As the brightness increases, the sky flushes with pink and red hues somewhere between birth and Armageddon.

She steps outside to be alone. The air has the clean snap of winter to come. She's thinking about the sky, the distance to the river, the mountains, the great unfolding of land. Even if one has no particular religious belief, the enormity of it is a spiritual experience. It reminds her to remain in awe as she faces into the wind. The ground, coated in frosty white dust, cracks underfoot. She hears her parents behind her, leaving the house.

"As long as you're happy," her mother says.

"Thrilled," her father says. "I'm absolutely thrilled. We'll be among the first."

Sonny, the ranch hand, is at the wheel, the scent of his morning cigarette leaking out of the cracked car window.

The bison are at the fence, their enormous eyes like great black globes of history, of memory, their wide nostrils pumping out air like steam pipes. She thinks of them as ancient animals somewhere between bull and minotaur.

The tires roll over the cattle guards, ka-thunka, ka-thunka, a marker between home and the rest of the world. She watches over her father's shoulder in the rearview mirror as the ranch recedes.

It seems strange: Yesterday she was at school in Virginia giving a report on the three witches in *Macbeth*. After class, she took a taxi to the airport and got on a plane that landed late last night. Now she is here, in a car, with her mother and father, on the opposite side of the country. There are many Americas; the language and the brand of orange juice might be the same, but they are very different places.

"I remember my first time," her father says. "My father took me."

"It was centuries ago," her mother says, laughing.

"Is it that funny?" her father asks.

"Did you go by horse-drawn carriage?" she asks.

"Actually, we walked," her father says.

"I'm just realizing that I didn't even register until after I was married to you. I wonder why I didn't participate then?"

There's a beat. A moment of silence.

"How'd you sleep?" her father asks her.

"Like a log." She'd gone upstairs, cracked her window, and let the night air slip in like the plume from a genie's bottle. The cold air, a little chimney smoke, the dirt and dung of animals on the farm, a couple of deep breaths, and she was out. "As soon as I get here, it's like I'm under anesthesia." She pauses and realizes he's waiting for a compliment. "And the warm milk was very good, thank you."

"Fresh air, fresh milk, you don't need much else."

"The cookies," she says. "Night cookies."

"I don't sleep well without them," her father says.

They are quiet as the car rolls toward town.

"Is it always on a Tuesday?" she asks, when the silence has become too loud.

"Yes," her mother says.

"For a reason?"

"For the reason that it has always been on a Tuesday," her father says.

Her mother scoffs. "I'm sure the men who originally picked the day had something more in mind than the idea that two hundred years later people would say that it's always been that way."

"Well then, look it up," her father says.

"Will it be crowded?"

"In some places they stand in line for hours," her father says.

"Not here," her mother says. "In this place three people is a line, five is a crowd, a dozen is a rock concert."

The car pulls into the church parking lot.

"It's at a church?" she asks, surprised. She secretly loves church: the ritual, the music, spacing out while "reading" the stories in the stained glass.

"My sentiments exactly," her father says.

"We've been here before," her mother reminds them both. "For the Mason boy's funeral."

"Horrible," her father says. "I don't know how you recover from something like that."

"You don't," her mother says.

They walk down the stairs into the basement.

She realizes that her mother and father are the only people who got dressed up. Her father is wearing a camel-hair topcoat over his suit. He's skipped the tie—but she has no doubt it's in his pocket, just in case. He always keeps a tie in his pocket. These days, after an incident with a melted chocolate Kiss, it's in a Ziploc bag. Her mother is wearing a red coat over a pair of nice slacks. That's what she calls them, "slacks"; it's always "slacks" unless she's going riding, and then they are "dungarees." Neither is dressed in a way that would keep them warm if they had to wait outside. Everyone else is wearing regular clothes: hats, gloves, parkas over long pants. Her own coat bears the symbol of an upscale company on the upper arm. A while ago she put a piece of dark duct tape over it, hoping perhaps that people wouldn't notice.

"Today's the day," someone says.

She feels like she's a small child being delivered for the first day of school.

"The moment is now," another man adds.

"Picked out your turkey for Thanksgiving yet?" her father asks one of the men. She notices that he's guiding the small talk away from the events at hand and toward more generic seasonal chat.

"No, sir," the man says. "This year I'm going to visit my brother up by Seattle."

"Fine man you are." It's charming how pleased her father is to be among these men and women. He's beaming; his excitement is palpable. He shakes hands, any hand he can get hold of. "You have to touch people; you have to look them in the eye and listen to what they have to tell you," he's said to her in the past. "You don't like it but you have to listen. We used to have a word for it—decency."

"Fine day," her father says to another man, who simply nods back.

"Nice to see you," her mother says to one of the women. As they move around the room, both her mother and father greet strangers as though they've met them before.

"Good of you to come out," a man calls out to them.

When she was younger, going places with her parents used to make her feel special; people paid extra attention; she imagined herself as a princess. When she stops to think about it now, she's embarrassed.

"Hello, Mrs. Hitchens."

"Hello, Jane, hello, Meg," her mother says. Other women call her mother Mrs. Hitchens and she calls them by their first names.

"Did your daughter have the baby yet?" Her mother is always asking after babies and young children.

"Soon," the woman says.

She tries her own hand at conversation. "That's a beautiful sweater," she says to one of the women. Her mother smiles, whispers, "Good girl." Her mother raised her with the idea that when women are together they talk about what they've made, their children, clothing, food; and what they've seen, travels, theatre; and if they're in the right crowd, what they've read, books.

"Thank you," the woman says.

"Wonderful colors," her mother chimes in.

Her father moves with a kind of swagger, occupying space in a way that might make you think he is the candidate. But he's not; he's the machine that makes it go—the money.

"Bull in a china shop," her mother once said when she was angry with him, and then she got defensive when Meghan looked shocked. "Well, you don't get rich being mister nice guy," her mother said and left it at that.

"They'll be coming," she hears someone say. "Just before lunch, and then again at the end of the day."

"People are gonna show up for sure; that's what they do when they have something to say."

"Some folks feel it's already been said," another one adds.

"Either way, it shouldn't be optional," one of the men says. "It should be legally required; if you're of age, you're required. That's just my opinion, but no one gives a hoot what I think."

"Folks don't like to be told what to do."

"You'd think they'd want as many people as possible to participate," another man says.

"A little naïve," her father whispers. "It's always interesting to hear how common people see it."

"Why do you say 'common people'?" she asks.

He looks confused. "What should I say?"

"Just people?" she says. "When you say 'common people,' it sounds like you see yourself as different from everyone else."

"I am different," he says. "I'm rich and proud of it. Common people should be glad to see me and be happy when I buy their products and eat in their restaurants; it's a sign of approval."

"Whose approval?"

"My approval."

"And because you're rich, your approval means more than someone else's?"

"If you were studying for a test, would you take advice from an A student or a C student?" he asks.

"Is this a test?"

"It's life," he says.

"It makes people feel bad, like they're less than equal," she says.

"It's not my job to make people feel equal."

"Are teachers less valuable than doctors? They get paid less; but without teachers, you wouldn't have doctors," she says.

"When I hear the word common, I hear Aaron Copeland's 'Fanfare for the Common Man,'" her mother says. "I attended a performance in New York years ago when you were just a baby." Her mother pauses. "What's nice about a place like this is that people are neighborly; they help out."

"It's the same folks who do everything from organizing the parades to the potlucks. They're the doers," her father says as they move closer to the check-in table. "Did you know that if you're sixteen you can be an election judge? All it takes is being a bona fide county resident, mentally competent, and four days of training before the event. A little pecker-schmecker who can't even tie his shoelaces gets to count things up and call it in. And they get paid; in a town that's not brimming with employment for children, it's not a bad deal."

Then it is their turn. Her parents step up and sign the book. You can see their signatures where they signed the last time—she finds it curious that a person's signature doesn't change over the years.

"Is this your first time, Meghan?" the woman asks, as she inscribes her name in the book.

"Yes."

"Do you know how it works?"

"In theory," she says. "But I do have a question."

The woman nods.

"Do you know why it's on a Tuesday?"

The woman smiles. "I asked my husband the same thing last night. He had no idea, so I looked it up. It turns out the founding fathers had something in mind; by November, the fall harvest was done but the weather was still mild enough for travel. And because folks used to have to travel in order to take part, they couldn't do it on a Monday because people wouldn't travel on the Sabbath, and it couldn't be November first because that's All Saints' Day, and some people care about that and so on." She pauses. There's a line forming behind Meghan. "Anyway, that's what I learned—do you know how this next part works?"

"Not really."

The woman hands Meghan a paper form. "You take this and go on over to one of those booths, make your selections, and then fold it over and bring the paperwork back over there and drop it in the sealed box. Easy-peasy."

The booths are mini stalls with cardboard side screens like blinders you'd put up to keep a kid from cheating on a test or keep people from peeping over their neighbor's shoulder.

"That simple?" Meghan asks.

"That's the way we do it," the woman says.

"How will they know who wins?"

"Tonight, after we close up, a few of us stay behind, open the boxes, and count 'em up."

Is that what the sixteen-year-old does? Meghan wonders. "And then what?"

"We get on the phone and call the number in; when my granddad was a kid, they sent the number via wire—like an SOS to the state capitol."

She's surprised at how rudimentary it seems, rinky-dink. She's not sure what she imagined, but it was definitely something more substantive, professional, modern, maybe a big machine with lights, bells, whistles, the kind of thing they have in arcades. She imagines matching the picture of the person you're supporting with their name, pushing the button, and then a lot of lights go off and simultaneously it registers on some great scorecard in the sky. Score one for the red team!

This, the paper form, the cardboard blinders, is beyond banal. All over the country people are doing the exact same thing? And by late tonight there will be a new order in the land? It's more like an activity you'd do at a school to pick the new head of the class.

She looks over and sees her parents carefully pushing their forms into the sealed box.

Her father smiles at her—he's passing the torch. His deep pleasure in this process reminds her of all the things they've talked about over the years—all the car trips and vacations they've taken to historical sites. This is the passion he shares. He doesn't talk about himself or his childhood. He talks about historical figures, battles, wars, treaties, and the three branches of government. She's been brought home to vote—to go on this electoral journey as a kind of indoctrination.

She ducks into her booth, fills out the form, folds as directed, then hurries over and stuffs it into the box.

On the way out, there's a table set up with an enormous industrial-size coffee urn, glass bottles of milk, and a box of fresh glazed donuts, still shining while the sugar dries.

She picks up a donut. Her mother sees her do it and looks horrified. It's hard to know if it's the calories, the idea of a donut for breakfast, or the fact that it's been sitting out and possibly touched by others. She's caught, donut pinched between her thumb and middle finger. The glaze begins to melt. She squeezes, denting the dough. As she's holding the donut, unsure what to do, her father leans over and takes a bite.

"Best damn donut I ever had," he says. "That had to be made within the last hour; I can taste it; the yeast is still rising."

Her mother reaches over, plucks the donut from between Meghan's fingers, and drops it into a trash can. The expression on her mother's face is one of enormous satisfaction—like she's put out a fire. Meghan is left with sticky fingers. She puts her hand in her pocket and thinks about when she might be able to sneak a lick.

"Well, that's all she wrote," Sonny says, as they're back in the car.

"Our duty is done," her father says.

They drive straight from the church to the airport. Sonny smokes with the window down—the smoke catches the air and blows into the back seat. Meghan can see her mother take a deep breath.

As soon as they're on the plane, her father turns to her and asks, "So, what did it feel like?"

She can't tell her father what she's really thinking; it reminds her of another first—her virginity and how losing that was also less spectacular than it was supposed to be.

She can't tell him that she finds the whole thing so basic that it is causing her a new kind of anxiety, the deep existential ache that nothing is as previously represented; nothing in reality is as good as the idea she's been sold. She can't tell him any of it because she knows it would break his heart.

Luckily, before she can say much, he continues. "Back in Connecticut we used to vote on a device that was gunmetal gray. You went in, pulled a little half curtain around you like in a photo booth, and then you'd toggle the switches up or down depending on which man you were for. When you were done, you'd pull an enormous lever with a black handle to register your vote. Every time I threw that lever to the right, I felt like I was doing something major, starting up a time machine or launching an atomic bomb, I was never sure which." He pauses. "I'm so proud of you. Getting yourself out here to cast your ballot with us means a lot."

"Thanks," Meghan says. "It meant a lot to me, too, we're making history one day at a time. I cast my vote in honor of all those who have come before me and with an eye to the future ahead."

"Is that a line from a poem?" her mother asks.

"No, I just made it up. What are we going to do when we get where we're going?" she asks.

"I expect we'll eat some lunch," her mother says. "Then I'll be taking a disco nap."

"I have some calls to make and later there's a cocktail event," her father says.

"A lot of standing around," her mother says.

"It'll be a reunion of the faithful," her father says.

"A very tense night," her mother says.

"There's gonna be a shit show if he loses, pardon my French," her father says.

"Is Tony coming?" Meghan asks. Tony is her godfather, her father's best friend from college.

"No, he's in DC, can't get out of the house on a night like this."

By house, her father means the White House, where Tony works as a special assistant to the president.

"It's a very big job," her mother says. "Too bad it's ending."

"Less a job and more like a calling," her father says. "It's like joining the priesthood; once you've worked there, you know things that mere mortals never get to find out. He's a good man to have around."

"Do you think he'll ever get married?" she asks.

"No," her father says definitively.

"I hope he doesn't get lonely."

"Tony is a very busy man," her mother says. "He doesn't have time to get lonely. He's what we call a confirmed bachelor."

"He has friends," her father says. "The man has a lot of friends, friends in all kinds of places."

Her mother has a drink on the plane.

"So early?" her father asks.

"You know I hate to fly. Did everything make it onto the plane?"

"Yes," her father says. "And if it didn't, that's what stores are for."

"Did you bring a dress?" her mother asks Meghan.

"Yes."

"It's good you're tall; you don't need heels. Young girls shouldn't wear heels anyway, but some just have to." She pauses. "Good gams go a long way."

"Remind me what a gam is."

"It's a leg, a shapely leg."

"Oh," she says. And she doesn't even want to begin to ask what her mother means.

"A nice ankle is also a plus," her mother says. "Let me see your ankles."

Meghan pulls up the legs of her pants; her ankles are covered in thick socks, not much to see. "As far as I know they're good."

Her mother makes a noise and goes back to doing the crossword puzzle. Her father reads the papers—all of them. And Meghan looks out the window and thinks about the events of the day.

The plane lands in Phoenix, and as they're getting off, she asks her mother, "Have we been here before?"

"I have no idea. Have we?" her mother asks her father.

"You would know," her father says, then turns to Meghan. "If I were younger, I'd take you on a cross-country road trip. Get a big old Caddy, and that's what we'd do this summer. I still might, you never know. It was fun when we went to Dallas, wasn't it? Did you like the soup? They're famous for their soup."

"Among other things," her mother says.

Last year, during spring break, Meghan went to Dallas with her father on a business trip. While he was in meetings, the Russian driver took her to see where Kennedy was shot. "We're getting close," the driver said, as they were approaching the grassy knoll. "We're there now," he said, as the car slipped through the underpass. "It's just there."

"Really?" she asked. "The little hill? That was it?"

"Ya," he said. "You want go around again?"

"Yes, please." So they circled it again—and again. After the fourth time, the driver asked, "You have enough?" It's less a question than a statement.

The grassy knoll is an example of the disappointment Meghan felt today. The grassy knoll is less of a hill or a mound, and more of a bump, or at this point in time—a blip? Is that true or has the scale of things changed? Does a place compact and get smaller over time? Does history shrink? She thinks about how a lot of her friends don't know the names of any of the presidents from before they were born.

They are in a black car driving from the airport to town. The interior is puffy leather that feels like a thick marshmallow. The faster they go, the quieter everyone gets as though they were sucked in, as though it becomes harder to speak, to move, like there's a force pushing them back— the mirage of the desert, the air, the day trapped between summer and winter. She glances over at her mother, whose eyes are closed, and her father in the front seat working his two devices. The driver catches her eye.

"Do you need more air?"

"I'm okay," she says. She loves being in motion, suspended between places. "This road has a different hum to it, a different frequency."

"It's true," the driver says. Later she will find out that this is actually true; the road was repaved with a mix that had recycled tires added in to quiet the sound and she will be pleased with herself for noticing.

When they pull up to the hotel, the car door opens and the seal is broken. There's an immediate shift in air pressure and temperature.

The hotel concierge brings them up to their room, an enormous connecting suite. A cellophane-covered fruit basket, cheese platter, and bottles of wine are laid out. The connecting room has a big bed and also a crib with a teddy bear wearing a bathrobe and a matching child-size robe. Someone took them seriously when they said they were "traveling with a child."

"I'll have housekeeping remove the crib and bring a larger robe," the man says.

"Honestly, this is perfect," Meghan says, picking up the teddy bear. She always feels younger when she's with her parents, imploded, her powers of speech and reasoning reduced. In the bathroom there is baby shampoo and elephant-shaped soap.

The family goes downstairs for lunch because her mother hates room service or, to be more specific, hates any room that smells like food for hours after it's been consumed.

During lunch, various men and women stop at the table to say hello to her father. Her father sees them coming and whispers, "Incoming." Some apologize for barging in; her father makes a show of putting down his knife and fork to shake their hands. They shake his hand, sometimes holding on too long, thanking him for his generosity. Each time her father blushes. "Trust me," he says. "It's not all about you; I have my own interests."

They make a point of saying hello to her mother, who gives a little nod while making it clear that no further engagement is possible.

Meghan feels sent back in time, like a child who should be sitting on a phone book to reach the table. At the end of the meal, a surprise arrives, a banana split, confirmation of her youthful status. "On the house," the waiter announces.

Her mother makes a face but then takes a taste. "Why is ice cream so good?"

Her father dabs chocolate sauce off Meghan's nose and Meghan shows her parents that she's learned to tie a cherry stem into a knot with her tongue.

"That's disgusting," her mother says definitively.

"Sorry," she says, spitting the stem out.

"Even worse," her mother says. "Use a napkin or better yet just swallow." Her mother's finishing school isn't for the faint of heart.

If someone asked, "What's your relationship with your mother like?" Meghan would say—good. She admires her mother, loves her deeply, but the relationship is prescribed. She sees how critical her mother can be. The disdain through which her mother views the world has grown over time, but it doesn't apply to her; she is either exempt or immune.

She thinks of the letter she wrote years ago thanking her mother for coming to school to visit the class. "Dear Mrs. Hitchens," she wrote, copying what was on the board for all thirty students to write. No one told her to change the salutation to Dear Mom. Her mother called the letter a classic and had it framed.

Once they're back upstairs, her father sets himself up in the living room. He has two televisions on as well as his computer and his devices.

She thinks it's cool that he's tech savvy despite his age and his thick fingers, which poke at the keyboard like stiff sticks of chalk.

Even though it is midafternoon, her mother has housekeeping pull the blackout curtains and lies down in the dark with her travel pillow, travel blanket, and eye mask. Her mother alternately says that she can sleep anywhere at the drop of a hat and that she never sleeps a wink. For the first time it occurs to Meghan that both could be true.

She sits with her father for a few minutes, and when he seems lost to this world, she announces that she's going to the pool.

"Do you need money?"

"No."

"Take a room key so you can come and go without waking Mother."

She makes a tour of the hotel. Cops with sniffer dogs walk in laps around the perimeter. A bus pulls in and two dozen men in suits get out. At first, she thinks they are part of some kind of delegation but then notices they're all wearing the same lapel pin and have transparent coiled earpieces going from under their jackets into their ears—Secret Service. She smiles; they don't smile back. Trucks from CNN, ABC, NBC, and CBS test their satellites and lay miles and miles of thick cable running in every direction.

She ends up in a restaurant by the pool called the Clubhouse, writing a draft of a paper that's due in two days.

"If you looked any more serious, they'd put you on Mount Rushmore." A man whose hair is too shaggy for his age is looking at her. "What are you writing about?"

"Termites."

"Seriously?" he asks.

She nods. "And you?"

"History in the making," he says, gesturing to the air around them.

"It's like New Year's Eve, waiting for the ball drop," she says.

"Something like that."

She looks at him. He's too old to just be chatting her up. She realizes that just by virtue of the fact that she's there, people must think she's older than she is—there are very few young people who just happen to be in Phoenix at this hotel on this particular day.

"Where do you live when you're not by the pool?" he asks.

"Virginia."

"As in Washington, DC?"

She shrugs. "Something like that. Didn't your parents teach you not to talk to strangers?"

"No," he says. "In fact, that's how they made a living." He extends his hand. "Mark Eisner."

"Did your father run Disney?"

"Same name, different family."

"Too bad," she says, sitting up. "What brings you to Phoenix on this balmy day?"

"The spirit moved me."

She waits for more details.

"Actually, I'm writing a book, or more like taking notes hoping that they will magically turn into a book."

"Have you written books before?" she asks.

"I have," he says. "My most recent was *Every Four Years We Begin Again*. I don't suppose you read it. I am a social historian."

"Does that mean you go around talking to strangers at parties?"

"Sometimes."

"The one you're working on now, do you have a hypothesis?" Despite appearing older, she is an eighteen-year-old high school student; everything must have a hypothesis.

"I'm looking at the evolution of political speechmaking."

What does one say?

The good news is she doesn't have to say anything; Eisner just keeps talking. "My father was a speechwriter; I imagine he wanted to be president."

"I hear it's quite competitive," Meghan says.

"I'm the black sheep."

She notices that the people walking by all have the same quality—trying too hard. She can't define it further except to say it's like they're waiting to be discovered.

"Why are they here? That's what I want to know," she says, pointing them out to Eisner. "Is it because they bought a kind of election ticket—if he wins, they win? They'll get jobs, a free move to DC, and a fresh start in life? They're definitely jazzed. That's the word my mother uses for when people are hepped up, that's the word my father uses. I just say cray cray. But whatever it is, everyone around here is acting a little cray cray like they have a case of premature Beatlemania. And by the way, who is the Beatle? Because this guy is a seventy-one-year-old politician, with what some would call a checkered history."

"That's good," Eisner says. "'Who is the Beatle?' Can I use that?"

She shrugs. "It's yours if you can give me something about termites."

He pauses. "Termite walks into a bar, asks, 'Is the bar tender?'"

"Try again."

"Pinocchio goes to the doctor's office and says, 'I think my prostate is enlarged; I'm leaking.' The doctor shakes his head. 'Your prostate is fine, but you have termites.'"

"Gross but okay." Meghan scribbles it down. "I can't include it in my paper and I'm not even sure I can tell it to the teacher for extra credit. The word prostate might not be allowed on campus. Prostrate, now we're talking." She laughs at herself. "Girls' school."

The historian laughs too. "Okay then. Maybe I'll see you later."

He didn't even ask her name.

There is no dinner, just a heavy snack at six p.m. from room service. Her mother, who never eats at cocktail parties, has a bowl of soup and a roll, with the excuse that she knows there will be drinking in excess, and while she doesn't usually eat carbohydrates, sometimes they are "required." Her father has shrimp cocktail because it reminds him of a time long ago when he had shrimp in this same hotel and they were the size of 45 records. She's not sure what that means, but he seems fond of the memory until they arrive and he remembers that he hates shrimp. She orders a burger—better safe than sorry.

Her parents dress as though the evening to come were an event, like a wedding. A lot of effort goes into it: showers, colognes, perfumes, jewelry, etc. When her mother washes her face, she never uses water; she uses something from an unmarked bottle dabbed onto a cotton pad. "Tap water is too harsh," she says. From the back, her mother looks like Nancy Reagan. She's thin but not skeletal. She does a lot of exercises on account of having had scoliosis as a child and having spent a year in a body cast.

"Can you imagine," she tells people, "a five-year-old entombed for an entire year. I was traumatized. I don't think I've recovered yet." When Meghan asked her mother whether she played sports at school, her mother told her, "We didn't have sports; we just had horses." She's from a Texas oil family, and Meghan's parents met through her mother's father—Papa Willard. "It wasn't exactly an arranged marriage," she says. "But it was certainly encouraged." "You were getting old," her father says, laughing. "It wasn't like I hadn't been asked," her mother says. "I turned down all the boys. I wanted a life of my own, but that was unheard of in my family. So I just held out until your father came along. And I thought he was all right."

While her parents are abluting their way toward dusk, Meghan puts on her dress, brushes her hair, and sits on the edge of the bed watching the early coverage.

"Do you think he's going to win?" she asks.

"I don't want to think about it," her mother says. "The professionals are not optimistic, but it's our job to be positive."

"Is it always like this?"

"Like what?" Her mother wants to know.

"Such a big deal?"

"Yes," her father says. "It is a big deal. The president steers the ship. Keep in mind it doesn't just affect us, it affects the whole country. Do you remember the dinner we went to for John and Cindy in Washington?"

"You took me as your date."

"We had a good time, didn't we?" Her father smiles.

"But what was the point of that dinner? It was a whole lot of people sucking up or trying to."

"Exactly," her mother says.

"You have to pull people in," her father says. "And keep 'em close." He turns to face them, pink-faced, his white hair neatly combed back.

"You look dapper."

"Thank you. Are we ready?" he asks.

"You know, I wouldn't mind just skipping the whole thing," her mother says.

"Out. Out the door." Her father ushers them through the door quickly before her mother decides not to go. It wouldn't be the first time that she was overcome by social anxiety and had to lie down.

They take the elevator up two floors. Her father has a schedule of parties. It's like trick-or-treating; you go from party to party and you see some of the same people from the last party at the next party, but as they progress, the snacks get fancier, the crowd gets smaller, the rooms get nicer, and the flower arrangements multiply.

At every stop, as soon as they're through the door, her father launches in. "How the heck are you?" He's shaking hands, smacking shoulders, working the room.

And at every stop, her mother heads for the bar. "Vodka with a splash of soda on the rocks."

"Twist?"

"Lime, thank you."

"Could I have cranberry and seltzer?" Meghan says.

"You remember what I told you about drinks at parties?"

"Never pick up a drink once you've put it down, always get a fresh one. And better yet, just bring your own bottle of water. You trained me well."

Her mother scowls.

"Did you know that some people are working on making something like a little Popsicle stick that you can dip into a drink to see if it has drugs in it?"

"When I was your age," her mother says, "the boys just tried to get us tipsy. Boys your age try to make you unconscious. You've never had anything happen, have you? If you did, you'd tell me?"

"Mother, I go to an all-girls school. The only thing that's happened is that two girls got made fun of for practicing making out. Personally, I think they're gay."

"Well then, just steer clear."

Meghan and her mother stand around—looking at the others.

She tells her mother what she knows about termites.

"I'm just so glad you're not like me," her mother says. "You seem so natural. After all these years and all these parties, I still don't have it mastered. If anything, it's gotten more difficult."

"Is gerrymandering named after someone I should know, like a historical figure?" Meghan asks her mother.

"No clue." Her mother takes a piece of celery from a crudité sculpture. "Have this, it'll keep you occupied and away from the—"

"Penis nuts," Meghan says.

Her mother smiles. Penis nuts. That's what her mother calls communal bowls of nuts. There are things one teaches a young girl: never eat the penis nuts. Men don't wash their hands after they use the facilities. They sink their paws into the nuts while they're waiting for a drink. If you must eat, take something that's sticking straight up, celery, a cheese stick, a carrot, but god forbid, don't dip it into anything; that's the other weak spot, double dippers.

The next party has someone stationed at the door with a check-in list and little photos of everyone. "No crashers in this crowd," her father whispers.

"Welcome, we're so glad to see you," a woman says, as they enter the room.

"'We' is a very wealthy old Arizona family," her father says.

A lot of the women in the room and a few of the men look like they've had repair work done; that's what her mother calls it, "repair work."

"You see that man over there?" her father says, nodding toward a distinguished-looking man holding court in the corner. "His son would be a good boy for you to meet. One day he's going to own most of the shopping malls in this country."

"Are you trying to sell me off?" Meghan asks.

"No. Just highlighting some of the options. He'd be a nice addition."

"And your children would always have hair," her mother adds. "Not many older men have such a thick head of hair."

"Ew," Meghan says.

"John's here," someone says.

"At the party?"

"No, he's upstairs. He's arrived at the hotel."

"I've heard people talk about the Keating affair. I feel terrible for Cindy," one of the women whispers to another.

"It wasn't that kind of affair," the other woman whispers back.

"Oh?"

"It was a political corruption case."

"I'm not sure I follow."

"A bunch of men were convicted, nothing romantic about it."

"I still feel sorry for Cindy," the woman says. "It's hard to be the wife."

"The Jewel of the Desert," Meghan hears her father say. "This is the same hotel where John and Cindy got married, May 17, 1980. It's their happy place."

"God willing," someone says.

An old man starts choking on a pig in a blanket and the room falls silent except for the televisions. Someone finally starts asking, "Is there a doctor?" while others pound on him and prepare to do the Heimlich. Just as a burly man gets behind him and is about to do the big squeeze, the old man coughs it up on his own. A chunk of baby hot dog flies out of his mouth and lands like a small turd on the carpet.

"Come with me." Her mother grabs Meghan's hand, pulling her into the bathroom. She closes the door quickly, locks it, then turns, sets her glass down, flips the toilet seat up, and vomits yellow bile. Twice. "I just don't have the stomach for it anymore."

"It's okay, Mama," Meghan says, patting her mother on the back.

Her mother looks at herself in the mirror, washes her hands, runs some tap water into her hand, and rinses her mouth. "Between us," she says, and doesn't need to say more.

"Pinkie swear," Meghan says. And they go back into the room.

At the fourth and final stop, Meghan sees people she has seen before, friends of her father's, maybe acquaintances is the better word; they are men he feels comfortable with.

Extra televisions are brought in for the occasion—there are at least two in every room. In one of the bedrooms a man is talking on his cell phone while frantically waving others away. "I'm on with the committee," he hisses.

"We all know where this is heading."

"It's like watching an accident."

"Are you sure?"

"Something is very wrong."

"A lot of things are wrong, very wrong."

"It's on us—we took our eye off the ball."

"It's her. He never should have picked her. She's an idiot."

"Don't you think he talked to her before he picked her?"

"Well, if he didn't, he's an idiot."

"Somebody talked to her, but they forgot to ask the important questions—like do you own your own clothes? Or what's the view from your kitchen window?"

"I can see Russia from here," someone says.

"Do you remember when Cindy had the drug problem?"

"She handled it so gracefully."

"I hear John is a gambler."

"A superstitious guy, my friend knew him in the navy, said he had a lucky charm he carried with him, a rock."

"He got out alive."

"I heard it was a compass; he had a compass."

"Feather," someone chimes in. "He keeps a feather. The staff went mental when he lost it on the campaign trail."

"Really, he lost his lucky feather? Did they find it?"

"No fuckin' idea."

Her father trades her mother's vodka and soda for just soda with a whisper of vodka on top. He hands her mother the glass. She smiles slowly and sips. She can't tell if her mother notices. All she can tell is that her mother is quieter. That's what happens when her mother drinks; she gets quieter and quieter and then goes to sleep.

Waiting for news. It's as though they were all at a hospital waiting for the surgeon to come out and tell them how it went. The suspense is rising, the air charged with contagious anxiety.

"John is going to stop by to say hello," someone announces. "A quick hello."

Her godfather, Tony, calls her father. Her father talks to Tony and then passes his phone to Meghan. "What's it like?" Tony wants to know.

"Weird," she says. "It's all weird. During the voting, I felt like I was in the short story 'The Lottery.' They check your name off in a big book like something Santa would have at the North Pole, then you duck behind a privacy screen, make an X mark on a piece of paper. You do that at seven a.m., and by the end of the day, all the Xs are counted up and we know who the president is. Is it just me or is it weird?"

Tony is quiet for a minute. "It's been that way for the last two-hundred-plus years."

"My point exactly."

"How's your mother holding up?"

"She doesn't like parties."

"Smart woman. Neither do I," Tony says.

"Where are you?"

"Home. I'm too old for this shit."

"If I remember correctly, you're younger than my father."

"I'm precociously aged. And I prefer to take in bad news alone."

While she's talking with Tony, Meghan spots Eisner, the historian, across the room. He catches her eye. He makes a gesture as if to say, Look around the room, then mouths the word termites.

"Have you ever noticed that people are weird?" she asks Tony.

"Daily."

"And for the most part, they don't have minds of their own?"

"The 'bystander effect,'" Tony says. "When you grow up, make sure you play an active role."

"Tell that to my father."

"What do you mean?"

"Mom and I are the bystanders. She knows him so well that she can read his body language and intuit what will happen next. 'Let's stop for a bite to eat. Let's use the bathroom.' Between the two of us, we have a joke—his nickname is Let's."

Tony laughs.

"But seriously, right now Let's looks worried. So now Mom is worried. I can tell by looking at both of them, all of them really. Is it definitely bad?"

But before Tony can answer, there's a lot of commotion in the room. "I have to go," she says. "The McCains are coming."

"TTYL," Tony says.

There's a palpable rush of excitement. Meghan notices the men pulling themselves together, giving their pants a tug up over their bellies while the women check their hair and lipstick. The effort to look good is so obvious, it's almost funny—almost.

And then there is a pregnant pause, waiting, waiting, longer than you would think. Across the room the speechwriter mimes blowing on a trumpet, as if announcing the arrival of the king. The sound of radios comes from down the hall, and the two men by the door are focused, transparent coiled earbuds go up the back of their necks into their ears.

A cloud of Secret Service agents sweep into the room, just their physical volume pushes the crowd back toward the wall.

As Cindy and John enter, the crowd breaks into applause and there's a forward surge—the desire for physical contact.

Someone offers John a microphone; he turns it down.

"I'm so glad to see all of you," John McCain says. More applause. "Cindy and I just wanted to stop by and thank you for the work you've done to make this campaign a strong one and for sticking with me through the unexpected ups and downs of the last few months."

There's a brief pause. "How's it looking?" someone shouts.

McCain shakes his head. "Well, right now, I wouldn't want to be me." He chuckles painfully. "But seriously, we all worked hard and I just wanted to come by and thank you."

Someone is hissing, like a low rattlesnake. The hissing builds; it's more than one person. Meghan's shocked. Then the hissing is overpowered by booing and she can't tell if they're booing McCain or the people hissing. "Don't be a pussy," the man next to her says loudly. His wife smacks him hard. "Shut up, you're drunk."

"We love you, John," someone shouts. "Don't quit now."

"We won't know anything official for a while," McCain says.

With nothing left to say, John McCain raises his arm as far as he can and makes a gesture somewhere between a salute and a send-off and gives

Cindy a little nudge, and they are quickly out of the room, enveloped by the Secret Service.

"Hopefully, no one will remember you," the wife of the drunk man says.

"I'm the least of his problems," the man says.

"I'm surprised he can come in here and seem normal enough."

"What should he do, start crying? He's got to put a good face on it. Who knows what he's doing upstairs."

"Smashing shit, that's what I'd be doing. I'd be fucking throwing the sofa through the window."

"That's it," the wife of the drunk man says. "I warned you. We're leaving now. Say nighty night to your friends."

"Good timing," he says, as they shuffle out of the room. "The shit's about to hit the fan anyway."

Meghan is surprised by how angry people are, like poor sports at a ball game.

"What happens if we don't win?" she asks.

"We have lost control," her father says, shaking his head.

A few women have started crying; one is weeping uncontrollably. "It's like when the *Challenger* blew; we all stood in front of our televisions sets, helpless," someone says.

"I wish they would call it," a woman says. "Put us out of our misery."

"Too early. They don't call it while polls are still open."

The rumbling continues.

Her mother asks for another drink and Meghan offers to go get it. On the way to the bar, she looks for the historian but doesn't find him. She orders the drink for her mother and the same for herself. It's the first time she's ordered a drink for herself.

As she's crossing the room back toward her parents, someone says loudly, "Oh my god." The room falls silent and all eyes focus on the television. "A Black man just got elected president of the United States. Oh my fucking god."

"Really?"

"It's over?"

"That's it?"

"Who called it?"

"I can hear my parents rolling in their graves."

"Wow," her mother says when Meghan reaches her with the drink.

"Is it true?" she asks her parents.

Her father looks pale. His eyes are darting back and forth.

"Dad?"

The news has hit the room like death. Waiters stop serving. Men, looking as if they might be sick, quickly steer their wives toward the door.

On the television screens the reporters are talking. "A truly historic moment, Barack Hussein Obama will be the next president of the United States; he is the first African American to be elected to the nation's highest office."

Those who haven't left the party stand dumbfounded in front of the television.

The network cuts to another reporter. "All over the country people are coming out into the streets; they're hugging one another, dancing, setting off firecrackers. We are here at a nursing home with Clarice Jones, one of the oldest Americans who voted today. She is 101 years young. Clarice, how are you feeling tonight?"

"I feel fine," Clarice says. "I got up this morning and cast my vote. And now look what we have, our first Black president. My relations were owned by White men and now look. Can you believe that in my lifetime this has happened? It's amazing and it reminds us to keep the dream alive when the night is dark."

"Thank you, Clarice, and back over to you, Tom," the reporter says.

"Let's go downstairs," her father says.

As they're leaving the room, Meghan overhears a man saying, "Just think, on Inauguration Day that man is going to be fucking his wife in the White House."

"Don't be crude," his wife says.

"I'm just telling it like it is," the man says.

"Downstairs," her father repeats. "It's time for Mother to go to bed."

When they get back to the room, Meghan understands why the hotel thought they'd need a crib. Her father has hired a babysitter—for her mother. He introduces her mother to Mrs. Stevens, who will keep her company while the rest of the family returns to the fray.

In the background the television set drones. "Shortly after eleven p.m. in the East, nine p.m. in Phoenix, Senator John McCain called President-elect Obama . . ."

"Is Mom drunk?" she asks, as they ride the elevator down to hear McCain's speech.

"I just don't like for her to be alone," her father says.

They have special passes that let them get up close. There's a singer on-stage and thousands of people are in the area she saw them setting up ear-lier. The crowd looks tired, baffled by what they perhaps already know but haven't fully processed. After a few minutes, the singer takes a bow and canned music begins to play. Stagehands come and go, moving things around.

The volume on the music goes up; the crowd recognizes the song "Raisin' McCain" by John Rich and begins cheering. Out from the edges of the stage come Sarah and Todd Palin and Cindy and John McCain. The crowd applauds wildly.

"Drill, baby, drill!"

"Go Maverick."

"The Mac is back!"

Meghan feels herself start to cry.

McCain holds up his hand to quiet the crowd. "The American people have spoken and they have spoken clearly," he says. The crowd boos. He continues, "I had the honor of calling Senator Barack Obama to congratu-late him on being elected the next president of the country that we both love."

As McCain is speaking, Meghan is overwhelmed with the feeling that something enormous has happened. She is a witness to history.

"I urge all Americans who supported me to join me in not just congratulating him but offering our next president our goodwill and earnest effort . . . to bridge our differences . . . defend our security in a dangerous world, and leave our children and grandchildren a stronger, better country than we inherited."

"What a load of crap," someone says.

McCain continues. "It is natural tonight to feel some disappointment, but tomorrow we must move beyond it and work together to get our country moving again. We fought—we fought as hard as we could. And though we fell short, the failure is mine, not yours . . . the road was a difficult one from the outset. You know, campaigns are often harder on a candidate's family than on the candidate, and that's been true in this campaign. I am so lucky to have such a wonderful family. A big thank-you for Cindy!" Applause and another pause. "Every candidate makes mistakes, and I'm sure I made my share of them. But I won't spend a moment of the future regretting what might have been."

A man next to Meghan picks a McCain/Palin hat off the floor and asks his friend, "Is this shit worth anything?"

The friend takes the hat, drops it on the floor, and stomps on it. "That's how I feel tonight, fucking crushed, fucking fucked," the guy says.

McCain carries on. "I call on all Americans, as I have often in this campaign, to not despair of our present difficulties but to believe always in the promise and greatness of America, because nothing is inevitable here. Americans never quit. We never surrender. We never hide from history. We make history."

And then he is done. He waves to the crowd.

"Thank you, and God bless you, and God bless America."

"I'm going to the bar," her father says.

"I think I'll take a walk," Meghan says.

"Fresh air is called for," her father says. "You need money?"

"There's nothing to buy. Air is free."

"You'd be surprised. Helium is five dollars a liter, that's up fifty percent from last year."

"You would know," Meghan says. It's a family joke given that one of her father's companies recovers helium from natural gas. "World's largest supplier."

"I'll be in the bar."

Outside, despite the fact that there are lots of cops around, people are smoking pot. The smell is heavy in the air. A grown woman in a ball gown is throwing up by the side of a car while a man holds her hair back. "I'm telling you it was the crab," she says, and vomits again.

People are standing around, doing nothing, while others start taking things apart. It feels like a failed mission, a rocket launch that didn't happen.

Meghan walks a little more and ends up by the pool. All is still. The underwater lights are on. The clear blue water looks like a morning sky. The umbrellas are down, the chairs tucked in. It's been neatly put to bed.

She sits, thinking without even knowing what she's thinking. There is no clear line, no logical order. Time passes. No idea how long. She's lost in thought as if thought is outer space.

"How are you holding up?"

Eisner is standing in front of her.

"No idea. You?"

"I'm fine," he says. "No skin in the game. Game being the operative word."

"Pretty big game if that's what it is. I've never seen people act so strangely. It's like I'm missing something. Is it really the end of the world? Armageddon comes to Phoenix?"

"It's a big deal. But is the world coming to an end? It depends on what your world is. For some people the world just got started." He takes off his shoes and socks, and stands at the edge of the water. "Put your toe in," he says, dipping his own into the water. "It's warm."

She laughs. "Are you being metaphorical?"

"No," he says. "I'm trying to entertain you; you look very sad."

"I found the expressions on their faces very upsetting. I've never seen my father look like that. Stricken."

They are quiet.

Meghan goes to the edge of the water, takes her shoes off, and walks down the first two steps, splashing heavily. "See, I can have fun."

"Advantage dress," he says, rolling up his pant legs and joining her on the steps. "Should we?" he asks.

"Should we what?"

"Go for a swim?" he asks, unbuttoning his shirt. "The water is warm. There's no one here. And it is the same pool Marilyn Monroe swam in." He unzips his pants and steps out of them.

"Very convenient that you happen to have a swimsuit on," she says. He's wearing black knit boxers and has a good body for an older guy. He plunges into the pool and swims off.

"There might be a molecule of Marilyn Monroe left in here," he says when he surfaces at the other end.

Meghan pulls her dress over her head and goes in. She's never done anything crazy like this before; well, maybe she has with friends, but never with a strange man, in a strange place, after such a strange day.

She swims back and forth and back and forth doing flip turns and several laps before she meets him in the deep end.

"Better?" he asks.

"Yes."

She loves to swim. She loves the water on her skin; she loves that despite the strangeness of everything she is back in her body and it feels familiar. They are like mermaids in the water—except that one is a merman.

The blue lights turn the pool into a lagoon, a dream.

He takes a mouthful of water and spits it at her. "I christen you with the waters of Marilyn Monroe."

She laughs. As weird as the rest of the day has been, this is magical. She thinks of herself as a woman in a foreign film.

"Look at you," he says, pointing to her reflection in a mirrored planter on the pool deck. Her hair is wet and slicked back, her face lit from below by the pool light. "There is hope, possibility, a future. Look at me," he says. "I'm twenty-five years older than you, that's five more elections. Mark this moment. You have lost your political virginity. You are baptized."

"Wait, how old are you?"

"Forty-three."

He is standing very close to her and there's the sense that something could happen, but then she dives under, turning double somersaults underwater. She pops up far away, in the middle of the pool. "To somersaults," she says, turning circles underwater, then breaking the surface. "I feel out of my mind. It has been the longest day ever."

After a while, they get out, grab towels from the stack by the cabana, dry off, and put their clothing back on. She slips her soggy bra off and leaves it tucked into a planter. They go back into the hotel and get into the elevator, skin covered in goose bumps, clean with the scent of chlorine.

"I'd invite you to—"

"I have to get up early," Meghan says, cutting him off. She's not sure if he's a making a pass and doesn't want to find out. "Flying back."

"Well then, goodbye for now," he says.

She walks down the hall to her room, her head high and wrapped in a towel turban. She likes him all the more because he lets her go.

She unlocks the door, slips in quietly, and peeks into her parents' room. Her mother is fast asleep, lying on the bed fully clothed, her shoes neatly side by side on the floor, with the red, white, and blue flickering light of the television replay bouncing off the walls.

She assumes her father is still at the bar downstairs. She covers her mother with the bedspread and goes to sleep in the other room.

Her father wakes her before the sun comes up. "Something to eat before you go? They have twenty-four-hour room service."

"I'm still stuffed from last night," Meghan says.

She'd been dreaming that she was riding a bike through one snowy village after another and asking people as she passed through if the next town was going to be the "real thing."

"I'm sure you're exhausted," he says. "Baptism by fire. We didn't win, but it was a real indoctrination." He pauses. "I got such a kick out of going to vote with you. More important, I don't want you to worry. I'm sure you heard a lot of talk last night about the world spinning out of control. As I said to the bartender last night, 'All men make mistakes, but you don't want to make the same mistake twice.' I just want you to know that I'm going to do whatever it takes to get things right."

"I know."

"It's important to see how the process works—and that you definitely did. I'm talking too much; you need to wash your face and get going. The car will be here soon."

She gets up, noticing how little her body disrupted the bed. She brushes her teeth and packs her bag, stuffing the little bear from the hotel and the baby products in with her clothes.

Her father is in the sitting area between the two rooms; the television is on, volume off.

"Are you up for the day?" Meghan asks him.

"No doubt," he says. He's wearing a hotel bathrobe over his pajamas, so at some point during the night, he must have changed. "I might take myself downstairs for breakfast or to the pool for an early swim." He pulls a hundred-dollar bill from the pocket of his robe. "Travel money."

"I have money."

"The only money you have is what I put in your bank account. Just take it; buy yourself something at the airport, a magazine or a chocolate bar. Your mother is still sleeping, but go in and give her a kiss."

Dutifully, she goes into her parents' bedroom. Her mother is now under the covers, so Meghan can't tell if she ever changed out of her party clothes. "Bye, Mom; I'm going back to school," she says, as she bends to kiss her. Her mother's face is warm and smooth.

"Bye-bye, big girl," her mother says and rolls over. "Do you know where my eye mask is?"

She hands her mother the pink satin mask, which was lost between the pillows.

"Here you go. One day I hope I have an eye mask just like yours."

"Christmas is coming soon," her mother says. "Travel safe."

After Meghan leaves, her father puts the Do Not Disturb sign on the door, the room key in his pocket, and goes off for a swim in the hotel's famous pool. He wears his trunks under his bathrobe and travels barefoot because he thinks hotel slippers make him look like an old lady.

He will swim in any pool, in every pool. He swims in every town, in every city, in every country he visits. He believes something is learned by taking the local waters. This was something he did as a boy with his father. Wherever they traveled, they took the waters; his father also took the liquor and the ladies. If there was a city with notable waters but he had no business there, his father started one. Hot Springs, Arkansas. Sharon Springs, New York, which he liked because that was where the Vanderbilts went. Saratoga Springs was a favorite because they also had horses and he could gamble. Sutherland Springs, Hot Wells. Mineral Wells in Texas, where a man could "drink his way to health." And Berkeley Springs, West Virginia, the same place George Washington had once taken the waters—that's what he remembers.

The Phoenix pool area is perfectly manicured, undisturbed and empty. Perfection. He goes to the deep end, curls his feet over the words No Diving, and makes a smooth racer's plunge into the water. Swimming is liberation. In the water he becomes an inventor, a superhero, a man capable of anything. He swims laps envisioning himself as a rescuer of those lost at sea; he swims laps and imagines what he still might do in life. His thoughts unspool; his energy increases; he feels flush with ideas about what should happen next.

He swims until he can swim no more, then he rests against the back of the pool and does a round of water exercises before getting out, taking care to slick back what's left of his hair. He puts the thick white bathrobe on and pads back up to the room.

His wife is still sleeping. She is flat on her back, pink satin eye mask on, her head on the matching travel pillow. The scale of the pillow, the motionless nature of her position, reminds him of seeing people in coffins with a small satin pillow tucked under the head. The reminder of her life is her breathing. She doesn't snore—she puffs. With each exhalation, her lips purse—and puff, as if she were saying, "Un peu, un peu," again and again. When her lips are dry and tight, they're like a perfect puckered asshole. He's mentioned it to her—the puffing, not the asshole.

He watches her. Her puffs shift from sleeptalking in French to a kitten purring and then to the strange wheeze and click of a respirator.

He gets up, opens the blinds, and lets the day in. His wife doesn't stir. He sits in a chair by the window waiting, wondering if she drank and took a sleeping pill. At ten a.m., when his own sense of the day leaking away gets to him, he goes over and shakes her shoulder gently. "Anybody home?"

"I'm here. I've been here the whole time."

Does she remember Meghan leaving at five a.m.? Does she want room service? Does she want to go for a swim before they leave? It might wake her up.

"Just coffee."

He calls downstairs for coffee. His wife lies there, looking up at the ceiling, still not having moved.

"Did you sleep well?"

"Like a corpse," she says.

Wednesday, November 5, 2008
Sky Harbor International Airport
Phoenix, Arizona
6:30 a.m.

In the Phoenix airport gift shop, Meghan buys herself a necklace, a silver phoenix rising. She writes in her journal: "The morning flight back to Washington is like being a passenger on Lincoln's funeral train. I am surrounded by the grief-stricken and bedraggled. As we boarded, someone said, 'It's like the last flight out of Saigon.' People laughed but I don't know why. The guy next to me is either a reporter or insane. He has a stack of thin spiral notebooks with words scrawled everywhere; his tray table is down, and he's typing frantically. One of the men is calling the stewardess Cindy even though her name tag says Katherine. 'You're Cindy to me,' the man says. 'You look like Cindy McCain, only younger, like you could be her daughter.'"

Meghan overhears two women talking. "I went up there last night; the door was open. 'Close the door behind you,' he said. 'It's not a fucking open house.' 'It's a shiva call,' I said. 'Leave it to the Jew to make a joke."

"My feet are a mess from having to wear serious shoes for so many months—I'll probably need surgery. Bunions."

The reporter sitting next to her stops typing and turns to her. "Are you writing it down?"

She looks at him. "Pardon?"

"Are you writing down what they're saying? That's what they call human interest or material for *Saturday Night Live.*"

"I got some of it," she says. "I'm journaling."

"Nice," he says. "I'm journalisting. I have to have the story ready by the time we land."

She lifts the shade and presses her cheek against the cold glass, looking out into the infinite.

Wednesday, November 5, 2008
The Biltmore Hotel
Phoenix, Arizona
10:40 a.m.

"It's a giant fuckup," the Big Guy mutters to Charlotte as they are checking out of the hotel. "I sent John a message this morning. It's not his error alone; whoever suggested that Palin woman to him should be court-martialed. If you want to appeal to women voters, don't pick an idiot. It was more of an insult than anything else."

"Is that what you said in your note?" she asks.

"Of course not. I said he'd run a strong race and that we are living in interesting times. Sweet and simple."

She nods.

The front desk clerk hands him a copy of the bill. He takes a good look at it.

"There's an error," he tells the man at the desk. "The lunch we had yesterday was not $137. I suspect I know what happened—they charged me for the banana split that we didn't order but that was sent gratis."

"Of course," the desk clerk says. "One moment." He clicks away at the keys and reprints the bill. "I have removed the ice cream and also the glass of wine as a courtesy. It was lovely having you with us."

"Thanks, kid," he says, taking out his Montblanc pen to sign the bill.

At the edge of the hotel driveway, a man is selling McCain/Palin hats—limited-time special, two for one or five for two. He's made himself a cardboard sign: "Please help. I put my whole paycheck into these hats and it's only Wednesday."

"Poor slob," Charlotte says.

The Big Guy has the driver stop the car. He opens the window and gives the man twenty dollars. "How many do you want?" the man asks.

"I don't want the hats. Buy yourself a cup of coffee."

The plane leaves at noon. The people in the airport look the same as they would have on any other day. There is no sense of change, of shock, or even of great joy, which would at least give him something to react to. He wants there to be a difference; he wants people to know something has changed and act accordingly. But it all goes on as usual. The flight from Phoenix to Palm Springs is short. Charlotte has a drink on the plane regardless. He watches her unscrew the miniature bottle of vodka, pour it over ice, and add the smallest splash of club soda. She drinks it with urgency, as if time were running out.

In Palm Springs, walking through the airport, he carries their heavy wool coats over his arm; his-and-hers pelts of defeat.

"Did the altitude get to your ears?" Charlotte asks.

"No, it did not."

At the house, Charlotte waits patiently while he searches for the key. He's never liked carrying keys, so at every house the key is hidden under a rock. The problem is that just outside this house there's an outdoor rock garden with a hundred rocks.

"Pick the one that looks like it's got something to hide," Charlotte says.

"I asked Craig to get things ready," he says, finding the key and opening the door. Every place they go has a set of caretakers, house watchers who turn things on and off in their absence.

He walks in, drops his bags, and begins to undress, removing his shoes, socks, shirt, and pants and leaving a trail of clothing behind him as he walks to the sliding glass doors overlooking the golf course. By the time he reaches the glass, he's buck naked. He unlatches the door and steps outside, picking up speed as he nears the water. He hurls himself at the pool, cannonballing into the water. It's his way of announcing his arrival.

"Holy mother of god," he shouts, as he comes back to the surface.

He exits the pool as though ejected. "It's a fucking ice bucket. Why can't he get something as simple as heating the pool right? I could have had a heart attack. Right then and there I could have bought the big one."

"Always good to dip a toe in first," Charlotte says.

"The toe should have already been dipped. That's what those phone calls are about. Make sure to turn the pool on by Sunday so it's warm for our arrival."

"Maybe the heater is broken."

"Maybe people are morons. Why doesn't anyone do their fucking job?"

"You mean why doesn't anyone do it the way you would do it?"

"That's what I said."

"I knew this would happen," she says. "You can see it coming from across the river like a thunderstorm."

"What are you talking about?"

"You were fine all day yesterday, and then as soon as we're on our own back at the house, just the two of us alone, you lose it."

"What's your point?" he asks aggressively.

"Nothing," she says.

"If I were you, I wouldn't say more."

She looks perplexed. "Why shouldn't I?"

"Now isn't the time."

"I have no idea what you're getting at."

"I advise you to leave it for now." He takes a breath. "The world is going to hell and I am not pleased."

"You're mad at the world and somehow it's my fault?"

"I didn't say that." He picks up his clothing.

"But at the moment I'm a contributing factor." She pauses. "I don't have the energy for this."

"Because of the drinking or the drugs?"

"Pardon me?"

"You don't have the energy because of the drinking or the drugs?" It's the first time he's mentioned it.

She says nothing. Just stands there, as if paralyzed. It's a staring contest—which he loses. He marches out of the room.

In his undershorts he marches around the side of the house, opens the closet where the heater is, and as he moves to turn up the temperature on the pool heater, a hedge trimmer falls out followed by a small axe, both landing dangerously close to his bare toes. "Fucking ass-ate," he says, and then wonders what ass-ate means. He turns up the heater; grabs the lawn tools, one in each hand; and heads off aiming for the bushes and palm trees. He attacks the yard with a vengeance, using the hedge trimmer like a machete, swinging it wide, wishing it was a sword, treating the greenery as if it were a thick-scaled dragon. He slashes wildly; debris flies in all directions.

When he's done, the ground is littered with dismembered branches, limbs that look like they've been hacked at by a murderer. Sweat stings the fresh cuts on his skin. A neighbor pauses as she's driving by. "You're gonna need to take care of all that junk or you'll get an HOA violation. And remember that the trash service doesn't take lawn cuttings."

He's tempted to scream, *Shove it where the sun doesn't shine*, but catches himself.

He bags the debris in Hefty bags and puts the bags in the garage. He'll let the house guy, or the lawn guy, or whatever guy there is figure out what to do with them. But he definitely doesn't want the public shaming of a homeowners association write-up or his neighbors pausing to reprimand him.

Streaked with sweat and now stinking, too, he jumps in the pool again, and this time it's warmer. He takes his own version of a victory lap, making mental notes to even out the hedges—some look like they got a bad haircut.

Then he goes inside and makes lunch. For his wife he makes an open-faced sandwich, turkey on thinly sliced white bread with a layer of mayo so thin that it's a film, a sweep, the essence of mayo. He puts the sandwich on a plate with four bread-and-butter pickles, pours her a glass of water, and delivers both to where she's sitting in the living room reading a book.

"Feeling better now?" Charlotte asks.

"Statement or question?"

"Question."

"Something has to change."

"Something did change—they voted for Barack." She's calling him by his first name, presuming an intimacy to annoy her husband.

He takes a pickle off her plate and pops it into his mouth. He hates bread-and-butter pickles. "It's like biting into a sour frog. And by the way, it's bigger than that. It's me."

"You're bigger than Barack?" Charlotte's eyebrow is raised.

"That's not what I mean. I'm trying to say that something needs to change. Something about me." This is not the kind of thing he usually talks about. "If I'd had a heart attack in that pool, which is maybe fifty-five degrees, you wouldn't have been able to fish me out. I'd have drowned and died for sure."

"I would have done what was necessary. I'm stronger than you think." She picks up a heavy book and hurls it at him.

"That's funny," he says. "Am I the only one who sees this as a turning point?"

"There were thousands if not millions of people in the streets last night," she says.

"They were celebrating; that's not the turning point I meant. The question is, what is expected of me?"

"By whom?" She wants to know.

"My country."

"Your country doesn't know who you are. It's only about what you expect of yourself."

"I can't live like this," he says. "I can't spend the next thirty years watching it all come undone." He shakes his head. "How can you not be in a rage?"

"I am not the same person as you. I have different desires. Someday you might ask what they are."

"I assume you mean something about me, some failure of mine, of the marriage."

Charlotte says nothing.

"I'm talking about something else; it's not about our marriage but a new America, an idea of who we're meant to be, like what the founding fathers talked about. What I realized last night was that there's something inside me, profound anger and grief at why I spent all my time trying to get rich but didn't do something more interesting with my life, something that might change the course of the world."

"Did you come up with an answer?"

"No."

She takes out a notebook and writes something.

"You know I can see you," he says.

"I am aware."

"What did you write down?"

"Just now I put today's date and I wrote, 'Weird.' Usually, I write what I've eaten. What I'm hungry for. What I miss."

He is silent.

"You know what Joan Didion wrote?"

He shakes his head.

"She wrote: 'Keepers of private notebooks are a different breed altogether, lonely and resistant rearrangers of things, anxious malcontents, children afflicted apparently at birth with some presentiment of loss.'"

"Is that who you are?"

"In part."

"It sounds like you're bored."

"I am."

"Me too."

It's the most honest conversation they've had in a long time.

"You do realize that the number of people who change the world is small." Her comment is meant to be comforting.

"I disagree. Every person changes the world in some small way."

"Since when did you become Mr. Spiritual?"

"I don't know—it's just coming out of me, bubbling up." He pauses. "Like bile."

The cabdriver who picks Meghan up at the airport is the same one who drove her from school the other night. He's one of the regulars from the local cab company; his rearview mirror is festooned with air fresheners, a cardboard banana, the Rolling Stones tongue, the classic Little Trees Royal Pine. All of it combines to create a sickly mash of sweet and sour fruits. It's like the driver is either desperate to improve things or masking some kind of unnamed horror. The girls at school call him Mr. Tooth— because he has bad teeth. A lot of people who interact with the girls don't have actual names as much as descriptions: tooth taxi, fat taxi, man-with-the-hair taxi, lady with the thick shoe at the health center, mailman with the missing finger.

"Do I look older?" she asks him.

"Older than you are?"

"Older than the day before yesterday? Have I aged?"

"Rough flight?"

"No. The flight was fine but I wouldn't want to be a stewardess."

"Oh yeah?"

"Yeah. The pilot sits in a little cabin of his own and does the fun stuff. If he gets hungry, they bring him something. If he has to pee, they block off the aisles so he can use the bathroom without anyone bothering him. Meanwhile, the stewardesses are banging around in the back of a tuna can wearing a uniform that's a cross between a gym suit and a cocktail waitress outfit, and dealing with the nonstop needs of the passengers. Why would anyone sign up for that?"

"I guess you're saying you don't want to travel the world and meet interesting people? I'd apply for the job but I don't think I'd look good in the uniform." He laughs, his broken teeth showing.

"People are rude to the stewardesses and they have to keep smiling and take it."

"Dealing with the public can be trying," he says. She doesn't pick up on the irony. "It used to be that landing a stewardess gig was a plum job. It was a way out."

"A way out of what?"

"Whatever it was that a woman wanted out of; there didn't used to be a whole lot of job opportunities. And for some it wasn't a way out—it was a way in."

There's a pause. She has no idea what he is talking about.

"It was a way to travel for free and maybe meet a guy from a different social class, you know, marry up."

"That's gross," she says.

"Is it? Where'd you go anyway? Did you go back to the future? Time traveling? Is that why you asked if you looked older?"

"Did you pick me up because I'm on your route or because it's me?"

"I take the jobs they give me."

"It's not personal?"

"Uh, no, it's definitely not personal."

"Do you remember when you picked me up and took me to the orthodontist and had to wait while they fixed my retainer?"

"I don't remember the details, Lady Girl, but I can comfortably say we have met before."

They drive for a while.

"Did you grow up here?" she asks.

"Nearby."

"I was with my parents for twenty-four hours. When I'm with them, it's like I evaporate; I barely speak. Seen and not heard. Every time I go back, it feels weirder and weirder. Is it them or is it me?"

"What's happening is not unique to you; they call it growing up," he says. "Books have been penned on the subject."

She doesn't reply.

"Over that way's where my great-grandfather was born; the house is still there. His brothers fought in the Civil War. That's what we are in my family, soldiers, farmers, and taxicab drivers."

"Which side did they fight on?"

"That's the big question, isn't it? They fought on both sides on account of living so close to the Mason-Dixon Line and having complex personalities. Where are your people from?"

"My mother is from Texas and my father is from Wilmington, Delaware."

"Home of DuPont, the folks who brought you forever chemicals and other problems like Teflon. You should ask your dad about his life. Every family has its stories, mysteries, and secrets."

"Maybe not every family. Maybe some are just regular."

The driver shrugs. "Anyone I ever met who seemed regular turned out to be a head case as soon as you scratch the surface."

"Do you still farm?"

"I grow some beans and melons, but I'm famous for my tomatoes."

"That's my favorite sandwich," Meghan says. "Tomato and sea salt on fresh bread."

"With mayo?"

"So much mayo." She laughs. "It was my great-grandfather's favorite as well, or so I'm told."

"Did you ever have homemade mayo?" he asks.

"There is no such thing as homemade mayo. It's like ketchup or mustard; it comes in a jar."

"Funny how young people are," he says to himself. "Acting like they know something."

A few minutes pass in silence.

"I voted," Meghan says.

"Oh." He pretends to be surprised.

"That's where I was. My dad made me fly out west to vote."

"Who'd you vote for?"

"John McCain," she says, as though it's obvious. "Who did you vote for?" she asks tentatively, knowing it's not considered polite.

"That's a bit like asking what side you fought on, but I'll tell you in a minute. First, tell me why you voted for McCain."

"Well," she says, "I voted for John McCain because he's the best candidate. He believes what we believe."

"And what is that? What do 'we' believe?"

"That this should be a good country, a strong country, and that we should all work hard."

"And the other guy? Does he believe the same?"

She doesn't say anything.

"Pretty much anybody running for president wants those things—the real question is what are his goals for the country. You can tell the difference between someone who is in it to make a name for himself or get time on TV and someone who really cares. A lot of guys are big old liars; they'll even tell you they served their country and it's not true."

"John McCain served."

"Yes, he did."

"And he was taken prisoner. I think McCain really cares. I've met him face-to-face and I believe in him."

"That's the first thing you've said that I can buy. You believe in him." He pauses. "And your parents voted for him?"

"Yes."

He nods. "So, in part you voted for him because your parents did."

She shrugs. It had never occurred to her to do anything else, but she wasn't about to tell him that.

"Why did you vote for Barack Obama?" Meghan asks. They're getting close to school; she wants him to go slower; she wants to keep talking.

"I didn't vote for Obama. I voted for McCain. He's a veteran and a maverick, and I like that. I might not always agree with him, but I'd rather have him calling the shots than some guy who does what the party says."

"Does Obama do what the party says?"

"I have no idea."

She feels like she owes Mr. Tooth an explanation for the confusion she feels. "I wasn't just in Wyoming. I also went to Phoenix. I went to be with John McCain when he accepted the victory, but . . ." She begins to cry. "Can we go around the block?" she asks. "I don't want to go in looking all puffy." Her mother has taught her that puffy can be cured by applying cucumber, tea bags, or a cold compress, none of which she has on hand.

Mr. Tooth does a few extra laps; the meter clicks higher, and then he pulls into the driveway of her school, drives past the stone pillars, and continues down the long road of arched oak trees. Entering the Academy is like stepping back in time. Everything is calm, contained, groomed, and well tended. There are rules, traditions, ways of doing things that have not changed since the Academy was founded in 1904. They don't walk on the quad; Sunday church is mandatory, as is the Wednesday morning all-school meeting. And every time the student body is together, they sing the school song, "We Look to You on High," which has an unofficial version as well, "We Look Like We Are High."

Mr. Tooth pulls up by the main office. The ride gets charged to her school account, but she wants to tip him and all she has is the hundred dollar bill her father gave her that morning. She hands Mr. Tooth the hundred.

"I suppose you want ninety back in change?"

"I just want you to have it."

"It doesn't work that way," he says, handing back the bill.

"I hope I didn't offend you."

"Take care, Lady Girl," he says, as she gets out of the cab.

Lady Girl. She likes it. She's not a lady and she's not a girl, and it reminds her a little bit of Lady Bird, Lyndon Johnson's wife, who was friends with her mother's mother.

Lady Girl, she has a new nickname for herself.

"I'm sorry for your loss," one of the international girls says, as Meghan walks up the dormitory stairs.

"Thank you," she says, not sure whether the girl is talking about the election or mistakenly thinks that someone in Meghan's family died—that's usually the only reason they let a student go home midsemester.

"In my father's country, when the government changes, many people die. That is why we left; he did not want to be there when the people would die. My mother tells a different story; she says that we had no choice but to leave. She said that it would not be safe. And so we came to America."

Meghan nods.

"That is the good thing about democracy," the girl says. "No one dies."

Meghan nods again, and as the girl is about to start talking again, she says, "Sorry, I'm late," and runs up the final flight of stairs.

"I hope you feel better soon," the girl calls after Meghan as she flies past posters announcing last night's Election Viewing Party and a note announcing that lights-out had been pushed to midnight.

She closes the door to her room and changes into her riding gear.

"The icing on the cake." That's what her father called it. When she was in eighth grade, her parents started talking about her education. When they moved to Wyoming, they felt the schools weren't challenging enough to shape her into a "global citizen." Her mother was convinced that girls learned better without boys around. And neither of her parents wanted to return to Washington, where she was born, or Connecticut, where they lived when she was younger. So they pitched Meghan the idea of boarding school. They visited with admissions people from several schools, who asked Meghan questions about how she saw herself and what she hoped to be and did she have any "special skills." To Meghan, boarding school was Harry Potter, so she confessed to the admissions person, "I'm afraid I have no magic." To which her mother added, "But she's an excellent rider." "Well, we happen to have a strong equestrian program," the admissions person from the Academy said. Her father chimed in, "If she goes to your school, I'll buy her a horse and that will be the icing on the cake."

The stuff they say about girls and horses is corny but sort of true. "That's the problem with stereotypes," her father says. "They start with a little bit of truth."

The icing on the cake was a beautiful black gelding named Ranger.

As soon as she is in the barn, she feels returned to herself. The physicality of the work, the familiar steps of getting Ranger tacked up, and the peppery leather scent of the stable brings her back into her body. "I'm here," she says, stroking him. "I missed you yesterday." She gives him a sniff of basil snatched from the herb garden outside. He loves basil.

"Don't look down; always look in the direction you want the horse to go," the instructor outside shouts to the younger girls learning to ride.

With a gentle kick of Meghan's heels, Ranger walks on. They loop around the short trail that encircles the school and trot off into the woods. Meghan has been riding since she was three. People are surprised her mother allows it, given how overprotective she is; they forget that Charlotte grew up in Texas on a ranch. Until recently, when Charlotte's back got worse, riding was something she and Meghan did together.

Charlotte thinks it's a perfect sport for a young woman; riding teaches control and posture and the unspoken—that's what she calls it, the "unspoken." What she means is communication without language. Meghan thinks that's mostly how she and Charlotte communicate, a look, a nod, a sigh.

Once they are out in the clear, Meghan leans into Ranger's neck and they are off, cantering through the cool Virginia air. A flood of the last twenty-four hours comes back. She sees John McCain's face in front of her. His eyes are a little too glassy, like marbles. In her mind's eye, she's charging toward him and he's glad to see her; there's a glimmer of recognition. She's reliving the moment last night when he came into the room to shake hands. But he didn't make a lot of eye contact. He didn't linger on anyone; it was as though he didn't want anyone to see too deeply into him. Previously, when she'd met him at a fundraiser in Washington, McCain looked at her intently. He took her hand in both of his and said how pleased he was to finally meet her. She felt something then, a connection, an inspiration. Now, as she's riding into the afternoon, she's feeling that again. She wonders whether John McCain might be relieved that he didn't win. Is it weird that she's thinking about what John McCain is feeling? She's doing the thing that she always does—revisiting what already happened.

It's late afternoon, the trees are almost bare and a chill is creeping into the air. There is a truth to nature that Meghan admires. Nature doesn't pretend; it doesn't hide; it simply is. Trees are expressive. Rocks hold history. These connections are more trustworthy than those with humans, some of whom have either the desire or the skill to conceal their emotions or manipulate. A rock doesn't do something to get the response it's looking for. A tree doesn't shed its leaves because it is jealous of another—but it might grow differently if blocked by another or if a different kind of tree grows next to it. She is pondering this when she realizes she has no idea where she is. Did she go too far? She was on a trail called Western Woods but wonders if she's gone off the trail. How long was she daydreaming? Using the sky and trees as her guide, she finds the Potomac River on her right. She and Ranger are high up on a ridge above the water; the view is majestic and a reminder that the world is enormous and not entirely knowable.

As the sun begins to set, the woods get darker. Light filtering in from above doesn't make it all the way to the ground. Up ahead a young fawn's flick of the tail catches Meghan's eye. She slows. The fawn stands fixed, looking at her. Something's not right. She dismounts Ranger and leads him into the woods. A doe is down on the forest floor. Holding Ranger's reins, Meghan moves closer. There's a large open wound on the doe's side and she's breathing hard. Meghan's heart races. The doe snorts, making a sound somewhere between a high-pitched oh and a whistle. She pulls Ranger back a bit and takes out her phone and dials 911. Nothing happens. She turns the phone off, turns it on again, and waits for it to power up. She dials 911 again.

"911, what's your emergency?"

"I'm on the trail with Ranger and there's a badly injured doe."

"You're a park ranger?"

"No, I am in the park with Ranger."

"What's your emergency?"

"Wounded animal," Meghan shouts, in case volume is part of the problem.

"You were in a motor vehicle accident with an animal? Are you injured?"

"No, I was riding Ranger, and we found the injured animal in the woods."

"What is your name, Ranger?"

"My name is Meghan Hitchens. I am not a ranger. I am on the back end of the trail. We passed the river on the right and I was heading up the back end and that's where the injured animal is."

"Are you in a car?"

"No, I'm on horseback."

"Horseback?" The woman's tone is slightly suspicious.

"Yes."

"And the animal is injured?"

Meghan can't tell how much of the problem is technological, the cell phone, or the woods. She finds herself getting agitated. "Can you send help? The animal is suffering and I don't know what to do. I don't exactly know where I am or how to get out of here."

"What street are you on?"

"I'm not on a street. I am in the woods, maybe across from Bear Island, maybe near Matildaville . . ."

There is a pause; someone seems to be asking the operator a series of questions in the background.

"I'm going to have to ask you to clarify so we can properly direct your call. You were NOT involved in a motor vehicle accident?"

"No. I am on my horse and there is an injured ANIMAL."

"I am going to transfer you back to the police department and will remain on the line."

"Police, what is your emergency?"

"Dispatch, I have a redirect from rescue over to you. The caller is on the line. Are you there, ma'am?"

"Yes. I am here. It's getting dark."

"Do you happen to know which trailhead you are closest to?" the police operator asks.

"I'm not really sure; I'm on the back side of Great Falls; I'm pretty sure of that."

"Are you able to meet the officer at the entrance to the trail?"

"No," Meghan says. "I'm deep in the woods where the animal is and I've got my horse."

"We don't just send officers into the woods," the operator says.

"If I told you I was lost, you wouldn't send anyone to look for me?"

"Are you lost?"

"I'm deep in the woods."

"What is your name?"

"My name is Meghan Grace Hitchens. If someone was trying to kill me, I'd be dead by now. I thought 911 was for emergencies."

"I have to inform you that all calls are recorded and that filing a false report is a crime."

"I am calling you for help," Meghan screams; her voice sends the fawn farther into the woods.

"Calm down." A pause. "We have an officer dispatched," the operator says. "Can I confirm your phone number is 307-656-7482. And where is that 307 area code?"

"Wyoming, which is where I'm from."

"You said that you are a student at the Academy?"

"Correct," Meghan says.

"All right. The officer is en route. Please do not approach the injured animal."

"Got it." She ties Ranger to a tree nearby and tries to get closer to the doe without completely chasing the fawn away. She can hear the animal more than she can see her now. The sound of the doe's breathing fast and hard leaves Meghan feeling helpless.

Twenty minutes pass and she dials 911 again. "It's getting very dark and cold out here," she tells the dispatcher.

"Are you in immediate danger?"

"Is there someone actually coming?"

"Yes, they are on the way." They confirm her name and phone number again.

"I don't have much battery left. I forgot to charge my phone last night."

"Keep it turned on if you can."

Forty minutes after she first called, she sees a light through the trees, distant but moving closer. An officer arrives on a bike. "I keep it in the trunk. It's a hell of a lot faster than on foot."

Meghan leads him into the thick woods to where the injured animal is.

"Probably had a run-in with a car," the officer says.

"Will she be okay? That's her fawn over there. Is there a vet who can come and help her?" Meghan's relieved when he takes out a flashlight and moves closer to the deer.

"I'm going to ask you to stand back," he says.

Meghan steps back, giving the officer room. As he goes closer, the doe tries to lift its head. Meghan thinks it's sweet; the doe is grateful for the help. The officer fixes his flashlight on the doe's face. Before Meghan can say or think anything, his gun is out of the holster.

Bang.

Ranger squeals and rears, pulling his reins off the tree and galloping off.

Bang.

Meghan runs after Ranger.

"Fuck," the cop says, running after Meghan.

She runs faster. "Get away from me."

"Stop running."

"I have to get my horse."

She dives into the woods where Ranger went off the trail. The officer is on his radio requesting backup. Both the horse and the girl have run off, and he can't see either of them.

"Can you hear me?"

She ignores him. "Ranger, where are you? Come on, sugar boy. Remember the promise we made—never to leave each other?" She is looking for her horse and making deals. "If you come back, I won't go home for Christmas; I'll stay with you and we can ride every day. Maybe I can take you on a trip. We could go back to that place down in Florida, what's it called? Wellington. Remember when we went there and you loved it. Sweet-sweet, where are you?"

She starts singing Christmas songs. "Westward leading, still proceeding." It's dark and she is thoroughly lost. She finds Ranger in a clearing between trees, dark against the dark. His saddle is hanging off to the side, like he's been through a battle. Meghan reaches down and picks up some dry leaves, crumbling them in her hand. The sound is like the wrapper for the peanut butter crackers she buys from the vending machine. Crackers he particularly likes. She can tell he recognizes the noise. "So, it's about my crackers?" she says, walking toward him, continuing to rustle the leaves. She looks at him square on through the darkness and keeps her eyes steady on his until he lowers his head. She puts her arms around his neck and takes the reins. "You scared me so much."

She is in a dark field stroking Ranger's muzzle. "I'm eighteen years old; I voted for the first time; that's where I was yesterday. I thought I was doing pretty well . . ."

Wednesday, November 5, 2008
Palm Springs, California
4:47 p.m.

At the exact moment of sundown, 4:47 p.m., Charlotte makes herself a cocktail. One of the nice things about the Palm Springs house is that the walls are glass; she always knows what time it is. Rye, sweet and dry vermouth, bitters, and one maraschino cherry poured into a cold glass. She keeps empty glasses in the refrigerator. The cherry is the one sweet thing she allows herself.

Supper. Usually, they stay home. Usually, he puts a piece of meat on the grill and maybe a pepper or a squash, and they call it a meal. But today he makes a dinner reservation. He feels the need for change, for shaking things up. "I'm taking you out," he says.

"Oh." Her expression is bemused.

"I made a reservation at Melvyn's."

Because they are concerned with how they're seen by others, they dress for the occasion. They clean up well. When they find each other in the front hall, each is pleased to see that effort has been made, not just for the world but for each other.

"You look nice," she says.

"Like an Easter egg." He's wearing yellow pants, a pink shirt, a pale blue sweater, and white Gucci loafers. "You smell like a grove of oranges," he says.

They leave the house at 5:45 p.m. They have become *those* people, the ones who eat at 6 p.m. and want to be home by 7:30. They don't like to drive in the dark and they want to get to bed early. Nine p.m. is prime time for bed, to be alone, to have themselves to themselves, to have finished the business of being a couple.

As soon as they are seated at Melvyn's, Charlotte orders another Manhattan. Then she orders steak Diane. He opts for the scallops and a scotch neat.

She has another drink. He's surprised she doesn't appear more inebriated. She's the size of a matchstick but holds her liquor well. When they were younger, it was something one aspired to.

"What if things had gone differently?" he asks.

"What if?" she asks. "There are a million 'what ifs' and only one 'what is,' which is where we find ourselves now."

"I like you," he says. "You've always been practical."

"Practical is rarely a compliment," she says. "Challenging has its good qualities. Mesmerizing is hard to sustain over time. But at least you didn't dip to well preserved."

"I would never." He pauses. "We are rather a miracle, aren't we? We have lived."

"Have we? I keep thinking, one day my life will begin."

"No time like the present," he says. There's a long pause.

Silence.

"I never meant you any harm."

Charlotte says nothing.

"I always wanted the best for you. I know I'm no cakewalk."

"You mean walk in the park?"

"I'm not easy."

"It's not all about you."

"Of course not," he says. "I see you suffering and I wanted to say something. There's so much we don't talk about."

"It just seems impossible."

"I'm not saying it's right or wrong. It's painful. I know you know."

"I do. Someday it might come out. It could leak or explode or just be exhaled in a single breath." She finishes her drink.

"It's important to me that you take care of yourself," he says.

"You're going to be okay."

"I'm not worried about myself."

The conversation tightens and chokes itself off. There are years of unexplored history. They each have their own version of the events at the heart of their disconnection. They have stepped back from each other in separate acts of self-preservation, in part out of fear of what might be said or the damage that might be done.

Charlotte signals the waiter for another round. He butters warm rolls for her.

"You always liked hot buns," he says, laughing.

"You're making me nervous. You know I don't eat bread. Just be yourself. What else did Tony say about last night?"

"People are sending out résumés and putting houses on the market. The ebb and flow has begun, but not as much as in the old days. Do you know that since 9/11 the number of 'top secret' jobs has expanded by hundreds of thousands? That's hundreds of thousands of desk jockeys somewhere between Bethesda and Alexandria."

The waiter appears with his cart of fire and prepares steak Diane before their eyes. It is her favorite meal. What she likes most about it is the smell.

"I'm undone by what happened," he says, as the waiter adds ingredients in a pan tableside.

"You didn't see it coming?"

"Apparently not."

The waiter visibly bristles, then fiddles with the heat beneath his pan.

"We care about our whole country; I don't think it's selfish not to want it all to turn to shit." He shakes his head. "I've not served my country well."

"Well, you were never military material, between the flat feet and the missing kidney."

"When we first met, we used to talk about who we wanted to be."

"Yes. You wanted to be Andrew Carnegie, but you felt the time had passed."

He nods.

"You didn't turn out so badly," she says. "You wanted to be rich and powerful and make a call and be put straight through."

"It's not enough."

They pause while the waiter serves them. He stands over the table until they begin to eat. She looks up at the waiter. "It's lovely. Thank you."

"Do you know what Tony wanted to be?"

"What?"

"Take a guess."

"Ambassador to France?" she says.

He laughs. "Nope. I'll give you a clue. They are most often seen at four in the afternoon or eleven thirty at night."

Charlotte is confused. "Sportscaster?"

"Talk show host," he says. "He was always enamored with David Frost and Dick Cavett. He didn't even try, too worried about what his family would think. Show business and all. They always gave him a hard time for being soft."

"Funny," Charlotte says. "When I was a girl, no one ever asked what you wanted to be; they only asked what kind of man you wanted to marry."

Deep in the woods, the sounds of radios crackle in the distance. Flashlight beams cut through the trees. "I'm here," Meghan calls out, worried that the idiot with the gun will shoot her. "Can you hear me? Are you armed? Are you going to shoot me?"

Before they get close, she hears them over their radios. "We've got her." Voices bounce through the woods almost as if the trees were talking.

"I'm Officer Robinson," a woman's voice calls out.

"Please don't shoot me."

"No one is going to shoot you." Officer Robinson is getting closer. "They're coming out with an ATV and I'll walk the horse back."

"I'm not leaving Ranger."

"We can't let you ride him in the dark. And it's a long walk," Officer Robinson says.

"I'm fine to walk," Meghan says.

After much squawking back and forth, Officer Robinson ties fluorescent green glow sticks to Ranger's tack and puts a few on Meghan.

When they get to the trailhead, cops form a ring around her. Officer Robinson stands to the side holding Ranger's reins. Why are they surrounding her?

"A lot of people have been looking for you," one of the cops says, like Meghan's in trouble.

"Tell that to the jerk with the gun," she says before she realizes that he is the jerk with the gun.

"I didn't know that you didn't have the horse in hand."

"Ranger was tied to a tree. If I had him in hand, it could have been a lot worse. When he reared up, he might have come down on me! It was a doe, a mother with her baby. Why didn't you help her?"

"Protocol tells us that if wild animals are injured we euthanize them as safely and quickly as we can."

"You shot her again and again."

"How many shots?" the top cop asks.

"Two," the officer says before Meghan can get a word out. "One to crack the skull, another to put it out. I was back about seven to ten feet so I didn't get spatter."

With that, Meghan starts sobbing. "Not okay. I am not okay. This is not okay."

"Do you want to tell us why you ran away from school?" one of the officers asks.

"Why would I run away?"

"You tell me."

"Wait, what?"

"You were upset this afternoon when you got back to school, and then you got on the horse and ran away."

"That is not what happened."

"One of the girls at school said she saw you and that you looked upset." The officer is now standing with one hand on a hip and the other on his gun.

"I went out for a ride on my horse because that's what I love doing most in the world. I came across a situation and I called for help because I thought you're supposed to. And then your guy shoots Bambi's mother like in a horror film. Did he tell you that her fawn saw the whole thing and now will most likely die in the woods alone? Did he mention the fawn?"

"You seem very upset," the cop says, sounding more judgmental than nice.

"I am upset," she says. "I feel like I'm losing my mind. This whole thing is crazy." The circle of cops standing around her pulls closer.

"Really?" he asks. "Did you take anything?"

"Anything like what?"

"Drugs?"

"Oh my god, are you kidding me?" She stands there shaking her head. "This is beyond the beyond," she mutters to herself. She turns away from the cop who has been quizzing her and takes out her phone. She calls Tony. She calls Tony because that's what her parents would do. Whenever they are overwhelmed or in over their heads, they call Tony. That's what best friends are for. That's what fixers are for—repair work. Tony does the repair work for the White House.

Tony answers on the first ring. "Hi, kiddo, what's up?"

"I don't even know what to say. But something is wrong. Something is very wrong and I need your help."

"Where are you?"

"I am by the side of the road with Ranger, surrounded by armed police officers who are asking me if I've taken drugs and a million other weird things."

"That doesn't make sense. Are you hurt?"

"I am not hurt. Although I easily could have been shot."

"Can you give the phone to the police officer?"

"Who is in charge?" she asks, waving her phone at the group.

"Who wants to know?" the cop asks.

"Tony Armstrong, from the White House. Special assistant to the president." She wouldn't normally drop a line like that, but it's all too out of control. "He would like to speak to whoever is in charge."

The cops look at one another, and then Officer Robinson finally steps forward to take the call. "Hello, Mr. Armstrong . . ."

Wednesday, November 5, 2008
Palm Springs, California
6:15 p.m.

Three-quarters of the way through the meal, both of their phones ring. His is in his pants pocket, hers is in her purse—he didn't even know she carried it with her. They look at each other—it can't be good.

People in the restaurant glare. He pulls out his phone and flips it open.

"Meghan is fine," a voice on the other end of the line says.

A cold sweat breaks out across his face.

"This is Mrs. Hayes from the Academy . . ."

The voice in the Big Guy's ear, initially alarming, drones on as color first drains from his face and then slowly returns when it becomes clear that the news is not dire.

"Everything all right?" Charlotte asks, as he hangs up. She signals the waiter for another drink.

He nods. "When both phones rang, I was sure it was bad. I thought the plane had gone down. Maybe it was too much for her, the travel, the excitement of voting, and then the letdown. These are the years when all hell can break loose, when you can lose them for no good reason."

"I thought they said she was fine?" Charlotte says. "You've done a good job with her. She respects you enormously."

"Doesn't matter how good a job you do; shit can happen. If anything, that's what these last few days have taught me." He signals for the check. "Clearly I'm not paying enough attention to you, to her, to whatever the hell it is that's going on"

"Have a sip of water."

He pays the bill in cash and adds a large tip. "Apologies for the ker-fuffle," he says to the waiter. "We had a bit of a scare."

"No problem," the waiter says.

"I'm shaken," he says to Charlotte as they are leaving. "That's the bot-tom line; I'm shaken."

The headmistress's door is three-quarters closed, but Meghan can hear people inside talking.

"She is to be reminded that riding the trail is a privilege, and it is suggested that for now she confine herself to the ring," someone says—she doesn't recognize the voice.

"One is expected to follow the rules; we are a community, and in order to function, we must all commit to a code of conduct."

Meghan is standing outside the office, listening, twirling the phoenix on the necklace she bought this morning.

"She needs to know what is expected."

Unable to bear it any longer, Meghan knocks on the door.

"Come in."

"I'm not the one who fired the gun," she blurts out.

"No one is blaming you," a teacher says.

"Then why are you punishing me?" Meghan pauses. "I hate it here, I hate everything. I hate my whole fucking life."

The headmistress and the others in the room stare at her.

"I've never done anything bad—ever. And now suddenly I'm in trouble because other people can't do their jobs? I quit. How about that? I quit. Pardon my French. I certainly won't have a day like today and then be punished for it. And I remind you, I don't have to be here at this school. I am not obligated to stay. I am emancipated."

"If you wouldn't mind excusing us," the headmistress says to the other two women in the room, who appear shocked by Meghan's outburst.

"Of course." They scurry out.

"Close the door?" one asks.

"Please."

"Sit," the headmistress tells Meghan, who doesn't want to but does.

The headmistress sits at her desk thinking. She has no idea what to do.

"It's unfair," Meghan says. "The day can start in one place where it all seems obvious and end in another where nothing will be clear again." There is no control, no certainty. That is the brutal awakening of this moment.

"Would you like something to drink?" the headmistress asks Meghan. Without waiting for an answer, she goes over to the little setup in the corner of her office and pours two glasses, one small, one large.

"This didn't happen," she says, handing the glass to Meghan. "Headmistresses do not pour drinks for their students. And there's nothing you can say that will convince someone that it did."

"It never happened," Meghan says, taking a sip.

"I don't think you should quit; you are just at the beginning. While your outburst was an earful, it seems you've found your voice and can do an excellent job advocating for yourself."

Meghan shrugs.

The headmistress finishes the drink and pours herself a second. Clearly a second glass is not in Meghan's future. "We were very concerned about you."

"If people were so concerned, why did it take the police forty minutes to come to where I was?"

"Because, as you noticed, not everyone is a rocket scientist." The headmistress finishes her drink and pours herself a third.

"What does it mean when the people you are supposed to count on for help don't help? They show up and act the opposite of what you would expect. Instead of saving a life, they take a life. I don't understand."

"I suspect you do," the headmistress says. "And that's why you are so upset."

Another virginity, Meghan thinks to herself but says nothing.

"Sometimes there is more to a story than one is aware of, information that has been left out."

"I told them who I was and where I was."

The headmistress takes a deep breath. "There is a story that will no doubt surface, so you'd better hear it from me. Actually, that's misleading and makes it sound like a fairy tale when, in fact, it's the opposite. I am telling you this not as an explanation or excuse but because it highlights the larger issue; there is often something we don't know, a backstory."

"Does it have something to do with me?" Meghan asks.

The headmistress shakes her head no. And over the next twenty minutes she tells Meghan the gruesome account of two girls—one who was attacked near campus and survived. The survivor was convinced that her attacker would return and kept telling people, but no one shared her concern; they wrote it off as a traumatic reaction. And then the man returned and grabbed another girl who looked just like the first one and murdered her.

"Where?"

"In the woods."

"Those woods?"

The headmistress nods. "Yes."

A brisk chill runs through Meghan. "She was murdered in the woods where I rode Ranger?" It was all fine until it wasn't.

For the first time she feels the threat of outside forces. Is this what the headmistress meant by loss of innocence? "Suddenly things don't make any sense. It's like there's something wrong with my brain."

"There is nothing wrong with your brain," the headmistress says.

Meghan is momentarily speechless. "I'm lost," she finally says. There is a pause. "Did they catch the murderer?"

"Yes."

"If I'd known, I might not have ridden into the woods."

"Indeed," the headmistress says. "That is the question. Does knowing empower or inhibit? Young women are prone to anxiety. Knowing what happened might make some feel unsafe; they might become trapped, entombed, by what they know."

"History needs to count for something," Meghan says.

"One would hope. In this case, the police did a poor job looking for the girl; if they'd done a better job, she might have survived. And today, did any of the people you spoke to know what had come before? One wants to believe that there are systems in place that protect us; but, in fact, we are all a little more on our own than one might realize." The headmistress puts away the things on her desk. "It certainly has been a long day. How about I walk you back to the dormitory?"

"Fine, but I'd like to say good night to Ranger." The headmistress nods.

"What was the girl's name?" Meghan asks, as they walk toward the stable.

"Shh," the headmistress says. "It's enough for one night."

On the way home, his phone rings; he pulls onto a residential street and parks under a streetlight. "Hello, Pigeon," he says, calling Meghan by an old nickname. "You okay? What the heck happened?"

As she's telling him the story, a coyote crosses the street about fifty feet in front of the car. He points it out to Charlotte. The coyote goes up a driveway. And then there are a lot of squeals and cats come flying out of the driveway and scramble up the tree overhead. The coyote skulks back down the driveway into the street—looking. He beeps his horn long and hard.

"Are you in traffic?"

"No, honey, I'm here in the car with Mother; we're just driving home from dinner. Your mother wants to know, is the horse okay?"

Inside one of the houses someone turns on a light and presses their face to the glass. He blinks his high beams, shining light on and off the coyote.

"Ranger is amazing," Meghan says. "The icing on the cake."

"She wants me to tell you . . . Here, why don't you tell her yourself." He hands Charlotte the phone and gets out of the car to check on the cats in the tree.

"In the morning, check the horse's legs; make sure he doesn't have any scratches," Charlotte says. "Sometimes when you go off trail, you can get scratches or abrasions that can get infected if you don't keep them clean. You're a good girl. Get some rest." Charlotte holds the phone out the car window.

"Sleep well, honey, and let's talk tomorrow," he calls out.

"Now what?" Charlotte asks.

"The cats are up a tree and the coyote is over there, lurking."

"And is your plan to stand in the middle of the street and see what happens? Are you sure it's a coyote and not a raccoon? Are you going to climb the tree?"

"Very funny."

He walks to the front door of the house where he thinks the cats belong and rings the bell. No one answers. He rings again.

"I'm not answering for a reason," a female voice says from behind the door.

"Okay," he says through the door. "I was just trying to tell you that your cats are up a tree and there's a coyote out here."

"This isn't a prank, is it?"

He can feel himself being watched through the peephole. "Do I look like a prankster?"

The door opens.

"Your cats are in the tree," he says, pointing. "And the coyote is there." His pointer finger pivots toward the neighbor's house.

The woman steps out, puts two fingers in her mouth, and gives a loud, sharp whistle. "Ginger, you come here," she calls out. "Right now, git over here."

And the coyote comes out of the dark and slinks toward the house. Overhead, the two cats hiss.

"Ginger, tell this man you are no wild animal."

Now that his eyes have adjusted and his pulse has settled, he can see that the coyote is no coyote or raccoon but a thin shepherd with tall ears and a long tail.

"All right then," he says, backing away from the house. "You have a pleasant night."

In the car Charlotte is laughing.

"Not funny," he says, getting in. "Not funny at all."

She puts her hand behind his head, tickling him on the back of the neck, a gesture of affection that's not been had in years. Blood changes direction in his body.

"You looked very good out there," she says. "Strong and authoritative."

When they get home, he impulsively wraps his arms around her and buries his nose in her neck. Orange blossoms. Hurriedly, he leads her down the hall to the guest room.

"The guest room?"

"Things have to change," he says.

It is less an act of passion than urgency, the need to relieve a cacophony of chemical surges, from the sickness of the phone call and the adrenalized response to the dog, from his rage and all else that has been unsaid for so long. Bang, bang, bang, it's like a mafia hit. Primal, hard, fast, like nothing that's happened between them in years. They have at each other and then collapse deflated, drunk on the bed.

It happens as though it were independent of either of them, as though they were overcome.

And then they are apart—strangers, stupefied. They remain dazed for an hour or so, and then he helps her up to the bathroom and down the hall to their room.

"I feel like a used condom," she says. "What did they used to call it—a johnny."

When she is tucked into bed, she rolls toward him of her own accord and they go at it again, this time slower, filled with familiarity, one might even say contentment, but that would be an exaggeration. That would be like the middle-aged word for passion. They made love contentedly—how awful.

They make love slowly because that's the best they can do. It's the first time in forever that they've done it more than once in a go-round. That's what they used to call it, a go-round. They make love slowly and whatever it was or isn't, it makes clear that what happened before was not just a fluke or an oddity. There is something one might call tenderness or appreciation, mutuality, stopping short of desire or, god forbid, lust.

Then inevitably, awkwardness, retreat. Neither wants to ask what it means or what turn in the relationship it might present. But it's a personal victory for each of them that neither wants to risk upsetting.

"I just want you to know I'm here," he says, wrapping his arm around her.

"Thank you," she says.

"Do you find it ironic that we were talking about things and then something happened?"

"Sex?" she asks.

"No. The phone call. I find it difficult. She's changing."

"She's becoming a person in her own right. She won't always be in love with you; she won't always do what you want."

"That's okay."

"You're lying."

"Not intentionally, I just hope that I'll get used to it. That I'll grow into it."

He snuggles next to her. "You know even Cindy McCain went to rehab; there is no shame. I bet she'd be happy to talk to you about it."

"I don't need rehab," she says tersely.

"You're very unhappy."

"Yes."

"Do you know why?"

"I forgot to have my life. I've been having your life for a quarter of a century. The last time I had my own life I was about eleven."

"And what were you doing?"

"I was taking tap dance lessons," she says without pause.

"Then sign up for tap again."

"I just might," she says, rolling over and putting out the light.

A pause.

"Have you gone through the change?"

"Pardon?"

"The change, that's what they call it."

"Why are you asking?"

"I was just wondering if it's happened."

"Yes. It's long gone."

He is thinking about Meghan and the horse getting lost and the wife asking if the horse is okay and not asking about Meghan. If he asked her, she'd say that she knew Meghan was okay, but they would both know there is more to it.

"Go to sleep," Charlotte says.

The long glass windows are shiny black. In the glow cast by the night-light, he can see his own reflection in the glass.

He doesn't hear her the first time because he's too busy watching.

"Go to sleep," she repeats.

The day begins with a test in history. A few of the girls know that something happened yesterday because word gets around, but no one knows exactly what. For Meghan, the bigger question is not who knows about her but who knows about the murdered girl.

"Are you okay? I heard you got arrested last night."

"I didn't get arrested."

"That's not what I heard."

"I heard the police were out looking for you. I'm surprised you're still here and they didn't kick you out."

"I got lost in the woods. They don't kick you out for getting lost."

"Two years ago, a girl got kicked out just for going into the woods."

"She didn't get kicked out for going into the woods; she got kicked out for selling drugs to another student who also went into the woods."

"I'm glad you're not dead," one of the girls says. "I thought you were so upset about McCain losing the election that you committed suicide."

"Why would I commit suicide over an election?"

"I have no idea; you know how girls are," the girl says.

"You are a girl too," one of the other girls says.

"Exactly," another girl says.

"I heard that Mrs. Webster from the admissions office was crying and couldn't be consoled. She said that it was because of her you have a horse; she felt responsible for your disappearance."

"You all sound hysterical," one of them says.

"That's what's often said about women," Naomi Widder says. She's the smartest one in the group.

"Ladies, ladies," Ms. Adams says, striding into the class. Ms. Adams is a twenty-three-year-old recent graduate of William & Mary with a double major in politics and women's history. She is the first recipient of the Woolrich Capstone Scholar Award, which invites a recent college graduate to spend a year at the school as a scholar-in-residence, doing their own research, and teaching a senior seminar. Ms. Adams is "of the Adams family," which gives her an edge, having grown up as a descendant and receiver of history. When the semester started, she presented herself to her students as someone who early in life "became mindful of the ways in which every family has a story. The story is identity. And those who don't agree with the story are black sheep." The course she is teaching is called Women's Lives: Windows and Mirrors Looking Toward a New American History.

"Today marks our midsemester, and instead of having a test, you will present your research projects. Naomi, how about you get us started."

The desks are arranged in a circle. Ms. Adams calls her teaching style the Harkness method, a unique model from which she benefited as a student at Phillips Exeter, where she "prepped" before college.

"Thank you, Ms. Adams," Naomi says. "As you know, I am a poet, and to be a poet one must study other poets. I zeroed in on Emily Dickinson because when I first started writing poems my mother gave me a book of Dickinson, not because she was the best woman poet but because she was the only woman poet my mother knew of who hadn't killed herself. What I am going to talk about today is what Dickinson didn't say and the concept of stone memory. The book *A Wounded Deer* by Wendy K. Perriman uses recent developments in trauma theory to unpack the idea that Dickinson was sexually abused."

"A wounded deer, just like you," one of the girls whispers to Meghan.

"I am not wounded," Meghan says.

Naomi continues. "What prompted me to explore this darkness in

Dickinson's life was an experience I had. Last spring I visited Dickinson's house in Amherst, and once inside the house, I felt uncomfortable but couldn't explain why. Around that same time, I discovered the idea of stone memory or place memory. This is a controversial idea first explicated in Charles Babbage's 1837 *The Ninth Bridgewater Treatise*, the idea being that buildings or objects store and can play back past events. Babbage thought that words leave a permanent mark on the air; even though one can't hear them anymore, they linger. Having spent time rereading Dickinson's work and visiting her home, I feel we need to reconsider Dickinson and the possibility that many women carry within their bodies a version of stone trauma that is passed down to future generations."

When Naomi finishes, the girls all applaud.

Meghan hears it all in the background while her mind is elsewhere. She's replaying the events of the last forty-eight hours as if they were a movie. She is thinking about the look on her father's face when John McCain lost. Fear. She was looking at him as the news broke; she saw color drain and a kind of cold white terror rise from his neck up. His eyes darted around the room, looking at the other men. "Game over," someone said, she doesn't remember who. Then her mind skips to the cab ride back to school from the airport and her conversation with Mr. Tooth. She had told him what she saw; she was almost afraid to say it, but she needed to tell someone. Mr. Tooth had nodded knowingly. "Like a bystander at the apocalypse," he had said. "I saw that look myself only once, in November 1963." "Election?" she had asked Mr. Tooth. "Assassination," he had said. "President Kennedy was shot. My father came home from work in the middle of the day and he had that same look, cold white terror. And it wasn't because my father liked Kennedy, he voted for Nixon, but because that kind of thing wasn't supposed to happen here. Reality and truth as he knew them were suddenly in question. And I can tell you that seeing the man I counted on for stability scared shitless, pardon my French, was something I never forgot."

She is in class thinking of Kennedy being shot, the bullet cracking his skull, and she thinks of the doe in the woods and she feels it in her body, the sudden snap crack of the first shot, an immediate jolt through her body, and then the second shot. She closes her eyes, winces.

"Are you okay?" one of the girls asks.

"What?" Meghan says. "Sorry, I . . ."

"You look like you saw a ghost."

"Take risks," Ms. Adams is saying. "Face what feels uncomfortable. Find language for your experience. Those are a few of the first words I shared with you this September when I talked about what I hoped we would do in this course. Thank you, Naomi, for pushing us to think about Emily Dickinson. Ashley, remind us what your subject is."

"My subject is women artists and the need for a women's museum," Ashley says. "When I was younger, my parents used to take me to museums all the time, and at first, I didn't notice that there were no women artists represented, and then I began to wonder why."

Nur presents her ideas on the luxury of being a housewife, cycles of the feminist movement, and does one have to hate men in order to support women. Haley discusses colonial brick and mortar and the dirt under a woman's fingernails.

Meghan can only think about last night: the deer in the woods, the fawn without its mother, the enormously loud crack of the bullet. She is thinking about the murdered girl. Her head is spinning; maybe it's not having breakfast, maybe it's a hangover from the small glass of sherry the headmistress had given her.

"Meghan, are you with us?" Ms. Adams asks.

"Sorry."

"Don't apologize," Ms. Adams says. "Women apologize too often."

"Right, sorry," Meghan says again, then takes a deep breath. "My project is called 'Riding Astride'; it examines how ideas about women, horses, and power have changed throughout history. My subject was influenced by my experience growing up as an only child with a mother who is somewhat formal. I admire my mother enormously but she is not cuddly. Riding is how we spend time together and it is where I have seen her demonstrate both physical strength and intellectual fortitude, skills that she has passed on to me. I have memories of my mother's eyes on me as I was cantering around the ring, the sense I had that I was pleasing her, seeking her approval, not a male gaze. The relationship of women to horses has been for the most part explored by men who see things as sexualized. Men believe that a woman on a horse is working out her sexual fantasies, her anxieties about men. I can tell you that my horse, Ranger, is not thinking about my butt or my thighs in sexual terms. My horse is experiencing the communication between my body and his; he is feeling my butt and thighs as command and power of body and mind. When I am riding my horse—I am empowered, confident, and free." Meghan continues to read from her paper. "Horses are the stuff of dreams and fairy tales, but they also have a place in women's historical narrative from Sacagawea to Annie Oakley and Inez Milholland. Deep and musky. Wise and gallant. Before the fourteenth century, women rode astride. Joan of Arc, burned at the stake at nineteen for the crime of being a witch, was a young woman ahead of her time. Joan of Arc rode astride. Catherine the Great, empress of Russia, was rumored to have died after having sex with her horse Dudley. Asking one to imagine Catherine in a sexual exchange with a horse was meant to show how 'unnatural' it was for her to rule as empress. Her freedom to rule, to take many lovers, bothered people who saw her behavior like that of a man. Catherine the Great rode astride. Anne of Bohemia, sent from Prague to England to be wed to King Richard II, was forced to ride sidesaddle, strapped to a horse because her family wanted to be sure she arrived 'intact.' The advent of the sidesaddle was to prevent accidental rupture of the royal hymen, which would render her unmarriageable. Anne was packaged and delivered like a parcel. When riding in public, Queen Elizabeth often rode sidesaddle as she did in 1987 for the ceremonial Trooping the Colour, but more often, she is seen riding astride, such as in 1982 when she and President Reagan rode together at Windsor Castle. Horses brought women full throttle into the future. Inez

Milholland, a suffragette, labor lawyer, and activist, led the March 1913 suffrage parade of eight thousand women down Pennsylvania Avenue in Washington, DC, in a white cape riding on her horse, Gray Dawn. In 1916 Milholland collapsed while giving a speech and died in Los Angeles, having given her life so that we may 'go forward into the light.'"

Meghan pauses, lip quivering, and begins to cry.

"What is it? What are you crying about?" Ms. Adams asks.

"Everything." Meghan sniffles. "I am crying about everything. It seems that if one wants to ride astride, to be powerful and independent, one has to leave things behind."

"Like what?" one of the girls asks.

"Like your family," another girl says. "Like everything that people expect you to be."

"Being a senior is hard," Ms. Adams says. "You're on the cusp of so much."

The girls look at Ms. Adams as if to ask, Is that the best you can do?

"We pretend things have changed, but have they? Really?" another girl says.

"She's crying about the dead girl," Ashley says matter-of-factly.

"What dead girl?" Ms. Adams wants to know.

"The one no one talks about," Ashley says. "A girl from here vanished and was found murdered in the woods."

"What do you mean, vanished?"

"You know the crappy school bikes that we ride downhill but never ride them back up? The bikes they put in the back of the truck and drive uphill?"

The girls all nod.

"One day, after chapel, this girl went off on her bike and no one noticed she was gone until dinner. The next day they found her body in the woods."

"Are you sure this is a true story?" Ms. Adams asks.

"My aunt knew her," Ashley says. "She said she was a very nice girl, among the nicest of the girls."

Naomi pats Meghan on the back as if she were burping her.

Meghan is still crying. She can't go back to things the way they were. None of this can continue.

"Are you crying for the dead girl?" Nur asks.

"I'm crying for all the girls," Meghan manages to say. "I'm crying for everyone."

"It didn't happen here," Haley says.

"It happened," Naomi says, and Haley begins to cry.

"Somewhere in the woods there is a fawn without its mother," Meghan says. "And there is a dead girl missing out on history."

Thursday, November 6, 2008
Palm Springs, California
5:00 a.m.

What Comes Next? He's scratched the question in large letters across the middle of his desk blotter with a blue Paper Mate Flair felt-tip pen. These are his favorite pens: blue, black, red, and green. Blue is for new ideas; black is for notes and signatures; red equals corrections or emergency; and the green, well, the green is for money, adding it all up. The Paper Mate Flair was first made by Frawley Pen of Oak Brook, Illinois, later acquired by Gillette.

He's got his stack of cocktail napkins from the Biltmore bar next to him and is working his way through them, deciphering his notes, some of which are stuck together with egg yolk.

He draws on the blotter paper, "sketching," he calls it, but really it's a map, a tree of ideas. He uses a set of symbols he's invented, including what he calls a "mental paper clip" and various marks that exist somewhere between logic notations and copyediting marks. It's a code understood only by its author—dots, dashes, squiggles, and a few newer familiar faces, :). He learned that one only recently from his daughter.

"What did your teacher used to put on your papers when you were a kid?" Meghan had asked, showing off her ☺ A+.

"Gold stars," he said. "She used to put gummed gold-foil stars on our papers. And what did we talk about most? The idea that Mrs. Worth had licked the back of the stars, that our papers had her saliva on them."

"When was that?" she asked. "The 1920s?"

"No," he said. "I wasn't even born in the 1920s. This was in 1950s Connecticut."

He uses his blue pen to put a couple of ☺s on the thick white blotter paper next to the ideas he's particularly fond of, watching each of the lines grow wider as the thick white paper stock drinks up the ink; the ·· in the ☺ expands like pupils dilating.

His idea is focused on what he sees as the failure of the Republican Party. Inspired by what he and the man in the bar discussed, he draws a series of large bubbles echoing the structure of the government and writes inside them: Executive, Legislative, Judicial. Then a series of smaller bubbles: Military, Finance, Health, Media. Coming off each of those in squiggly lines like small waves or a wake from a boat, he scrawls: choir, footslogger, pawn, man on the ground.

With his map before him, he spins around in his chair, opens his filing cabinets, and begins to dig. He has a row of three wooden cabinets that have been retrofitted with serious locks. He has three sets of the same cabinets, one in each of his homes, each with the same contents. He calls them the vaults. Everything in the vaults is filed in chronological order, oldest in the back, newest up front.

When he's trying to figure something out, he works the vault. It's like his own Rubik's Cube; what he's looking for are the right elements, the recipe. The common ingredient is money, a lot of money. What is in the vault? Everything. Lists of the meetings he's had every year, the business deals he's been offered, what he's taken, what he's turned down. He has files on his friends. "Your own little FBI," Tony once called it.

For this endeavor, he makes a chart of men who are connected to one another through business, where they went to school, where they play golf, their wives and families. He's trying to figure out what he can build where the parts can act both synchronously and asynchronously without the workings being exposed, something operational and yet scrambled well enough so the identity of those pulling the strings can't be traced.

He knows this idea is not unique; he is well aware men far greater than he have made plans of their own in the past—but where are they now?

In general, it's best not to tell the Big Guy what can't be done because he will find a way; a wall or the word impossible is not a barrier, it's a source of excitement, a challenge in a life that has otherwise become far too routine.

By this point, he's pulled out files, notes, and stacks of business cards, and is connecting the dots. As he works, he's reminded of the tools of childhood: Erector sets, plain wooden blocks, scraps of wood, old bricks he used to find in the yard. He always enjoyed building a world of his own design. He knows that kids still do that, but now the Lego kits come with instructions and contain only the pieces to build the thing in the picture on the front of the box. He knows that kids build worlds on their computers and play virtual war games, but whatever he's making, he likes to be hands-on, to feel it, to touch it.

Networks. That's the key to the whole caboodle. He is fully engaged for the first time in a long time and thrilled with the feeling. This is how it used to feel, like anything was possible.

He moves from the file cabinets to his favorite tool. He grabs the heavy black knob of his dual-barreled Rolodex and gives it a spin. The Rolodex is the true power broker's tool, and as with all things, he has rules that must be applied. You don't remove the card of the deceased; you simply mark it with a slash of black marker and the date of death. All cards contain name, birth date, contact info, name of personal assistant, spouse(s), children, and any other pertinent info—allergic to nuts, etc. Methodically, he works his way through the alphabet, starting at the letter M (the midpoint), as he believes that familiarity and fatigue can set in when always beginning the same way.

He's asking himself who would be an asset to this undertaking. Who has imagination, insight, and money to burn? Who might be at a stage in life where they don't feel as compelled to play by the rules, who for reasons of their own or a philosophical, moral, or cultural inclination might desire a change of game plan? Who likes a challenge? Who can be trusted?

By seven a.m. in the East, he's on the phone with Tony. "I don't know what it looks like from where you are, but on this end, it's an official apocalypse. We're going to have to do something."

"Like what, ask for a recount?" Tony says, reminding the Big Guy of the call they made last time around to Florida's secretary of state, Katherine Harris, whose father, George W. Harris Jr., was an old friend.

"No. Something bigger," he says. "More long-term. I want to bring together a few people to start talking about it. Now that the game is over, can you come out?"

"Where?"

"Where I am sitting right now, your home away from home, Palm Springs."

"When?"

"This weekend."

"Is it that much of an emergency?"

"Tony, you've been in DC too long. We barely got out of 2000 intact. And now this? When are you going to look outside and see what color the sky is?"

"At the moment, it's a lovely nonpartisan light gray," Tony says.

"Well, where I am, storm clouds are gathering," the Big Guy says. "When are you gonna stop hugging the center line? You've been doing it since Nixon departed; it's not exactly becoming to a man of your caliber."

"I goes along to get along," Tony says.

"At some point you're gonna have to stop doing other people's bidding and have the courage to do some of your own."

"All the more now that we're officially lame duck; there are things to be done—my future awaits."

"My point exactly."

"I was half kidding," Tony says. "As Alfred North Whitehead said, 'True courage is not the brutal force of vulgar heroes but the firm resolve of virtue and reason.'"

"Your education has held you in good stead," the Big Guy says. "I have a few names to run by you, a core group to see if my idea will hold water."

"What kind of names?"

"Men I would trust with my life." There is a pause. "I'll just say the names, and if they pass your bar, no need to respond."

"I hate this game," Tony says. He and the Big Guy have been having these kinds of one-sided conversations ever since *All the President's Men* came out.

The Big Guy begins. "Edwin? Roger? Martin, not the one who first comes to mind but the quiet one? Albert?"

Tony interrupts. "With Edwin, you'd be fishing in troubled waters; he's about to be indicted for fraud. Roger is Roger for better and worse. You can't go to Martin, there's something fishy going on with his private life."

"You want to say more?" the Big Guy asks.

"I'm at the office. In the tank. Even big fish feel rough seas." The fish idioms are Tony's revenge for hating the game.

By the time they are done, the Big Guy has a short list of names, the "first wave," he calls it, and Tony has agreed to take the red-eye out on Friday night. "Anthony," the Big Guy says—he only calls Tony Anthony when he's dead serious; he doesn't even realize he's done it. "Anthony, they were crying in Phoenix."

"Their tears are not lost on me."

"There's one more I'm interested in," the Big Guy says. "A guy who was there last night, he seemed to know his way around."

"What's his name?"

"Well, that's the funny thing, I didn't get his name but I got his phone number—DUpont 7-8354."

Silence.

"Interesting. DU in 2008. Old-school."

"Exactly. He talked about rain on Mount Weather," the Big Guy says.

"I'm at the office," Tony says, cutting him off.

"Let me know what you find out and I'll see you on Saturday," the Big Guy says, hanging up.

After Tony, he calls Bo McDonald. The Big Guy would be the first to say that he doesn't know Bo McDonald terribly well, but he has known him a long time, and he knows his history. If ever there was a man one would characterize as sound or reliable, it would be this guy—his father was one of the founders of the OSS and the kid grew up knee-deep in it. William McDonald VII, known as the Boy Prince, worked "with" Washington until he got fed up with the bureaucracy and returned to California and started an aerospace corporation. His father's old friend Howard Hughes taught him to fly planes when he was a kid. "You ready to kiss the sky?" Hughes would ask the boy, while simultaneously slapping a Hershey bar with almonds into his hand like it was cold hard cash. "I loved Howard," Bo would often say. "Loved him until there was nothing left to love." And if anyone speaks of Bo's short temper, the comment is always followed by the disclaimer that Bo is the way he is because he has nothing to lose and nothing to gain. There was never a chance that he could do enough to impress the only man who needed impressing—his father, William McDonald VI, aka Big Will.

The McDonalds were members of a generation of men who climbed mountains before breakfast because they believed it built character. They were of the variety who called one another "boys" until their fathers died. Bo was among the last of the boys raised to run an empire, and as outdated as that might seem, it gave him the kind of perspective the Big Guy thinks is perfect for this situation. He knows Bo is fond of him. And he knows that after a third marriage went sour, Bo sold what remained of his aerospace interests, including the plans for an outfit that was going to make reusable spaceships designed for commercial travel to the moon. He bought himself a vineyard somewhere up near San Francisco. In magazines like

Cigar Aficionado, he is depicted as a gentleman farmer, if that's the right word for someone who's got a thousand acres and is looking for more.

The Big Guy waits till the sun is up in Sonoma before letting his fingers do the walking on the telephone dial. "Bo," he says, in an ebullient voice. "Bo," like he's about to bestow him with some kind of award. "It's Hitchens. Good to catch a glimpse of you the other night."

"You still in Phoenix shaking off your dick?" Bo asks. They'd run into each other in the men's room.

"I'm in Palm Springs, wondering what you're doing this weekend; maybe you'll come down for some golf and a conversation?"

"What are we having now; isn't this a conversation? What time is it?"

"Apologies about the hour. Did I wake you?"

"Not possible," Bo says. "I haven't slept more than ten minutes in at least five years. What is it you want to talk about that's so interesting I'll have to leave the house?"

"Freedom," the Big Guy says, almost as though it's a suggestion or an open question.

"Are you hitting me up for money to conserve some kind of puffin sanctuary? Or lakes on the moon, Sea of Tranquility?"

"I'm asking you to help me figure out how to save the world— otherwise known as the Democracy of the United States."

"Why didn't you just say so in the first place?"

"I was trying to be discreet."

McDonald grunts. "What's the weather supposed to be like?"

"Nice," the Big Guy says. He has no idea what the weather is supposed to be on the weekend, but it's almost always nice.

McDonald is well-bred enough not to ask who else will be there. He simply asks for the address and what time they'll be gathering.

"Eleven in the morning on Saturday."

"What's the nearest airport?"

"Bermuda Dunes. That said, sometimes I use Thermal, which goes way back; it was an old military base. For a while they called it Desert Resorts and now it's Jacqueline Cochran."

"Thermal indeed. That was General Patton's purview," McDonald says.

And the Big Guy wonders, Is that true? Patton in Palm Springs?

"Saturday at eleven," McDonald says, and hangs up.

"Is the golf any good?" Henry Proctor Kissick wants to know. "And who else is coming?" H. P. Kissick is a guy who needs a lot of information. He's not versed in the lingo of rain and mountains and unique area codes. Why does the Big Guy want him? He wants Kissick because they can't all be from inside the box. At the moment, all the Big Guy has is money and a desire for things to be different, which he's smart enough to know, if used correctly, equals authority and then some. He needs Kissick because Kissick is exceptionally good with money. He was an economist who became a tax lawyer, and in his first job at a white-shoe law firm, he noticed something about how the firm was doing its accounting, made a change in the system, and saved the firm something like eighty million dollars in the first year. Then Kissick realized that if he could do things like that for others he could do it for himself. He started his own company, insuring the assets of others, making money off anxiety, off the what-ifs. He and the Big Guy have made hundreds of millions banking on people's stress. Insurance companies take in more premiums than they pay out, but the real play is in investing the float, the money they're holding in anticipation of future claims. Imagine that, making millions off the anxiety of others. Kissick lives in the suburbs of Nowhereville, Florida, in a modest house with his wife and their five children, all girls.

At 7:45 a.m. Charlotte is still sleeping. He leaves a note in her bathroom: "Gone Out/On an Errand."

At 8:00 a.m. the Big Guy is in the grocery store. He could have made a shopping list for Craig, the house manager, or the cleaning lady, but he's so excited about his plan that he wants to do something. There aren't many 8:00 a.m. customers. One of the clerks asks if he is okay. "More than okay, I'm inspired," he says, loading his cart with mixed nuts, pretzels, goldfish, the little cans of soda they have in hotels and on planes.

"You're up to something," Charlotte says when he gets home with bags of groceries. A can of ginger ale tumbles to the floor and they look at it like it's a grenade that might go off. He waits a moment and then picks it up, dented but not leaking.

"Indeed," he says. "I've invited a couple of guys to come hit some balls this weekend and talk about next steps. I should have asked you before I went ahead, but you were sleeping and I didn't want to lose momentum."

She shrugs. "What kind of next steps?"

"I wasn't kidding when I told you I can't live like this, watching everything I worked for come undone and this country turn into some kind of socialist experiment or, worse, just weaken and leave itself open to being overrun by who knows what, could be Russians or aliens from another planet."

"Ah." She nods. "Your plan to save the world."

"It's incumbent on me to take the necessary measures."

She makes a face.

"It's not personal," he says. "I'm not doing it for myself. It's on me in the larger sense. Me, meaning men like me, men who have the ability, the means, that's what I'm talking about, the means to take action."

"Who?" she asks. "Besides Tony."

"Bo McDonald," he says.

She's surprised. "The guy whose father was a spy and who killed himself because he couldn't get it up anymore?"

"I'm not sure about the last part."

"I am."

"Who else?"

"H. P. Kissick."

"Kiss-it Kissick?" That's her private nickname for Kissick because she thinks he's endlessly kissing up to the Big Guy.

"He's very smart. I put in a couple of other calls, but I'm going to keep it small for now."

"A regular brain trust you're putting together. It's fine," she says. "You know I don't care. I'm half teasing you."

He sighs. "It really isn't like me to just invite people."

"I know. And the good news is, it doesn't matter. I'm leaving."

He looks baffled.

"Maybe you forgot? I scheduled myself for a cleanse."

"Did I know?" He doesn't usually forget.

"When you made the plan to go to Phoenix, I booked it. I figured, win or lose, I'd have eaten too much cheese and would need a good cleaning out."

"You didn't eat any cheese," he says.

"Yes, but it was everywhere. In every room. It'll be good for me. I need to get away."

"Will you at least stay until Tony arrives?"

"You'll be fine," she says. "If I stay, I'll be anxious and tempted to eat. I'm already thinking of scrambled eggs and toast. Fixated on it."

"Let me make it for you."

"Our activity last night left me very hungry this morning."

"I've heard that can happen." He smiles.

She doesn't.

"Maybe I should go a day early. Given it's a weekday, I bet they have room and I could check in a day ahead of schedule and get a jump on things."

"You need to eat something."

"If I have an egg, just one egg, do you think it will ruin the cleanse?"

"No, I'm sure some people stop at In-N-Out Burger and check in on a full stomach. I bet they're so anxious about not getting any food that before they enter they stuff a Double-Double in the piehole."

"That's disgusting. And I can't believe you said Double-Double to me. You know that I feel the same way about a burger that other people do about truffle pasta, once a year, maybe twice. A Double-Double, what I wouldn't give to just eat one without having to think—at what cost?"

"It's human nature. People need to eat in order to survive."

He cooks her an egg. He wants to get this right. He takes out the small pan, fries her an egg, toasts a piece of bread, and puts it on a plate with a few slices of tomato, a sprinkle of salt and pepper, and brings it to the bedroom.

She's not there. The sliding glass doors are open.

She is outside on the diving board—naked.

"I wanted to see what it felt like to be you," she says, bouncing on the board. Her breasts jiggle up and down. He wonders whether the neighbors can see.

"I called Green Valley; they can take me today. I don't have to wait until tomorrow. Isn't that great news?" She jumps into the pool.

When Charlotte is gone, he is bereft.

Whatever happened in the last two days, call it a rekindling of what once was, has left him stunned and wondering—was it real?

The house is silent. Whatever happened, it was so unfamiliar, so unusual, that he and the house can hardly hold it. The place is a mess. The egg pan is in the sink, cold and greasy. He scrubs it. Then he makes the bed, tidies her bathroom, makes a circle all around the house, cleaning up after her. It's unlike Charlotte to leave a mess; she lives like a ghost; you'd never know she'd been there. For a moment, he finds it sexy, a sign of life, and then it makes him anxious and he's compelled to put everything back in its place.

Tony calls back. "Regarding DUpont 7-8354. His patois is that of having attended the same school."

"Can you repeat that in English?"

"He's one of us."

"And I suppose asking for his name would be pushing the boat out?"

"See you on Saturday. I would offer to bring crab cakes but they don't travel well."

The Big Guy is at the dining-room table with a stack of what Charlotte calls recipe cards and what he calls index cards. Funny how women have one name for something and men another.

He likes writing things down—instructions for how to make something, a cake or a new world order. Every idea gets its own card. Whole treatises are drafted on these cards—not just instructions for sour cream coffee cake or lemon drop cookies.

He writes his welcome: "Have a seat, make yourselves comfortable. Get something to drink, have a slice of salami."

Then he digresses and gets lost in his thoughts, remembering his grandfather, who felt a man should win on personality, not possessions. That said, the old man, Millard Hitchens, was fond of boiled Valencia peanuts and carried a brown paper sack of them everywhere he went. The Big Guy remembers thinking it wasn't classy enough, but everyone seemed to love talking about his grandfather and his boiled nuts. When he thinks about it now, it occurs to him that the peanuts were something that he'd grown up with in the South. No one up North ate boiled peanuts. They were a conversation starter, a way of making a connection. His grandfather often bragged that he could talk to anyone about anything. The Big Guy was closer to his grandfather, who made his money in extruding metal and later plastics, than to his father, who was kind of an ass. His grandfather was an old-school Southern gentleman who had a lot of respect for men who got their hands dirty, working men. He made his money off the labor of others. His father, who moved North at sixteen, liked to make his money off money itself. The two men didn't get along, and as a young man, the Big Guy was often put between them—as referee. He's never gotten over how his father took advantage of the Big Guy's wedding by making a deal with Charlotte's father and uncles that allowed him to recover helium from her family's gas fields. Historically, Charlotte's family had been resistant to outside investors but the marriage made him kin. Later, his father bought out a uranium mining operation in that same area, and to show his gratitude, he offered the Big Guy part of the deal and actually made a sizable profit off his own son. At the time the Big Guy hated him for it—now he just chuckles. Clearly the Big Guy learned a thing or two from both of them. He now owns the helium company in its entirety, and one of the first investments using money his grandfather left him was buying more Walt Disney stock. When the Big Guy was a child, his grandfather gave him a thousand shares as he believed it was useful for children to understand "where the fun came from." Taking a cue from his father's way of doing business, the Big Guy would double down on Disney whenever he had extra money. The day after JFK was shot, the stock market went down almost 3 percent and closed early so people could mourn, but before it closed, the Big Guy bought in. He did the same thing with the Cuban Missile Crisis and when Nixon resigned, and then again when Reagan was shot. When others pulled back to "wait and see," he went forward, like a looter. It's not the kind of thing he brags about—but if pressed, he will tell you that he always loved the elephant. What elephant? The Republican elephant? "Not that elephant, the real Dumbo," he would say. "I love Dumbo. But I don't like being taken for a ride." He had plenty of other investments and punch lines but that one gave him the biggest kick. Meanwhile, he's noticed that the market is down about five hundred points this morning—but he's not buying.

This time he's keeping his cash on hand, thinking that soon he'll need spending money.

He takes out a fresh index card.

We are among the last of an era, a generation where phrases like noblesse oblige, and haberdashery and supper, along with a warm glass of milk at night and a stiff shot of scotch during the day, were all a piece of something. We summered in one place and had Christmas in another. We had manners and a code of conduct, good men, men who thought beyond their own betterment.

He sounds like his father and his grandfather. Maybe that's okay. Maybe they meant it then the way he means it now. The world is changing; he has no son who one day will do this same thing. Tony has no children. Bo McDonald lost a boy to drugs and has another child, a girl with problems of some sort, he can't quite remember what. The guy from Phoenix, Eisner, the historian, has no known children. Kissick has five daughters who keep him under their thumb. He remembers running into Kissick and his family at an event and Kissick leaning over to say, "Everyone says they look like princesses; clearly I'm the frog. I can pay the bills, but I'm allowed to use the bathroom in my bedroom only when my wife isn't in it; otherwise, I have to use the half bath at the back of the house. In order for them to feel good about themselves as girls, I have to accept that I'm disgusting. So be it."

The Big Guy, relieved to have found language for something ephemeral that had been nagging at him, makes a card noting that none of the men have a son to carry on after them. There is no succession plan—there is nothing in place to say who will run the world after they are gone.

Saturday, November 8, 2008
Palm Springs, California
6:30 a.m.

Saturday morning, Tony calls to say he's landed in Los Angeles and is en route.

Bo McDonald rings the doorbell exactly at eleven a.m. The Big Guy assumes he's been sitting out front for a while because it's difficult to arrive right on the dot. McDonald carries a small duffel, like a gym bag.

"Bo, good of you to come," the Big Guy says.

"Nice of you to invite," Bo says.

The Big Guy shows Bo around the house because that's what people do; they show off the spread. He takes him down the halls, shows him the bedrooms. "I've put you by the pool," he says, opening the sliding glass door, showing off the golf course in the distance and pointing out the fancy plants that they've put in over the years. "I used to have an amazing gardener who specialized in exotics. All well and good until it turns out he was also dealing in exotics of other kinds—human trafficking." There's more space at the ranch and he half wishes he'd hosted the event there but reminds himself that the house is fine; it's big enough, filled with sunlight, sitting right on the golf course—and the men he invited said yes, so it can't be too far beneath them.

Tony arrives next and goes into the pool immediately. "Just a quick dip. Much needed. DC has been cold and rainy." Tony is long and lean and, unlike the Big Guy, still looks good in swim trunks.

Kissick, the tax man, comes through the door already irritated. "Have I mentioned how much I don't like traveling? On the other hand, it's nice to see you. I'm cheap; when it's just me, I fly coach commercial. I add to the money I'm saving and I love it. I feel like Warren Buffett buying breakfast at McDonald's. I sit there folded up like human origami and the service sucks. But that said, I did talk with someone interesting, and that doesn't happen when you fly alone."

"Maybe you should jump in the pool with Tony and wash off the ride?" Bo suggests.

"I only swim at night," Kissick says. "I limit my time in the sun. I had a great-uncle who died of sunstroke. I never met the guy, but the idea of his dying alone in a New York hotel on a hot July night sticks with me. I took my wife and daughters to Rome last summer; it was unbearable, like a pizza oven. In all the photos I am dripping sweat."

"The whole damn Tilt-A-Whirl is off course," Bo says.

"I tell people that I live in Florida for tax reasons, but I won't go out from ten a.m. to four p.m. for atmospheric reasons. 'Atmospheric,' that's what my eldest calls it. I wear a bucket hat. I look like a man about to be arrested for selling pornography as I run furtively from place to place. Duck and cover; my brother got a melanoma behind his ear, didn't really notice it until it was too late. Not me, nothing fucking invisible like a ray gun is going to get me; I'm going to die of something old-fashioned like colon cancer or a ruptured hernia."

"I've heard that logorrhea can be fatal," Bo suggests.

The historian, the scribe from the bar in Phoenix, arrives in a cheap rental car looking like a pizza delivery boy. He's a good fifteen years younger than the rest of them. The Big Guy didn't realize how much younger until he sees him in the daylight.

"I remember you," Bo says, slightly surprised. "Last time I saw you was at our beloved club in San Francisco and you were wearing a dress."

"I would assume that I was in a play," the scribe says. "That was something I used to do—acting."

Bo shrugs. "You might call it that."

"It was most likely my last role, the Emperor Norton. Just another of the crazy things one will do to please their father. Despite my best efforts, I was an endless source of disappointment."

"Your dad was a gifted man but not easy to please. Someday ask him about the times we spent together in France in the 1950s," Bo says. "He's got some good stories. Things that couldn't be said then—but now it's fine."

"Like what?" The guy wants to know.

Bo shrugs. "They're not mine to tell."

"My father is no longer with us," the scribe says.

"Sorry to hear that," Bo says, but doesn't offer anything more.

Meanwhile, Kissick is just standing there looking at the guy, waiting. "I never knew your father, but I am sorry for your loss," Kissick says.

"Eisner," the scribe says, offering his hand to Kissick. "Mark Eisner."

Eisner looks at the Big Guy, makes eye contact, and repeats, "Mark Eisner."

"I could have sworn the name used to be different," Bo says.

"My father was Einhorn. But I changed it after high school."

"Hiding the Jew?" Bo asks.

"Not exactly, far from observant. It was more the horn jokes, horny and so on. So now it's Eisner, Mark Eisner."

"Pleased to meet you, son of a horn," Bo says. "Your father was a sp—"

"Speechwriter," Eisner says, finishing it for him. "He wrote for Eisenhower."

"Do the names Malcolm Moos or William Ewald ring a bell?" Tony asks.

"Moos was president of the University of Minnesota—which is where my dad's family is from," Eisner says. "It's the land of a thousand lakes, L'Etoile du Nord. He grew up fishing on the St. Croix River."

"I didn't know Jews fished," Bo says.

"Where do you think lox comes from? And the Jews of the Midwest were quite assimilated; they fished, they played poker, and they even drank."

"I'm sure you know that Malcolm Moos wrote Eisenhower's farewell speech that foretold the rise of the military industrial complex," Tony says.

Imitating Eisenhower, Eisner intones, "'Only an alert and knowledgeable citizenry can compel the proper meshing of the huge industrial and military machinery of defense with our peaceful methods and goals, so that security and liberty may prosper together.'"

"Which brings us to this morning." The Big Guy jumps in, trying to get a handle on a situation that gives herding cats a new meaning—try herding cats who each have a certain male need to dominate.

The Big Guy stands before the group scrubbed pink and new, refreshed by having been brought back to life by Charlotte twice in one week.

He pulls out his cards. "I'm glad you're here. I'm looking forward to hitting some balls with you, grilling some meat on the fire, having a drink or two, and talking with you about this fix we're in." They smile and nod. "What happened in Phoenix has been happening right under our noses. We have known for a while that within the party things were going south, and we elected, pun intended, to do nothing. We can no longer not know what we already know."

"Quit beating around the bush," Bo says. "Just spit it out."

The Big Guy stops and takes a breath. "What happened in Phoenix ..." Overcome with emotion, his lip quivers and he skips ahead. "As I watched the returns coming in, I felt as though I were watching the Hindenburg going up in flames. Only it was us; it was the American dream on the pyre. I looked around the room and everyone was blank, dumbstruck. 'Maybe it's not as bad as we think,' I heard someone say. 'He's a good-looking man,' another said, speaking of Barack Obama. What I saw in that Phoenix hotel room was the grim face of defeat, having backed the wrong horse in the absence of a better horse. And worse yet, knowing it wasn't a horse race anymore, it wasn't even a rat race, it was a farce, buffoonery."

"A pasquinade," Tony says softly.

"Oh, the big words," Bo says.

"It was clear to me that a mockery had been made of the system that had for two hundred years anchored the land of the free, home of the brave." The Big Guy's voice crescendos as he reaches the word brave. "In the past there were times when I thought it didn't really matter which side a man was on as long as he loved America. Being in that hotel room on Tuesday, listening to men speaking in platitudes, was a night unlike any other. It was the long goodbye, the end of not just an era but the end of the America as dreamed by our fathers." The Big Guy's eyes mist, like he might actually cry. He looks up, biting his lip, blinking the mist away. His eyes return to the room. 'Are you bitter?' Someone asked me that on Tuesday night." He pauses. "'Are you bitter?'" He says it slowly. "I said to him: 'Bitter is an aftertaste. At the moment I'm pissed off.'" He makes a fist, thick and meaty. "Someone needs to grab this country by the balls and wake it the hell up." He thumps himself in the chest with his fist. "I take it personally as a failure. My failure. We are here today because I didn't take responsibility." He thumps himself again. "My fault." He's apologizing and it's making the other men in the room uncomfortable. "You might be saying to yourself, it's not his fault; if he thinks it is, he's got delusions of grandeur. Exactly! If it is not all on me, then what? Then it is on US. It's not John McCain's loss, it's our loss. We are the ones who had every tool to see this coming, to take steps; and instead of paying attention, we stopped looking outward, we closed our eyes."

"Fucking blind is what I'd call it," Bo says.

"Let's take a moment to ponder that and then we will begin again." The Big Guy takes a breath and blows it out as if to clear the air. "Let's start with this; we are lucky men, members of the good fortune club and the school of hard work and elbow grease, which is wonderful because we will need both in equal measures for what comes next." He delivers his remarks in such a way that it's clear he stayed up late ordering and reordering his sentences.

"We're old-fashioned Americans, not assholes; we care about our country," Bo says.

"This conversation is entirely reasonable, that we don't want it all to turn to shit in some kind of socialist experiment—which, by the way, won't work," Kissick adds.

"And you, sir, you are a phoenix rising from the ashes," Eisner, the scribe, says under his breath. The Big Guy looks at him. He heard it, but there's no need to say anything.

"We can ask ourselves, what's the call we've not answered? We are conservatives. We believe in free markets, individual liberty, the freedom to do what the hell you want. We come together with wisdom and experience and the awareness that democracy was not created in a heartbeat. Democracy is fragile, more fragile than any of us are comfortable admitting."

"Dangerous times," Kissick says. "It wouldn't be surprising if what we think of as democracy is not the same as what *they* think of."

Bo interrupts. "It bothers me that these 'new right' rodeo boys, as I call them, are getting in; they're taking up seats that used to be ours."

The Big Guy continues. "These last few months have been a roller coaster; it's getting out from under us. Bottom line is, we've lost control of the Republican Party and it's not just our ability to steer the course of the country; the party itself is about to blow into a thousand little pieces."

"The party is already blown," Bo says.

"I blame the young," Kissick says, looking at Eisner.

"The young don't know diddly," Bo says.

Tony stands up, which immediately draws all eyes. He stretches his arms high over his head, abruptly bends his torso right and then left. His vertebrae audibly pop. "Very good introduction, putting things on the table. I want to go back to what you said about being a passionate conservative. Yet you feel we need to get involved. I'm hearing that we f'ed up, took our eyes off the ball, and woke up on Wednesday to find ourselves in a different place."

"Correct."

"Let's keep it in context," Tony says.

"This moment is happening at a specific time and place with history behind it and eternity ahead," Eisner says.

"That's a good line, history behind us and eternity ahead," Tony says.

"Yeah, my father put something like that in a speech for Eisenhower or maybe it was for one of the Kennedys."

"Must be nice to insert words into the mouths of powerful men," Tony says.

"If I understand correctly, you're about to be out of a job," Bo says to Tony.

"The situation is fluid. My position often stays with the office rather than traveling with the man."

"Interesting," Bo says. "So you'd be willing to work for him?"

"I'm interested in supporting the office," Tony says.

"Can we get back to the subject?" the Big Guy says. "We have lost our beacon, our North Star. Let's remind ourselves of who we are and use history as not just our guide but as our inspiration to put things back on track."

Bo jumps in again. "Among these rodeoers are extremists and we need to be careful not to align ourselves too closely with them."

"Perhaps there is something these 'extremists' can offer?" Tony suggests.

"What's that?"

"Cover," Tony says.

"Are you suggesting we use the extremists to do some of the work for us?" Bo asks.

"It's worth thinking about," the Big Guy says.

"I'm not necessarily suggesting that they work for us but that perhaps their activities don't work against us. Flamethrowers create noise and distraction, which can make our point of view appear more moderate. Depending on how things evolve, they're potentially an asset."

"I'm not looking to be moderate," Bo says. "But I don't want to look like a fool. To me, that's what those boys are, fools."

"What we're gonna get from Obama is more government intervention," Kissick says. "That's something that even fools don't want. In fact, it's the last thing they want—liberal hobbyhorses on gun control and social intervention."

"Transparency," Eisner says. "That's one of their favorite words."

"The Constitution is about to be ripped to shreds," Bo says. "Keep that in your crosshairs."

"The Republican Party has a constitution of its own, did you know that?" Eisner says.

"Lovely," Tony says, taking a handful of nuts and passing the bowl. "Perhaps we can read aloud from it tonight at dinner."

"If I can pull us back into one conversation, the question is how to reclaim our America, a traditional America that honors the dreams of our forefathers. When you look at our peer group, which I define as conservatives of a certain age with an extra decimal point or two in the bank, there are already some things happening, early efforts to recapture the flag. We're not looking to replicate what's already out there."

"You're talking about what the brothers are doing? The gatherings?" Bo asks.

"They're calling them 'seminars,'" Tony says.

"There are the seminars and the conversations we have at our beloved club up north and at Bilderberg," Bo says.

"I always feel nervous at the Grove," Kissick says.

"Like someone's going to mistake you for a stick in the mud and take a leak on your leg."

"Something like that."

"Old men like to see one another. We get lonely," Bo says.

"Back to the plan—between the club and the brothers, there is philosophical overlap and alliances to be made, but what most of us have done in the past, throwing money at it, isn't working," the Big Guy says.

"Correct, and that money is buying more rubber-chicken dinners. I fucking hate chicken. And I am not interested in policy. Or think tanks," Bo says. "Been there, done that."

"All these years, I didn't risk anything except money," the Big Guy says. "I played it safe and now I'm unhappy."

"Well, that's why we're all here," Tony says. "To jolly you up."

The Big Guy smiles. "Thank you, Tony."

"Would anyone like a glass of orange juice?" Tony asks. "There is nothing better than fresh-squeezed orange juice."

"Sure," Bo says. "Hit me."

Bo crosses his legs, revealing the bare ankle of an old man, hairless and very white. On the ankle is a red-hot wound, a thick brown scab at its center. The red zone spreads out to a pale pink, like an exploding chrysanthemum or fireworks.

"You want some antibiotic cream for that?" Tony asks.

"It's fine," Bo says. "Better than it was."

"He can't help it," the Big Guy says, talking about Tony. "He takes care of people."

"A giver," Eisner says.

The Big Guy clears his throat and looks down at his index cards. "The only reason we didn't lose in 2000 was because we had control in Florida and in Washington, and Gore is a doughboy. We were able to hang on because he and the Democrats didn't have the balls to fight—they didn't know what hit 'em and we did well with the court. But that wasn't what you'd want to call a win. That was one of our wake-up calls and we missed it."

"Hit the snooze button," Bo says.

"You're right; we're has-beens. A new world is emerging and we have done ourselves a disservice by clinging to the past," Kissick says.

"The world around us has changed but our little bubble has remained the same," the Big Guy says. "Obama won because people wanted something new, something different—hope.

"So," the Big Guy says, referring to his last index card. "The election makes it clear that we have been through a period of upheaval even if we were blind to it. Upheaval is an indicator, a bright red warning light, which if not heeded spells the end of democracy as we know it." He stops for a moment, pauses as if for applause.

"Do you mean the end of democracy or the end of the Republican Party?" Tony asks.

"The Republican Party is officially a stale cookie—just crumbs," Bo says.

"Here's my question: What is the man in the middle of America thinking tonight? I bet he's scared shitless. He's losing his footing, the factory is closing, his job is gone, his pension isn't what he thought it would be, people coming into the country illegally are taking what he thinks should be his. And his wife is haranguing him: Why aren't you doing more? It's a wonder he's not killing himself or everyone else. I often find myself thinking that if I wasn't successful in the ways I am, I might be a murderer. What we're looking for here is pretty clear," the Big Guy says.

"Is it?" Kissick asks. "You would be a murderer?"

"I would be very unhappy. Is that better?"

"Are you really concerned about the average Joe or is that just a line you wrote down?" Bo asks. "I suspect that there are many Joes who don't know the difference between Democrat and democracy. And personally, among friends, perhaps we can be a little more honest, what we care about most is ourselves."

"Whether or not I care about Joe is irrelevant," the Big Guy says. "We need to harness the power of Joe; there are millions of Joes in this country; we need to bring Joe into the fold. And if Joe doesn't know the difference between number one and number two, that's fine—we just have to tell him what to think. We remind him that in America democracy is capitalism, guns, and lower taxes. Because Joe is the one who is going to get the work done. This isn't about money; it's about power."

"Don't say power, say freedom," Eisner says. "Substitute freedom for power."

"This isn't about money," the Big Guy says. "It's about freedom."

The doorbell rings. The local sandwich place in town has made lunch for them. The delivery guy comes in and sets it up on the dining-room table.

"Looks good," Bo says.

"We can eat turkey sandwiches and talk about our Pilgrim past," Kissick says.

"Actually, the Pilgrims were on the evangelical side; John Winthrop's sermon from 1630, the 'city upon a hill,' our 'beacon of hope,' comes from the New Testament," Eisner says.

"I thought it was Ron Reagan who said that," the Big Guy says.

"I would have pinned it on Kennedy," Bo says.

"Let's eat," the Big Guy says.

At lunch they talk about their health. They are obsessed with living as long as they can, preserving whatever they can. They are of the belief that if you can't take it with you, then whatever you have damn well needs to last a long time.

They talk about bread and carbs and what foods to eat. They talk about how people don't think men care about that stuff but they really do. And they talk about businesses they've bought and sold, what they won or lost—each has their own version of a greatest hits album.

"I've had some repairs done: a heart valve, a knee, and a little work on one shoulder. I feel like a million bucks and it only cost about half that." Bo laughs. "I'm divorced more than once with a kid who doesn't talk to me because she thinks it's my responsibility that we lost her big brother as a teen. It would be better if she was angry at the drug dealer or her brother's friends, but it's easier to hate your father." Bo looks at Eisner. "How do you feel about your father?"

"Haunted," Eisner says.

"Still waiting for that stamp of approval?" Tony asks.

"Something like that."

"Because I do like the sound of my own voice," Bo says, "I'm going to tell you that a lot of the problem is related to what you'd call progress, connectivity, and outsourcing. Lehman was the tip of the iceberg. When this global economy contracts and everyone sees how intertwined it's become—there's gonna be even more pain. No one wants to admit that it's all been knit together now like an ugly Christmas sweater."

Kissick claps. "Just the word derivative gives me pains. Lehman had more than a million derivative contracts, notational value of almost forty trillion dollars. No one seemed to understand the global implications."

"Can we get back to business?" Tony says.

"Yes, please," the Big Guy says. "And I want to say, it doesn't bother me if we differ on some things; I was thinking about it during lunch and I really do care about Joe America. We are all Joe America."

"On some level," Tony says.

"I'm sure you care, old man," Bo says, slapping him on the back. "It's one of your better qualities. It's not that I don't care, but sometimes what's good for me and what's good for the average Joe aren't exactly the same. Hard to have your cake and eat it too."

"Speaking of which," Tony says, carrying a carafe of coffee and a large plate of cookies back into the living room. "Shall we continue over dessert?"

The Big Guy takes a sip of his coffee, strong and black and hot, the way he likes it. Charlotte calls it burned because he often pours the coffee from the coffee maker into a saucepan and fires it up to boiling. He sips the coffee and takes a look at his second set of cards, wrapped with a rubber band, marked Morning Part 2. "I thought it would be useful if we each shared our concerns. Tony, you want to start us off?"

Tony spins 360 in his chair for effect. Big and bold. "I'm going to use a word I haven't heard from anyone in a long time. *Vision*. That's what's missing. Vision. Our leaders, whether elected, appointed, or hired through the civil service, lack vision. There is no one stepping up and laying out a game plan, a strategy. It's all election-cycle thinking, how can I get from here to there, short distances. There's no one training for a marathon. They say what they have to say to get the votes and then nothing—poof."

"Good point," Kissick says. "Short-term thinking is very expensive."

Tony continues. "My other, bigger issue is that we're a divided country, now more than ever since the Civil War. We are economically, racially, and gender divided, and that divide is part of the chasm that we're too busy navel-gazing to notice. But when that sucker splits, we're all going down."

"How's it going to split?" Bo asks.

"Random tipping points," Tony says. "Things you never thought of, like the weather. Hurricane Katrina. Civil unrest. Crazy shit like O. J. Simpson in a Ford Bronco live on TV. Floods, fires, pestilence, killer bees. It's coming soon and it will be live on TV and all over your phone. The age of small and regional is over; everything goes big. Any of those could spin entirely out of control." Tony spins full circle in his chair.

Bo nods. "He has a point."

"Does that make you nauseated?" the Big Guy asks. "The spinning?"

"I like it," Tony says. "It feels like flying, like the merry-go-round I used to play on, and it reminds me of Plato, the spinning top and the principle of opposites."

"You're giving me a headache," Bo says.

"Because I'm spinning?"

"Because you're talking about desire versus reason and the parts of the soul. The thirsty man who refuses to drink. It's not like I haven't heard it before."

"We're all that man," Tony says. "An object won't change its motion unless force is applied. Newton's first law. When force is applied, it gets interesting. The acceleration of an object depends on the mass of the object and the force applied."

"Yes, and?" Bo says.

"When one object exerts force on another object, the second object offers equal and opposite force. But what happens when there is an out-of-balance situation? That's a nonreciprocal interaction."

"Why are we having a physics lesson?" Kissick asks.

"Because this is what's happening. There is a greater amount of force being applied resulting in acceleration. It will continue to grow," Tony says. "And it cannot be contained."

"That's a big one," the Big Guy says. "Capitalism and fundamentalism in a race toward the rapture?"

"Something like that," Tony says.

"I have a fear of my own to share," Kissick says.

"I can't wait to hear it," Bo says.

"Cyberattacks," Kissick says.

"That's a good one," Bo says.

"We're not prepared," Kissick says. "WW3 is going to happen and it won't be a conventional war. Not a drone attack. It'll be about the national grid." He pauses. "Do you know that National Grid, the firm that powers the Northeast, is actually based in England? In 2006 they bought KeySpan, a gas producer, then they picked up a subsidiary of Southern Union Company and now they're laying cable between the UK and the Netherlands. If our most basic needs are being provided offshore, we have less control. What is the investment of Americans in America? Foreigners own a heck of a lot of US debt; just wait till they come calling."

"You're all over the place," Bo says, "banking, the national grid, gas supply; can you boil it down so I know what to hold on to here?"

"Yes," Kissick says. "One word. China."

"Gold star," Bo says.

"Are you being facetious?" Kissick asks.

"Not at all. I am in agreement with your assessment and I would add one more word—Russia. China holds substantial US debt; they have an investment in the US that's doing well, but Russia, apart from using us to launder dirty money . . ."

"You're on to something," Tony says. "No one talks about Russia, but there's a lot happening there; the economy is unbalanced, meaning only a few are making money but they're making it in spades. Their technology is evolving and they have people with good skills. I wouldn't put it past them to launch a cyberattack in the next few years, like a thorn in the side. There are things coming in from the outside and we here on the inside are not doing enough to protect ourselves. If the situation is allowed to progress, our government will erode, like rust under a car, and we won't discover it until they are 'in the house' or our feet sink through the boards."

"There are numerous threats on the horizon," the Big Guy says.

The men all nod.

"Getting back to what Tony was saying, I've got a few things stuck in my craw," Bo says. "One is the religious right. I don't care what people believe in, but they sure do, to an extreme. I think we're underestimating their impact. They're relentless zealots and their beliefs are encroaching on government in a way that is antithetical to our footprint. For the last thirty years, they've been creeping further and further into the party. You know who I'm talking about . . ."

"Weyrich," Kissick says.

"And his kind," Bo adds.

"Ralph Reed, Norquist, Pat Robertson," Tony adds.

"Do you remember when Reed attacked John McCain in the South Carolina primary?"

"Like I could ever forget. We do ourselves a disservice to be in bed with them. The other issue that's gotten even more out of control is the size of the government itself. There is no way people working in the government can even know what other people working in the government are doing. If we cut the workforce by half, we wouldn't even notice. The bureaucratic bullshit world would remain bureaucratic bullshit and all the rest would be the same. I can point to the moment when it happened. That's the thing about getting old, you hold the history . . ."

"In 1970 there were six million government employees," Bo says.

"That's impossible," Kissick says.

Bo doesn't even bother to reply.

"Where do you get these numbers?" Kissick wants to know. "I'm the numbers guy and I can tell you with confidence that you're wrong. The government workforce has not kept pace with private sector growth and, in fact, is smaller than it was."

"Fuck me with the numbers," Bo says. "My point is that during the 1970s government turned into a bloated bureaucratic potbellied pig. It used to be that when one administration came in the other one went out, but in the late sixties and into the seventies, Washington became a place people wanted to stay, raise families, and all that crap. They may not all be government employees in the old-fashioned sense—but these contractors, lobbyists, bureaucratic hangers-on, whatever you call them—they're excess baggage."

"Political groupies," Eisner says. "That's what my parents were."

"That's not what your parents were," Bo says. "But you are correct to say political hangers-on linger in Maryland, Virginia, even some neighborhoods in DC. Real estate in Washington was dirt cheap after the riots."

"What riots?" Kissick asks.

"Really?" Bo asks. "What did you study in college?"

"Math."

"The rest of us took some history courses and 1968 should ring a bell because—"

Kissick realizes his error. "I'm a total ass. Fuck me. Bobby Kennedy was assassinated. And you were there. I remember you telling the story about how you were there."

"I was there, but that's not what changed the housing prices in Washington."

"Martin Luther King," Tony says, throwing the bone in the middle. "I hate the tension."

"There were four days of riots in Washington, more than a thousand fires. That's why real estate was cheap," Bo says. "It was crazy in 1968 when you look back on it; everything that could arise did arise."

"You seem to be familiar with Eisner's father, but may I ask what your father actually did?" Kissick asks. "I've always wondered."

The room gets noticeably still; it's the question everyone wants to ask but no one ever does.

"What didn't he do is really the question," Bo says, avoiding answering.

They nod.

"This is all such good stuff," Eisner says, eating it up.

"Is that so?" Bo asks. "You know, of course, that the modern meritocratic civil service can be traced to Imperial China?"

"I did not know that," Eisner says.

"Humor me for another five minutes," the Big Guy says, as he hands out paper place mats with a map of America printed on them and small packs of crayons. "I picked these up this morning at the local pancake joint."

Tony laughs. "You never fail to entertain me."

"A little mental exercise. I want to see where our heads are in color and where we think the blue and the red states are."

Bo raises his hand. "Do you mind if I take a leak?"

"You don't have to ask; it's down the hall on the left."

"Well, you're running the room like it's third grade so I wasn't sure."

The men take the crayons. Tony, Kissick, Eisner, and the Big Guy diligently color in the maps. Tony sits cross-legged on the floor. He would look like an eight-year-old except that he's six foot three and his legs are a mile long.

Bo comes out of the bathroom, takes his map and his crayons over to the dining-room table. He does his thing, then folds his map into a paper airplane and sails it back toward the Big Guy. Then he goes back to the lunch food and starts picking at things. "My favorite meals are eaten standing up," he says. "Tastes better that way. These are very good olives. What are they?"

"No idea," the Big Guy says. "The bottle is in the fridge."

"Dirty olives, marinated in vermouth," Bo says. "No wonder they're so good. I just ate about a dozen of them." He blows a raspberry to the room.

"When you're done, let's come back to center and we're going to talk about the maps," the Big Guy says.

"I'm gonna drop a fact ball here," Tony says. "Barack Obama's total vote will turn out to be the highest vote won by a presidential candidate. More than 130 million votes were cast; that's more than 43 percent of the population. Historically speaking, 1964 was blue, 1968 red, 1972 more red, then in 1976 it was very divided; 1980 and 1984 were red, 1988 turned blue again, then 1992 was split, 1996 more red, 2000 nice red."

"Is he like an idiot savant with the numbers or a rapper?" Bo says.

The Big Guy unfolds the paper plane, on which Bo has scrawled, "Fuck This."

Bo shrugs.

"My point is, we're divided and we can't afford to be. When you look at these maps, you'll see that part of the Midwest is blue and it shouldn't be like that."

"What's the takeaway from our coloring project?" the Big Guy says. "We all have different ideas about where the power lies but agree that there are centers on the East and West coasts."

"It's not fucking nursery school, gentlemen," Bo says. "And by the way, you're out of olives. I could eat a gallon of them."

"If this shitstorm shows us anything, it's that we're increasingly in the minority," Kissick says.

"Now that you know what's on our minds, the question is, what are you going to do about it?" Bo asks the Big Guy.

Saturday, November 8, 2008
Palm Springs, California
4:00 p.m.

The Big Guy takes the men for a ride in his golf cart. Bo rides up front; Tony, Kissick, and Eisner are sandwiched on the bench seat in the back. He tells them stories of who else owns houses on the golf course, the history of the place, buried treasure, poisonous snakes. Over hill, over dale, and then off the trail until they arrive at an empty lot where a man and a couple of helpers are inflating an enormous hot-air balloon.

"Getting the lay of the land is all about perspective," the Big Guy says. "And keeping in mind that we don't know everything. We can't know everything."

"Are you shitting me?" Kissick says. It's not clear if he's thrilled or upset.

"I've always wanted to do this but never have; it's one of the few things still on my list," Bo says.

"Pretty great," Tony says, laughing. "You got me, I'm impressed."

"Tony, when you said 'vision,' I thought, Just you wait and see. It's spectacular. Especially this time of year. The other night when I cooked this up, I thought we should float over America from on high and have a moment of contemplation."

Kissick climbs into the basket. "My wife would kill me if she knew I was taking off in a helium balloon. I'm supposed to stay alive and support the family. They need me."

"I'm sure you have more than enough life insurance," Bo says.

Kissick shrugs. "That might be true."

"Didn't one of these catch fire and crash a few months ago in Pennsylvania?"

"We've been flying for more than thirty years," the balloon man says. "And have never caught fire."

"I don't think we're all going to fit," Bo says.

"Not a problem," Kissick says, moving to climb out of the basket.

The Big Guy tosses his car keys to Eisner. "You be the chase car. Follow the leader in the 4x4."

"Why does he get to be the chaser?" Kissick asks.

"Because he's our witness, the one who will live to tell the tale," the Big Guy says.

The burner ignites with a loud whoosh and the balloon rises in the late-afternoon sky.

Kissick sinks to the floor of the basket, sitting on the Big Guy's feet.

"You okay, buckaroo?" Bo asks.

"Fine," he says. "Just fine, perfect, right where I want to be—in a picnic basket going into the woods with Little Red Riding Hood."

"It's safer than driving at night in Florida," Bo says.

"Amazing," Tony says, as they float over palm groves and wind farms. "Beautiful."

"Stand up. Take a look," the Big Guy tells Kissick, "the scale of the land, the glory of it all."

Kissick gets up on his hands and knees, and peers out over the edge. "Oh Jesus, how high are we?"

"About nine hundred feet," the balloon man says.

"Look at the landscape," the Big Guy says. "The enormous untapped potential."

"All I see is barren desert," Kissick says.

"I think it's a national park," Tony says.

"It's an example of the parts of this country we have yet to tame," the Big Guy says.

"Reminds you why people fight for their country," Bo says.

"Did he say tame or claim?" Kissick asks.

"It kind of puts it all in perspective," Tony says. "We are flying over America in a vehicle that is lighter than air, riding in a gondola of the past through the present and talking about the future."

"Profound," the Big Guy says.

Saturday, November 8, 2008
Palm Springs, California
8:00 p.m.

Back at the house, it's like a eulogy for an America that perhaps never was. The air is awash with the scent of unsmoked cigars chewed on, gone wet—damp with the drool of men still dreaming.

They pause, pour themselves drinks. They swim, they drink, and they eat.

The only thing missing is fucking. "You're not bringing any girls in?" Bo asks. He is sitting shirtless at the dining-room table with a thick incision down the middle of his chest. He notices the other men staring. "That's the way they used to do it at the Cleveland Clinic; they cut you in half like a chicken and go in with a Roto-Rooter. I look like shit but I'm alive."

The other men nod.

"So no girls?"

"Not this time," the Big Guy says. "Short notice."

"Bad form," Tony says.

"Okay," the Big Guy says. "We all agree—we're going to make change, because if we don't, the American way will be forever lost. We want a new government."

"Anyone going to mention the T-word?"

"Tits?" Bo asks.

"Tricks? Dirty tricks?"

"The crime of betraying one's country?" Tony asks.

"Is trying to get back to our roots, to what made us strong, is that treason?" the Big Guy wants to know.

"Not everyone sees it the same way," Tony says.

"What are we actually asking people to do? Write a check? Get four friends to write checks? Assassinate someone?" Bo asks, looking at Eisner.

"Are you looking at me?" Eisner asks.

"Yes," Bo says. "I see you as either a bagman or an assassin."

"We're asking them to do their jobs," the Big Guy says. "We're asking them to do what they were hired or elected to do. We are the legacy generation, the living link to a time when wars were fought for reasons, when it wasn't a giant pissing contest. We're not doing this for ourselves; we have what we need, what we want, but it's terrifying out there. We're doing it for our children, for whoever comes next; we're doing it for history, to protect and preserve the America of our founding fathers—the real America."

"Enough already, how are we doing it?" Bo wants to know.

"This is serious stuff, the kind of thing that costs people their lives. We are respectable men, and until the tide turns, until we get a majority on our side, we are going against the current," Kissick says.

"We talk to people, we find out who's capable, we enlist the help of those with the skills," the Big Guy says.

"Please, let's not be all talk; let's goddamned do something," Bo says.

"The distance between political action and treason is large," Tony adds.

"You don't think we'll be marching in there and saying, 'Excuse me, we've come to take back the government, so if you don't mind, clear out your desks and don't forget the photos of your wife and kids'?" Kissick asks.

"I don't see an appetite for revolution," Tony says.

"Perhaps that kind of appetite can be created over time," Bo says.

"I'm gonna be frank with you. This election proves that the Republican Party isn't what it used to be; there is no respect, no consensus, and what ten years ago would have been a strong voice has turned into hysterics who are turning politics into political end time. A less inflammatory word for revolution is change. And change doesn't evoke the T-word," Tony says.

"Change is a great word," Eisner says.

"What are you, like the Scrabble police?" Bo asks.

"So what would this change look like?" the scribe presses. "Would we actually see it? Would we know it was happening?"

"Right there, you hit on something. We don't all see the same thing; we see what we want to see. That's a big shift. We don't all watch the same TV shows, read the same papers; we see what speaks to us. We look for confirmation of what we already know rather than having to deal with ideas and information we might not agree with," Tony says.

"I have no idea why, but I'm thinking about Lou Gerstner," the Big Guy says.

"Gerstner, the guy who turned around IBM?"

"I was thinking out of the box. We are all in a box. We are trapped and we don't even see the box. You're right about that, Toes." Toes is the Big Guy's old nickname for Tony. "We're being fed specific information, whatever it is that 'they' want us to know. And we don't even know who 'they' are."

"Is this going to get all weird and paranoid? We're not like geese being turned into foie gras; we are men with minds of our own," Kissick says.

"We are who they are," Tony says.

"We have to reach outside of our box into the playgrounds of others," the Big Guy says.

"I am game for action. I haven't had dirt under my nails since I was a Boy Scout. I like the idea of a mission. I'd happily go into training," Bo offers.

"How many revolutions happened in the first four hundred years of England or France?" Tony asks.

No one has the answer.

"What would it look like if your plan were to succeed?"

"We would know we were in control."

"How big does it go? How far does it get?" Tony asks. "I'm not saying this to scare anyone but as a reminder that our loyalty to the project must be unquestionable."

"It's fine if some of you don't have the stomach for it and want to excuse yourselves. Once things get rolling, it could get bumpy," the Big Guy says.

"We're talking about creating a plan that disrupts," Tony says.

"As far as I'm concerned, what happened on Tuesday night was a disruption in the worst way," the Big Guy says.

"Fucking fine with me," Bo says. "I'm not going to spend the next however many years sitting around whining and chopping pieces off my dick to see how small I can live with; I want to get something done."

"If we can't win control, we need to assume control," the Big Guy says.

"Speaking of which, where is your wife?" Kissick asks.

"When we returned from Phoenix, she said she needed to take a break; she'd eaten too many cheese cubes. It happens to all of us at some point in the course of our lives—we all have eaten too much cheese and need to step back, turn inward, collect one's marbles, whatever that might be."

"That's what I always liked about Charlotte, she is no bullshit. She's comfortable flippin' the bird to what is and what is not," Kissick says.

"The vodka has been watered down," Eisner says.

"Jesus, really?" the Big Guy asks.

"It's like spring water with essence of alcohol."

"Vodka is not expensive," Kissick says, baffled.

"Try the scotch or the bourbon, she doesn't touch those," the Big Guy says, looking down at his index cards. "Whatever this is; this moment in time, it should be a long dark night of the soul; if it's anything less, it's a joke." The Big Guy puts down the cards with an audible snap on the coffee table.

Eisner is slouched on the sofa, sipping scotch on the rocks, pumping his khaki-covered legs back and forth like he's fanning his balls. He's either anxious or overexcited by the energy in the room.

"Imagine," the Big Guy says. "On January twentieth, a Black man will be setting up shop in the White House."

"I do believe one can be a Republican and not be a racist," Tony says. "You talk about missing the boat and the wake-up call. You guys are out of your minds."

A long silence follows.

"I'm sorry," the Big Guy says.

Another long silence, like a hefty pregnant pause.

"Really, I'm sorry."

"That could mean so many things," Tony says.

"It means I didn't mean to offend you."

Eisner sits up, pulling himself together. "A Black man is going to be the president. No matter how you slice it, it's hugely important."

They all nod.

"Some events change the course of history, shape the evolution of a country, the pathos and ethos of a society. What happened in Phoenix on Tuesday was without a doubt one of those events," Eisner says.

"And to all a good night," Bo says, leaving the room.

"I'm not following you; I'm taking myself to bed," Kissick says, following Bo down the hall.

Tony and Eisner linger in the living room, picking up the debris of the day and bringing it to the kitchen. The Big Guy puts on an apron and does the dishes. "I am beneath or above no man," he says.

"Whose line is that?" Eisner asks.

"Deepak Chopra."

In the middle of the night, the Big Guy can't sleep. He goes into Tony's room—Meghan's room—and pulls out the trundle.

"Can't sleep?" Tony asks.

"Would you be surprised if I said she has a drinking problem?"

"Meghan?"

"God no, Charlotte."

"Based on what?"

"She drinks. She drinks every day. Alone. A lot. She has little bottles in her bag; she's never without. She's basically catatonic."

"Have you spoken with her about it?"

"Not so easy to do. It's not like we argue, but on Wednesday after we got back, I was in such a crappy state of mind that I was unpleasant. I mentioned it then and not in the best of ways."

"Did you apologize?"

"Yes."

"I'm sure she has disappointments of her own that she keeps to herself," Tony says.

"We all do." A beat passes. "The whole thing with Meghan scared the shit out of me. I had taken Charlotte out to dinner to be nice, and all of a sudden both of our phones rang. I thought the worst. I nearly vomited." Another beat. "Do you think there's something going on with Meghan?"

"No," Tony says. "What happened in Phoenix rattled her and she went for a ride to clear her head. She's a good kid, but it's a big deal, realizing that life isn't a Disney film. The real world is darker and stranger than she knew. If Tuesday was a wake-up call for you, it was a panic attack for her."

"I'm having a four-alarm fire myself."

"No doubt that's part of it," Tony says. "She's very connected to you and your expectations of her."

"What does that mean?"

"She wants to do well, to impress you."

"That's nice, right?"

"Do you ever talk about any of this with her?"

"I wouldn't know where to begin. That said, she seems to tell you things . . ."

"I'm a good listener," Tony says. "And I'm not her parent. What did your father do when you were a kid; did he answer your questions?"

"What are you now, a shrink? You knew my parents. If I learned anything, it was by accident. I'm surprised they ever had children; I can't imagine them in a room alone together, much less procreating." A moment of silence passes. "Do you remember when we were in college and I'd be up at night sweating a test? You'd tell me to take my mind off the subject so my brain could refresh itself."

"How could I forget? You used to recite everything aloud all night, from math equations to Roman history."

"You talked me down with stories about Maw-Maw, Paw-Paw, Aunt Pepper, who liked to dance, and Uncle Joe, who fished for muskie in the New River, and how one time he caught a fifty-pound fish that had to be seventeen years old."

"Pepper is still alive. She's gonna be ninety-seven in June."

"Fine thing."

"All that dancing kept her in good shape; she can't see and she can't hear but she can still move . . ."

They laugh.

"I only told you the good stories, not the reason I spent so much time with Maw-Maw, Paw-Paw, and Pepper."

"I had some idea."

"The ever-present threat of violence," Tony says. "When I was a boy, my father wouldn't strike out in front of others, but it got to a point where he didn't care who was around. By then no one wanted to be around him. Not my mother, not her family, and not me."

"That's a rough start."

"I became deeply attuned to fluctuations in everything from the barometric pressure to vicissitudes of temperament in all things around me, be they plant, animal, or human. My sociability, my affable nature, was meant as liniment to counter the ornery or choleric disposition of my blood kin."

"I'm really sorry," the Big Guy says.

"I got out alive," Tony says. "And I'm still here, which is more than can be said for some."

A long pause. "You're a good man, Toes, the best I've ever known." Then another pause. "How do you think this is going?"

"It's certainly interesting, but what is a fish without a river?" Tony says.

"Do you really believe what you said about everything speeding up on a crash course?"

"All I can say is that our situation is not sustainable. The pace and impact of what I call the global weave—technology and money—exceeds man's ability. What is technically possible may not yet be humanly possible. I'm in it for the long game. My goalpost is not yet on the horizon."

"Well, if we can get the boys to sign on and actually do something, we stand a chance. I don't think we're alone in our thinking."

"Speaking of alone, where did Charlotte go?"

"Some kind of a diet place about forty-five minutes from here."

"Maybe it's a chance for her to dry out without announcing it?"

"Maybe."

"She tries hard," Tony says.

"We all try hard."

"You know Obama isn't a bad guy," Tony says.

"Oh yeah, how well do you know him?"

"I got to know him when he was in the Senate. We've played golf a few times."

"Where does an African learn to play golf?"

"Right there, that's part of the problem," Tony says. "There's nothing funny or cute or good about it. You're a racist. It won't happen in your lifetime but it will in Meghan's; the majority won't be white."

"Fuck all," the Big Guy says.

"That's the part that makes you really anxious, the idea that old white men will be obsolete."

"You're not wrong," the Big Guy says.

"Think ahead," Tony says. "'Imagination is the highest kite one can fly.'"

"Nice. Who said that?"

"Lauren Bacall," Tony says.

They are quiet for a while. The Big Guy starts to snore.

"Are you going back to sleep?" Tony asks.

The Big Guy grunts.

"I don't think it would look good if the other men saw you leaving my room in the morning."

"Are you kicking me out of bed?"

"I am," Tony says.

The Big Guy gets up. "My wife is a drunk, my kid is running off into the woods, and the people elected an African as president, but it sounds like you think that's all par for the course, pun intended. Sleep well, old friend," he says, and leaves the room.

"We'll see each other again soon," the Big Guy says, sending them off wearing temporary tattoos, carrying rolled-up maps of the fifty states hand-colored in red and blue, a couple of good cigars from his secret stash, and in the case of Bo, an empty olive jar.

"Sooner than you might think," Bo says, and the Big Guy has no idea what he's talking about.

Each of the men has been given an assignment to come up with a list of other men they can tap, men with the necessary skills to take the enterprise from thought to deed. The tapping process will be much like that of the societies many of them joined in college—interviews, vetting, and an initiation process.

The Big Guy tries to get Tony to stay until Charlotte comes home—he offers to helicopter him to LA so he can take the red-eye east. But Tony needs to be in DC on Monday morning. He's got a nine a.m. at the White House.

The housekeeper has washed and ironed everything, buffed and polished the surfaces so not a fingerprint remains. She is so thorough that she could work for a government scrub agency.

To make conversation, he asks what she thought about the election.

"If you are happy, then I am happy," she says.

"Did you vote?"

She looks away.

He kicks himself. Dimwit. Of course she didn't vote; she's not legal. As if to repair the damage, he says, "Well, I don't like the fella who won and I want you to know I'm going to do all I can to make sure America remains a country where there is opportunity for everyone."

"Thank you," she says.

"You deserve it," he says.

"Pretty flowers. Did your friends bring them?"

"No. I ordered them for Charlotte, for when she comes back."

The housekeeper nods but says nothing.

Charlotte is not fond of flowers.

He knows people who have personal florists who come every week with flowers for every room, flowers that match the house. At parties, he's overheard women talking about their "flower men." But Charlotte resents the responsibility of flowers. She feels like it's her failure when they wilt. He ordered them anyway, hoping she can learn to live with something alive.

"They are very nice," the housekeeper says.

She is almost done. Vacuuming is what she does last. Mowing, he calls it. She is mowing the carpet in the living room; he can hear the occasional peanut or goldfish as it clatters up the pipe. He notices that when she mows the carpet it leaves tracks the same as one sees on a freshly cut lawn.

He remembers the story of Charlotte's mother and her living-room rug. The children were not allowed in the living room, but if, god forbid, they made their way in, they had to back out on their hands and knees, smoothing the carpet as they went, erasing their footprints.

When the housekeeper leaves, he gives her an enormous bag of leftovers, sandwiches, chips and dips, cookies—things they will never eat.

"It shouldn't go to waste," he says. He pays her double for the extra effort, for coming on Sunday, for not telling him he is a dimwit. She has done such a good job cleaning that it is as though the weekend never happened. It has been erased. There is no evidence.

Sunday, November 9, 2008
Palm Springs, California
6:42 p.m.

A car pulls up and Charlotte gets out. All she has with her is a small tote bag. Who goes away for two days with only a half-full tote bag? He carries it in for her.

Something has changed; there is a lightness to her, like a weight has been lifted. He makes a joke about it. "You look lighter, like you're floating."

"Floating on air," she says. "I'm bilious, filled with gas."

He watches as the driver backs out of the driveway crookedly and takes out a cactus. He can't bring himself to run after the guy and shout, Come back here, you crushed my cactus.

She is talking. He tries to stay focused but wonders if he goes out now, if he sets the cactus upright again and repacks the dirt, will it survive?

"I did whatever they told me to do, drank whatever it was, went on walks when I could and spent a lot of time sitting on the john. I expelled things that may have been prehistoric, dinosaurs from the depths of my colon. At one point I lay flat on the cold tile floor of the bathroom, counting the little squares to keep myself from passing out. I may even have hallucinated."

"Are you sure you went on the right cleanse, not one of those aya-huasca experiences where you're tripping through the desert?"

She pauses in the front hall. "Do you want the polite version or the truth?"

"Truth."

"It's torture, paid-for abuse. I don't know why anyone does it—save self-loathing. It's equal only to how much we are at war with ourselves."

He holds up his finger. "Give me a moment," he says, overcome by anxiety. He opens the front door and hurries to the end of the driveway. His *Pachycereus marginatus* is lying on its side. At first, he attempts a bare-handed rescue but finds it's not possible.

"What are you doing?" she shouts out the door. "I just got home and already you're out there, running away."

"I'm not running away; the driver ran down my cactus."

"Which one?"

"Pachycereus marginatus."

"The giant dildos by the end of the driveway?"

"Yes."

"Can it wait till morning?"

"I guess," he says, returning to the house.

"Why are you smiling?" she asks.

"You're fiery," he says. "Biting. I like it when you don't hold back."

"You have no idea. They stuck a tube up my ass and flushed me out. And while they were doing that, I was breathing in some kind of enhanced air otherwise known as oxygen while two women from south of the border were doing a special massage on my stomach." She lifts her top and shows him her belly, which looks lightly bruised, yellowy like a banana going bad. "Not only did I shit my brains out, I shit out things that had been in there for years, rocks, stones, pieces of coal, a little gold necklace my grandmother gave me; I swear I saw it there in the bowl shining up at me. Then I started vomiting. All the colors of the rainbow, like a horror movie. They brought in the doctor, who gave me a yellow bag of fluids; they put a little oximeter on my finger."

"Was the vomiting supposed to be part of the cleanse?"

"Who knows. They say it's different for everyone; it's all about how much you're holding in. For me, it was the history of the world in four parts. They actually wanted me to stay longer, another day or two for rest. 'I'm fine,' I said. 'I've done all we can and the car is coming in an hour.'" She pauses, and then, almost as if speaking in an aside, says, "On the way home I had to ask the driver to get off the road. I opened the door and got out. I didn't even have a chance to take my pants down. I lost it in my pants and took out some clean clothes and left the soiled ones by the side of the road. I gave the driver all my cash for his discretion. He couldn't have been nicer."

"Except that he mowed down my beloved plant."

"I guess that may have been more truth than you were looking for." She leans against the wall; it comes off as nonchalant, as though she were at a party smoking a cigarette and leaning her hip against the wall, a laid-back gesture, physical commentary, as if to say, Can you even handle the truth?

He thinks she's lost her balance. She seems to sway, to move between a state of profound consciousness, an epiphany, to something akin to nodding out.

He leads her toward a chair.

"Shower first," she says.

He steers her toward the bathroom, turns on the shower, and sits outside, perched on the small stool of her vanity. He sees that she's left her clothing in a pile on the floor. She never does that. She never leaves things on the floor. He tries not to look. He wishes the housekeeper was there to deal with it.

She emerges bright pink like a half-boiled lobster and slides on her robe.

"Tea?" he asks.

"Please."

He makes her tea with honey even though she likes it black. She needs the sugar.

"How were the boys?" she asks.

"Good," he says. "Better than good, on the cusp of life changing, or at least when we're done, I hope that's what it will be. I'm excited."

"Who was here besides Tony?"

"Kissick and Bo McDonald and a kid I met in Phoenix, Mark Eisner; he's not really a kid, but he's younger than we are, a jack-of-all-trades. A historian who's writing a book."

"But you hate the media; I'm surprised you let him in the house."

"He's not that kind of journalist; in fact, I dubbed him the scribe. His father was one of Eisenhower's men. Can I make you something—soup?"

As soon as he says soup, nausea sweeps across her face. "I wouldn't be able to keep it down. Gut rest. I have to give my gut a rest. It's been wrenched."

He sits in the chair near the sliding glass doors and looks around the room. "Watercolor," he says, landing on a painting she made years ago. "Remember when you did that?"

"Yes. I enjoyed it until the teacher told me that my colors were too washed-out and that the world was a much brighter place. She turned me off—too earnest."

"Maybe the woman wasn't smart enough to be your teacher."

"I bruise easily," she says.

At around nine p.m., she gets out of bed and makes herself a drink, then another. He gets a jar of peanut butter and a spoon. "You have to eat something," he says, forcing it into her mouth.

"I can't eat it plain," she says, gagging.

He returns with oyster crackers.

"I love an oyster cracker. They remind me of Chanel purses. They're quilted."

He feeds her oyster crackers dipped in peanut butter.

"I am not okay," she says.

"I know," he says.

"I've not been okay for a very long time."

"I know."

"I am never going to be okay."

"Well, I'm not so sure about that. The fact that we're talking about it says something."

"It says nothing. There is nothing I can say; there is nothing you can say that will ever make it okay. It is not okay."

"I get it," he says. "Sometimes things turn into a shit show, like the election, but there's no going back. It is what it is; that's where you have to begin—start where you are."

"What it is," she says, then pauses. "I cannot accept it."

"I know."

"I have tried and I cannot."

Despite what he said to Tony, he quietly wonders if she really tried. He thinks she is unwilling and doesn't see that her steely reserve, which she mistakes for strength, has left her crippled by grief.

"I really have tried," she repeats, as though reading his mind.

He nods.

"And I cannot." She pauses. "I will not."

Touché, he thinks but says nothing. Touché.

She has come back from her cleanse resolute. Whatever happened between them, whatever moment of closeness, cannot continue. She can't maintain this openness. It's too much to bear.

It's not personal, but they can't suddenly have a better relationship. She doesn't have the emotional will for it. Even the possibility of a relationship, the memory of it, the temporary feeling of closeness, the physical nature of what recently passed between them, was too much; and rather than cracking a door open, it seems to have cleaved her in half. Now she is broken and unable to bind the two halves together. Two halves, before and after, each pulling at her so she is actually breaking apart.

A crack has quickly become a fissure, a crevice, an ever-expanding rift that cannot be stopped, capped, sealed, or repaired.

Between the fallout from Tuesday's election, the flash of unexpected intimacy combined with their conversations over the last few days, and the cleanse, something has tripped a wire in Charlotte, uncorked the genie, whatever you want to call it. Whatever it was or is, all that's never been said, a quarter century of unexpressed everything, has risen to the surface and she can't contain it any longer. She drinks more.

For years, he has told himself that every family has its secrets, things they wished they'd handled differently.

He sees this as an opportunity for yet another revolution.

We should not fear revolution. What we should fear is changing the story to make it sound more palatable, the use of fact to weave a choking kind of floss.

Is he thinking about his family or his new plan?

Why is it enough for some people and not for others? What compels a person to want more, to push things further? Is it ambition? Greed? Or desire?

This comes in the middle of our lives when we know what brought us to this moment. Where do we go from here, do we give in to it, do we throw our hands up? Do we cave or do we fight for what we want?

He is having this conversation half with himself and half aloud with her.

"I want nothing," she says. "I want absolutely nothing."

She can't sleep. She can't sleep because she is drunk. She can't sleep because her metabolism is racing like an electric meter. She is wired. She is gutted, eviscerated. She doesn't know if this is new or the way it has been for a very long time, but she feels it.

At 1:15 a.m. she gets up. He hears her knocking around in the medicine cabinet.

"You okay?"

"Peachy," she says, swallowing two sleeping pills.

She is out. The breath of death, hot and sour, slips out of her lips in puffs like stale smoke rings.

"Where is the baby?" she asks at three a.m.

He wakes—startled.

"Where is the baby?"

"You're talking in your sleep."

"Don't gaslight me," she says. "Where's the baby?"

"Meghan is at school," he says.

"Don't treat me like a fool," she says. "Where's my baby?" She is insistent.

This is the hardest part. He wraps himself around her. He is pushing himself to do what doesn't come naturally; moving closer when he would otherwise move away.

She is drunk, drugged, malnourished; her body is a loose sack of bones in his arms. She is either losing her mind or coming to know her mind. He is so agitated by her middle-of-the-night wake-up that he can't go back to sleep. He goes outside to look at his cactus with a flashlight. Using thick oven mitts, he lifts it upright. Two limbs have been crushed and are oozing. He gets a large serrated knife from the kitchen and cleaves them off, thinking that might save the rest of the plant. He presses the soil firmly around the plant and goes back into the house. He throws the mitts, now embedded with cactus spines, into the trash. "Fuck it," he says loudly at five a.m. "Just totally fuck it to hell."

Eighteen hours later, when she wakes up, the window has closed.

He is in his office but comes in to check on her. She is breathing, calm, regular, steady. Should he rouse her for tea? He makes her a bouillon cube and leaves the steaming mug by the side of the bed. Covers her with a blanket, opens the shades, closes the shades.

He goes back to work. A few hours later, he finds her at the bottom of the pool.

Does she mean to be there? Did she faint? Is she okay? He must have seen or heard something—because he was suddenly pulled outside, as if called to find her at the bottom of the pool. When he dives in, he finds she has tied bags of pennies to her arms and legs, baggies of spare change from the jar in the kitchen.

He raises her to the surface and puts her on the concrete at the side of the pool.

Was she trying to kill herself? Is she out of her mind?

He turns her on her side and presses on her belly. Coins spill out of her hands.

"Don't stop me," she says. "I don't want to talk to you."

He's not even sure she knows who he is. "What were you doing in the pool?"

"I was meditating."

"We need to go to the hospital or something to make sure you're okay and didn't breathe in any water."

"I've been holding my breath for years; I'm very good at it."

He leaves her and goes into the bathroom. He pretends he's urinating, but he's sobbing over the toilet. He makes some calls. He calls his friend Tom, the orthopedic surgeon. "My wife is a very unhappy woman," he says. "She's spiraling."

"Does she want help?" the surgeon asks.

The Big Guy chronicles the last few days. "She's crying for help whether or not she has the words. All week she keeps trying to kill herself, between the pills, the drinking, the pool."

"Do you think it was intentional?" the surgeon asks.

"Does it matter? If you wake up dead, you're still dead whether you planned it or not."

"If this is an emergency, you should hang up and dial 911."

"I'm asking for your advice, not how to operate the telephone. I need to know where to take her and how to make the arrangements."

"She's stable for now?"

"Yes."

"Don't let her have any more alcohol and I'll call you back as soon as I have news."

She falls asleep by the pool on a lounge chair. He covers her head to toe with a blanket and pulls the umbrella over to shield her from the sun. She is stick thin, a social X-ray, not even anorexic because those women never ate—ever. Social X-rays grow up on crustless sandwiches, watercress, de-caffeinated coffee, and hard liquor. Their insides are pickled. At least the men ate steak and lamb chops with mint jelly.

He's always been a little proud of how much she was able to hold in for so long.

While he's standing over her, she lets loose a long thin fart in her sleep, the leftovers of the cleanse.

He packs a bag for her, an old blue suitcase that's been in the closet. He's never been in her drawers—somehow that feels more intimate than having had sex with her.

Underwear, slacks, tops, everything is folded insanely neatly—so neatly, it moves him.

When it's time to go, he tells her that he's taking her to a spa, like the ones in Switzerland with doctors. He tells her they will make her bouillon like on a cruise ship, that they will make turkey sandwiches, very thin, the way she likes.

He tells her that in life people go through seismic shifts and that this week in particular has been difficult. He tells her that he wants her to feel better soon. "The holidays are soon upon us, Thanksgiving and then Christmas." He mistakenly asks if there's anything special she'd like to do. A trip they might take?

She looks at him blankly. She has no plan to be here for that—no will to live.

He helps her get dressed and out to the car.

"Are we going home?" she asks.

"Soon."

"I'm sorry."

"About what?"

"The other night." She pauses. "I know it meant a lot to you."

He nods.

"And I'm sorry your man lost."

He nods again.

"He won't run again," she says. "That was it."

"I know."

"You're going to have to find a new hobby or you'll be at sixes and sevens. You could go back to work; you've been depressed since you retired. You're not really the retiring type."

"I'll be fine," he says, touched that in the middle of all this she's thinking about what he should do next. "It's not over till the fat lady sings. I've always hated that saying; it's so down on fat ladies singing. There are plenty of hummingbirds that like to sing."

"Maybe you'll get the boys together again soon."

"I plan to," he says.

She is still drunk when he brings her to the Betty Ford Center. When he made the arrangements over the phone, he said that he would come in with her and that together they would sit down and explain things.

He pulls up to the front door, takes her suitcase from the trunk, gives it to the man who is waiting outside, then hands Charlotte to him as well. "I'll be right back," he says. "Just going to park the car."

She has no idea what's happening.

He tells her that he is going to park the car but he drives away. It's not intentional. At first, he drives in laps around Betty Ford, thinking he'll go back, thinking he'll go in, and as planned they will explain things together. But the circles are ever widening, and then he's driving a long straight line, his foot flat on the gas, grateful for the open road.

IN THE WEEKS between Palm Springs and the inauguration, things happen. Bo sets up a meeting for the Big Guy in San Diego, code name Twinkle Toes.

The Big Guy is given instructions to drive to a Denny's near San Diego. He takes a table, thinking the guy he's supposed to meet will show up. While he's waiting, he orders a club sandwich. The sandwich arrives with a note pressed under the toothpick: "When you finish your breakfast, leave your car keys on the table and go outside. A white Chevy Malibu will be waiting. Get in." He skips the sandwich, pays the bill, and goes out. The car is waiting. "You could have gotten a box for the sandwich," the man says.

"Didn't know you wanted it," the Big Guy says. They take off, drive this way and that, making a lot of turns and zigzags that seem less than a direct route. The car stops outside a popular fast-food joint. "Buy a vanilla shake and wait for a woman in red," the man behind the wheel says.

"I guess this is where I bid you adieu," the Big Guy says, getting out of the car. He buys the vanilla shake and comes back outside. A woman with red hair and a red dress driving a red convertible with the top down pulls into the parking lot. She beeps. He goes to the window of her car. "Vanilla?" she asks.

"That's what the doctor ordered," he says, handing her the shake.

"Okay, so now you're gonna cross the street, go into the massage place in the strip mall, and ask for Barry."

He can't help but laugh. "Who's paying for the shake?" She steps on the gas, burning rubber across the parking lot before pulling into moving traffic without so much as a pause.

It's a bit much, but there's a sense of intrigue and what he hopes is play to the whole thing, so he figures why not cross the street and see what comes next. And it's not like he can easily walk away because he has no idea where he is or how to get back to his car. He pushes the walk button, waits for the light, and crosses. He's sweating now and can't help but wonder how many people are involved. Who is the woman in red? She was sexy and the milkshake looked good. His hand is cold and wet from the cup.

The massage place is dark and smells like boiled sauerkraut.

"Barry?" he asks the woman at the front desk. "Is there a Barry here?"

"Lunch in back," she says. "Lunch in back." He has no idea what she means until she takes him by the arm and leads him down a narrow hall.

Along one side of the place are cubicles divided by cheap shower curtains. He hears the sound of flesh being pounded and a few random sounds of people moaning unhappily. The whole thing makes him uncomfortable. It's tawdry and the kind of place you see on the news when cops bust rings of whatever. As they get down the hall, the smell of food intensifies, a vinegary sweet-and-sour odor. There are three rice makers on the floor. Are they really rice makers? They look as much like rice makers as IEDs, homemade land mines that could detonate at any moment.

"Sorry about the club sandwich," a bald burly man says, as he stands up from behind a small table. Despite the dark, the Big Guy notices that he's got piercingly clear blue eyes.

"You must be Barry," the Big Guy says, putting out his hand. Barry doesn't shake it or show any acknowledgment of his name. "Thanks for making the time . . ."

"Sit," the bald guy says, returning to his own seat.

The Big Guy sits. Even on a chair, Barry towers over him. Perhaps Barry's name isn't Barry—and he misheard everyone from the very start. Baldy. They've all been calling him Baldy except Bo, who called him the General. Now he's wondering if Baldy is, in fact, a general or if this meeting they're having is a "general" one, meaning they're supposed to discuss things in general rather than drill down into specifics.

There's a bowl of pea pods on the table. Baldy is eating the beans rapidly, sucking them from the shell, throwing the empty husks into the space between them. "Edamame," he says. "Help yourself."

"I don't think I got your name," the Big Guy says.

"That's right," the bald man says.

"I thought we were meeting at the restaurant?"

"Denny's? I never heard it called a restaurant before."

"We have a friend in common, Bo; he put me in touch with you . . ."

"I don't know who you're talking about. Someone asked if I'd sit down with a Mr. Money Bags and reassure him the country isn't going to hell. They said you'd had a panic attack the night of the election and couldn't carry on until someone who had a grip on things reassured you that the bases are covered. So I offered up my lunch hour."

"I'm not sure that's the most accurate description, but thank you."

The bald guy holds up one of the beans. "One day they're going to make hamburgers out of this stuff and they'll be so realistic that they'll ooze pink juice like blood. But they'll be one hundred percent fake, made in a lab. Cow farts. That's what's taking us down. Bovine emissions. There are 1.5 billon cows on the planet ripping too many fucking cow farts into the world's air supply. Each one puts out something like forty-six gallons of methane every day." He shakes his head. "I gave up meat years ago but not for the reason you think. Remember when they had that mad cow outbreak in the UK? Let's just say I was made aware of things that I'd never been privy to before. The meat market in this country is not what it once was; it's dirty, dark and dirty. You ever heard of pink slime?"

Two women appear carrying large buckets of water. One of the women stops in front of him, puts the bucket down, and gestures that he should take his shoes off and put his feet in.

The Big Guy notices that Baldy is already barefoot and that his toes are exceptionally long—so long and well-defined that they look like fingers.

"I can do tricks," the bald guy says; it's not the first time someone has been awed by his feet. He moves his toes through a selection of top hits: crossing the toes, snapping the toes, picking up objects with the toes. "I can play 'Für Elise' on the piano, although I have to warm up first."

"Nice," the Big Guy says, at a loss for words.

"I like to think we all have a little something extra, surprises for special occasions," Baldy says.

"Your feet are the health of your heart," the woman says to the Big Guy, as she squats on the floor and rolls up the legs of his pants. He wasn't expecting this. He's got very thin legs, nearly hairless at this point.

"Say again?" the Big Guy asks.

"Your feet are your heart," the woman says, picking up his feet one by one and putting them in the water, which is tinted blue and scalding hot.

Immediately the Big Guy's face flushes red. "Sweet Jesus."

"At least twice a week," Baldy says. "Reflexology. California is a great place for cheap body work. Hedonistic but healthy. But that's not why you're here. The foot rub is on me. I'm always trying to get new converts. You're a flag buff, a lover of all things organized and military, even though you never served. Your grandpa fought in WW1 or your father in WW2 or something like that, but you, you missed your moment; the military wasn't in vogue. You went to the right schools, you met the right men, you made the big bucks, now what? You need our help. Are we like school crossing guards? You can't get across the road without us?"

"Not exactly," the Big Guy says, but it doesn't matter, the bald man keeps on talking.

"We had six presidents who served in the navy: John Kennedy, LBJ, Richard Nixon, Gerald Ford, Jimmy Carter, and George H. W. Bush. Every one of them has some kind of crazy cockamamie story; Gerald Ford was basically a gym teacher; Jimmy Carter was about to be the captain of a submarine when his father died and he had to go home to Georgia—thank god. Can you imagine him out there during a battle? 'Hey fellas, how about we surface and offer the enemy a prayer and some peanuts? I'm not a violent man. I may have had lust in my heart, but not war.' In *Playboy* magazine no less, he needed to confess his adulterous hard-on."

The Big Guy looks like he might barf. The woman rubbing his feet has hit a very tender spot.

"You have clot," she says.

"No," he says. "No clot."

"You have gout," she says.

"Yes," he says, wondering how she knows. "I had gout once about five years ago."

"You bad boy."

"This isn't what I normally do," Baldy says. "I'm not a therapist, I'm more of a—"

"General?" the Big Guy asks.

Baldy makes a gun with his fingers and fires. "Gun for hire. Retired from official duties or at least that's the story." He laughs. "I've got my three stars tattooed on the back of my balls and an American flag between my ass cheeks in case anyone feels the need to check and see where my loyalty lies." He shakes his head. "Fuck me and you're actually fucking with the US of A." He laughs, a rat-a-tat, rapid-fire chortle. Romantic. Poetic. "What can I say, I live for this shit. My father did and his father too. Me, I don't have any kids, had my lines tied long ago, didn't want to be firing any man-made missiles. I always was a bit of a wanderer, an unconventional player in a game that's all about the rules. But this isn't about me; this is about you. What part of the whole charade put your tail in a spin?"

"I'll be blunt if I may . . ." The Big Guy looks Baldy square in the eye. The bald man nods.

"We are concerned." The Big Guy pauses. "In the event of decapitation, that we don't go all Humpty Dumpty and . . ." He can't bring himself to finish the sentence but looks at Baldy to confirm that the content is clear.

"We are prepared," Baldy says. "Like an alien life form—we walk among you. There are those who say the system of checks and balances has been gravely injured. But they need to know that the backbone of America is protected. Continuity of government goes beyond the Constitution because, in the event of the kind of emergency we anticipate in the twenty-first century, the provisions of the Constitution take too much for granted, including the idea that there are survivors and a government to succeed the one currently in place. Not only are systems in place but there is institutional memory. We are lifers. That's what the military is—a calling. Politicians call themselves public servants, but that's a load of crap. Schoolteachers are public servants, firemen are public servants, but people who run for office are pulling on your pud. The system has been moving rapidly in that direction since the end of WW2 and the rise of bullshit. Speaking of WW2, that's where this all started. Our plan has been in place since Eisenhower was in office. We have bunkers. We have copies of all kinds of historical records, from phone books to tax forms to Social Security checks. We have antivenom, cake mix, helium for your birthday balloons, and your favorite beer. COG plans run deep, with redundancy built in. We even have a cohort in the US Post Office, come rain or snow or nuclear fallout. The bases are covered. Plans have been made, keeping in mind everything from knowing that those who are alive will have lost their minds to locations where we will bury the dead. It's been set down in great detail. I hope what I'm saying reassures you. Yankee Doodle Dandy will ride high upon his pony."

Baldy talks like someone from the movies, like George C. Scott playing Patton. He would be Patton except that they're in a strip mall somewhere near San Diego with their feet soaked, sanitized, and dried with sandpaper-rough towels now being manipulated by Korean women with jackhammer strength who squat with their asses floating two inches off the floor.

Baldy is in love with the sound of his own voice. "Continuity of government—COG. I always found that an odd turn of phrase. Like a cog in a machine, like those tourist stops where you put a penny in, turn the crank, and get your penny back, but now flattened with the face of Abe Lincoln looking like you made him into Silly Putty. In 1958 and 1959, Eisenhower sent letters of authorization to ten men giving them special powers in the event of a national emergency. These letters had no expiration date." Baldy takes a long thin breath as the foot queen snaps each of his toes hard and fast in succession; it sounds like old-fashioned stove-top popcorn. "George Bush declared a state of emergency on September 14, 2001. When he did that, he set in motion the basis for five hundred dormant legal provisions—everything from censorship to martial law. They've never been made public. And here's the big news, no one's revoked that state of emergency. It's all still in place. Right here, right now. We train for shit you don't even dream about. Lone wolves, Waco, outer space shit crashing to earth, insects that no longer exist coming back to life, a spectrum of biological incidents—lettuce that can kill you in twenty-four hours, brain-eating amoeba, viruses that pass invisibly through the air two feet in front of you and can kill thousands of people a day. I know I'm not telling you anything that well-informed people don't already know or suspect. Know that it is real—it's not a question of if but when. It's the when that we are ready for."

"When the when comes, how will you know when it begins and what to do?"

Baldy laughs. "This is just the surface," he says, gesturing to the world around them. "What's key is what happens below. It's the only way to get things done—in the dark. The best-laid plans can sour at any time. We remain vigilant. The minute you let down your guard—shit happens. It can be naturally occurring or man-made—a change of public sentiment. Any one thing or a series of things, a cascade, can trigger an unfolding. Civil unrest, riots. News spreads fast. So does dissent. People feed off one another, the vibe of discontent."

"When do you let go of the kite string?" the Big Guy wants to know. "Who decides when you begin and when you're done?"

"We are in a unique moment; the fact that we're even having this conversation is unusual. We don't discuss operations with civilians or anyone not already in the program."

"This is an extraordinary time and none of us can be considered civilians anymore—we are all in this army."

"Aww," Baldy says, with a voice usually reserved for throwing candy to children at parades. "What a lovely thought, all of you in an army. But it's not like a marching band you can buy with your loose pocket change."

"Billions," the Big Guy says, insulted. "Our loose change is billions."

"It's like finger cymbals on a belly dancer. We're talking about a ten-layer plan that's been in the works since the day we dropped the bomb on Japan." He catches himself. "What am I even saying? It's not ten layers anymore—we're easily up to fifteen, twenty-four, or more. We've got layers on layers. After 9/11, we added so many more layers that you'd be hard-pressed to find any one man who knows what really goes into the mix. That's the beauty of it, always a little bit of a question mark." He lifts up both arms as if to say, Look Ma, no hands. "Who is driving the bus?"

"That is among our questions. When the when comes, who will be at the helm?" the Big Guy asks. "What can we do for you? How can we ensure that when the moment comes the wind doesn't blow the whole show south?"

"We don't typically work with civilians, but there is certainly historic precedent. The Eisenhower Ten were scions of industry, communication, and banking. It's helpful to know that there are men willing to serve. For those of us doing the work, sometimes it feels too insular. There are times I've wondered whether I was making the whole thing up, like a giant novel written in the sky."

"I hear you. My group has interests in a variety of areas and is keen to be of use. Who is your commander?"

"I can't answer," Baldy says.

On cue, a Korean woman comes in with a large plate of steamed dumplings. The pile of bean husks has disappeared and a dish of brown sauce has appeared along with two sets of wooden chopsticks. Baldy separates his sticks, rubs them together so fast and fierce, sawdust flies. He pinches a dumpling, dunks it in the sauce, and pops it into his mouth. "So good," he says, breathing out the steam and quickly popping more into his mouth. Speaking in Korean, he asks the woman what kind of dumplings they are. "Homemade," the woman says in perfect English. "Wild mushroom. I picked them myself."

"Fuck me," Baldy says. "The one thing I'm allergic to." He whips an EpiPen out of the side pocket of his cargo pants, slaps it down on the table, and starts checking his pulse against his watch. "It's nothing to worry about until my heart stops."

The Big Guy is sweating. Sweat trickles down his head, forms tributaries over his ears, the sides of his nose, and then rivers down his back into his pants. Minutes pass; everyone is focused on the second hand of Baldy's Rolex Milsub. The Big Guy isn't into "stuff," but he knows watches.

Suddenly, down the narrow hall comes the woman in red carrying two cups from the carry-out across the street. She hands the Big Guy one of the cups.

"You okay?" she asks Baldy, putting the other drink in front of him.

He takes his fingers off his carotid artery, abandoning the pulse check.

"Either I'm not allergic anymore or the mushrooms weren't really wild."

A sigh of relief. The Big Guy takes a long pull on the red straw sticking out of the cup. Vanilla milkshake. For a second, he thinks it's the original milkshake, but that's impossible, it would have melted by now. This one is fresh and thick with ice cream crystals that melt on his tongue.

The woman in red looks at the Big Guy, her face stricken. Is something wrong? Is he being poisoned? He feels fine, but there's something odd about her expression. "I'm so sorry," she says. "I couldn't help it." He looks at the drink and sees that the red straw has the darker red imprint of her lipstick.

"It looked so good, I had to have a little taste."

"No worries," he says, taking another long pull on the straw, cold and creamy and as perfect as perfect can be.

"So, we're good?" Baldy says.

"I'm good if you're good," the Big Guy says—lost in a boner and brain freeze.

"Do you have any singles?" Baldy asks him.

For a moment, he's distracted; is Baldy asking if he's single?

"Singles," Baldy repeats. "Dollar bills? Greenbacks?"

The Big Guy checks his wallet. Nothing smaller than a hundy.

"Forget about it." Baldy passes him a couple of dollars.

"What's this for?"

"The valet out front." Baldy slides him a parking ticket. "I don't think you're going to want to walk all the way back to Denny's. Your shake will melt."

"That's it?" the Big Guy says. "We're done?"

"For now."

When he goes outside, the valet appears with his car. He gives the guy the two bucks and gets in.

He stops to get the car washed on the way back to Palm Springs. He stands watching through the glass as the car is pulled through the machine, foam wash, wheel cleaning, wax. As he watches, he's sucking up what's left of the shake, the red-and-white paper straw now a limp wet noodle between his lips.

When they're vacuuming the car, they find something and give it to him.

"Button?" they ask. It looks like a cross between the brass button from a woman's coat and a coin from a foreign country. It's not something he's seen before, not off his blazer or Charlotte's coat. It's a bug; they planted a bug in his car. He takes it from the guy, goes to the men's room, and flushes it down the toilet.

When he gets home, Bo is waiting in his driveway, sitting in his car, blasting the AC even though it's a beautiful seventy-three degrees outside.

"So, how'd it go?"

"Sew buttons," the Big Guy says. "Weirdest fucking meeting I ever had. It was like fucking *Apocalypse Now*. Was it all a ruse, a stress test to see how I responded? A psychological car wash? What was the vanilla milkshake about, a temptation offered, then removed, and then delivered? Was it my reward for jumping through weird-shit hoops?"

"Slow down, old man. I have no idea what you're talking about," Bo says.

"You set me up. I jump through a thousand hoops, turn right, turn left, knock twice, code name Twinkle Toes, to sit down with this wackadoo who tells me that basically he's been asked—I assume by you—to peel me down off the walls, to offer reassurance from the 'highest levels' that things are well in hand. Stand down and thanks but no thanks."

"What did you expect?"

The Big Guy snorts. "What did I expect?" He pauses. "I have no fucking idea, but it wasn't what I got. I sound fucking insane and I suspect they bugged my car."

"I bugged your car," Bo says.

The Big Guy looks at him—WTF?

Bo shrugs.

"Is that supposed to make me feel better?"

"It's supposed to show you how much I care," Bo says. "Seriously, did you think that you could actually walk in there and say, 'Oh hey, General, my buddies and I are unhappy with the way things shook out and we're wondering if we can partner with you and—you know—flip the switch.' This isn't some kind of upside-down Banshee or Montu roller coaster. You can't just walk into the military and go wink, wink, I know and you know that there's a secret 'other' room and I want to do business in it."

The Big Guy shrugs. "I'm not used to hearing no."

"What if he'd said yes? What if he said, 'You bet, we've been waiting for a guy like you to come along. How about I stop by your place on Wednesday night and we figure it out?' Would you think he was a man you want to be in business with? Would you trust him? You don't know him. He doesn't know you. These things take time. The meeting went well. You got what you wanted; you wanted him to tell you to fuck off. You wanted him to tell you—it's not going to happen, there's no place for men like you in our world."

"Interesting," the Big Guy says.

"Now you're on his radar and you can bet he's gonna be watching you. He's gonna figure out if you're serious or not—Rome wasn't built in a day."

"Yeah, but it burned pretty fast." He pauses.

"If it's going to happen, you want him to come to you, to think it was his idea to invite you to the party. Let them think the wheel is their invention."

"Smart," the Big Guy says. "Question for you. When you called it Operation Twinkle Toes, did you know I was going to have to take my socks off and let some lady rub my feet so hard that I doubt I'll be able to walk tomorrow."

"No," Bo says. "I called it Operation Twinkle Toes because something about the way you move reminds me of Fred Flintstone. Remember when Fred and Barney would go bowling?"

The Big Guy shakes his head no.

"Fred would go down the lane on his tiptoes trying to be light on his feet. The sound was a rapid tinkle of the piano keys?" Bo looks at the Big Guy; still nothing. "When we were all here and you ran across the patio and jumped into the pool, it reminded me of Fred Flintstone. To me you are—Twinkle Toes."

"I need a drink," the Big Guy says. "You staying in your car or coming in?"

The two men go into the house; the Big Guy makes them both a drink. The booze is disgusting, weak, watered-down. "I might actually cry," the Big Guy says.

"I'm happy to take you out and buy you a drink."

"I don't care about the drink. I had a milkshake with the General. I'm just sad. Sad."

Bo gives him a big bear of a hug.

"Is now a good time?" the Big Guy asks, when Meghan answers the phone.

"Sunday night study hall—doing homework."

"You've always been first-rate at that," he says.

"My whole life you've been telling me that my job is going to school and that I had to work my way up the ladder so of course I'm good at it."

"Fine thing," he says. "And the horse is well?"

"Still skittish about the woods. The trainer and I have been going on some rides together. Ranger picked up on my stress, which has stuck with him."

"Keep at it," the Big Guy says. "One foot after another, sometimes that's all you can do." There's a pause. "I have some news." He clears his throat. "It can't have escaped you that your mother . . ." Another long pause.

"You okay?"

"Fine. I meant to lead with that. We're fine. Everything is going to be okay."

"That's good," Meghan says, unconcerned until now.

"What I'm trying to talk about, not very successfully, is drinking. Your mother's drinking."

"Vodka?" Meghan asks. She's not entirely clear about why he called; did he call to tell her that her mother drinks?

"Yes. Vodka."

"She told me the reason she drinks vodka is because it has the lowest calories."

"Fascinating," the Big Guy says. "I thought she drank vodka because it doesn't really taste like anything. But the point is, the reason she drinks, it's not about the calories. She has used alcohol to help her manage her days and it's clearly not helping. There is something I need to tell you."

"Okay."

"After the disappointment of the election, she made a big decision to seek help."

There's another long silence.

"I don't mean to be weird, but I'm not sure what you're saying."

"Your mother is an alcoholic. She's gone into treatment at the Betty Ford Center. It's one of the best places in the country for this kind of thing." The tension in his voice ratchets up. He stops and takes a deep breath. "You might remember we spent some time with the Fords years ago when you were little. The father, Gerry, was VP under Nixon and took over the presidency after Dick resigned, a thankless job if there ever was one. And Betty, she was the powerhouse; God bless her for coming forward with her problems. Do you remember years ago when we went over to their house? It was Easter. Their son, Jack, was visiting with his boys."

"I'm not sure," Meghan says. "Mostly, if I think about going to visit people, I remember you and Mom being nervous in the car before we went to anyone's house and Mom checking to make sure my dresses were long enough and my shoes were clean. Also my nails—she always checked my nails."

"Your mother cares a lot about how she's seen."

"She was worried about how drinking made her look?"

"She's concerned about her privacy, about what people know about her or that she's being judged by others. It's important to her that others see her in a good light."

"So, this Betty Ford, is it like a hospital? Is she locked up on a psych ward? Last fall a girl here took some kind of drug and had to be tied to an office chair in the infirmary until they could get her to the hospital. She kept saying she was God and the nurse on duty kept saying, 'God is a man and you're a lovely young girl,' which aggravated the girl even more."

"She's not on a psych ward. Your mother's not crazy."

"Is she on an IV?"

"I don't think so. My understanding is that it's a good environment for people who have this issue. They talk to one another about what drives them to drink and how to handle things differently."

"This was something she wanted to do? She's not usually big on talking about problems."

"It was what she needed to do," the Big Guy says, trying to get things back on track.

A long pause. "Was she driving drunk?" Meghan asks.

"No, she'd never do that. She never wanted to put anyone in danger. Things got to a certain point and she had to take action. The reason I'm telling you is that it will affect Thanksgiving. We won't be making our usual trip to be with you, which is disappointing, but I talked with Tony and he's going to have you join him in DC. You'll probably have a lot more fun with him than being with your mother and I in a hotel somewhere."

"Your mother and me, that's how you're supposed to say it; your mother and I is not grammatical."

"Well, fancy that you know something I don't," the Big Guy says. "It's pretty cheeky of a kid to correct her father. I suppose I should be glad you're a confident young woman. Speaking of which, are you in good shape with your college applications?"

"It's a work in progress," she says.

"If there's anything I can do, let me know."

"Can I ask you a question?"

"Yes."

"Were you born in Delaware?"

"In Wilmington," he says. "You do know that Delaware was the first state?"

"Literally the first in America?"

"Literally," he says. "In 1777 George Washington fought a battle not far from Wilmington, and in December 1787 it became the first of the thirteen states to ratify the US Constitution."

She laughs. "How much do you love George Washington?"

"As the father of this country, he is as much my father as pater Hitchens."

Another pause.

"Do you think Mom ever wanted to do something . . . ?"

"Like what?"

"I don't know, like go back to school?"

"No," he says, without a pause. "Why would she? Your mother is an exceptionally intelligent woman. If you gave us both IQ tests, I have no doubt that she'd score higher than I would."

"I wondered if there was something else she wanted to do, some dream that she had or . . ."

"She's going to be fine," the Big Guy says.

"Is there anything I can do for her?"

"Nice of you to ask, but I don't think there's anything right now."

"Should I call her?"

The thought hadn't occurred to him. He doesn't think of them as having that kind of relationship, has no idea whether Charlotte would want that. He realizes that for more than a week the girl has had no idea her mother was in the hospital; it's all he could do to tell her now, and if it wasn't for the holiday, he thinks it unlikely he would have said anything. "Well, I don't quite know how that works—I'm not sure she has a phone of her own, but I could find out for you."

"I could talk to her and say something encouraging like they did with Bambi."

"Who is Bambi?"

"The deer, Bambi, from the movie. It's a way of saying I'm rooting for you."

"Maybe send a card?" Is there such a thing as a dry-out card? *I'm sorry you're in the bin but here's hoping you make new friends and stay off the sauce.* Staying dry sounds like an advertisement for incontinence pants. *Having problems with bladder leakage?* He imagines a television commercial that starts with a woman playing tennis, then cuts to a man playing golf before ending with an older, formerly famous actor holding up what looks like a trash bag and saying, "Perfect for keeping an active lifestyle."

"Is there an address to send the card? Do I write her name and then Betty Ford Center?"

"Just wait," he says, imagining Charlotte's name on an envelope with Betty Ford Center written on the line below. "With any luck, she'll be home soon." He pauses. "You okay over there, kiddo?"

"Yeah, I'm fine," she says. "Do you think she can shop while she's there?"

"What do you mean?"

"Christmas is coming and she always does a lot for Christmas."

"I have no idea," he says. "But I guess you'd better work up a list and be sure to pass it along to Santa Claus."

"You're not going to start that again, are you?" Meghan asks.

"Start what."

"The delusions."

He laughs. "I guess not."

"Do you think Mom cares about me?"

"Of course she does."

"Then why did she do this?"

"I don't think it's about you or I."

"You or *me*," she corrects him again.

"I guess that's what I'm paying the big bucks for, a grammarian."

"What do you think caused it? Did something happen?"

"Yes, something happened," he nearly says but catches himself. "You saw it right there in Phoenix, a generation of hard work flushed down the toilet. That's what it is—it's not four years, it's not nothing, it's an entire generation of men who worked to build this country and now it's flushed, that's what happened."

"Was it something I did?" she asks. "Like did I vote the wrong way, wear the wrong thing, say something I shouldn't have?"

"I don't think you should take it personally," he says.

"But I was in Phoenix, with you and Mom."

"You're being too literal. What depressed the hell out of her in Phoenix was seeing how old everyone looked; that hit her worse than the election result. You don't get another go-round; there is no going back; realizing that was a shock. It had been brewing for years; Phoenix was the tipping point. Your mother has certainly never asked anything of us before; she's not interrupted our lives in any way."

There's a long silence.

"Maybe she's going through something you don't know about; maybe it's not that people looked old but maybe she feels like she wasted her life, that it was all for nothing?" Meghan suggests. Another pause. "Who do you want me to be?"

"I'm not sure what you mean."

"Am I supposed to be like Mom? I mean isn't alcoholism genetic? Am I supposed to marry a rich guy and have babies and drink vodka?"

"Am I actually supposed to answer that?"

"How is it I'm eighteen and know nothing?"

The Big Guy laughs. "You know some things: colonial history, geometry, European literature, and grammar. Women aren't really supposed to know all that much."

"Did you really just say that?"

"Didn't say a word," he says. "Let's talk again in a few days. And until then, take good care of yourself and that horse. You know where to find me if anything comes up."

"Love you," she says, hanging up.

A couple of days later, Tony calls.

"Do you think it's surprising?" she asks. Meghan is in her dorm room at her desk; in front of her is the spreadsheet for her college applications, her essay, and other supplemental materials.

"What?" he asks, not about to give away anything.

"That Mom's in rehab?"

"Do you?"

"At the moment, everything is surprising. I don't know whether I've had my head in the sand or if suddenly things are coming out."

"Could be a little of both. As you get older, perhaps you pick up on more and they say more."

"Do you think she has a drinking problem?"

Tony is quiet.

"Should I take your silence as a yes?"

"Kiddo, I'm not a medical professional and I don't live with your mom, but I've known her a long time. In the long run, it's promising that she's taken herself for treatment. What do you think?"

"I think she likes her vodka. She counts the hours between the wine at lunch and cocktail hour. She says that when you fly it can really mess things up. Especially going from east to west."

"That sounds about right," Tony says. "Five p.m. in DC is only two p.m. out West; that's a long dry afternoon."

"Are you sure she's an alcoholic? Because she never seems drunk, she doesn't do stupid things, and she sometimes stops drinking entirely for weeks at a time. Like when she goes on a diet."

"Maybe something changed," Tony says. "Things get to a point where a person feels they need to act and need help to make changes. About Thanksgiving," he says, switching subjects. "I'm hoping that you'll come with me to a friend's house in Georgetown."

"What do I need to wear?"

"Simple but classy. Even though the first settlers landed far north of here, Washingtonians think they own Thanksgiving."

"Maybe my colonial woman's work costume from the school play? It's a print dress with a red apron and bonnet."

"Perfect," Tony says.

"I guess Dad already told the school that I'm not leaving because I got an invitation to visit a local church and go apple picking. Gives new meaning to the phrase 'Black Friday.'"

"It's a day like any other," Tony says.

"Not when you go to boarding school and all the other girls pack up and leave on Tuesday night and don't come back until Sunday. I bet even most murderers have Thanksgiving plans."

"Oof," Tony says.

She can't help it. She keeps thinking about the murdered girl. The night she went missing, the police searched but didn't find her. The next morning her father came with the family dog and found her right away on the hill behind the chapel. Ashley's aunt said that after the murder the family left the country. Meghan imagines that's what you have to do when something truly awful happens; you have to seal it off, bury it not just in the ground but so deep within yourself that it can't ever come loose.

"Don't worry," she tells Tony, half trying to convince herself. "I'll be fine. I'm going to use the time to rewrite my college essay."

Since Phoenix, she's been thinking about how people see the world around them. In Phoenix her father's friends stood in front of the television looking shocked, as if they hadn't seen it coming. Terrifying was the word her father used and the word stuck with her. What happened in Phoenix was terrifying but in a different way, a new way.

She has always been aware that there is a darkness, a threat no one mentions that lives at the edge of the woods. She thought it was a fake, some kind of grown-up problem, like worrying. Now she feels it for the first time. It's big and it's terrifying.

Thursday, November 27, 2008
Palm Springs, California
9:00 a.m.

He's been on his own for days. It's a strange kind of independence that wasn't asked for. He belongs to no one, is accountable to no one; no one is watching. What might feel like liberation to others is becoming increasingly terrifying.

The first day or two it was simply odd. If anyone had pressed, he might have said there had been an accident of some sort, an enormous misunderstanding that involved the swimming pool. He might have said that Charlotte had briefly fallen through a psychic crack—that's how he would describe it, like a crack in the cement—he's still finding pennies in the pool.

If you asked a pool man, they might say the crack was due to hydrostatic pressure. He loves those words. Hydrostatic pressure has to do with the downward force of gravity from above. That sums it up. Charlotte cracked due to increased hydrostatic pressure.

If you said that to some people, they might nod their heads gravely and say how sorry they were to hear it; they might go home and tell their wives that Charlotte had suffered something akin to a stroke. Some might take the pool metaphor more seriously and announce that her water had broken; most would avoid saying that she'd cracked, although that was the most accurate description. Charlotte had cracked, and after he'd dropped her off at Betty Ford, he didn't know what else to do. He'd driven around until it started to get dark, then he went home. A day or two passed in a fog. The sun went down, then it came up again, and that happened a few times, and at first, he was afraid to even go into the pool so he used the skimmer to try to scrape up the pennies from the bottom, then finally he just dove in and he rather liked the game of it: holding his breath, going to the lowest point, and picking up the loose change.

The restaurant starts serving Thanksgiving dinner at noon, but he waits until one p.m. to leave the house. He doesn't want to seem desperate. A race is being run and streets are closed. In an effort to navigate the detour, he nearly clips a runner with his side-view mirror. His system flushes with adrenaline, a rocket-fueled cocktail of shame and rage. He slams the horn just because and guns his way down the road.

He drives past the Betty Ford Center, circling it a couple of times thinking he might see something that would give him a clue about what's going on inside—but there's nothing. The place radiates a big blank. He hasn't heard a peep. When he dropped her off, he figured it would be a week or two at most. He assumes that at some point they'll want money. He thinks maybe they did a little digging and calculated that he could afford it and decided to keep her. There's nothing worse than feeling both taken advantage of and helpless. It's a bad combination.

He parks at the restaurant, takes off his tie, and stuffs it into his pocket. He can't wear a tie at one p.m. and he can't go alone into the restaurant. He brings a legal pad and pens.

Once he's seated, he immediately orders a drink. The waitress brings his scotch and the menu for the day. Oysters, chestnut soup, roasted squash and goat cheese salad, roast beef au jus or free-range turkey with sausage stuffing, sage and pancetta gravy, mashed Yukon Gold potatoes, mashed sweet potatoes, creamed spinach or green beans with crispy shallots. Dessert is a choice of pumpkin pie, three-berry crumble, pecan tart, or homemade ice cream.

The menu itself is an antidepressant.

The last time he had Thanksgiving dinner alone was 1978. He knows because he remembers it vividly and he keeps datebooks. He's always kept datebooks and makes annotations in them in part in case the IRS ever asks for them and in part because it's what he does. He is old-school—makes notes in margins, writes things down, ideas, fragments of conversation, bad jokes and who told them to him. Thanksgiving 1978 alone. And it wasn't really alone. He was in DC working and was invited by a friend of Tony's to his family home in Chevy Chase and ended up spending the weekend with them. He remembers it not because it was his first and only Thanksgiving alone but because it was like a fantasy Thanksgiving. There were easily forty people—friends, neighbors, a Supreme Court justice—and after the meal, the "boys," meaning four seventy-year-old males, went outside and played football, then came back in, watched football, and ate leftovers. In the morning, the lady of the house made him a sandwich he still remembers, white bread with turkey, cranberry sauce, and stuffing. Then she panfried the sandwich. He still remembers it as the best thing he ever ate. He also remembers that the guy who invited him to Thanksgiving blew his brains out ten years later when he was about to be outed for being gay. He got arrested in a public bathroom with another man in what might have been a setup—it made the evening news. And overnight the guy drove out to Great Falls, hiked out to a rock, and shot himself clear through the head. That stuck with the Big Guy. It depressed the hell out of him that someone would kill themselves over being queer. Only years later did it occur to him that perhaps Chip had been Tony's boyfriend. He never asked Tony about it, but he makes a mental note to ask him now that the cats are coming out of the bag. He always thought he was doing Tony a favor by not talking with him about his homosexuality—in retrospect, he thinks he did the opposite.

The waitress comes to take his order. "Chestnut soup and turkey." Does he prefer dark or light meat? "Light." Mashed white or sweet or both?

He's a grieving man, and despite that he has made a billion and more decisions, today he is absent the ability to ask for what is good or what is right. "Both," he says. "Some of everything. And then some more."

Although he has at times thought of himself as soulless, when the waitress brings him his soup, he says a brief prayer. Who thought it would come to this, alone on Thanksgiving; his wife in the dry-out clinic; his kid, who doesn't know the whole story, having Thanksgiving with her closeted queer godfather; and he is down deep in Palm Springs, California, secretly plotting what some might call a domestic disturbance, but first—a little prayer that sanity and balance restore themselves over chestnut soup.

The soup has thyme cream and wild mushrooms on top. It is warm, slightly nutty, an earthy delight that he should know from the first spoonful is too rich for his stomach. But it is so good. He's become a man who speaks to his soup. "So good," he says to the bowl, and drinks it down. In a maneuver that would send Charlotte off the rails, he breaks off a large wad of his popover and runs it around the inside of the soup bowl, wiping it clean.

"Saving the best bite for last," the waitress says, refilling his water glass.

He blots his lips with his pumpkin-colored napkin.

Lunch. That's what he's calling it even though the restaurant has billed it as an all-day Thanksgiving dinner. This isn't dinner; this is lunch. A working lunch. He is immersing himself in his project in this new world. He's eating his soup; reading his book, *Democracy in America*; and taking notes. He is recommitting to his values and getting this job done. It's the thing that's keeping him going while the rest spins out of control.

His plate arrives piled high. And there's a basket with two fresh hot popovers. "Do you need a side of gravy?" the waitress asks.

"Thank you."

"I like to take care of fellas like you on their own," the waitress says.

Is she hitting on him? God, he hopes not; he can't handle that.

"Much thanks. My wife is away and my daughter is at school."

The waitress shakes her head. "It's difficult, isn't it?"

He's eating Thanksgiving dinner by himself at one in the afternoon, and as he eats and reads and writes, he's reviewing his life, flipping through a mental photo album from Thanksgiving to Thanksgiving. He cut out brown-paper turkeys and thumbtacked them to the wall outside his elementary school classroom; he had ideas about hope and abundance as a young man, which transformed into a competitive desire to win, to earn, to become an empire builder—master of the universe. But knowing what we all know, that money and success don't isolate one from pain. He's left with loneliness, anxiety, and the rising question, What's it all about, Alfie?

This dark afternoon alone in Palm Springs is unfathomable to him and yet it is happening. The whole thing has gone tits up; nothing is what you'd expect it to be; nothing is the way it was, and that's the way it's going to be. Unfathomable. Unexpected. That's what happens in life—just when you think you know where it's going, it takes a turn.

"For dessert?" the waitress asks.

He shakes his head, speechless. The meal was enough to feed a family of four.

"Don't fret, honey; let me figure it out."

"Is that you, Hitchens?" A man in a cowboy hat comes to a stop at the Big Guy's table.

The Big Guy looks up.

"Keyes?"

"Keyes to the city." The man laughs and extends his hand.

The Big Guy stands up and gives Douglas Proctor Keyes, a retired judge from Texas, a warm welcome. "I haven't seen you in a dog's age. What brings you to Palm Springs?" The Big Guy looks over the judge's shoulder expecting to see his family filing in after him. "Where are your people?"

The judge laughs. "I ran away."

"From home?"

"From Las Vegas. A few years ago, my twin girls, Melanie and Melody, married a pair of brothers, Byron and Bruce. Somehow they decided we should all have Thanksgiving in Vegas—on me! You can't make it up. We get there, and last night, as we're sitting down to dinner, Byron and

Bruce call me Old Man and offer me a seat at the head of the table. Old man? What the hell? I fucking made the table; I fucking own the hotel—along with Adelson. One of the grandchildren called me Gampy. I thought they said Gimpy, but does it matter? It was all I could do to get through dinner without blowing the two bustards a giant Bronx cheer and walking out. This morning I woke up thinking I don't need this shit. I left. I told my wife to tell them that I was under the weather and staying in the room—so as not to infect anyone. I felt like I couldn't breathe, like I was trapped in Houdini's box. Took me an hour and a half to get from there to here—door to door. I already feel so much better. I popped the bubble. I just needed to know I could get out. I'll go back tonight—but for the moment, it is a joy. I am free." The judge does a little jig.

The waitress, returning with a platter of deserts, says, "I see you met a friend."

"An old friend of the family," the Big Guy says, motioning for the judge to sit down. "Care to join me?"

The judge sits. "I'm going to pretend I'm not a little diabetic."

"And I'll pretend that I didn't have gout last year. I just came out to get a little bite; my people are in DC today," the Big Guy says, preempting the question. "So here I am."

The waitress brings Keyes a set of silverware and a hot cup of coffee.

The two men dig in and between the pumpkin pie, the three-berry crumble, the pecan tart, and the melting ice cream, they talk about everything from the election to a particular kind of male depression that they believe is unique to men of a certain class and age. They talk about oil and tobacco and how the judge made his money—it had nothing to do with his early years on the bench and more about the "capture" of calls, natural resources, and real estate. "Vegas is a perfect example," the judge says. "People come into town, stay in a hotel with marble bathrooms, eat a steak thicker than their hand, and believe that they stand a chance of coming away with a piece of the pie, but it's a delusion. They don't see us right there with vacuum cleaners cleaning up after them, sucking up every last nickel and dime. And for whatever deluded reason, they leave with a smile. 'Better luck next time.' It's crazy."

The men talk about their desire to do something more. "Despite having abandoned the bench in pursuit of greenbacks—I remain active behind the scenes," the judge says, spooning the last of the pie into his gullet. "Not that I'm self-interested, but the trick is to keep your eye on judges, that's where the action is. What we want over time is to control the bench—that means appointing Article III federal judges on our watch."

"What is Article III?"

"The US Constitution," the judge says, surprised that the Big Guy doesn't know. "Article III judges are lifetime appointments, not just the Supreme Court but the US courts of appeals, the US district courts, and the Court of International Trade. At the moment, there are more than eight hundred of them."

"I had no idea," the Big Guy says, as he hands the waitress his credit card. "You and I need to spend more time together."

"Indeed we do," the judge says. "This day has turned a corner."

After lunch the Big Guy heads back to the house, circling Betty Ford again on the way home. That Charlotte is in there is eating at him. He would go around again, circle a few more times, maybe even go so far as to beep the horn, but his stomach is hurting. He's past the point of comfort. Distended. As he's driving, it swells more. Even though he finished eating twenty minutes ago, his belly continues to inflate. How crazy was it that Doug Keyes was in Palm Springs? How crazy is it that he's not the only man alone on Thanksgiving? He has no idea how many desserts they ate, but he has to unbuckle his pants as he's driving; uncouth though it may be, he has no choice. He pulls into the driveway, quickly throws the car into park, and rushes into the house.

He spills his lunch into the toilet again and again. To cover the stench of his stomach having run afoul of the holiday, he sprays an entire can of Lysol, which leaves him wheezing.

Wrapped in his bathrobe, he goes outside and lies by the pool. The air needs to clear. He needs time to recover. He tells himself that it was the soup, the richness of the chestnuts. He thinks of his lunch with the General, the venerable man with his EpiPen poised to stab himself in the thigh. He thinks he should get an EpiPen in case whatever happened should happen again and escalate.

He thinks of the prefix epi, as opposed to prix fixe dinner. Epi: over, before, near . . . Over, before, near death. He lies outside in the afternoon sun thinking that in his abrupt spill, the loss of his lunch, he has narrowly avoided death this afternoon. That's how it feels in the moment.

The phone rings. He would say it scared the crap out of him, but there is no more crap left in him; he is empty, involuntarily cleansed. He hurries into the house, not waiting for the machine to screen the call. He's sure it's Charlotte or maybe Meghan calling to wish him a happy day.

"Are you all right out there?"

"Who is this?" he asks.

"It's Godzich, your loyal employee. I'm calling to see how you're doing."

"Are *you* all right? You've never called me on a holiday," the Big Guy says. "Is something wrong? Are you under arrest? Did you siphon my funds? Whatever it is, you scared the bejesus out of me."

"I called to say we're thinking of you and Charlotte. I'm not sure if you know it, but my wife went through something similar. If there's anything we can do, we are at your disposal."

A flush of shame and rage. Of course you are at my disposal, he thinks, but knows enough not to say, "You work for me."

"I'm fine," he says. "Nothing to worry about."

Godzich has worked for the Big Guy for years, more years than he'd care to count. They have grown, if not old, deeply middle-aged engaged in the same endeavor. The funny thing is, he never liked the guy. Godzich trained as a lawyer and makes more than a decent living. Charlotte often teases the Big Guy that he's surrounded himself with A+ minds that have C- lives. Godzich is devoted to the Big Guy. He's been peculiarly effective over the years, managing and diversifying the Big Guy's holdings, among them shopping malls, hospitals, residential apartment buildings, and more. The Big Guy was never into real estate but saw it as a parking place for some of his "winnings."

"I'm fine," he says again, lying to Godzich. "I'm back from a lovely lunch—with Doug Keyes who happened to be passing through town. All day I've been thinking about how wonderful it is—what we have done. We have provided food, clothing, shelter, and—with the movie theatres—pleasure to so many Americans. We made life good, better than it used to be. These are quintessential American experiences: being able to eat in the same restaurant no matter what city you are in and have the food taste exactly the same; being able to shop in malls and know exactly where each store is. It is full service; all your needs are met. We have made America rich and bountiful, and we have created the desire for more." The Big Guy waxes poetic with such grace that he impresses even himself. He goes on talking, a split from the reality of the moment, and yet it is a strange but true story he's telling. "These are the stories we tell ourselves when we are going to bed," he says. "These are the stories that let us sleep." There he is, an old whale in a bathrobe by the pool having eaten himself sick in an effort to blunt the pain. "I'm right here, Godzich, taking the day to myself. I've got a pad of paper and a stack of books. *The Conservative Mind*, *The Conscience of a Conservative*, and I dug out *God and Man at Yale*, and of course there's the ball game, the Tennessee Titans against Detroit, that's the first game of the day. All is well."

"How is Charlotte doing?" Godzich asks.

"No idea."

There's a pause on the other end.

"These things can take a while . . . And Meghan? Is she aware?"

"Yes, she's been informed. She's spending the day with Tony in Washington so she's in good hands. Listen, Godzich, thanks for reaching out. I appreciate it. Don't worry. The ship isn't about to sink; in fact, the ship is in good form. I've got a lot of ideas, nothing I want to talk about right now, but suffice to say, I'm taking the time off to reflect and shape a future. Always good to step back and evaluate. Don't worry about me, I am optimistic, energized, excited for what comes next." He's blithering and realizes that he might sound half out of his mind, but he's not going to back down. "So thanks for the call and we'll check in again on Monday— during regular business hours." He doesn't wait for Godzich to reply. He hangs up the phone.

He pauses. And then he calls the Betty Ford Center. "Just checking in to see how my wife, Charlotte, is doing. Do you people need anything? A pie?"

"We appreciate your call and the offer. We've got everything we need. All is good here. We've got a full day scheduled, lunch, some meditation, football, a movie later in the afternoon."

"I was thinking maybe I should come by and visit," he says, testing the waters.

"What a lovely thought, but we discourage any kind of visit on a holiday. It can be a difficult time for some; ill will may get ignited, dashed dreams, guilt, anger, the pot is stirred. Imagine if some guests got visitors and others didn't. How that might feel."

"Guests?" he says, not even realizing he's speaking out loud.

"Yes," she says.

"Honestly, it's weird for me."

"Try to be with friends," the woman says.

"I don't have friends, I have people who work for me. My 'friend' is in Washington with my daughter. I thought of flying there this morning, but it felt too last minute." There's a pause. "I find it odd that no one checks to see how I'm doing."

"Have you ever thought about going to a meeting?" she says. "I can give you a link to locate one near you."

"What kind of a meeting?"

"Al-Anon. There are lots of Al-Anon meetings today. You're not alone. You may feel alone but you are not."

A meeting, spouses of drunks. "Not going to happen," he says. Most drunks are men, so the spouses are women. The last thing he's going to do is sit in some folding chair in a moldy church basement listening to women bitch about their drunk husbands while avoiding the box of powdered donuts someone was "generous" enough to bring. No thank you.

"How about putting on the TV?" the woman says. "Watching the parade?"

"You know Gerry and Betty were old friends of ours," he says.

"Very special people. I hate to let you go, but I've got to get back to work."

"Not a problem. What did you say your name was?"

"Shirley. Shirley Jackson."

"Well, Shirley Jackson, you have a good Thanksgiving."

"Thank you, same to you."

He sits with that for a while. It went well, or at least good enough. He wonders what to do about his second Thanksgiving dinner. Is he up for it? Has his stomach sufficiently recovered from the first? He bought himself some frozen turkey dinners earlier in the week—just in case. He didn't know which was the best, so he bought them all, Stouffer's, Hungry-Man, Lean Cuisine, Marie Callender's. With no one cooking Thanksgiving, there will be no leftovers, the best part, so the frozen ones will get eaten one way or another.

He sits around for a bit, contemplating all things, flipping through a few of the books that he's been "studying." It's gnawing at him. Charlotte. He needs to talk with her. It's not right, her not being home. What if she's not happy? What if she feels she's being held against her will? What if she feels she's being brainwashed and turned against him? He calls Betty Ford again and asks to speak to Charlotte.

"I'm sorry, sir; that's not possible."

"Why is that not possible?" he asks.

"We're not able to put calls through to patients without prior authorization."

"Authorization from whom?"

"The team leader. I don't see that Charlotte has any calls authorized."

"I'm the one who authorized Charlotte to be there and I'm the one who authorized paying you however many thousands of dollars it costs to be there. So I should be able to authorize a phone call with Charlotte."

"I'm sorry, sir, that would have to come from her team leader."

"Great, put the team leader on the line."

"Unfortunately, the team leader isn't here today."

"Then give me the assistant team leader," he says, assuming it's like football or any sport. There's always an assistant.

"Not possible."

"Terrific, then how about you put my wife on the line."

"I'm not able to do that."

"Is Shirley there?"

"We don't give out that kind of information."

"She works there, Shirley Jackson; I spoke with her not that long ago."

"Shirley Jackson isn't a person."

"Pardon me. I spoke with a lady named Shirley Jackson; are you telling me she isn't real?"

"Oh, I didn't mean to imply that . . . I meant she isn't part of our therapeutic staff. There's someone named Shirley who is part of the cleaning crew. She may have been answering phones while someone was on a break. We're a little understaffed due to the holiday. Do you want me to put you in touch with your wife's team leader?" the woman on the phone asks.

"What is this, high school? Her team leader?"

The woman says nothing. The silence extends.

He hangs up then immediately calls back, punching the now-memorized number into the touch-tone keypad of the kitchen Trimline.

"Charlotte," he insists.

"One moment." He thinks he's made progress until he hears, "This is Grace Underwood, team leader. I'm not here to take your call; if this is a medical emergency, hang up and dial 911; if not, leave me a message and I will return it when I am back in the office on Monday."

He hangs up and calls again. "You sent me to voice mail. I was calling to talk with my wife. I wish to speak with my wife." His voice is escalating.

"I'm sorry, sir; that's not possible."

"I'm not sure why that's not possible. Do you know how much I'm spending a day for my wife to be there? Are you sure you're the person whose job it is to tell me it's not possible?"

"One moment, please," she says, putting him on hold again. And this one is a long one. Finally, someone picks up.

"Good afternoon."

"Yes," he says. "I'm calling for Charlotte Hitchens, my wife."

"I understand and we appreciate that, but this is a therapeutic community and we can't just put people on the phone because someone calls and says they want to talk with them. Maybe it's not good for your wife right now. Maybe she's working through things and a phone call, however well-intentioned, would disrupt that process. It's interesting that you keep calling back. Escalating. Each time you're more agitated when we're not able to do what you want. Take a moment. Ask why. Ask how can you meet your own needs."

There is a long pause.

"Who exactly are you?" he asks.

"I am the on-duty leader. You were sent to your family member's team leader's voice mail and I can transfer you to that number again and you can leave a message, but for now I'm going to encourage you to go about your day and not keep dialing this number. If you continue to call, I will file a harassment claim, which could result in a referral for a restraining order." There is a pause, a silence. "Goodbye."

The line goes dead. He hurls the mustard Trimline across the room toward the window and the pool. The only thing that stops it from smashing through the plate glass window is the cord, which jerks the receiver back to earth. The phone is old, from the days when things were built to last. The hurl has no impact on the device, no crack, no sign of damage. The receiver lies on the gray and white terrazzo floor bleating with the off-the-hook sound.

He is disconcerted. Shamed. Who talks to him that way, reprimanding him like a child? He works hard. He has earned the right to get what he wants. He has earned the right to demand to speak to his wife. "Bitch," he yells. "Goddamned son of a bitch." His voice brings the house to life like a shock treatment. The window vibrates. He feels the glass shaking and is tempted to do more, to throw more, to smash it all. He feels like he's been smacked down, as if he were a child. It's embarrassing, confusing. Now he's flush with rage, energy that he can barely contain. Is it time to go to dinner—again?

This time he wears the tie; this time he orders the roast beef. It's a different place, more crowded because it's later in the day. Lots of families, lots of children in high chairs and grandparents with walkers parked in the aisles. He gets a table near the bar, which has two large televisions, sound off, football on. The chaos is a relief. The television an old and familiar companion. Thanksgiving football is the best; there's a specific joy that comes with the crisp snap of autumn. Despite thinking he's not hungry, he eats a lot, gets cranberry sauce on his shirt and gravy on his tie. This time he has apple pie for dessert, no ice cream. He doesn't mean to go nostalgic, but all he can think about is how much he loves being an American. He can't imagine being from anyplace else. This is the country he was bred into; this is the country that made him and that he is determined to preserve. He is a man whose eyes water when the national anthem is played. The phrase "O'er the ramparts we watched" swells him with pride. One thing men of his age and older have going for them is national pride, a passion for something larger than themselves.

He's remembering the men he knew in college whose fathers and grandfathers were titans of industry who all at one time or another had served their government in addition to working for Nabisco, GE, the

Campbell Soup Company. Their patriotism and good intentions were assured.

Among younger men there seems to be none of this. They expect a seat at the table just because they've shown up. That's one of the issues: presumption plus arrogance and disrespect. They are bullish on themselves, survival of the fittest; I got mine you get yours. They don't ask what they can do for others. They are focused on what's next for them, their new house, bigger boat, second wife.

He laughs at himself; the idea of what one can do for others sounds downright socialist. But were it not for that desire to serve, to build and shape a country that governs itself, there would be no America. First and foremost, that is what he is, American. The quintessential American man manufactured in 1944 with a 1945 issue date. He catches the eye of another Thanksgiving soloist a few tables down, an older man sucking on some sort of bone.

The horrible sucking sound catches the Big Guy's attention. The man has thin white hair slicked back like it's still 1962. He makes a sort of half smile, flashing his bottom teeth, which look like organ pipes going from large in the middle to smaller and smaller. A human chipmunk with hands like thick paws, fingers like sausages.

The Big Guy has to look away. He flags the waiter. "Check, please."

Back at the house, it's game time. Not just football. He's been promising himself all week that today he can play. On an ancient and expensive pool table in the basement, World War II is happening—Dunkirk to be specific. A few feet away on a foosball table is Korea. The Big Guy has staged the Battle of Inchon with actual water. This is where the US Eighth Army won a major victory against North Korea with a well-conceived, if ambitious, amphibious landing. He's got General Douglas MacArthur in charge, aka a soldier with extra medals painted on his chest, and in his head, a whole mental list of moves that need to be made for the battle to be successful. The Big Guy puts the soldiers in boats and moves them through the water—a series of blue plastic emesis pans brought home when he spent three days in the hospital with a kidney stone. Across the room, Vietnam spreads across the Ping-Pong table, the green net still up. He likes that part, finds the boundary ironic. He has figures and weapons for each engagement, the right men and the right tools for the job.

Today he starts in World War II, that's where his heart is, that's where he thinks patriotism ran deepest. He immerses himself, speaking aloud in various accents and arguing about who and where our allies are and can one eat the rind on French cheeses. He makes the moves, but today it's too depressing; he can't handle the defeat and can't wait for miracles. He rips it apart. Now it's not Dunkirk. Now it's Normandy, June 1944, Operation Overlord, 1,200 planes, 5,000 boats, soldiers parachuting in under cover of night and the landings on the beaches: Sword, Juno, Gold, Omaha, Utah. Around 160,000 troops crossing the English Channel. Splish-splash, better have your wellies on. Something like 6,000 Americans dead in one day. Bloodiest battle of the war, but in the end, they won. He makes a giant mess of it. He's got men down everywhere, water everywhere. He's flying planes, pushing small groups of soldiers up a hill. Wounded men are crying in pain, shot, knowing they will die on this hill. "I have news for you," he says, as a spy knifes a snitch in the stomach. "War isn't pretty. War is hell. A nightmare one never wakes from. Nice knowing you and thanks for all the clues." Disinformation. Fliers dropped like confetti from a plane. Concealment, keeping things under cover. Feint, the mock attack in an effort to distract. This is his idea of a good time, reenactments, skirmishes. His men are the highest quality, tin, lead, mixed metal. He hates plastic and uses it only as a last resort. When there is fire involved, plastic fails; it melts into a molten puddle of toxic sludge. He keeps a box of baking soda on hand when playing with fire—and an extinguisher should anything really get out of control. He has a thing he likes to do with roll caps. He bangs his men down on them, their heavy footfalls and the nail of his thumb setting off the small land mines, grenades, explosions. Every now and then he drops a bigger fused load from above, usually something he's purchased at a side-of-the-road fireworks stand where he stocks up every summer.

Today nothing is a good enough distraction; everything is a downhill ride. His mind is muddy; his aim is not true. He buries the dead, pouring sand over them. The sand spills through the edges of the table down onto the floor. If Charlotte was home, she would sense the war going wrong. She would call across the house, "Everything all right in there?" And he would perhaps ask her to pass him some paper towels, but for this moment, he is living with being slovenly, he is living with being grotesque. There is no avoiding the darkness. This is bleak. What are we doing? That's what he wants to know. He leaves World War II behind and goes to Vietnam. The country is spread across the Ping-Pong table, North and South. He's used palm fronds and other greenery from around the yard to give a realistic feeling to the landscape; rice paddies are made out of grass cuttings. He flies a US Air Force C-123 over the "jungle" he's built and has it drop "Agent Orange"—undissolved orange Jell-O powder that he heard about at a war-game convention. He calls this Operation Ranch Hand, Operation Trail Dust. Today he is using rainbow herbicides, orange and strawberry mixed together, to defoliate the trees. People were allergic to it. Vietnamese babies were born deformed. Soldiers claimed it gave them everything from acne to diabetes to heart disease. Maybe the stuff wasn't perfect or wasn't handled properly, but people have to quit complaining; they can't be expecting everyone to take care of them. This is war.

The locals come running out of the trees, farmers, men, women, children. The soldiers gun them down; they don't ask questions; there isn't time. Today they want to kill without having to ask why. They are confused; they are enraged. They are American soldiers in this strange and unfamiliar country, and no one knows what it means to be an American anymore. At home people are protesting this war, saying it is not theirs to fight. Tell that to the man who got his legs blown off yesterday. They want to kill because it is Thanksgiving. Turkey and cranberry sauce are flown in by chopper; they thank God for the food they are about to receive; someone jokes that it's a two-paper-plate day, but nothing is funny. One of the dead guys was supposed to go home tomorrow. The whole thing makes him sad. The American dream is spilled over sporty tables in his game room. But this is no game. These men died. Can you imagine charging another man, gouging out the insides of a stranger with a bayonet, not to protect yourself but because your country is asking you to? He knows that war isn't fought this way anymore; there aren't hundreds of thousands of dead. Wars are now fought with a joystick, a toggle, and a pull of the trigger from thousands of miles away. The mechanics of war have changed, but the human cost hasn't. He gives up for the day, filled with confusion about what it all means, about what being an American means. He leaves the army figures with their arms and weapons reaching up out of the orange, looking like they are drowning in Jell-O that is turning into wiggly mucus, phlegm of war, stuck on everything. The Ping-Pong table is doused in sugary powder, the foosball table is dripping under the sludge of Inchon, and the sands of Normandy and young lives never lived are dropping onto the floor. He turns out the light as he leaves the room—no doubt field mice will snack on the remains, and whenever he returns, all will be as he left it, each of the surfaces a little more warped, a little less playable, and covered with tiny black turds, like unexploded ordnance dotting the battlefields.

Friday, November 28, 2008
McLean, Virginia
3:00 p.m.

By the time Thanksgiving weekend is over, Meghan feels like she's been inserted into a movie or someone else's dream. It is as though she'd stepped out of her own skin and made an appearance in another world.

Yesterday she wrote a letter to the dead girl's family.

Dear Mr. and Mrs. XXXXX,

I am a student at the Academy and recently learned about your daughter and what happened to her. I'm not sure getting this letter will make you feel better or worse, but it seemed important to let you know your daughter is not forgotten. Parents send their daughters to what is portrayed as a "safe and nurturing place where a young woman can grow emotionally, spiritually, intellectually." We all know that our parents send us here because they are trying to protect us from something: bad influences, drugs, sex, the big world; what that something is varies for each family.

We wear key cards on lanyards around our necks. The lanyard is designed to break away if pulled hard enough so we can't accidentally harm ourselves if one got caught in a door. The campus is not fenced as several public parks divide the land as does the river. We have blue-light stations on campus and two old men from buildings and grounds drive around in pickup trucks from six p.m. to midnight. No one is allowed to walk after dark without a "buddy."

But does that change anything? Does it make us safer? Do we want to be locked in, kept under wraps? Is that what the future for women is, being kept inside, living in fear? I am sorry that your daughter was killed and even sorrier that you had to discover her body yourself. I recently had my own experience with the local police and was not impressed. What we as a student body at the Academy have asked for is to be listened to, to be heard and not dismissed. Had people been listening, I believe your daughter would still be here. We, the next wave of young women, are actively listening to one another and advocating for one another and those who have come before. A piece of your daughter and her history lives within us. Enclosed please find a phoenix that I recently bought at the Phoenix airport. It is meant as a token to represent the idea that your daughter is here among us and will rise with us.

Sincerely,
Meghan Hitchens
Class of 2009

She wrote the letter, put it in an envelope, and got dressed for Thanksgiving supper.

Promptly at four p.m. she rings the bell of the town house on P Street. Through the living-room window, she sees people with drinks in hand talking animatedly. No one comes to the door. She rings again and finally a man opens the door.

"I'm supposed to meet Tony here," she says.

"Of course you are," the man says jovially.

She extends a clumsily wrapped package.

"Let's save that for the hostess," the man says, ushering her in.

"You have a beautiful home," she says.

He laughs. "It's not mine. It's Peggy's place; let's find her."

"Where have they been hiding you?" Peggy, the hostess, asks when they find her at the back end of the living room. She is busy adding more place settings to an already impossibly long Thanksgiving table. "This year may be a record; we're up to thirty-six."

"Thank you so much for including me," Meghan says.

"Well, of course. We 'orphans' must stick together."

Meghan extends the package she's brought. Cookies she stole from the dining room over the last few days. "They're not the most artfully wrapped but they are famously good."

"I have to tell you something," Peggy confesses. "Tony will back me up on this. I knew your father many years ago; it's a lifetime, but we went out a couple of times and what I remember was that he was a good kisser, a very good kisser. And a very sweet man. Stalwart. That was the word Tony used. 'Stalwart and well-intentioned,' a phrase I took to mean he wouldn't try to get me intoxicated and take advantage." She pauses. "Imagine if I had married him, I would be your mother! Isn't that wild?"

Beyond wild, Meghan thinks to herself.

Tony puts his arm around Meghan. "Happy Thanksgiving, kiddo."

"The kiddo brought cookies," Peggy says, waving the cookies at Tony. Peggy opens the cookie package, which is wrapped in pink tissue.

"Yum," she says, biting into one. "These are the most delicious cookies I've ever eaten.

"I read somewhere that in some countries it's customary to eat a sweet before dinner, that it keeps you from overeating. I might have to have another."

"She's as high as a kite," Tony whispers in Meghan's ear. "She got so stressed about how to seat everyone, not sure whether to mix or separate the Democrats and Republicans, that her back went out and she took a couple of Percocet about an hour ago. Peggy is known for her ability to make social pairings, but the election took a toll. Some of the regulars won't be here tonight and a few new faces will be auditioning. It should be interesting. They say that Thanksgiving at Peggy's is training for Alfalfa in January and warm-up for Gridiron in March."

"Let's see if there's anyone here of your generation." Peggy looks around the room.

"Jordon?" another guest suggests.

"Jordon goes to Georgetown and is studying medicine," Peggy says.

"I'm still in high school," Meghan says. "A senior."

"You look older."

"It's the dress. If I wear a short dress, which my mother says looks cheap, people know how old I am, but if I wear a dress that covers my knees, I look like someone's cousin visiting from rural England, a place that has yet to discover fashion. Unfortunately, fashion doesn't make good clothing for eighteen-year-olds."

"Touché," Peggy says, and she means it. Everything is like a fencing bout. There are points to be scored. "Oh, William, have you said hello to the goddaughter?" Peggy stands over Meghan repeatedly pointing her finger at Meghan as if to say, Look here, look here.

William glances up, looking slightly stricken or caught off guard. "Come on, say hello," Peggy says.

So William, a gentleman with close-cropped hair and dark ebony skin, and sporting a beautiful turquoise sweater, gets up from the sofa and makes his way across the crowded room.

"It is very nice to meet you, Meghan," he says, shaking her hand. "I've heard so much about you over the years. How are the college applications coming along?"

"Oh," she says, unsure of how William knows anything about her and her college process. "After the election, I decided to throw out my essays and start again."

"Ah," he says. "A change of plan. I started out at Winston-Salem, then came up here to Howard before I went to Hopkins. There is no one road to take. Any idea what you're going to study?"

"History. I am in deep with history."

"We are ready," Peggy says, coming out of the kitchen swinging a carving knife wildly. "The show is about to begin."

A good-looking older man relieves her of the weapon. "Thank you, Richard," she says. "You are always there to save me, the perfect second-husband-in-waiting."

"What are you waiting for?" one of the guests calls out.

"The embers to cool," Peggy says, fanning herself.

The energy in the house is herky-jerky, as if they were riding on a carousel with each guest mounted on a different horse, moving up and down and dancing to a different tune.

The meal is served in a manner that, like much of Washington, is formal, prematurely aged, and feels a bit like an immersive theatre experience or a historical reenactment. Each food and serving dish is presented with a provenance, a raison d'être, as her French teacher would say. Meghan half suspects that curators from the Smithsonian are among the guests and have authored the "liner notes" recited by Peggy and Richard. Heirloom carrots are served in a dish that was "Mother Taylor's." The gravy boat is a turn-of-the-century gift from the Tyson family. The herbs in the stuffing are direct descendants from those in Aunt Bishop's garden. Every name has a dimly familiar sound: Coleridge, Hancock, Tierney, Cumberland.

Peggy is dressed in what Meghan's mother would call "hostess wear," clothing that is between a costume and an outfit—more than a dress, less than a ball gown. There is a roaring fire in the fireplace and the windows are open because it is about a thousand degrees inside. There are paintings hung salon-style on the wall that remind Meghan of some she saw long ago: landscapes of early America, expansive views, expressing unfettered optimism for this new world.

Meghan watches everything very carefully. Life has gone from 2D to 3D; just the serving of the food is an action sequence. She clocks everything, especially people drinking. What is normal and what is too much? Most people at the table are drinking except those who are actively not drinking and instead are consuming large quantities of mineral water. "Is there any more mineral water? Could someone pass the mineral water?"

In the middle of the table is a large green porcelain turtle.

"That is my mother's turtle soup tureen," Peggy says. "Now no more than a decorative object. What can one put in a tureen made for terrapin soup? Besides cayenne pepper and lemon juice, I'm not sure. No one eats terrapin soup anymore."

"Because it's illegal to hunt turtles," the man next to Meghan whispers.

"I make a delicious cold zucchini soup," one of the women says. "It would look lovely in your turtle. I'll give you my recipe. Do you have an immersion blender?"

"A what?" Peggy asks.

"Immersion," the woman says. She makes a back-and-forth hand gesture that in another setting could mean something very different.

"Really?" one of the guests says.

"Like a vibrator?" Peggy asks.

"I'll tell you later," the woman says, laughing.

Eyes roll all around the table. Meghan feels a rush of what her mother calls "social anxiety." She's never felt it until now.

"Good shoes," the woman sitting next to her says.

"Oh, thank you," Meghan says. "I'm at a funny age where I have big feet and don't want to wear little-kid shoes, but I also don't want to look too 'available,' as my mother calls it."

The woman laughs. "I'm at a funny age too. I need to look serious and feminine, but I have to be able to run down the hall very fast and navigate marble stairs."

Meghan laughs and glances at the woman's place card, Ms. Rice.

"They talk about the glass ceiling, but no one talks about marble stairs. It's very hard to move quickly and gracefully especially when there are people watching you."

Farther down the table, one of the guests who has been drinking a lot asks William, "Did you make these biscuits?"

"I did not," William says.

"I thought you were a boy who likes biscuits?"

"Let's not start," Peggy says. "Not tonight, Charlie."

The man presses on. "I am just curious. I bet you are pleased about the election. Your time has come."

"Charles, there is a name for what you are doing," William says. "And why would you do that here at a holiday meal with your good friends?"

"Here we go," the woman next to Meghan says. "Charles is poking the bear."

As the voices escalate, the men in suits move farther into the room. Meghan noticed them before; neither sat at the table; they were hovering near the front door and the kitchen.

"Secret Service," the man next to her whispers. He'd been talking with the woman on his left until now.

Interesting, Meghan thinks. Why are Secret Service people at Thanksgiving dinner?

The woman beside her keeps talking as if intentionally trying to distract Meghan from what is happening at the other end of the table. "My parents were very involved in their church. My father was a preacher. Thanksgiving was and remains my most favorite holiday. My mother made wonderful candied yams and pecan pies."

She smiles at Meghan, a lovely warm smile.

"I go to church every Sunday," Meghan says, leaving out the fact that it's required.

Meanwhile, Meghan is picking up snippets from the other end. "Your hostility is more pointed than usual, Charles," William says.

"Do you have a favorite teacher?" the woman asks Meghan.

"Ms. Adams."

"Having one great teacher can change your life. Never take other people's no as definitive. A lot of people will tell you what you can't do for one reason or another. Be your own guide."

Meghan's discomfort grows. On the one hand, the woman next to her is trying to distract Meghan from what is some kind of race-related incident at the other end of the table. On the other hand, it makes it hard to focus on what is happening.

"For twenty-eight years I was a Democrat, and then I 'converted.' The downfall of the Russian government was a pivotal moment for me," the woman says.

The turtle tureen seems to be shaking, but it might just be the rising timbre of voices.

"You people think you can own the world," Charles says.

William shakes his head as if to ask, When is enough enough?

"You may be excused, Charles," Peggy says, looking deeply unsettled.

Meghan notices that Tony is standing behind William. Tony puts his hands on William's shoulders to both calm and confirm. The gesture is at once familiar and intimate. Meghan is struck with the sudden awareness that William is Tony's boyfriend.

"I have known Tony for more than twenty years," the man beside her whispers. "That is the first gesture of public affection I've ever seen. He's like James Bond, enigmatic, sexy, unpossessable."

Meghan can't swallow. She can't think. "Excuse me," she says, getting up from the table. She makes her way into the hall in time for Charles to blow past her as he is leaving. Her equilibrium is off; every fluid in her body is shifting, the bottom falling out, the Thanksgiving meal rising in the back of her throat. The bathroom is occupied so she goes farther down the hall into a small library. She stares at the bookcases. William is Tony's boyfriend. Tony is gay. "Dedicated bachelor," that's what her mother says. She must know. They must know. How did she not know?

There is a bar in the library, heavy crystal glasses on a mirrored tray. She pours herself a glass of vodka. It tastes like a cleaning product, like something you'd use in the event of an emergency to dissolve grease and grime. There is nothing about it that says *Drink me*. But she does. She drinks the whole glass, then carefully sets the glass back in place and returns to her seat and has another biscuit with butter before the cakes are served.

"Football," the woman sitting next to her says. "That's what we always used to play after Thanksgiving supper. My father was a football coach as well as being a preacher. We would all go outside and play ball, even the girls."

When Meghan gets home, she writes another letter to the dead girl's parents.

Dear Mr. and Mrs. XXXXXX,

Things are not what they seem. This might not be news to you. But to me it is a great awakening. The things that I took to be "truths self-evident" are not truths at all. These are ideas that I grew up believing that were indoctrinated into my thinking as truth—it was part of the narrative, part of the story of my life, a story that fit so well that I believed it without question. But it turns out the story is larger and more complex than those around me are willing to admit. Lies. Untruths. This awakening has made clear to me that much of what I took to be fixed as fact is simply a story, a fiction told to me, and a story that fit so well that I believed it without question. In my awakening I have discovered that one must question, one must look with one's own eyes and think for oneself. This awakening comes with a new kind of terror. The fear that truth is an elusive thing, that history is not fixed in time and space but subject to fluctuation and interpretation and to the possibility that there are other stories, other narratives, that are potentially as strong, as believable. History changes as the world around us changes. Whose history is being recorded is dependent on who is doing the reporting and what lens they are looking through. What is clear to me now—in my awakening—is that the subject is not history. The subject is histories. I don't want to just study it; I want play a part in it. I want to make history, to live in history, and to be the history of the future.

Tony is the first to mobilize. "As discussed, there are areas of the country that need representation. I consider the Midwest a flyover, but Chicago is the place to go for the Oracle."

"The what?" Bo asks.

"Fortune teller?" Eisner suggests.

"The guy who tells us which way the wind's gonna blow," the Big Guy says.

"Sometimes I just wish you boys would speak English," Bo says. "It's six fuckin' o'clock in the morning—do me the favor."

They are on a Saturday-morning conference call. Tony is standing outside his Georgetown town house just in case the house is bugged. Tony watches his neighbor, a retired general, come out in his pajamas to get the Sunday paper. The man picks up the paper and salutes Tony, who salutes back, and then the retired general turns and goes back into the house.

"Even in ancient times, people wanted to know what was going to happen next, half out of curiosity and half so they could be ready for it," Kissick says.

"Exactly," Tony says. "I'm sending you to the guy I use when I need to see over the fence."

"Is this man aware that we're not looking to hire someone, that this is pro bono and then some?"

"He is. At first, you might wonder—why this guy? He lives in a plain house on a plain street and is a most discreet, inconspicuous, unremarkable man."

"I hope we don't accidentally knock on the wrong door," Bo says. "How would we know if he's so indistinguishable?"

"I've met him before," the Big Guy says. "Despite being inconspicuous, he's not someone you'd forget."

"Exactly," Tony says. "He and I worked together thirty years ago."

"I remember," the Big Guy says. "You came back from reading philosophy at Cambridge and took a job selling chocolates in Chicago. I thought you were nuts."

Tony corrects the Big Guy. "Actually, it was hard candy."

Bo chimes in. "We used to call those suckers."

"I'm going to pretend that you all just said, 'What an inspired idea, thank you; and we'll talk again soon,'" Tony says, hanging up.

Tuesday, December 9, 2008
Winnetka, Illinois
12:00 noon

Bo and the Big Guy are in a Lincoln Town Car outside the plain house on the plain street. It's snowing lightly. Flakes are collecting on the windows. Every few minutes, Bo opens and then closes his window to clean it.

"I need to be able to see," Bo says, apologizing for the burst of cold air. The driver turns the windshield wipers up a notch.

"How do you know this isn't a setup, some kind of sting? Tony would have every reason to want to take this down before it even begins."

"Because Tony is the man I trust with my life," the Big Guy says, busy texting with Meghan about Christmas plans. "And I've met this guy before. He's the real deal, the Oracle."

"We're sitting ducks," Bo says.

A car pulls up behind them.

"Who the fuck is that?"

The Big Guy turns his head. "The scribe."

A minute later there's a knock on the car door. "May I join you?" Eisner asks.

"Take the front seat," Bo says, rolling down his window. "And take note, we're not alone." He nods toward the driver.

Eisner climbs into the car. "I drove down from Madison. It took longer than I expected, what with the weather. I was visiting my mother."

"No one cares," Bo says.

"Is Tony joining us?" Eisner asks.

"No," the Big Guy says.

"I understand that he's your best friend, but the fact that he plays for both teams is a thorn," Bo says. He's clearly in a bad mood.

"He doesn't play for both teams," the Big Guy says.

"Then why is Obama going to keep him around?"

"One of Tony's gifts is that he's willing to touch what no one else wants to."

"Meaning what?" Eisner asks.

"He deals with a lot of shit." The Big Guy puts his device away. "If anything, when it comes to politics or taking sides, Tony is a soloist."

Kissick pulls up in a taxi.

"Game time," Bo says, getting out of the car.

The Big Guy rings the doorbell. Bo, Eisner, and Kissick are lined up behind him.

Snow is landing on the back of Kissick's neck. "Among the reasons I live in Florida," Kissick mutters.

The Big Guy rings again. The cover of the art nouveau peephole slides open and he feels an eyeball on them. The door opens and they are greeted by a thin man wearing a white lab coat.

"Friends of a friend," the man says. "Welcome."

"Good to see you again, Twitch," the Big Guy says, stepping into the house.

"Welcome, like the mat," Bo says, wiping his feet on the thick doormat. Bo shakes the man's hand and is surprised. He looks down; the man is wearing white latex gloves with the words Matfer Bourgeat written on top.

"Apologies," the man says, pulling off the gloves. "I was doing some sugar work."

"Well, that's a relief. I thought perhaps you were Dr. Strangelove," Bo says.

"Twitch," the man says, shaking Eisner's hand. "Twitchell Metzger."

"Tony tagged you as a mad scientist," Eisner adds.

"I'm making caramel; come in quickly before it burns," Metzger says, ushering them in.

As they enter, fumes envelop the men. The smell is like a toxic Halloween meltdown, hot sugar and ash. Inside the house, the air is foggy, dense with tobacco particulate.

Kissick whispers to Bo, "They've done studies on retained tobacco smoke, but this is a whole other level; I feel like I'm licking ashes."

"You live alone?" Bo asks.

"How'd you guess?"

"Children don't like eating Pall Malls for breakfast," Bo suggests.

Metzger leads them through the living room into the kitchen, which is set up more like a chemistry lab than a kitchen in *Martha Stewart Living*. He checks the temperature of what's on the stove, lowers the heat, and pours some bourbon in, stirring. "It's all about avoiding caramelization," he says.

"I feel the same way," Bo says.

On the kitchen table are four bright pink 11x14 sheets of what looks like foam insulation.

"Home repair or Christmas presents?" Bo asks.

"Boozy marshmallows," Metzger says. "Made with Rumple Minz and pink food coloring. You're going to see a sizable uptick in liquor-infused foods globally. Chocolate consumption in the United States is rising, but Europe is the real sweet spot. You know that's how I met Tony?"

"We know," Bo says.

"I'd be curious to hear more," Eisner says.

"It was his first job, but for me, it was a homecoming. I grew up not far from here; the men in my family were butchers in the beef markets of Chicago, laborers in the steel mills. They made cars in Detroit. But when I was a kid, I was an idiot. Life was all about the sugar coating, all about the candy. Vita, Dulcedo, Spes."

"Is he speaking in tongues?" Bo wants to know.

"Life, Sweetness, Hope," Kissick says. "It's the Notre Dame motto. His alma mater."

"I met Tony when we both landed in Chicago. Back in the day, Chicago was the candy capital of the world. Lemonheads. Brach's, Boston

Baked Beans. We traveled the Midwest in search of regional sweets. Sunshine Candy, Jujyfruits. Now and Later." He pauses. "Any of you know what the shelf life of a Twinkie is?"

They all shrug.

"Twenty-six days. What does that remind you of?"

"No idea," Bo says.

"The female menstrual cycle," Metzger says.

The men look pale.

"I thought that was twenty-eight days," Kissick says.

"Close enough. You might wonder why I'm wearing a lab coat in the kitchen."

"Yep," Bo says.

"I find aprons too feminizing." Metzger takes the caramel pot he's stirring off the heat. He points to the fridge. "Take a look inside."

Eisner opens the refrigerator. The four shelves inside are filled with trays of candy. "Looks like what my grandmother used to call turtles," Eisner says.

"Turtle gophers," Metzger says. "A spin-off of an old recipe from Savannah's. Go ahead and try one."

Eisner peels a turtle off the wax paper and hands it to Bo, who demurs.

"Go ahead," the Big Guy says. "You need it."

Bo tastes the candy. "Rich," he says, smiling. "But delicate."

"The contemporary palate leans more toward the salty than previous generations do. I use lemon juice as well as cream of tartar. Both are acids that break down the sugar molecules—an inversion. Instead of boiling, I simmer. Gives me the flavor I want and minimizes the crystals. I have always maintained that if you want to sell something you need to know how it's made and what it means to people. I can't sell something that I don't know intimately."

"You and Tony handled the Atomic Fireball?" Bo asks.

"Briefly, long ago. At the moment, I'm tinkering with a dream confection that will ease my way into retirement. But I don't think you boys came all this way to talk about my hobbies. How about we take a seat in the conference room."

"Pass me a couple more of those turtle pies," Bo tells Eisner.

"This was my great-grandmother's dining table," Metzger says, leading them into the dining room. "I've got snacks and I've got smokes."

In the middle of the table is a giant candy dish filled with Halloween leftovers and a brass globe. He pushes a knob on the globe and it opens, fanning out cigarettes in assorted shapes and sizes.

"Cowboy killers." Metzger takes one for himself and gestures that the others should feel free.

"My first job was in Richmond, Virginia—Cigarette City. Wherever I've traveled in life, I've picked up one bad habit in each place." He unwraps a chunk of milk chocolate. "Switzerland," he says. A twitch in the corner of his mouth jerks his lip upward. "I do my laundry there," he says with a dry wheeze, clearly pleased with his own comic timing.

Bo smiles, which makes the Big Guy smile; so far, so good.

Eisner reaches for a Butterfinger. "Haven't had one of these since 1979."

Metzger lights his cigarette and takes a drag.

"I can barely breathe; can you open a window?" Kissick asks.

Like deadweight falling through the air—ker-fucking-plunk—an enormous fat cat jumps from on top of the china cabinet, landing squarely on all paws, tail sweeping the air like an antenna trying to catch a signal. The cat walks the length of the table, hops onto Metzger's lap, then jumps to the floor.

Bo's face drains. His expression implies that he could easily have shit himself. "What the fuck?"

"My pussy," Metzger the smoker says, straight-faced. "I can't open a window because my pussy will get out."

And Bo, who looks like he might kill someone, busts out laughing. "You are fucking demented."

Metzger pours him a drink from a decanter.

Bo knocks it back and does a spit take. "What is this shit?"

"I call it ball water," Metzger says. "I make it myself, bourbon poured over marijuana and left to steep. I drink it before bed; puts the hair back on your balls."

"I fucking love you," Bo says, offering the glass up for a refill.

"What's the story?" Metzger wants to know. "What are you shopping for? I assume it's not magic tricks."

"We're looking for someone who thinks along the same lines as we do," the Big Guy says.

"Cut to the chase," Bo says. "Postelection problem. America is in the crapper and we need to do something about it. We're not going to stand by and wait to see what happens; we're going to make something happen and we need someone to put that idea out there in front of people."

"You want to spread ideas like a virus," Metzger says. "You want them to be comforting like peanut butter and jelly, like Sunday dinner. You want to lull and seduce, to numb them, so in the end it's not a surprise because they saw it coming and they want it too."

"Yes," the men say, nearly jumping up and down. "That's exactly what we want."

"And if I told you that's not what I do?"

"It is what you do; you just did it to me," Kissick says.

"I told you what you wanted to hear," Metzger says.

"Exactly."

There's a long pause.

"You know what my father did during the war?"

They shake their heads. "It may still be top secret, so let's keep it between us. He was in the 23rd Headquarters Special Troops. They were a ghost army. They had inflatable tanks and jeeps and radio trucks. Basically, they were like a circus that played near the front lines."

"Sorry, say that again?" Kissick says, stumped.

"He thought he was going as a mechanic, but they put him in covert programs. For the longest time, I couldn't understand how he managed to have so much fun in the war. All the other kids' parents were totally traumatized. When he came back, he got a job selling cars—used cars, because he thought that was kinder than talking folks into buying new. I watched him sell; the key to his pitch wasn't to pitch. He was a listener. Because he listened to their stories and got to know the customers, they felt as though they'd made a friend and they'd buy a car off him. And then in a year or two, they'd come back and get another car."

The men nod.

"Good listener," the Big Guy says.

"What I like to do is drive. He sold cars; I drive cars. I drive to think. I drive across America like an anthropologist. I get my jollies looking at people. I go to big box stores and follow people while they shop. I like to see what catches someone's eye. I like to see what feels helpful or off-putting. Anticipating desire, need, a place for something. Old-school, I guess you could say." Metzger picks up a lighter and flicks it. "Flint-wheel ignition. You know why people like lighters?"

"Cigarettes," Bo suggests.

The Big Guy is lost in thought, remembering the man at the bar in Phoenix, the man who kept rolling his finger over the flint and saying, "Windproof."

"Nope." Metzger shakes his head. "The capacity to summon fire. It's about power and mastery, man's conquering of the physical world; that's what Dichter said, among other things. Did you ever read Ernest Dichter's *The Strategy of Desire*?"

They all shake their heads no.

"Absolute genius."

"I'm open to bringing him in on this," Kissick says. "If you think he's good."

"He died about seventeen years ago," Metzger says, taking a deep drag and holding it longer than you'd think possible. "What's in it for you boys?"

"We don't go out limp," Bo says. "We worked like dogs, we built empires, or whatever came after empires."

"Kingmakers," Kissick says. "Pillars of society."

"Titans of industry, fat cats, industrialists, tycoons, entrepreneurs," Metzger says.

"The Man," the Big Guy says.

"Panjandrum," Metzger says. "The big cheese."

"Do you have family?" Bo asks.

"Where?" Metzger asks.

Bo laughs again. "Exactly!"

"After the second wife, I gave up. I can take a hint. I'm not exactly fit for human consumption."

"In the end we want to do whatever we have to do to make things right again," the Big Guy says.

"The same words can mean different things depending on when they are said, and by and to whom," Metzger says. "Radical Republicans were a faction of the party from 1854 to 1857, and what did they want? The eradication of slavery. And yet that wasn't what brought about the election of Lincoln in 1860; he got only forty percent of the votes. It was the split between Northern and Southern Democrats. Now you say the words Radical Republican and what do they mean? Do we even know?" A pause. "My point is that there are always forces at play that one doesn't anticipate."

"I can tell you right now, there's a set of fresh-faced yahoos out there who call themselves Republicans, but they're not like Republicans I know," Bo says.

"Charting sociocultural evolution, tracing the processes that increase the complexity of a society, while at the same time monitoring the degeneration/degradation of systems—that's the way we do it."

"I have no idea what he just said," Eisner says. "Sounded more like math than advertising."

"Funny you say that," Metzger says. "It's a little like the work I do for the quant funds. By tracing evolution and recognizing patterns—we can identify a vision of the future and drill down on how that, along with cultural, social, economic, and environmental shifts, will affect consumer behavior. That's why I stay here; I'm the Big Noise from Winnetka, the Einstein from the Dance. I am embedded with the American consumer."

The fat cat jumps back onto the table, meowing loudly, its tail curling around the decanter of ball water.

"You are all that and more," Bo says, standing up. "But seriously, thank you."

"Sometimes you have to just say yes and not resist," Eisner says.

Kissick checks his watch. "Told the family I'd be home for dinner. Can I ride back to the airport with you?"

"Really great to see you again, my friend," the Big Guy says.

"Tell Tony I said thanks and that I look forward to seeing him in person next time we meet."

"Do you think your pussy would let me pet her?" Bo asks.

"Not a chance," Metzger says. "She's vicious. Bit me once and I came down with cat scratch fever. First time in fifteen years that I had to go to the doctor."

Bo laughs. "I like that; she's a real bitch."

"I've called her worse," Metzger says.

"How do I reach you?" Bo asks.

"Here's my fax number. I assume you've got a fax machine." Metzger opens the china cabinet in the living room. Inside is an ancient fax machine so old that the ivory plastic has turned piss yellow.

"A man after my own heart," Kissick says.

"Thanks for making time," the Big Guy says.

"The Forever Men," Metzger says, shaking their hands as they go. "That's who you are. I might have called you the Great Awakeners, but it's too evangelical. The Forever Men feels right," he says, standing inside his front door.

"See you soon," Eisner says, wiping snow off his windows before getting back into his car. "I promised my mother I'd be home in time for dinner."

"Of course you did," Bo says.

"Forever Men is good," the Big Guy says, climbing into the Lincoln Town Car, which has been idling at the curb for hours.

"If ever there was a man I'd trust to get the message out, it's that guy, the Big Noise from Winnetka," Kissick says, joining the Big Guy in the back seat.

"I like him," Bo says, squeezing into the back next to Kissick.

"You're giving me the hump?" Kissick says.

"I paid for the car," Bo says. "What's good about that guy is that he understands how people think, what they need but aren't saying. He's like an undertaker. He knows what box to put you in."

"All three going to Midway?" the driver asks.

"Yes, thanks," the Big Guy says.

"I figured it out," Bo says.

"What?" Kissick asks.

"Who he reminds me of."

"Who?"

"The undertaker, the smoker, the candy man, what's his name," Bo says.

"Metzger," the Big Guy says. "Twitchell Metzger. Twitch for short."

"He reminds me of William S. Burroughs," Bo says. "When he was talking about Ernest Dichter, the guy who knew about fire, I got a twinge; it meant something to me."

"Burroughs, the guy from *Firing Line*? The guy who talked like this." Kissick starts talking through his nose. "The one who got everyone to think that to be a true American conservative you had to have gone to Yale. 'Conservatism is rooted in tradition.'"

"Opposite end of the fishing line," Bo says. "I'm talking about William S. Burroughs. You're thinking of William F. Buckley. The guy I'm talking about was a junkie who shot his wife in the head—accidentally. I spent July 4, 1997, in his backyard watching fireworks, drinking Coke with vodka, and smoking pot."

"What are you talking about?" Kissick is so baffled that he seems on the verge of being frightened.

"I have lived many lives; you know only the tip of the iceberg. William S. Burroughs wrote a whole slew of books and had one character named Dr. Benway. That Twitch asshole reminds me of Benway, a surgeon who smoked cigarettes while leaning over open bodies, flicking his ashes into slick, wet cavities."

"Who the fuck was Burroughs if he wasn't Buckley?"

"He was a *fahncy* boy from a *fahncy* family, went to Harvard, then medical school in Europe. He was also a military man who wanted to work for the OSS but got turned down; I believe he actually got kicked out—they thought he was nuts. His glasses were like Twitch's, old G-man-style heavy black frames from the 1950s. Burroughs was like that—dressed like the straightest arrow and then was off his rocker, completely off his rocker. The quintessential weirdo. Loved cats and drugs, and had the driest, drollest voice, a WASPy aristocratic groan. When that cat jumped on the table, holy mother of god, my reflexes kicked in and I almost hurled it across the room before I knew what was happening. I had the sensation of an incoming grenade, fire in the hole." Bo is positively invigorated by the later part of the day.

"I wish I had any idea of who you are," Kissick says.

"I am who I am," Bo says.

"That belongs in only two places," Kissick says. "Exodus and *Popeye*. What's he going to do for us? That's the question."

"What are we going to do for ourselves?" the Big Guy says.

"Who are you now, John Fucking Kennedy?"

"He's going to figure out how to sell it, that's what he's going to fucking do," Bo says. "He's going to take our plan and turn it into peanut butter and jelly sandwiches that Joe America and his whole fucking family will be willing to die for. Whoever the fuck that weirdo is, he is now mission essential as far as I am concerned."

"You saw his car?" Kissick asks.

"The old green thing?" the Big Guy asks.

"It's not some old green thing—it's a Gran Torino," Kissick says. "That's the new Clint Eastwood movie. I mean isn't that weird that your weird friend has the car from the Clint Eastwood movie?"

"You're losing it," the Big Guy says.

"I'm going to spit something out," Bo says to Kissick. "I felt like you were almost mocking me when I was talking about Burroughs. I didn't like it. And I don't especially like you, but you already know that. When I told you about Burroughs, I was telling you something about myself. I have lived more broadly than you, and because I haven't driven down the little narrow lane of tax law and banking regulations doesn't mean I should have to dumb it down when I'm with you. The problem is yours not mine."

"What Kissick was saying was that we should get Clint Eastwood in on this. He'd be a good spokesperson for our plan," the Big Guy says, stepping in as mediator. "Think of Eastwood in a commercial at 9:49 p.m. on CBS. Close in on his face. 'Are you worried about what's going on in America? This is Clint Eastwood here to tell you that we've got your back. People for the Resurgence of the American Way is waiting to take your call, your money, or your complaint about your neighbor's landscaping. If you pay in cash, we offer a punch-in-the-nose service and will come over and fuck up anyone you want—for a price. Be prepared to bleed. Operators are standing by. Call now.'"

"You're actually pretty funny," Bo says, laughing at the Big Guy. "I had no idea."

Thursday, December 11, 2008
Palm Springs, California
5:00 a.m.

No rest for the weary and then some.

There is a brief period between Thanksgiving and Christmas where business still gets done; call it a limited-capacity portal surrounded by a dead zone. The dead zone has been growing in recent years; now it starts the Friday before Thanksgiving and goes until the Monday after New Year's Day. Ten years ago, it was a day off. Then it became a three-day weekend, then a week off. And finally it became impossible to close a deal between November and New Year's if you didn't catch the fumes of the first ten days of December despite the financial implications of December 31 deadlines.

Now they've got their communications and misinformation man, Metzger from Winnetka; Frode, an eccentric doctor from Bethesda brought in by Kissick; and Doug Keyes, the judge from Texas the Big Guy knows through Charlotte's father. And things seem to be progressing with the General. At Bo's suggestion, the Big Guy recently sent him a "thinking of you" gift and got a vintage Denny's postcard in the mail with "One day we'll celebrate with a Grand Slam" written in red block letters on the back.

That said, the Big Guy needs to bring them all together one more time to make sure they're ready to start the clock just after the new year.

More important, he wants to get it done while Charlotte is still at Betty Ford and before Meghan comes home for the holidays. Some men might find this a lot, a double-whammy stress ball, but he kind of likes it, yin and yang as he used to say; it is the balance or unbalance of things that keeps him on his game.

From Palm Springs, he makes the calls, inviting the boys to a "hunt club" weekend at the ranch.

"What's a hunt club?" Kissick wants to know.

"If anyone wants to go hunting, I've got a couple of guides who will take them out on horseback for a day."

"Live ammunition?"

"Yes, Kissick, real men don't hunt with Nerf guns."

"What about paintball or rubber bullets?"

"That's called play fighting; this is called hunting," the Big Guy says.

"But it's optional, right? It's not like the balloon thing where we all have to go?"

"One hundred percent optional. You can stay home and take a bubble bath if you like. I'll put you in Meghan's room; you'll feel right at home."

"I'm not a gun person."

"I know. And listen, Kissick, I want you to present your findings on the composition of the project, and we need to discuss the price of the buy-in and sharpen our expectations."

"What am I supposed to say to my wife? Every time I'm running off on one of these weekends or to meet with the guys, I'm likely to miss one of the girls' holiday spectacles or a ballet recital. Do you know what it costs me in family currency?"

"Kissick, you are a businessman; they spend the money faster than you can make it. Tell them you're traveling for work; put your lovely wife on the phone—I'll tell her myself."

Kissick declines. "Is Bo coming?"

"Yes. Bo is coming and bringing a special guest. I can't say more at the moment, but I want to be ready to push the big red button the day Obama takes office."

"When you say 'big red button,' what do you mean? Are you talking rogue nuclear?"

"No," the Big Guy says. "I'm using it as an expression—a synonym for launch."

"And when you say 'General'?"

"I didn't say 'General.'"

"I know about the General," Kissick says. "I've been doing the work."

"Whatever," the Big Guy says; he's not about to confirm or deny.

"Is he really a general or just a guy who likes to play dress-up?"

"Good question," the Big Guy says. "In theory he is a general. Or as I like to say—in general."

There's a silence. Then a little kind of crackling on the line, like someone fumbling with a candy wrapper. "And, Kissick, we have to stop meeting like this." The Big Guy hangs up.

The Big Guy gets in touch with Sonny, the ranch hand, and arranges for Sonny and his wife, Mary, to prepare what is needed for the guests. He tells Sonny to line up the hunting guides and any extra help they'll need.

When the Big Guy gets to the ranch, he and Sonny take the taxidermy collection out of cold storage, also known as the basement, and rehang everything. He's got an antelope, a bear, a bobcat, a caribou, an elk, a moose, and a mountain lion. Meghan made him take them all down years ago—they gave her nightmares.

The Big Guy goes over the menu with Mary. On arrival, hot coffee and coffee cake. For lunch—make your own sandwich bar, a big salad on the side. And potato chips, preferably ridged. Who doesn't love chips?

"I don't know if I ever told you about how as a boy I would go to my father's golf club, sit by the pool, and order club sandwiches with potato chips and a bottle of pop. I'd sign the paper chit with my father's name and think I was quite the man—little Mr. Big Shot. Yoo-hoo—that was my drink back then. You ever had a Yoo-hoo?"

"Not that I'm aware of," Mary says.

"You would know," the Big Guy says. "It's unforgettable. Put it on the list; we'll get some for the weekend."

"I'm not sure they sell that here."

"Figure it out," he says, which means spare me the sad song and make it happen.

"To get me out of his hair, my father was always sending me off; 'Go down to the club,' he'd say. I thought he owned it. It wasn't until I was in college that I made the mistake of saying something about it and he bristled, and said, 'For the amount of money I've given them over the years, I damn well should own it.'"

There is a pause, a silence. Mary has nothing to say.

"For dinner on Saturday night, we'll have steak, baked potatoes, green beans, and ice cream," the Big Guy says, like a kid planning a sleepover. "Full breakfast on Sunday with sausage and bacon."

Tony makes it out of Washington late on Friday night and comes in through Denver with one of the new men, Dr. Frode. The Big Guy leaves the side door unlocked. Tony knows his way in and claims the small room off the kitchen, formerly known as the cook's room. Dr. Frode is also downstairs on the fold-out chesterfield in the den.

In the morning Frode is in the kitchen digging through the vegetable bins of the refrigerator looking for things he can "run through" the juicer he brought with him. "Anything green, anything leafy."

"Whatever you find. Make yourself at home," the Big Guy says somewhat facetiously. It seems a little odd that a veritable stranger would feel so comfortable rooting through the kitchen of another.

"Can I make you one?" Frode asks. "I am, after all, a medical professional and I swear by it."

"No," the Big Guy says. "I'm constitutionally averse to the consumption of grass cuttings."

"Que sera sera," Frode says, flipping the switch. The juicer sounds like an unmuffled garbage disposal as it grinds whatever the doctor shoved into its pipe and excretes a thin dark green stream.

"Did you know that Dr. Frode is a vegetarian?" Mary asks the Big Guy.

"I did not."

"Mary and I have been adapting recipes," Frode says.

"Since six thirty this morning," Mary says.

The judge flies his own plane in and arrives as the above is underway.

"Nothing better than being ten thousand feet in the air at sunrise," he says. "And I brought a couple of guns with me—loving the idea of a hunt. I packed a few bricks of .408 Cheyenne Tactical, which I get retooled, tapped out by my wildcat cartridge. They're supersonic to fifteen hundred yards. I love the history of it—modeled after the .400 Taylor Magnum, which, of course, is based on the .505 Gibbs—you know it as the English big-game cartridge. When I'm banging them out, it feels like I'm of a piece, keeping it in the family."

"Is that a fact," the Big Guy says.

"Wasn't someone in your family the Royal Gatekeeper?" Tony asks.

"You certainly do your homework," the judge says.

"It was Kissick who did the homework," Tony says.

"Kissick is why I'm here," the doctor says. "The man is an accounting genius."

"With a soft spot for mad scientists," Tony whispers to the Big Guy.

"My relative was the Royal Gatekeeper in the 1500s," the judge says. "He married a relative of the queen without her blessing and was sent to prison. I'm surprised you even know about it."

"I'm the knower," Tony says. "That's what they call me at the office, He Who Knows Too Much."

By the time they have sorted the judge's guns and lineage, Kissick, Metzger, and Bo have arrived and are partaking of Mary's coffee cake. "Special ingredient—yogurt," the Big Guy says. "She uses yogurt and protein powder because it's healthier and that way you can call it breakfast cake."

Eisner arrives at the kitchen door looking the worse for wear. He's got the remains of an external-frame backpack strapped onto his shoulders, a bag of gear bungeed to his chest, and a broken shovel.

"What's the matter, Little Prince?" Bo asks. "Did your jet pack fail?"

"Mission accomplished," Eisner announces. "With a mild case of frostbite."

"Please don't tell me you hiked the whole way here."

"I was boondocking," Eisner says, shedding his gear on the kitchen floor much to Mary's chagrin.

"Burying a dead dog?" Bo asks.

"Kind of."

"He was on a sensitive compartment mission," the Big Guy says proudly.

"Really?" Bo asks, now interested.

"You'll hear more about it later, I promise."

Now that everyone has arrived, the Big Guy herds them into the living room surrounded by taxidermy.

"Did you shoot all this yourself?" the judge asks.

"Absolutely not," the Big Guy says. "I bought it at an estate sale. Listen, I know you are all busy men and how hard it was to get here, so I want to thank you for making the effort. I wanted us to have a chance to talk unencumbered. Looking back on November fourth with the benefit of hindsight, it seems too obvious, like rewatching a movie and noticing how inevitable the 'surprise' ending was."

Bo jumps in. "First things first. Just to be clear, whatever is said here stays here. And more to the point, this meeting never happened. When you leave here this weekend, there will be no swag, no nice sweater or golf hat for you to bring home. If you leave anything behind, it will not be mailed. You'll notice that your cell phones don't work here. If you need to call home, I can give you a connection and it will appear to whomever you're communicating with that you are in Minneapolis–Saint Paul at a 3M factory. And yes, Kissick, you can call the baby ladies to say good night. We'll be having cocktails and you'll be reading *Little Red Riding Hood*. You can thank me for that."

"Thank you, Bo," the Big Guy says, taking the cue. "Now some of you have heard me talk about this before; I've been thinking a lot about fathers. Whether we were in love with our fathers or not, they had a profound impact on who we are as men. When I contemplate where we go from here, I am aware that I have no son to carry it forward, to indoctrinate; there is no succession plan, no answer to the question, Who will run the world when I am gone? Maybe it's a coincidence, but I suspect the anxiety caused by that void and the lifelong desire for paternal approval is something that bonds us—the need to create and ensure a future that is externally manifest. Is all this for naught? This is what I ponder when I can't sleep."

"Naught," Eisner says to Tony. "Did he ponder naught in college as well?"

Tony shrugs.

"On the one hand, the lack of a successor buys us freedom to operate without concern for our legacy, and at the same time, each of us has worked too hard to leave this earth without having made a lasting impression."

"Hear, hear," the judge says.

"I second the motion," Eisner says.

"We are not doing this for ourselves," the Big Guy reminds them. "We're doing it for our history, to protect and preserve." The Big Guy is practically singing off his index cards.

"All right already. We've heard this before, but how are we doing it?" Bo asks.

"Vision," the Big Guy says. "I've been thinking about Tony's comments on vision when we were in Palm Springs. V.I.S.I.O.N.: Vital, Invisible, Succession, Insurance. Our (or octogenarian). Nation. Judge, I hope it's not tales out of school to tell the boys that you're not only a member of the club up north but also the International Order of St. Hubertus."

"That explains the love of the hunt," Kissick says.

"It adds to our reach and geographic diversity," the Big Guy says. "We have representation from Texas, Chicago, Florida, San Francisco, Princeton, and Madison for our scribbler, Texas and Georgia for the judge, Palm Springs and Wyoming for me, and the doctor is DC born and bred. Kissick and the scribbler have done us the favor of meeting with each of you privately and we'll get a report on that shortly."

"Is he saying 'scribbler' as an insult?" Metzger whispers to Kissick.

"Doubtful," Kissick says. "Sounds like he believes he's hitting the right note, could be a pronunciation problem."

"In case you haven't noticed, the group of you who have been tapped for this project echo the Eisenhower Ten, the group of citizens secretly appointed to keep things going in the event of a national emergency. The men Eisenhower selected were from a variety of areas he felt would be essential in the case of an emergency. Our plan will echo the original structure, which has managed to stay mostly secret all these years. Among us, we have representatives of the business community with expertise in energy and minerals"—the Big Guy takes a little bow—"and the areas of finance and law, medicine, agriculture and intelligence, media and communication."

"Is the hunt going to happen?" the judge wants to know. "I'd like to get something in the bag before supper."

The Big Guy is aware that usually a whole lot of nothing happens when a bunch of blowhards get together. It's bonding time, man time, a chance for them to feel good about themselves. And when the time is right, if so moved, someone might mention a little something important, something game-changing. That's the plan. Fun and games, and then the "plan."

"It's happening," the Big Guy says. "But we have a lot of ground to cover, so before we get going, Kissick is going to give us an update. Since we last saw one another, he has been on a coast-to-coast tour, meeting with each of you individually, gathering information, and creating the organizational blueprint, which will be shared with the group for the first time today. Pretty exciting stuff."

"Sweet, how you toot his horn," Bo says.

Kissick steps to the center of the room. "It was a pleasure meeting with each of you in your geographic or native state and having a chance to dig deeper into the details. As you know, I took my oldest with me, and we looked at colleges along the way; I can report that she felt the Texas schools were too large, San Francisco too artificially intellectual. In terms of a major, my Cherise is torn between poetry and political science, and I fear that she at heart is more Oberlin than College of Wooster."

"At least your kid is going to college," Bo grumbles. "Mine abandoned ship and makes six fifty an hour pulling shots of espresso and thinks she's 'going places.'"

"His Cherise is the same age as my Meghan," the Big Guy says. "I took my girl to a couple of places, including my alma mater, and then she very politely said she'd seen enough. I still don't know what she meant."

"Enough chitter-chatter," the judge says.

"Thank you for keeping the train on track," Kissick says. "Our plan will be organized around the concept of rings of power and authority with an inner circle."

"That's us, we're the inner circle?" Bo asks.

"That's us, with the highest level of authority, call it the rhodium ring. A first outer circle, platinum, has less power but is still significant for planning. Then a golden ring is made up of people putting our programs into service. After gold, I went with palladium rather than silver because I want to make clear we're still discussing an organization operating at a very high level—rare and precious. Palladium is a white-gray metal valuable because it is both stabile and malleable, and does well under extremely hot conditions. 'Hot' being a euphemism for active or dangerous conditions."

The men nod.

"Once the plan is developed and active, most of the visible activity will be in this outermost palladium ring. We will see the effects but will be personally removed from the events."

"We will not have exposure," the judge says.

"Correct."

"That's the way to do it," the judge says. "Limit the exposure to anything questionable."

"This is new territory. It requires strategic thinking, coalition building, and passion," Kissick says.

"Passion is a lady word," Bo says. "I'm suspicious of men who use the word passion."

"Determination," Kissick says. "And trust."

"Better," Bo says.

"I'm going to talk a bit about how we'll organize and regulate ourselves," Kissick says.

"We're all big boys and I don't think we want to police one another and I doubt we want to elect a top dog," the judge says.

"I'll do it," Bo says. "You can't have a company without a CEO."

"Well, actually, you can," Kissick says.

"Ambiguity of authority can slow decision-making," Bo says. "We want to be able to move quickly, deploy assets, cut our losses when we need to. Chain of command. Who reports to whom?"

"For organizational reasons, we should hire an executive director," Kissick says. "Someone who is minding the store day-to-day. Among ourselves, we'll have a division of labor, skill sets, and personalities leveraged to add value."

"You definitely need someone in charge, someone who has run big things—like cities, airports, even wars, because that's what this is—big," Tony says.

"A former military man," Bo says.

"What do you think of Dick Cheney?" the Big Guy asks.

"You friends with him?" the judge asks.

"No one is friends with him," Bo says.

"I find him very interesting, inscrutable," the Big Guy says.

"It sounds like you have a crush on him," Metzger says.

"He doesn't play well with others," Bo says.

"I saw Dick and Lynne at a party recently," the judge says. "Tight-lipped as ever."

"Do you think he even smiles when he cums?" Bo asks.

"I'm sure the man hasn't ejaculated in years," the judge says. "He can't afford to fuck since the heart attacks. That's part of why he's such an ass-hole."

"Back to our assignment," Kissick says. "Who are we to ourselves and the larger world?"

"In Doug Coe's 'family,' they keep an eye on one another; someone once told me they have veto rights over one another's lives," the judge says.

"What does that look like? Veto power over my life?" Metzger asks.

"I don't give a crap who the boss is, I want to get something done," Bo says.

"Back to the money," the judge says. "How much will we need and what will we be spending it on? Are we buying lunches for politicians or are we buying guns? How big are we going to get?"

"Millions," Kissick says. "Hundreds of millions."

"Used to be you gave a man ten thousand dollars and you had his ear forever," Bo says.

"Inflation," Kissick says. "As more people have more money to throw around, it costs more to get things done. Our organization will be bigger than you can see with the naked eye. That's intentional. We don't want to be seen. We'll build alliances with existing enterprises and activate their constituencies in a way that will seem entirely organic. We will need contingency plans for everything from replacing ourselves in case of incapacitation to establishing financial backups, so the ball will keep rolling once we are in motion."

"What is the one thing that will not change an object's motion?" Bo asks. "Inertia. That's one thing we cannot have."

"Exactly," Kissick says.

"Do we go offshore?" the judge asks.

"Or stay in cash? Consider gold? We also need a bank," Bo says.

"I thought I was the finance guy?" Kissick asks.

"You are, but we need an actual bank," the Big Guy says.

"In the United States or offshore?" the judge asks.

"If we're concerned about intrusions or tracking, I'd stay out of the United States and go with Switzerland," Bo says.

"A lot of people use the Cayman Islands these days," Kissick says.

"That's nouveau riche," Bo says. "I like a bank that's a bank, not a Club Med laundry service. Also, a real bank has history, a credibility that might encourage others to engage with us. Does anyone have a special relationship in Switzerland? I'd like to know that our assets will be cared for by a friend. Kissick, no offense, but how much do you bank offshore?"

The Big Guy jumps in. "I'll tell you something about Kissick that he won't say himself—Kissick has clients whose clients have clients who have clients. He's a schlub, a family man, doesn't golf or play tennis, has no hobbies beyond fixing old adding machines."

"Typewriters," Kissick says. "I like to fix typewriters. You know what my favorite key is?"

Kissick waits for someone to ask what his favorite key is. There is silence.

"Shame on all of you," Kissick says. "My favorite key is zero. Whenever you can hit that zero again, it's a big moment. More than a keystroke, it's a measure of success."

The Big Guy continues. "Anyway, my point is that he's the most boring man in America and the best man for the job."

"Can we please start the hunt," the judge says. "If I don't kill something soon, I'm gonna die; I'm a vampire like that."

"It's happening," the Big Guy says. "The horses are outside and ready to go. But before we depart, I want to share something I'm particularly pleased about." He pauses. "You might have noticed that our scribe—"

Metzger corrects him. "Scrivener. 'Scribe' sounds like a scab, and I am not interested in being part of any organization with scabs. The way things sound is of great importance. In that spirit, I rebrand the man—the scrivener."

"All right then," the Big Guy says. "The scrivener was late for breakfast because he was on a special mission."

"Mission impossible?" Bo asks.

"Mission accomplished," the Big Guy says. "As the youngest and most physically fit of our group as well as our official archivist, Eisner was tasked with taking a custom-made time capsule to a secret location and burying it for posterity. Scrivener, you want to tell the boys about it?"

Eisner goes to the front of the room. "As a political historian, I have studied the organization and operation of power in large societies after the fact. Now, in our group, I am working to design and implement those structures. We do not know yet if history will see us as heroes or martyrs. As the resident historian for the last several months, I have worked with a carefully selected company to build a time capsule—designed to last for five hundred years. This capsule is unique in that the contents—ranging from the cocktail napkins from November fourth to transcripts and draft plans, the ephemera that would be our liner notes were we a boy band— have been vapor-phase deacidified, fitted with Viton rubber gasketing, and the oxygen replaced by argon gas; and as of last night, the capsule has been interred underground, the location marked with a GPS tag."

"How about a round of applause," the Big Guy suggests.

"Here's to our wandering Jew," Bo mumbles, clapping.

"So while we will not be lost, neither will we be easily found," Metzger says.

"It is my hope," the Big Guy says, as the applause dies down, "that this capsule is just the first of many and that in time the wilds of Wyoming will be dotted with hidden silos of history."

The judge inches toward the door.

"If I might take a moment," Bo says. "I want to introduce a special guest, a fellow we have been talking with for several months and, well, it just warms my heart to have him here."

On cue, the General walks into the room wearing a helmet that he removes, revealing a Special Operations Command baseball cap, which he takes off, exposing his truly enormous naked head that he tips toward the group, bowing with such depth that they can see the American flag tattoo at the base of his skull.

"Feel free to call me Mt. Baldy," the General says, pulling out of the bow. "I'm honored to be with you."

"Just like I said," Bo whispers to the Big Guy. "He came to us."

"I suspect when they looked at their 'contingency plans,' they couldn't tell the left hand from the right," the Big Guy says.

"Sometimes you just need to prime the well. Toss in a couple of coins and make a wish."

"Mímir lived in the well of wisdom," Frode says, inserting himself into their sotto voce conversation. "In Norse mythology, Odin threw his right eye into the well in exchange for wisdom and the ability to see the future."

"What a pleasure, truly honored, thrilled in fact," the Big Guy says, extending his hand to the General. "You're the man I'm banking on."

"Very glad to see you again," the General says. "It's a treat for me to get out of town."

"Welcome to the club, General," Bo says. "Will you be joining us on the hunt?"

"I will not," the General says. "At this stage of the game, I must confine my game to the theatre of war. Outside that arena, there is the risk that I might perceive a threat where there is none. I could accidentally murder you all."

There is a long pause, a loss for words. And then the judge says, "Bo?"

"I'm in."

"I'll go for the ride," Eisner says. "I used to love riding on a pony."

"Kissick?" the judge asks.

"I do not mount animals."

"Metzger?" The judge is calling their names as though each man were casting a vote.

"I love to shoot," Metzger says. "But my balls can't take the ride anymore."

"I'll ride," Tony says.

"I'm planning to get myself a bull," the judge says.

"A bull what?" Eisner asks.

"Elk, moose, caribou, it just means a big boy," Bo says.

"Indeed it does," the Big Guy says, sending off the hunters with the guides.

Metzger is still standing in the foyer waxing poetic about shooting. "It didn't occur to me to bring my own guns. When I was a kid, we learned to shoot long distances, now everything is up close, one hundred meters. Used to be that three to four hundred was considered long range. The velocity of a Remington round is about 3,790 feet per second while a .308 Winchester is 2,680, and for context, consider that a Boeing 737 cruises at about 600 miles per hour, 880 feet per second."

"What are you getting at?" Kissick asks.

"I'm unpacking the meaning of 'faster than a speeding bullet.' I'm talking about the marketing of Superman. 'Truth, Justice, and the American Way.' It is fascinating to look at the evolution of that singular character from his creation in 1938 until now, that's what I'm doing, Mr. Kissick."

Kissick, the Big Guy, and the General are waiting for what comes next.

"Not that anyone is asking me, but I prefer a Ruger," Metzger says dryly. "Not only are they reliable, accurate, and nice to look at, but you can repair them yourself if you are inclined."

They're staring at Metzger because it seems so odd that he's a gun man; they'd be less surprised if he said he was a scholar of medieval texts.

"You know, of course, that the 'grain' of ammunition is based on the weight of a grain of rice," Metzger says. "The grain is also used to calculate the weight of gold a dentist uses to fill a cavity and the hardness of water and the dose of an aspirin tablet; 325 is five grains. There was always the weight of wheat or barleycorns, and one carob is equal to four wheat grains or three barleycorns. Just the word barleycorn . . ." He looks off into space. "Then there's the English penny. Twenty pennies make an ounce and twelve ounces make a pound. Then there's the tower pound, 240 silver pennies."

Metzger may never stop.

"Maybe we should take this outside?" the Big Guy suggests.

"I have no need for trophy shooting, but I wouldn't mind a little target practice," Metzger says. "All this talk has me primed to fire a few rounds. Have you got the gear?"

The Big Guy looks at Kissick and the General, both of whom shrug as if to say, Sure, why not.

"Yeah, I have the gear," the Big Guy says. He goes into the kitchen and opens a cabinet. Inside the cabinet is a lockbox, and inside the lockbox are keys. He gives the key to the gun cabinet to Kissick and tells him that he'll meet them outside in the clearing between the barn and the house.

The Big Guy goes back into the kitchen and asks Mary to give him a hand in the attic. It doesn't matter that he hasn't been in the attic for years; he knows what's there.

With Mary's help, he extracts an enormous red dress form that Charlotte used for a few months about a decade ago when she was into making her own clothing and comes banging down the stairs with it. Mary follows with a laundry bag filled with Charlotte's collection of heads and wigs. The heads range from muslin-covered orbs that look like oddly shaped bowling balls to faceless white Styrofoam forms with hairpieces, falls, and bangs pinned onto them to a half-dozen flesh-colored faces complete with long eyelashes and red lips, sporting hairstyles that range from Jackie O tailored flips to blonde beehives piled high like donuts of the mind.

When they get outside, it's snowing; there's maybe an inch on the ground. As the Big Guy hauls the dress form past the house to some bales of hay, where in the past the family has been known to have a bonfire or drinks, it looks as much like he's dancing with a woman in red as trying to maneuver her to the right spot. Mary dutifully follows, bouncing the laundry bag of heads. When they get to the site, she hands him the bag. "If there's nothing else, I'll leave you to it, whatever it might be."

The Big Guy thinks there's something Irish in Mary's accent, but Sonny has said that if it's anything it's likely Alaskan, as that's where her grandparents were from.

"You sure your wife won't notice?" Kissick asks.

"Positive," he says. He can't remember when Charlotte last used these items. "In fact, she might even get a kick out of it." He's lying. Charlotte's Texas roots are riddled with violence, and the idea of a bunch of guys blowing the heads off a dress form would rub her the wrong way. She would define it as a perfect example of sexism or, worse, misogyny. And she would be correct. The Big Guy isn't saying it aloud, but sacrificing these specifically female objects is giving him a giddy pleasure. He's angry at Charlotte for being a drunk. The whole situation makes him mad and, if he was being honest, afraid. He has no idea where it will leave him or their family. As he jams the plastic faux head with the long eyelashes and bright red lips down on the metal knob at the top of the dress form, a perverse pleasure courses through his veins.

"Her head is not on straight," Kissick yells from about fifty yards away. He's holding a long gun in each hand as Metzger takes turns trying out each of the three that they've taken from the gun cabinet.

The Big Guy looks back at the head; it's cocked off to the right, listening to the wind, with the hair fluttering in the breeze as it picks up flakes of snow. He straightens the head on the knob and then extracts two long straight pins from either side, gets the hair on right, and pushes the pins through the skull back into place. He looks back at Kissick, Metzger, and the General. The General, with his helmet on, gives him a double thumbs-up, and the Big Guy calls, "Hold your fire," and walks back toward the men.

"Are we going to do it all at once like a firing squad or take turns?" Metzger asks. There is silence.

Despite his guilty pleasure, the Big Guy can't; it's a step too far. If he shoots, he's shooting Charlotte.

"Would it come as a surprise if I said I've never used a gun?" Kissick asks.

"Never too late to take your shot," the General says, relieving Kissick of one of the long guns, so his hands are free to raise the other.

"What is this one called?" Kissick asks, bringing it up to his eye.

"It's a Remington," the Big Guy says. "A classic."

"Lower your shoulders," the General says in a calm, instructive voice. "No reason for your shoulders to be in your ears. Close one eye, look through the scope, and tell me what you see."

"The gates of hell," Kissick mumbles. "I'm an accountant, not an assassin."

"Every man needs to defend himself if push comes to shove," the General says gently. "It may not be safe for me to shoot outside the theatre of war, but I am always primed to teach."

"Fine," Kissick says. "I see the woman in red."

"Good job," the General says. "Currently, your weapon is not loaded, but when it is and you pull the trigger, be sure you stay steady. Every weapon has a kick, the rearward thrust of the bullet exiting the barrel. The heavier the bullet, the more recoil. With this gun, you have a nice stock, that's the part up against your shoulder, and a longer barrel—all of which give you accuracy."

Kissick lowers the weapon, his face twisted into a knot. The Big Guy is sure he's about to walk away in disgust. Kissick hands the weapon to the General. "Load me up."

The General loads the weapon and hands it back to Kissick. "You are now an armed man. Face forward."

The Big Guy takes five steps back.

Metzger takes two.

The General raises his right arm straight up in the air. What a minute ago looked like a regular-length arm becomes a yardstick with fingers. He holds this arm straight, high. "Raise your weapon and find your aim." And then the General swiftly lowers the limb and simultaneously shouts in a booming voice, "Fire."

Kissick fires, sending the shot high and well south of the mark.

"Prepare for round two," the General broadcasts. "When I raise my arm, take a breath in and hold your innards tight and steady. Exhale when you pull the trigger." The General raises his arm again. "And fire!"

Kissick pulls the trigger; better but still no prize. Again and again. With each round fired, Kissick's face unwinds a little bit. When the ammo runs out, Kissick lowers the gun; his face is glowing.

"You all right?" the Big Guy asks.

"As I was shooting, I remembered that I have done it before, on the boardwalk. You know the one where you aim a water pistol into a clown's mouth to blow up a balloon to win a stuffed animal. I'm very good at that, excellent at getting the water in the hole."

"Well, you didn't win anything this time," Metzger says. "But maybe you'll do better later when we play piss on the Cheerios."

"Who's next?" the Big Guy asks.

"I'll go," Metzger says, taking the Browning from the General. Like a pro tennis player, he does a few things akin to bouncing the ball before serving. He raises the gun into position, adjusts his shoulders; moves his head back and forth, audibly cracking his neck; then sinks into his knees, bracing himself, anchoring his legs to the ground, the snow compressing under his wing tips—the Big Guy hadn't noticed the wing tips until then. They are old but well maintained, likely custom-made.

"Maybe you should try the Remington that I used," Kissick suggests.

"No," Metzger says. "Guns need to recover after they've been abused."

Metzger—thin, his pants belted with a narrow black strap—raises the weapon, his arms steady and stronger than one would expect. His face is unmoved but for the pink tip of his tongue poking out from between his lips. The first shot goes clean through the middle of the head—blowing it off the knob. The Big Guy thinks that this might be enough, but Metzger continues to fire. The second shot pierces the dress form, ripping the chest open, causing the form to teeter but not fall. The next shot, like a gut punch, sends the form pitching forward onto its stomach. In the final two rounds, one skips off the dirt and wedges into the fabric; the last blows the base off the dress form, separating the stand, or legs, from the body.

"The man is an assassin," the General whispers to the Big Guy.

"It helps me think, clears my mind," Metzger says, handing the gun back to the General.

The men continue taking turns; after each round, the Big Guy resets the stage. He goes back out to the dress form although there's less of it each time, the stuffing poking out like spilled intestines, burn marks on the torso, entry and exit wounds. It's like the reset at a bowling alley. He hikes back to the form, sets it upright again, props it up using bales of hay, and puts a fresh head on top.

After a while, the Big Guy takes a turn, blowing a Styrofoam head to smithereens and taking the left side out of an old muslin one. The smell of the gunpowder, the strange heat in the cold air, stirs an unfamiliar violent passion that is relieved only by going another round and then another until his shoulder hurts and his emotions are spent. They continue rebuilding the target using whatever is left: the dress form, the bales of hay, the hair, the heads, hitting them again and again until there is nothing left, until the surrounding area looks like some strange ritualistic sacrifice has taken place. Meanwhile, it has continued to snow, enough to dust everything with a fine white powder that the Big Guy thinks Charlotte would appreciate. The sacrifices of these encumbrances of female life are the things she likely resents even more than she's willing to admit. He imagines Charlotte watching them from an upstairs window and thinking that they are asses, then coming down and taking either the Remington or the Browning out of Kissick's hands and showing the boys how it's really done. He might be angry with Charlotte, but he admires her enormously and misses her as well.

By the time they are finished, the blonde beehive is two hundred feet in one direction and the head with the long eyelashes is split open one hundred feet in the other. There is a serious debris field of 1970s fashion carnage.

"Not a pretty sight," Kissick says, surveying the damage.

"I could teach you boys how to make a little napalm and we could light it up," the General suggests.

"You know how to make napalm?" Kissick asks.

"Yep, easier than Toll House cookies. One bag of packing peanuts, two gallons of gasoline, half a container of table salt, and a large container to mix in. And, of course, a stick to stir. You mix the gas with the peanuts—and when you've got as much gas as the peanuts can absorb, add a bit of salt, or window cleaner if you need to thin it. Mix well. And as they say, 'Unite and ignite.'"

"That's crazy," Kissick says.

"I finally figured it out," the Big Guy blurts out. He's had an epiphany.

"What?" the General asks.

"Who you remind me of," the Big Guy says. "When we first met, it was George C. Scott as Patton, but now I realize it's more Marlon Brando in *Apocalypse Now*."

"'I love the smell of napalm in the morning,'" Metzger says.

The General smiles. He is enamored with Metzger, who is as wily as the General himself. Both men have an affinity for esoteric, mostly useless information shared in great detail.

"I once went negative for a stomach product, planted a rumor in medical circles that the product ate holes in the lining of a stomach, worse than an ulcer. And because the first sign was pain, 'victims' were wrongly instructed to take more of the medication over a period of days, and by then, it was too late. The firm didn't last eighteen months." Metzger tells the story with an absence of affect as though it were the score in a ball game and not a life-or-death application of misinformation. "What about you, General; you ever stir the pot?"

"Well, I'm not one to brag, but there have been times I've put someone who wasn't up to the challenge in a difficult spot to see him squirm. But there's always a point, a lesson to be learned. 'The Only Easy Day Was Yesterday; Facta, non Verba; We Quell the Storm and Ride the Thunder; Whatever It Takes; Balls of the Corps.'

"Kissick, are you always good? Do you ever cheat, steal, or lie?" the General asks.

"I'm not as perfect as I seem," Kissick says.

The Big Guy snorts so hard that he sounds like a water buffalo.

"What was that for?" Kissick asks.

"The 'as I seem,'" the Big Guy says. "It implies that to others you seem perfect—you don't."

"In what ways are you not perfect?" Metzger asks.

"Change," Kissick says.

"What?" the General asks.

"If someone gives me the wrong change, I don't correct them."

"You mean if they give you too little, you eat it?" the Big Guy wants to know.

"Of course not," Kissick says. "If they give me too little, I correct them, but if they give me too much change or simply undercharge me, I let it go. The world can handle that, my making a few extra cents here and there. One year I calculated it at $451.26, that's what I took from the world that wasn't mine. But then there's also the calculation for ways in which I was robbed."

"Robbed in what way?" Metzger asks.

"Sometimes overcharged, or a parking meter that runs fast, a taxi that's cheating, a wrong price at the checkout, a food item that you order but don't receive."

"You keep track of that?" the General asks.

"I have been known to."

"It seems painful and minor," the General says.

"It was $1,843.89 the year I kept track of it. Over ten years, that's easily 20K that goes unaccounted for. At 6 percent interest, that's another $15,816, and at 10 percent, it's $31,874 in interest. But as you know, we have some 19 percent funds, so the total would be $113,893 with $93,893 of that in interest. And I often do better than 20 percent a year. What looks like pennies to you is tens of thousands to me."

The Big Guy is both impressed and agitated. Metzger and the General love it.

Kissick continues. "I look at investments in a holistic way. I like to aggregate money, gather my sources together; and I'm a huge fan of compound interest. It's something I have a true passion for. My greatest fear is poverty. My parents constantly talked about the times their parents couldn't pay the bills and lost their homes and their cars; sometimes they didn't have money for food or clothing. My father went into business for himself when he was sixteen; he financially carried his whole family out of poverty into a different world. But there was no amount of money in the bank that was enough for him. There was no amount that would make him feel safe, and so he diversified; he had money in banks, in the market, in real estate; he bought and sold almost anything he could get his hands on and managed to build a little empire. Land was cheap; he built housing developments and named the streets after his relatives. Ursula Way, Fishwick Path, Robert Road, Donald Street. And you know what part I'm proudest of?"

"What?" the Big Guy asks.

"He built quality houses; he used good materials. No one ever complained about Dick Kissick's construction."

"Impressive," the Big Guy says. He can't help but notice that Kissick is tearing up as he's telling them all this. The crying makes him nervous.

The Big Guy pats Kissick on the back. "How about we head inside. I'm sure Mary has a little something special for us." He takes the guns from

Kissick, carries them back to the house, and puts them back under lock and key. For the moment, he doesn't put the key back in the lockbox but hides it in his office. He's not sure why, just a feeling.

Mary has made cookies and a giant pot of hot cocoa.

"I highly recommend it with bourbon and a little cayenne pepper," the Big Guy says. "It sounds strange, but a dash of the hot stuff cuts the sweetness and gives it a kick."

While they're snacking, the hunt team returns; the judge has something with him in a bag that he drags into the kitchen.

"A little trophy to take home?" the Big Guy asks.

"More a memento than a trophy," the judge says. "It was Tony who bagged the prize."

"I got a mountain goat," Tony says. "It'll make a nice rug or maybe an antler lamp."

"Whatever," Eisner says. "At least you brought the whole thing back." He turns to the judge. "Watching you cut that animal apart was something that will leave me permanently changed."

"It's called field dressing," the judge says.

"Dressing in any form is not what I saw," Eisner says. "Unless you're calling spilled blood mixed with snow and dirt dressing."

"There's a lot you don't know."

"Like what?" Metzger asks, putting himself into the mix.

"Like you don't cut the throat to bleed the animal if you're going to mount it. Leave the feet if it's a bear and think about the shape of the mount, basically cut down and around the shoulder."

"I like the idea of bear feet," Metzger says. "I'm surprised that no one has used it as a product name, hell of a lot better than Bag Balm."

The judge's game bag is taken by Sonny to be packed in ice for its return flight and finishing in the Lone Star State. Tony's goat is already being processed by Sonny's brother, who wants to know if it's okay for them to give the meat away.

"Please do," Tony says.

"You know," Bo says, smiling. "This is great. This is wonderful. Today reminds me of days I had as a boy. The whole family would be on a trip, skiing in Austria or the Swiss Alps, and we'd either be out on the slopes or in a restaurant having a family dinner and a stranger would appear out of nowhere and hand my father something. It could be as big as a suitcase or as small as a cigar. No one said anything; my mother never let on that it was strange. Whatever my father was doing or saying, he'd just keep going. I thought that was normal. I thought that fathers worked all the time, day and night, around the world."

"Remind me, what did your father do?" Metzger asks.

"He worked for the government," Bo says.

"In a particular department?"

"In an agency," Bo says, and leaves it at that.

The men take a break to refresh themselves, especially the hunters, who have the metallic stink of hot blood gone cold. The Big Guy notices dried blood under the judge's nails. He takes Mary aside and asks her to put a nail brush in his bathroom.

When they reconvene, drinks are poured and dinner is served. Mary has outdone herself with steak and potatoes and green beans with slivers of almonds. Christmas-style is what Mary calls them. A good red wine is aerating, bold and deep in flavor, and is poured as the conversation progresses.

Dr. Frode has brought to the table an ancient doctor's satchel. He pulls out a glass bottle and proceeds to wash his hands at the table.

"It's not you, it's me," he says, as each of the men clocks his activities. "I know too much."

"As far as I know, the only way to really clean your hands is to piss on them," Bo says.

"Correct," the doctor says. "But this I make myself; it smells terrible but cleans great."

"Frode, that's not a common name," the Big Guy says. "Is that correct or a typo?"

"Nordic," the doctor says. "It means wise and clever. First name is Gunnar, 'he who stands alone.' Turned out to be prophetic when my father left my mother for the widow next door and I would go back and forth between the houses in a sad domestic version of Red Rover. As in Red Rover, Red Rover, we call Gunnar Frodeover."

"Were your parents Vikings?" Bo asks.

"Not really. They were dermatologists in Los Angeles."

"Smells like turpentine," Bo says.

"Elements of that," the doctor says. "Among other things." Frode has a long beard, too long for a man in his late fifties, and has an old-fashioned corncob pipe sticking out of his mouth.

"Recognizing that we are not well-known to one another," the doctor says, drawing the judge's focus across the table, "I return to your question, Who am I? Like you, I am not the person I appear to be on the surface. Where to begin? I was always unusual—"

Bo makes a sound. "It's a bio, not a birth announcement."

"I'm not sure I asked him a question," the judge says to Eisner. "Did you hear me ask?"

The doctor ignores them. "How best to describe myself? I'm a catastrophic thinker. I go as dark as possible and then some. My wife thinks I'm paranoid; I call it prudent. We live in Bethesda, which to me is political ground zero; we've got air purifiers, filtration systems, a fallout shelter, all the bells and whistles. Given the information I see on a daily basis, I can tell you that it's only dumb luck that we're all still here."

"Interesting," the judge says.

"I have a whole other life as a tinkerer; that's where the money comes from. A number of years ago, I came up with some medical items: stents and adhesives and whatnots that turned out to be quite lucrative. Every year I launch a few things; this year it's kosher pet chews—Jew Toys. Now, if you don't mind, I'm going to check the kitchen before we eat. It's a habit I can't quit, food preparation, safety, and all that." The doctor excuses himself from the table, taking his mystery satchel with him.

"He's going to inspect the kitchen? I bet that's a first," Tony says. "I wouldn't be surprised if Mary clocks him."

"Do you think he's carrying drugs?" Eisner asks.

"What kind of drugs?" Bo asks.

"I'm sure he has drugs," Kissick says. "My brother is a dentist and even he travels with all kinds of drugs, just in case."

"Not regular drugs, mind drugs like they make in labs—LSD and MDMA and the kind of stuff they used to use for experiments." Eisner starts singing Jefferson Airplane's "White Rabbit."

"You're out of tune and I don't think he's carrying anything with him," Bo says. "His ego is so big, it's all he can manage."

"What's with the pipe?" the judge asks. "What's he smoking?"

"He doesn't smoke it; he sucks on it," Kissick says.

"Smells like mothballs and peppermint," the judge says.

"It's herbal," Kissick says. "He makes it himself."

"Marijuana is herbal," Bo says.

"I hope he's not in the kitchen doctoring our dinner," Eisner says.

"You're being paranoid," Tony says.

"I'm being careful."

Metzger pipes up. "Brand-wise, he reminds me of Colonel Sanders."

"How do we know he doesn't have a wire in that beard?" Bo asks.

"If you fellas don't think he's a good fit, there are others, medical men who were in the military. I know a guy who worked at Plum Island," the General says.

"Is that a tropical retreat? The atoll where they tested Castle Bravo?" the judge asks.

"No, it's where they did all the bioweapons experiments off the coast of Connecticut," Bo says.

"Long Island," the General says.

"Both," the Big Guy says. "It's between the two."

"Brief delay," Mary yells from the kitchen.

"When I was younger, I had a bit of a problem," Eisner says. "That's why I'm so fanatic about exercise—I need the endorphins."

"Cocaine," Tony says. "Look, Eisner, we know everything about you. I can assure you that Dr. Frode is not in the kitchen fucking with your food; he's more likely quizzing Mary about how long the butter has been out on the counter. He's a stickler for microbes."

"He'll be fine," Kissick says. "He wants in and he can contribute on many levels. He's very crafty; there's money streaming in through various sources, arranged almost like the human body, capillaries into veins, veins into arteries. If he wasn't in medicine, he'd be a brilliant moneyman."

As they are segueing to dessert and the Big Guy is about to ask Kissick to explain the shape of the organization and why it cannot be structured like a company, the General interrupts. "Before we get into how the FBI took down the Mafia using RICO laws, there is something else we must discuss." He stands and begins walking in laps around the table. "The gray zone is not a movie about a zombie apocalypse. The gray zone is neither here nor there; its boundaries are indeterminate and not covered by an existing set of rules. That makes it the ideal place for you folks to do your work. In this zone you can take advantage of known vulnerabilities; you can disrupt and disable, exploit information, use proxies and the disinformation campaigns that Eisner and Metzger design. These are time-tested tools that have been used with excellent results around the world. Today, we find ourselves in a unique position, in a more modern world that has yet to be truly explored, or should I say exploited; and by that I mean technology, communications, social media, changing public opinion by creating public opinion. One of the finest tools in the gray zone is language—what you say and to whom you say it. Historically, we have used everyone from New Orleans jazz musicians, abstract expressionists, and lady chefs who liked a nip of sherry; we have used film and radio and television to sell Americans and the world on a vision of what this country is all about."

Eisner chimes in. "Reference point: the phrase America First isn't the same as the American dream. The ideas behind the first phrase can be traced to Thomas Jefferson and his relationship to other countries. The dream phrase was coined in 1931 as a criticism of individual wealth and was meant to spur a return to equality and wealth for the nation over the individual. The Progressives thought it undemocratic to be a millionaire. By the 1950s, it had metamorphosed; the American dream was both a symbol and a vision of success and prosperity, and we sold it not just at home but around the world."

"What he's saying," Bo says, "is that manipulating the mainstream media is a cheap and effective way to get the message out."

"Exactly," the General says. "A program I call 'the half-baked potato restuffed,' meaning that you eat it because you like the way it tastes, but you have no idea what you're eating."

"And then there's just shit we make up," Metzger says. "Science fiction, pure fantasy."

"How do you know the difference?" Kissick asks.

"Difference?" the General asks. "What difference?"

"Between what is real and what is made up."

"I'm not sure that I should be the one to break this to you," the General says, "but it doesn't fucking matter; the only important thing is that people believe what you're telling them."

"On a technical level," Metzger says, "the difference is that misinformation is bad intelligence shared without harm. For example, 'the world is flat.' Disinformation is bad intel shared with the intention to harm: 'if you jump off that building, it's okay; you'll bounce back up.' And malinformation is genuine information shared with the intent to cause harm: 'just between us, the stock market will crash' or 'your family is in danger.' A great example of this is when Mark Antony, defeated in the Battle of Actium, hears the false rumor that Cleopatra has killed herself. He then kills himself."

"You create the bullshit and then you spread it," the General says. "Getting good spread, echo, and repeat is how you make it real. The more times it is repeated, the more real it becomes. By real I mean true—your fiction becomes fact. And at this time, despite the fact that the first television was sold in 1929, the majority of people don't know the power of technology to influence decision-making."

"Some of it is old-school," Metzger says. "You start a radio station, a TV network—in many ways, it's easier now than ever; you can do it online—it's not like when David Sarnoff started NBC and competed against William Paley at CBS. Sarnoff was a boy from Minsk who came to America and got a job working for Marconi sending telegraphs. We're in the twenty-first-century version of that same moment—and it's called the internet."

"I thought you were going to say it's called FOX," Bo says.

"Too new to be true," Metzger says.

It's a love fest between the General, the doctor, and Metzger. Bo and the Big Guy are smiling at each other. Bo is fucking glowing, but that might also be because he's near the fireplace.

"The ancient Chinese general Sun Tzu believed the indirect approach to war was about deception and uncertainty, creating confusion, dividing allies. What you're playing is the long game that evolves under the radar," the General says.

The Big Guy looks at Metzger and sees that his face is reptilian, snakelike—big eyes, narrow jaw, cold skin that looks preserved or more like petrified by forty years of Pall Malls, Camels, and Kools.

Metzger meets the Big Guy's glance and, as though reading his mind, says, "I started smoking when I was eight; I had a butane lighter from Esso. I loved to set the flame up high. I'd light up pretty much anything I could get my hands on just to watch it burn."

Bo steps in. "The shift in the political waters has its own riptide. The fracture on the right, the extremism, will find its voice or voices and will roll in; then like a rip current, it will pull away from shore, sucking and drowning those voices as it does—they will be lost at sea. And while it may appear that we, the party, are lost at sea, the sea level itself will be rising and the tidal wave, initially imperceptible, will build and slowly roll in. There will be a seamless transition unfolding in the corridors of power, a slow turn to the right that no one sees coming. In the name of what it means to be an American, we will spearhead the development, within the military and outside it, of separatist soldiers who believe that they are following the true wishes of their leaders culminating in the erosion of civil liberties under the guise of protection. This combined with the withering of local law enforcement, economic setbacks, and failing infrastructure will become part of a picture that coincides with a period of economic, social, and political unrest; the destabilization in this country will give rise to rogue nonpoliticians."

"If I'm hearing you right," the judge says, "what you're outlining is a coup of sorts that will sweep across this country largely unnoticed until it is too late—until the American people have been decimated economically, intellectually, and spiritually. It comes together on a decision day that results in the emergence of a new America."

"Yes," the Big Guy says. "And no one will read it as an inside job. It's a new American dream."

"There comes a point," Bo says, "where there is no going back, a moment of great faith, of activation, a call to arms."

"This is for the common good," Kissick says. "Let's be very clear that what we're talking about is a return to American values—family, home, the right to succeed."

"This is serious stuff," the judge says. "The kind of thing that costs people their lives—we are respected men, good men, our loyalty must be unquestionable."

"I declare us brothers—like a blood-bonding ceremony. I once knew a guy who had a rabbi come to his house for his son's circumcision, and because my friend wasn't circumcised, he felt bad that he wouldn't understand what his son experienced, so he asked the rabbi to make a little cut on his dick. My friend reported that it hurt like hell and he couldn't scream because all the relatives were right outside. The guy used a blade on him," Bo says.

"Look, I don't want to step on your party plans, and as you know, I'm not really here in any official capacity, just a 'guest,'" the General says. "But FYI, you can go with some kind of private military contractor, but you're gonna need an internal interface. It's not so much a show of force as invisibly rocking the boat in such a way that either no one notices or the rocking becomes lulling, and soon it's something you desire and can't live without."

"What's the rollout?" the judge asks

"At least fifteen years," the Big Guy says. "Any faster and our cover will be blown; slower and it's too late."

"Do we take it all at once?" the judge wants to know.

"The more invisible we are, the more powerful," Kissick says.

"Lie down in peace, rise again to life," the General says.

"That's your second Bible quote of the day," Tony says. "Are you a religious man?"

"I was raised in a house of prayer."

While they are talking, Metzger is roasting one marshmallow after another in the fireplace, perfecting a toasty brown skin and then pawning them off on the others—the General seems to have an endless appetite for them. Every now and then Metzger loses his focus and one goes up in flames. When that happens, his face lights up; the glow of the flame reflected in his dark-rimmed glasses gives him the look of a demented jack-o'-lantern.

A distant thrumming noise, which at first could be dismissed as a car engine or an old oil furnace or maybe a generator of some sort, starts to hum louder and louder until the windows are actually vibrating.

"You don't get earthquakes here, do you?" Kissick asks.

"Nope," the Big Guy says.

The judge grabs a knife off the table and is going for the door. Bo grabs a fire iron and is just behind the judge. Metzger pulls a decorative sword from China off the wall and they head outside. "We're under attack," Kissick yells, holding a snowshoe out in front of himself as if it were a shield.

The din increases. The men can't hear one another, and the visibility is down to zero, the air spinning like a night tornado.

On the side of the house near where they were shooting the heads off the mannequin, two helicopters land as if falling from the sky, the doors slide open, and teams of heavily armed soldiers disembark. There are flash-bangs, heavy white smoke, and then, kapow, bright white floodlights go on as if a switch has been thrown.

The men are face-to-face with twenty soldiers.

"I am one hundred percent going to die," Kissick says.

"I told you," Eisner says. "He fucking doped us. It's coming on. Strong."

"It's not dope, it's real, we are busted," Kissick says.

"Our toast is burnt," Metzger adds.

"I already have a fucking record," Eisner says.

"For what?" Kissick asks—after all, he's the one who's been doing the vetting.

"Gambling," Eisner says. "I was a professional player for a while and then I lost my touch, but it didn't keep me from playing. And cheating, that's what the record is for, robbery."

"How did I not know that?"

"I did community service," Eisner says. "I taught poor children how to write fiction and then I taught guys in jail, the kids' fathers, how to read. Maybe the record was expunged."

"Identify yourself," the General bellows to the soldiers.

"Sir, we have a mass casualty situation," the first soldier out of the chopper shouts.

"There were no shots fired?" another shouts.

"Sir, we must have encountered something in the LZ; there is debris everywhere."

"What the fuck?"

"Sir, please advise."

The engines on the choppers are cut back, the thwomping blades slow to a dull spin.

"Gentlemen," the General shouts to his friends. "This is what decision day looks like. What you have before you are two UH-60 aircraft and two highly trained private military contractor teams. I can get you as many of these men as you want for $1,200 a day per man. I've got 5,000 trained, and by the time you're ready to go, I can double that. That, of course, doesn't include time on the aircraft, which runs about $2,250 an hour just in costs. We have teams around the world that can be deployed with the drop of a geographical pin."

"What is he saying?" Kissick asks the Big Guy.

"He hired these guys; it's a party trick."

Metzger cracks up. A high-pitched Appalachian tee-hee-hee escapes with a wheeze followed by a sputtering cough. "Holy mother of cows. If you could see the looks on all your faces."

"Sir, I repeat, we have a mass casualty situation," the first soldier insists.

The white floodlights make it impossible for the men to see past the soldiers.

"Did you know he was going to do this?" the Big Guy asks Bo.

"Not specifically," Bo says, clearly enjoying the presence of these two massive helicopters. "But he did ask me for a lot of information—dimensions of everything, a map of the land, all kinds of crazy stuff. I just figured he was a security nut."

The pilot kills the engines; the smoke and dust float off into the night. The front door of the bird opens and the pilot comes out. He looks out ahead of the chopper into the night and promptly vomits.

"Not good at vomit," Kissick says. "Vomit begets vomit." Kissick retches.

"What the fuck are you barfing about?" the General bellows.

"The bodies," the pilot moans. "I can see the bodies with my night-vision glasses. We fucking tore them apart. There are heads everywhere." The pilot falls onto his knees. "I so fucking shouldn't say yes to things when I want to say no," he says to himself.

"If there was a spare pilot among this group, I would fucking shoot you," the General says. "I would write it off as friendly fire, collateral damage. Those are not real heads. Those are props from a game earlier today. Take a look. Do they look real or like 1960s go-go dancers?"

"I was born in 1984, sir," the pilot says.

"You're killing me," the General says.

"I feel the same way, sir."

"This is amazing," the Big Guy says. "So much better live and in person than on a Ping-Pong table in the basement. Maybe we should give these boys a drink of Mary's cocoa before they head back to wherever they came from."

Kissick, out of his mind, makes a snowball and hurls it at one of the soldiers. "What you gonna do now, shoot me?" he taunts the soldiers.

"Is that a real gun or just a Nerf?" Metzger asks dryly.

The soldiers do not respond or react. They are brilliantly robotic and restrained, holding the line.

The General goes over to the pilot, who is now just out-and-out weeping, and pokes him with the fire iron. "Pull yourself together, man. There are no bodies."

"Just in front of the chopper. Sir, you can't see it but I can; there are heads that have been severed; there are parts of people." The pilot vomits again.

"Stop," the General orders. "You're just chumming now."

"Chumming?" the pilot asks.

"Burleying; your vomit is like an angler using fish parts as bait, bone blood, it draws sharks in the ocean, bears on land."

"They're all dead," the pilot says. "No one is moving."

The General wants to take out his pistol and put the pilot out of his pain—but there's an additional fee for that, something like $250,000 for a pilot, so he puts his hand on the man's shoulder. "Why don't you come inside, soldier. Have a cup of Mary's cocoa or maybe something a little stronger."

Tuesday, December 23, 2008
Palm Springs, California
1:00 p.m.

When Charlotte said she was coming home for Christmas, the Big Guy was so relieved that he didn't ask questions for fear of jinxing it. That said, he's surprised when she knocks on the door just after one p.m. with only one small blue suitcase in hand.

"Why didn't you let me come get you?" he says.

"Then I'd have to tell you where I live."

In his version he would have picked her up at the sober house. She would be ready to go, bags packed. He was expecting that this would be it, her last hurrah, graduation from the program. She'd wave a tearful goodbye to her counselors and the other residents. He's been expecting all kinds of things but is afraid to ask questions for fear it will push her further away. For years Charlotte went along with everything because she didn't have the strength to stand up to him. He should have paid more attention to her efforts; he should have noticed the clues.

He understands that now. After what she's been through, she's not about to return to the old way of doing things. But where does it leave them? That's what he doesn't know.

Just before the weekend at the ranch, he went to a family meeting; he did what he thought was a good job listening to her talk. He didn't defend himself. He's been in business long enough to know that coming off like a bully and shutting people down doesn't work. He just listened. When they asked whether he had anything to say, he said he was sorry for any pain he had caused her, sorry for any of his behavior that made her life more difficult. He said he was sorry again and again and started to cry, and then said he was sorry for crying but that listening to her was painful.

Near the end of the meeting, he went to hug Charlotte and the counselor got between them and said, "No." The Big Guy flushed red with shame and anger, and sat down in his chair, vowing never to do this again. He didn't understand. What had he done wrong? Was it wrong to try to hug his wife? It seemed like a nice gesture. He wanted to know what the problem was but wasn't about to ask. There are limits to the amount of humiliation the Big Guy can expose himself to in a given day.

And now, at one p.m., when she walks in the door and sees how hard he worked to make it nice, she gives him a soft pat on the back.

"It's beautiful," she says. "It looks like a Christmas fantasy."

"Thank you. I would say I did it myself but it's not true. I had some help."

"So much effort," she says.

He nods.

"That only makes it harder."

"Why?"

"Because it's not a pleasant occasion."

"It's Christmas," he says.

"You promised me that we would tell her. That's why I came back."

A pause.

"We will tell her but it is also Christmas, and even though you're not in the mood for it, others might be. We have to make up for having messed up Thanksgiving."

"That's what we did? We messed up Thanksgiving? I thought I was doing a good thing. Taking care of myself."

"That's not what I meant and you know it."

"We have to tell her."

"I agree. But we don't have to do it the minute she comes through the door. Welcome home, sorry about Thanksgiving, and by the way, we're about to detonate a bomb in your life. The kid is coming home for Christmas."

"I've been sitting on this for years," she says.

"Right, which is why it's not an emergency."

"It's your secret. I'm not keeping secrets anymore. The secret store is closed. That's the reason I'm here. I came to back to tell her."

"You're not staying?"

"Not for long."

He doesn't say anything.

"It's not personal," she says.

"Unlikely."

"Maybe it is personal but it's about me; it's not about you. I have to continue my work."

"And that's not something you can do from here? You could even have the group come here to the house."

"It's not possible," she says.

He moves her suitcase from the front hall into the bedroom.

She moves it back to the front hall.

"I promise you'll be able to get out quickly," he says. "But you don't need to leave the bag in the front hall. You can have the bedroom, I'll take my office."

"No."

"Fine." He opens the front hall closet and puts the suitcase in there. "Does that work for now?"

"What time is she due in?"

"Between three and four. Are you hungry?"

"I'm not," she says. "I'll just sit outside and read. I brought a book."

"You could go for a swim."

"I didn't bring a suit."

"As though that's ever stopped you."

She shrugs.

"I'm sure there's one in your drawer."

"Could I please have something to drink and maybe a nut?" she asks.

"Of course."

"Do you happen to have pineapple juice? Or a Sierra Mist?"

"No, but I have pretty much everything else. Cranberry? Fresh lime?"

"Maybe."

"It's your house too," he says. "Make yourself at home. You can serve yourself."

"I don't feel comfortable doing that."

"There is no liquor in the kitchen; you don't have to be afraid of going in there."

"This is so awful," she says.

"It's all gone; I cleaned everything out, removed temptation." He's done his homework and has all kinds of juices and soft drinks, things to mix to give the feeling of a cocktail, of celebration. He's got crudités and nuts.

"You know what I discovered that I just love?"

"No idea," he says, as he's making a cranberry and seltzer for her and one for himself.

"Goldfish."

"Oh."

"The crackers. I just love the goldfish crackers. Did you ever notice that they have faces, that they smile at you while you're eating them?"

"I didn't notice that," he says, handing her the drink. "But they're tasty."

"And graham crackers," she says. "I hadn't had a graham cracker since I was a child. I didn't even know they still made them."

"We could get some."

"No need." She moves around the living room, touching the various decorations. "Is the tree real?"

He laughs again. "I forgot to ask."

"We never had a tree here before."

"It's a first," he says.

"It looks nice against the windows, with the golf course in the background."

"I didn't know what to do; I had Neiman's come style the place like a window on Fifth Avenue."

What he doesn't tell her is that he also had them do the shopping; he gave them some ideas and they came back with a list. Family pajamas, sweaters, mother-daughter roller skates, headphones, hairstyling. A nice black dress and a red one, too, for each. Cozy soft sweatpants and cashmere sweatshirts. Something from Burberry. Something from UGG. Something for everyone. Glass icicles. Snowmen in globes for the tree. Rigaud candles, Christmas table decorations, oven mitts and aprons, a waffle maker. No barware this year.

"It's a little much, isn't it?" she asks, looking at the enormous pile of gifts.

"I did what I could," he says. "I wanted it to be nice for everyone."

"Reparations."

He doesn't answer. She picks up a box and shakes it. "What did you get me?"

"I'm not telling you."

"You should. Christmas is not my holiday. I would be relieved to know what's in the box."

"Why?"

"Because I didn't get you anything. I didn't get anyone anything."

"I got something for everyone."

"You always were very generous."

"Just because you are going through this doesn't mean everything has to be shit. Every minute of every day can't be excruciating," he says.

"You'd be surprised," she says, and there's another long pause. "You know what's been interesting?"

"What?"

"I've learned to live with less. In the old days I couldn't have done it. But this time I did. No special mattress, no good pillow, everything at the facility was designed to be wiped off and reused. There was nothing personal, nothing pretty, nothing nice in any way. And the food was terrible, flavorless and heavy, as if it were made for an army. I had to learn to let it all go, to accept that I'm not special, that if I don't sleep with my special pillow I would survive. It was very difficult. I could have pitched a fit. I could have said that I need this for my soul, like when you need things not for your comfort but for your spirit, but I decided not to. At first, I accepted the situation as a kind of self-punishment. I told myself that I deserve to be uncomfortable. I was so mad at myself, at you, at them. And then I moved from being angry to thinking, Fine, I will tough it out; I will show them that I'm not so fragile, that I don't think I'm so special. If I die, so what? I started looking around and noticed that no one was complaining about their pillow or their blanket and that no one else needed fruit that wasn't as hard as a rock. I realized that they either didn't notice or didn't care, but most important, it seemed easier that way, and I wished I could be like that. I wished it could be easier for me. I practiced just accepting what is. Years ago, I would have thought they were fools for not knowing there was a better version available, and now I realize they're not stupid; they're sparing themselves the disappointment, the pain of longing, of desire. They're not obsessed by perfection. Everything doesn't need to be perfect. That's why this is all too much." She gestures toward all he has done. "It's perfect."

"Thank you," he says. "I'm going to take that as a compliment."

"But it doesn't need to be perfect, perfection equals pressure."

"You could just enjoy it. And decide to feel no pressure. You could just accept that I tried to do something nice for you."

"If I could do that, I would be a different person. You see, it's all still a work in progress." She laughs.

He feels thoroughly confused.

They sit for a while. A beam of sunlight cuts through the glass and moves slowly across the living-room floor, using the Christmas tree like the gnomon of a sundial.

"What time is it?"

"Almost three fifteen," he says.

"I think I'll go for a walk."

"Now? Meghan will be here soon."

"Yes," she says, preparing to go. "I trust you can hold down the fort."

"I can."

She slides the glass doors open and takes off across the patio, past the pool, and toward the ninth hole of the golf course.

Not long after she leaves, Meghan arrives.

"How's my big girl?" the Big Guy says, greeting her with a strong hug.

"Good," she says, hugging back. She inhales deeply. "The house smells like Christmas."

"It's a candle."

"I always associate that smell with the ranch in winter."

"Rigaud cypress," he says, carrying her bags into her room.

"Wow. The house is so decorated."

"Nice, right?"

"It's Christmas inside out. It's snowy and there are icicles inside, and outside there's the desert and palm trees. I like it. It's wild, with all the white and silver and everything crusted with make-believe snow."

"They call it flocked."

"So good," she says.

"The guy who installed it kept saying he thought Palm Springs was perfect for flocking, and honestly, I thought he was talking about the other F-word." He laughs. "Apologies for the crudeness but I thought it was very funny. He just kept saying flocking and finally I had to ask."

"Where's Mom?"

"She went out for a walk."

"Before I got home?"

"Just a little while ago. She's anxious."

"Should I go look for her?"

"Absolutely. She left a few minutes ago and was headed toward the ninth hole."

Meghan cuts across the patio in the same direction as Charlotte. A few minutes later, she's back, looking distressed.

"Did you find her?"

"I saw her . . ."

"And?"

"I hope she didn't see me."

The Big Guy is bewildered.

A pause. "She was, uh, uh . . ."

"What?"

"Smoking pot."

"What?"

"I saw her smoking something skinny and white, and it had the unmistakable scent of a dead skunk. I'm a teenager; I've been to parties; I know what marijuana smells like."

"That makes no sense. Number one, your mother doesn't smoke, and number two, she's living in a sober house. It must have been someone else."

"She was wearing yoga clothes and a pink baseball cap."

"Jesus. The fun never ends."

They hear the sound of the screen door scraping open.

"Smell her," Meghan whispers.

"I'm back," Charlotte calls out. "Is she home?"

"She's home," Meghan says, coming out to greet Charlotte. "I'm so glad to see you." Meghan goes to hug Charlotte, who is thin, as flat as a board, and doesn't so much hug back as brace herself. The image in Meghan's mind is that her mother is crispy like a saltine. "Are you doing okay?" Meghan asks.

"Truthfully, I have no idea," Charlotte says, going into the kitchen to pour herself some water.

"Do you want me to get that for you?" the Big Guy says, following her and trying to sniff her without being obvious.

"Why are you following me?"

"I was just being solicitous," he says, backing off. "Meghan, how about you? A drink?"

"Sure," Meghan says. "Travel is so dehydrating. I don't really understand how people do it as a career."

"Some people don't have as many choices," Charlotte says, coming back with a club soda and lime. "It used to be a way to meet a man with a good job."

"I think it's unhealthy to be up there where the air is bad, going back and forth, and having to deal with drunk people."

There's an awkward silence.

"Uh, sorry," Meghan says.

"I'm not drunk," Charlotte says. "I stopped drinking. And I was certainly never drunk on an airplane."

Neither the Big Guy nor Meghan says anything.

"You look very thin," Meghan finally says to her mother.

"Thank you," Charlotte says, because there is nothing else to say.

"It's been a while," her father says to Meghan.

"Not so long," Meghan says. "November fifth until now is seven weeks."

"Well, it's felt like a long stretch."

"What did you do for Thanksgiving?" Charlotte asks. "Where'd you go? I didn't hear anything about it."

"Tony took me to someone's house in Georgetown. It was fine but I kept thinking how much I missed our Thanksgivings. I love going to those old hotels and how decorated and festive it is. Remember the stuffing in those individual pewter pans, the bread pudding, and that crazy peanut pie?"

"Pecan pie," the Big Guy says.

"It always felt like a party at some grand old house in England."

"There is no Thanksgiving in England," Charlotte says. "Thanksgiving is about the Pilgrims who escaped from England."

"I didn't mean Thanksgiving in the literal sense but the feeling of a grand party." What Meghan doesn't tell them is how much of Thanksgiving Day she spent alone thinking about the murdered girl from her school and how she wrote letters to the girl's parents.

"Do you remember whose house you went to?"

She shakes her head. "Peggy somebody. I had a funny encounter. I was sitting next to a very nice woman who told me all kinds of things about how her father was a preacher and a football coach, and how she had been a Democrat until she was twenty-eight and then became a Republican. It was so interesting."

"What was the funny part?" Charlotte asks.

"After we left, Tony asked what I thought of her. I said that she was very nice and Tony said, 'She's the secretary of state.' 'What state?' I asked. 'The United States,' he said."

"Seriously?" Charlotte says.

"Uh, yep. Tony didn't want to tell me ahead of time in case I froze up."

"Condi Rice?" the Big Guy asks.

"That's the one."

"It was also funny because the man sitting on the other side of me told me that there were Secret Service agents in the house and I didn't understand why. One of them stayed in the kitchen the whole time. I thought he was helping the cook."

"Making sure the cook didn't poison anyone," the Big Guy says.

"Exactly," Meghan says. "Thanksgiving in Georgetown. The secretary of state, a couple of people from the TV news, one guy out on a special weekend pass from prison, and a bunch of kooks." She wants to say something about meeting William but is distracted by the tension in the room. She pauses.

The three of them are sitting in the living room; the beam of sunlight has crossed the living-room floor entirely; and the autotimer on the Christmas tree has activated, and the lights are twinkling.

"Can I ask a question?" Meghan says. "Is something wrong?"

No one answers.

"Do you have cancer?" she asks Charlotte.

Charlotte looks stricken; that's the last thing that would have occurred to her.

"It's been a difficult time," the Big Guy says.

"I brought your mugs," Meghan says, handing Charlotte a box. "The annual painted pottery mugs. This year I did an Americana political theme on them."

"Lovely," Charlotte says. "Perfect for tea."

"You certainly haven't lost your wits," the Big Guy says to his wife. "Political theme, tea . . ."

"I wasn't trying to be funny. I gave up caffeine along with the liquor."

"Oh."

"It's hard to know where to begin," Charlotte says. "There is something I need to tell you."

"Now?" the Big Guy asks. "Right now?"

"I can't breathe until I do it," she says.

"What?" Meghan says. "Do what?"

"Let the cat out of the bag," the Big Guy mumbles.

"Before you were born," Charlotte says, "we had a baby."

"I have a sibling?" Meghan asks excitedly.

"The baby had problems," the Big Guy adds.

"Is the baby coming home? Is he like in a wheelchair or something?"

"We did everything we could. Medical technology was different from what it is today," her father says.

"How long ago?"

"Twenty-one years."

"The baby was a boy," Charlotte says. "When the baby was born, we were told not to bring him home, that he was too ill, but I wasn't about to leave my child behind. We brought the baby home and cared for it for a very long time."

"The baby didn't grow or develop. It just kept getting sicker and sicker despite everything we did," the Big Guy says.

"The baby died," Charlotte says. "That's what happened."

"That's awful. Such a sad story," Meghan says. "But why are you telling me now?"

"Because we need to," Charlotte says. "You need to know. I need you to know."

"There's more," the Big Guy says.

Meghan looks baffled.

"I'm not your biological mother," Charlotte says.

"Like I'm adopted?"

"No."

"Donor egg?"

Charlotte shakes her head no.

"I don't understand."

"I didn't give birth to you."

"Does that mean you're not my mother?"

"I don't know," Charlotte says.

"Of course she is your mother and I am your father. Maybe we could have handled this better, but we did the best we could, the best we knew how."

"Daddy is your daddy but I am not your mother."

"It's my fault," the Big Guy says. "The onus is on me."

"What are you talking about?" Meghan cries. "Why are you saying this?"

"Because I can't live with the secret any longer," Charlotte says.

"You've known all along?" Meghan asks.

Both Charlotte and the Big Guy are a little startled.

"Well, of course I've known. I would have known if I'd given birth to you, wouldn't I?"

"I heard some people forget that it's so awful, that after it's over all memory of it goes away, which is why people keep having children," Meghan says.

"I didn't give birth to you."

"Well then, where did I come from?" She starts to cry. "I don't under-stand."

"On some level you do," Charlotte says.

When Meghan finds out that her mother is not her mother, she vomits into her own mouth without warning. She swallows. The hot bile burns in both directions. There is a pause. A blank. Then she vomits again, the contents of her stomach, her soul, emptying onto the gray terrazzo floor.

"I'm sorry," she says.

She has to stop the impulse to get down on her knees, shove the vomit back in her mouth, and eat it. She knows that her parents don't like a mess.

"I'll get some paper towels," her father says.

"I'm sorry," Meghan says again.

"Maybe we shouldn't have told you," the Big Guy says.

"That wasn't an option," Charlotte says. She is sitting in the living room doing breathing exercises. If Meghan hadn't vomited, she would have.

Covered in hot, sour, pink vomit going cold, Meghan runs into the bathroom. She takes off her sweater and throws it in the garbage. She looks at herself in the mirror.

"Can I come in?" her father asks.

"No," she says. "No. I don't know who you are. Whose house is this? Where am I? Where did my family go?"

"We're right here," he says through the door.

"Oh my god, I am losing my mind. I'm losing my mind. I just came home for Christmas. All I wanted was a normal vacation. It's so messed up. I thought my life was one way. I thought I was a certain kind of person with a certain kind of a family, and it turns out none of it is true."

"Some of it is true," he says. "You are who you know yourself to be."

There's the sound of crying, nose blowing, sniffling. "Is this why we don't visit Mom's family?"

"No," Charlotte calls out from the living room. Both Meghan and the

Big Guy are surprised she can hear what they're talking about. "The problem with my family is unrelated."

"They're Texans," the Big Guy says. "Not easy folks."

"Well, who else knows?" Meghan asks.

"No one knows."

"Tony?"

"Yes, Tony knows."

"Great. No one knows but someone knows. You cheated on Mom. That's disgusting."

"I'm not proud of it."

"I'm sure that's why she drinks. That's the big news that she wanted me to know? You replaced a dead kid with one you had with a hooker."

"Not a hooker."

"Are you sure?"

"I'm sure. Look, Meghan, I don't know how to have this conversation, neither does your mother. We're not people who deal in the business of emotions. None of this is your fault."

"Of course it's not my fault," she says. "I would never have done these things."

"None of it has anything to do with you except it's at the core of what your mother has been dealing with all these years; she's been sitting with these very difficult feelings."

"You say it's not my fault and that it has nothing to do with me, but it's about me. It's about where I came from. My creation. Somewhere out there is a lady who is actually my mother."

"Yes."

"Is that another surprise I should prepare myself for? Is she in the garage waiting to meet me?"

"All your mother ever wanted was children. She had a terrible time with the baby. We should have told you long ago, but we didn't want to burden you with all that had come before. We wanted you to have a good life. I hope this helps you understand how she's been overprotective at times and distant at times. It's my mistake for not telling you sooner."

In the living room, Charlotte, who can hear everything he's saying, has started to cry.

"Do you even know who my real mother is?"

"I certainly do."

"Does she know that I know?"

"No," he says. "I've not spoken with her in many years."

"You're going to have to now," Meghan says.

The Big Guy says nothing. It hadn't occurred to him that he'd have to call her, but Meghan's right.

"I feel like I'm in a nightmare, like this isn't real. You're not real. I want to be back in Virginia. I want to run away."

"Take some deep breaths."

In the background there is the sound of the glass doors sliding open. Charlotte steps outside.

"You should have just given me to strangers, to some poor family who didn't already have a dead kid."

"History is a funny thing," he says. "This happened to both of us, to your mother and me. We had a sick child; that was something we did together. When the child died, we buried him and we each dealt with it differently." This is the part that he's been telling himself; this is the speech that he's practiced in his head. "People are not the same; couples are not one person; parents are two separate people who feel things differently."

"Whatever. I have the worst headache now," Meghan says. "I don't want to hear anymore."

"There are some headache pills in the cabinet," he says. "You're probably dehydrated."

There is the sound through the door of Meghan opening the cabinet and turning on the water.

"Where's Mom now?"

"Out by the pool talking on the phone. Maybe she's calling her sponsor."

"She has a sponsor, like Nike or Lancôme?"

"No, like an antidrinking coach, a former drunk she calls for support."

There's another long pause.

"Does she hate us?" Meghan asks.

"Who?"

"Mom?"

"No."

"If I were her, I would hate you. You did this."

"I did."

"To Mom and to me and to some other poor lady who had to give her baby away. I always thought you were a good guy, the great provider, and it turns out that you're kind of a jerk."

"That's a nice word for it."

Another long silence passes.

"Did you have a funeral?" Meghan asks.

He's not sure what she's asking. "For who?"

"For the baby."

"No. Your mother didn't want one. Everywhere we went after that happened, people just looked at her with such sad faces. That's what started the social anxiety and maybe even the drinking. She stopped going out, couldn't look at people, couldn't bear the way they looked at her."

Meghan opens the bathroom door. Her face is puffy and tear streaked. "While the shit's hitting the fan," she says, "I have to ask you something. Is William Tony's boyfriend?"

"That's a fair guess."

"Why did no one ever tell me that Tony's gay?"

The Big Guy says nothing.

"Do you know William?"

"We've met."

"How long have they been together?"

"A few years. Tony used to go through a lot of boyfriends, but it seems he's settling down."

"Tony is over sixty. Why do you call them boyfriends?"

He doesn't answer.

Charlotte comes back inside. "I had to buy a vowel."

"What?" the Big Guy asks.

"I needed some advice."

"Who did you call?" Meghan wants to know.

"A friend."

There's a pause.

"I have to go," Charlotte says.

"Where?" the Big Guy asks.

"Back to where I came from."

"Are you leaving me?" Meghan asks plaintively.

"I'm not leaving you," Charlotte says. "I'm just going someplace safe."

"I need you."

"I need a moment," Charlotte says.

"Mommy."

"A moment."

"Okay, I'm leaving too," Meghan says.

"Where are you going?" the Big Guy asks.

"No idea. I just have to get out of here."

"You're both leaving?"

"For now," Charlotte says.

"Can't you stay here?" the Big Guy asks.

"It's like a panic attack," Meghan says. "I have to hurry. I have to go somewhere. Can you call me a cab?"

"We can go wherever you want," the Big Guy says. "We don't have to stay here. We can go to Aspen or Paris or Hawaii; we're already halfway there."

"No," Meghan says. "I have to go outside." Now it is her turn to slide the glass doors open and wander onto the golf course. Meghan has always prided herself on figuring things out on her own. But as her foot slips off the green and she slides into a sand trap, she cries out. She is stuck, trapped in Palm Springs, a living fossil. She pulls herself out of the sand and hurries back into the house. Charlotte is still there; she's standing in the front hall, clutching her blue suitcase, waiting for her ride.

"We could all go to a meeting together," the Big Guy suggests.

"I'm sure we will one day," Charlotte says. "But not yet."

"You're both leaving me? What if I freak out?"

"Deal with it," Charlotte says.

"The way you're both acting is the reason why women have bad reputations," the Big Guy says.

"Pardon?" Charlotte says.

"The female of the species is known for being erratic and flying off the handle."

Both women stare at him.

"What? It's true. You don't think that people think women are difficult?"

"When you say people," Charlotte says, "you don't mean people, you mean men. Men find women difficult."

"Yes," the Big Guy says.

"That's because women are different from men and men expect them to be the same. Women don't expect as much from men; they know better," Charlotte says.

"Women are smarter," Meghan says.

"Now you're ganging up on me?" he asks in disbelief.

"Were you smoking pot outside?" Meghan asks Charlotte.

Charlotte says nothing.

"I saw you and I smelled it."

"Are you going to tell on me?" Charlotte wants to know.

There's a pause.

"No, I'm not going to tell on you. But given what you've been through with the drinking, it seems odd that you're smoking pot. And besides, it's illegal."

Another pause.

"I find it very difficult to be here," Charlotte says. "It's not you personally—it's the situation. You are terrific," she says to Meghan. "I couldn't ask for more."

"Where'd you get the dope?" the Big Guy asks.

"It won't happen again," Charlotte says. Outside, a horn beeps.

Charlotte picks up her bag. "Till soon," she says as she leaves.

"I feel really weird," Meghan says.

"Don't," the Big Guy says. "Your mother is going through something. It has nothing to do with you."

"She just told me she's not my mother; I feel like that definitely has something to do with me."

"The fact of it is about you. The rest is about her."

"Can you call me a cab and have them take me somewhere?"

"When you call a cab, they want to know where you're going."

"Into town."

"Where?"

"Where did Mom's ride take her?"

"Betty Ford? The sober house?"

"Denny's," she says.

"I could drive you there. We could have breakfast for dinner."

"I need to be alone."

He calls her the cab and waits with her in the driveway. "You know that we're old for parents. You may have noticed, most of your friends' parents are much younger."

Meghan nods.

"We love you very much. There are just some things that are part of a marriage that are very hard to talk about."

"Are you sure she doesn't hate us? I've never heard her talk like that."

"Like what? With feeling?"

"With anger."

"We had lives before we got married."

"I know Mom almost married some guy named Chet, but you convinced her to call it off."

"His name was Chip and Papa Willard hated him so I was brought in. Your mother was the most beautiful woman I'd ever met. She was spectacular, in full possession of herself."

"Except she's apparently not my mother."

"There's a sound in your voice."

"My feelings," Meghan says.

The cab pulls into the driveway.

"Do you need money?" the Big Guy asks, taking out his wallet.

"No," she says. "You throw money at people as if it fixes things."

"It fixes nothing but sometimes it makes things easier."

"I'm not okay," Meghan says. "I know I seem sort of okay, like I'm talking coherently, but I'm not. I have no idea what to do with this. Everything I thought I knew is now a fake. I'm applying to colleges as what, the illegitimate replacement baby?"

With that, she gets into the cab. As they drive toward town, she tries to chat with the driver. He's nothing like Mr. Tooth. She's upset; tears and snot keep leaking out of her despite her efforts to suck it all back in.

"Hey," the driver says. "You seem sad."

"I am," she says. "Thanks for noticing."

"Hey, maybe we could do something about it."

"Like what?"

"I don't know," he says. "I have some friends and we could party or something?"

She doesn't say anything. Just looks out the window.

"Does that sound good, partying?"

She feels uncomfortable. It's dark now. She doesn't know Palm Springs.

"In theory," she says. "But I have to be at Denny's. I'm meeting a few friends there."

"We could all party, the more the merrier," the driver says, looking at her in the rearview mirror.

"No. We made this plan a long time ago. We go to Denny's, then we go to church. We're really into church." She starts to sing. "Star of wonder, star of night, star with royal beauty bright, westward leading, still proceeding, guide us to thy perfect light . . ." Singing not only helps her feel less panicky but she's breathing more deeply. It's her favorite song.

"No problem," he says. "Church. That's cool. I respect that." His eyes are back on the road. At Denny's she thinks of giving him a big tip for not kidnapping her but worries he might take it the wrong way, so she gives him an extra dollar. "Thanks," he says. "By the way, you have an excellent voice. You shouldn't party—it might wreck it."

She goes into Denny's and orders hot tea and a blueberry muffin. She hasn't eaten since breakfast unless you count the pack of pretzels on the plane. Two days ago she was singing in the Christmas concert at school, the voices of one hundred girls lifting her—"westward leading, still proceeding"—she hums the song over the steaming cup of tea and starts to cry.

The waitress comes over and asks if she needs anything, and Meghan manages to stop the waterworks. "No. I'm okay," she lies.

"Do you need help?"

Meghan nods.

"Are you pregnant?"

She shakes her head no.

"In an abusive relationship?"

Again Meghan shakes her head no.

"Struggling with a substance?"

She shakes her head no again. "I want to go to a meeting. How do I find a meeting?"

"Oh, honey, it's a rough time of year. Hold on. I know who to ask; the guy in the kitchen knows where all the meetings are."

In a few minutes the waitress comes back with an address scribbled on a napkin and a map of how to walk there from Denny's.

"Be careful on the corners; the cars really can't see you at night, so wait until you have the Walk sign. Then if they hit you, they at least have to pay to repair you."

"Thank you." Meghan leaves Denny's and walks to the meeting. It's in an empty store in a strip mall. All the windows have been covered with paper and For Rent signs. When she opens the door, the bell jingles and people turn their heads and look back at her. It's crowded. She takes a seat on a folding chair.

"First time?" the guy sitting next to her asks.

She nods.

"This one is AA/NA, mostly people who have been around for a while. You don't have to talk; you can just listen."

She nods.

"Welcome," the guy says.

"Thanks."

The stories she hears are harrowing; one man talks about how he lit a crack pipe and ended up in the burn unit. A woman details living on the streets with her two cats. It's entirely heartbreaking. Meghan sits there thinking that she's an asshole for thinking she has problems. Her life is so different from these people's and that's on purpose. Maybe her mother sent her to boarding school to free her or to protect her from all of this. Meghan doesn't even remember how the idea of going away to school came up except that it seemed like her parents wanted the freedom to move around, to travel at will. It was around the time she went through puberty. She remembers her mother trying to have the "talk" with her and how excruciating it was. Maybe that was part of it; men were starting to look at her differently. She saw it; her mother saw it. Meghan thinks about this past week at school. The seniors had tea with the headmistress and the board of directors. The girls all wore twinsets, barrettes, and skirts, and had their hair combed back. Each girl was presented with a single strand of pearls—the school tradition. The girls joked behind her back that the headmistress was still wearing her hair in the same style as when she'd graduated from a similar school about fifty years earlier. Now Meghan's sitting in an AA/NA meeting, fingering the strand of pearls around her neck, thinking that maybe her mother doesn't really hate her. Maybe her mother wanted something for her that she didn't have for herself. Autonomy. Freedom. Maybe Charlotte wants Meghan to go into the world on her own terms, as an independent person not beholden to a marriage or a man.

The meeting ends, and even though she hasn't said a word, she feels better. Outside, it's cold. In the parking lot she spots a taxi with its light on. She goes to the driver's window.

"Are you available?"

"Were you just in the meeting?"

She doesn't answer.

"Where are you going?"

She tells him the address.

"I can take you," he says. "No problem."

She gets into the car; the vinyl seat is cold, which makes her realize that he was also in the meeting. He's blasting the heat; the car warms up fast, and he's got nice classical music playing on the radio. He puts on his indicator light, makes a right turn out of the parking lot, and all seems good. She's so spaced-out, looking at the city at night, the flickering lights along the way, that they're halfway home before she notices he didn't put the meter on.

"The meter?" she asks.

"I can't charge you."

"Yes, you can."

"Really, I can't. It's just my thing. I'll drive anyone to or from a meeting."

"That's very nice," she says. "But I can afford to pay you."

He shakes his head. "It's something I have to do. I can't make amends to everyone I hurt. I don't live near them now. So I do what I can for others. That's my way forward."

"But you have to make a living."

"I do," he says. "But not from taking people to and from meetings, that's like chasing ambulances."

"That's admirable."

"I wouldn't go there. I used to be a bartender; my drinking put me out of work. Then I was a drug dealer and that put me in jail. I like jobs that are self-directed and I like contact with the public. So this seemed like a good option. I own the car; I make my own hours." He pulls into the driveway. "Stay strong."

Meghan goes to the front door and realizes she doesn't have a key.

She presses the doorbell hard. Her father comes in his bathrobe, phone pressed to his ear.

"Well, look who's back," he says.

"Who are you talking to?" she asks, as she comes into the house. The Christmas lights glitter like a hypnotists' convention.

"Who do you think?"

"Mom?"

He shakes his head no.

"Tony?"

He nods. She takes the phone from her father and goes down the hall toward her room.

"I assume you know," she says.

"Know what?"

"Everything. The story of the nuclear family meltdown and all about me, everything I never knew about myself until tonight."

Tony does the verbal equivalent of nodding along in conversation. "Um-hum."

"Why didn't you tell me?" she asks, taking the phone into her room. "Why didn't you tell me that my mother isn't my mother?"

"It wasn't my job to tell you," Tony says.

"What do I do now?"

"You probably don't want to hear it, but perhaps you should give your parents some credit. They have been dealing with some big stuff for a long time, and it may not be pleasant but at least it's out there and now there's no mystery. All your dad wanted for you was the best. He and your mom have done everything to make sure you have every opportunity."

"At the moment, I'm busy being traumatized. I find out that I'm replacing a dead kid and my identity changed without warning—and you're telling me that Mom and Dad always wanted the best for me? It does not compute."

"What are you looking for, pumpkin?"

"A simple 'I'm sorry' or 'that sucks.'"

"I am sorry," Tony says.

"Thanks. On top of everything, you know what really sucks?"

"What?"

"That I didn't know who Condoleezza Rice was."

Tony laughs.

"I should have recognized her. And it sucks that my parents didn't trust me with the truth. Only because Mom is having an actual breakdown did they decide to tell me."

"I don't think it was about trust."

"Well, there's no other excuse," Meghan says.

"Shame is a powerful thing," Tony says.

Wednesday, December 24, 2008
Palm Springs, California
10:00 a.m.

On the morning of Christmas Eve, Charlotte calls the Big Guy. "Let's make a deal."

"What kind of a deal?"

"I'll come home for Christmas if you buy me a car."

"We have a car."

"I want you to buy a car for a friend of mine."

"What friend?"

"My roommate from Betty Ford; she's moved over to the sober house now and I'd like to buy her a car. If we have a car, we can go places."

"You can go places in our car."

"She loves to drive," Charlotte says. "It would be a nice gesture. A celebration of her sobriety."

"Can't she buy herself a car?"

"If she uses her family's money, it comes with strings attached. This is about independence, giving something that has no strings attached. That's why I'm asking you."

"I'm sure you already know this," he says. "You can just write a check. There is plenty of money in your name."

"I don't want to use that money. I want you to do it for me."

"Fine," he says. "I assume you have a car in mind. A Ford? A Chevy?"

"I have my eye on something. It's at the Mercedes dealer. There are two. I can't make up my mind. The 190SL seems small. Maybe the 220SE. I like the cream but there's also a red one—red is a great color for a car."

"Hell of a nice gift," he says. A Mercedes is triple the cost of a Ford. Clearly this isn't just for transportation; there's an element of style in the mix. "You drove them both?"

"I did."

"Did you go with your friend?"

There's a long pause. "I didn't tell her that I was looking for her. I made it seem like it was for someone else."

"Like who?"

"You. I told her that I felt bad for all I'd put you through and that I wanted to get you a sporty little gift as a kind of reparation."

He laughs. "Well, how do you want to do it? Want me to go over there with the two of you and square it away?"

"You and I should do it," Charlotte says. "And then I'll give it to her tomorrow on Christmas Day."

"Fine. I don't know how easy it is to buy a car for someone. Does she have a driver's license? Is she insurable? No DWIs or other arrests? You can't drive it without insurance."

"Her last car was a Harley-Davidson. And I don't feel comfortable riding around on that, so I want to get the car. I have a copy of her license and Social Security number, and if need be, we can put my name on it too."

"Fine thing."

"I just want to give her this. A gift outright. Like the Robert Frost poem. I'm going to write the poem out and leave it on the front seat."

"Sounds like you've given it a lot of thought."

"I want to be clear," Charlotte says. "This is what they call pay for play; I'm not coming home in the way that you want me to come home."

"I understand. Are you spending the night?" he asks, phone still tucked under his chin. At this moment he has some leverage.

"Yes."

"Where are you sleeping?"

"On my side of the bed."

"And where am I sleeping?" he asks.

"It's not like I wanted to hurt anyone, I hope you know that," Charlotte says. "I feel terrible about all of it. It's the most awful thing I've ever had to do, and I'm sure now she thinks I am against her or that I have no feeling for her and that's not true. What's true is that we don't really know each other. Hopefully over time we will form a new relationship. She's the only child I have, and despite everything, I have tried hard to be a good mother."

"You have been a wonderful mother."

She says nothing.

"A fine mother," he says.

"At least now it all makes sense," Charlotte says.

He looks out the window; Meghan is in the pool swimming determined laps back and forth down the middle of the pool.

When he's off the phone, the Big Guy calls Godzich, and tells him about the car. Godzich says he'll call the dealer and get things going. Then the Big Guy says, "On a more personal note, I need the contact information for my old friend Irene."

There's a silence.

"Irene, from the dentist's office."

"I'll locate that and call you back," Godzich says.

Five minutes later Godzich calls. "I have an address and a phone number."

"Just the phone, thanks."

"I have some personal details if that's helpful."

"Like what?"

"Additional information."

"Go ahead."

"She's married with children."

There's a pause.

"Good for her," the Big Guy says. "What's the number?" Godzich gives him the number. The Big Guy writes it on an index card and slips it into his back pocket.

Meghan is still in the pool. She has been swimming laps for hours, as though the motion will help her process things. She's swimming, always swimming. The water is her think tank. She is swimming under; she is swimming through. She is swimming laps and thinking of Charlotte. She is thinking of Charlotte and of all the ways she tries to be like Charlotte.

Meghan has been replaying the meeting she went to last night. As much as Charlotte was not a warm, cuddly parent, she tried very hard. Charlotte was always teaching Meghan something. Meghan had no sense that Charlotte was withholding—she just thought that's who Charlotte was and that this was as much affection as one got from her.

Theirs was a life lived by rules. Charlotte believed that manners were a path through anything. Charlotte told her that etiquette was helpful because it was a guidepost you could turn to when you didn't know what to say or what to do. There would be those moments, times when one is at a loss; that's just the way life is. Things would take you by surprise. Be prepared.

Meghan is swimming and remembering things she and Charlotte did—long horseback rides at the ranch, mother and daughter spa adventures, Charlotte taking her for a mani-pedi and Meghan feeling so grown-up. The two of them bought matching purses, or dresses and shoes; these things meant to her that they were attached, they had something in common. She is thinking of Charlotte and the Girl Scouts—her mother was a Brownie briefly and got her into it, selling cookies, hosting meetings when she was younger and they lived in Connecticut.

Those were times Meghan felt that her mother was giving her useful lessons in how to be a woman.

Charlotte often reminded Meghan to pay attention to the outside world; the life cycle of the natural world is a source of comfort and regularity.

Meghan is thinking of Charlotte and plants. She was always planting something, always tending to something, an African violet or an orchid. She was in conversation with plants. At the ranch there was a shelf in the pantry where Charlotte's dormant orchids rested. Multiple pots of orchids with labels indicating when they last bloomed. When she was not at the ranch, one of the people who worked there managed them for her. There was nothing she liked less than people failing to care for the plants. The plants were like children, dependent on humans for survival. "It's our minimal duty to water them, to give them the key ingredients of life," Charlotte had been known to say.

Was Charlotte always like that or was that something that came after the baby? If she couldn't keep her own child alive, could she keep an orchid alive? Remembering that her mother's absolute pleasure and actual tears when an orchid rebloomed seemed odd at the time, Meghan now realizes that her mother's disproportionately large emotion for a plant made sense.

As she is swimming, Meghan is thinking of Charlotte and nature. She is thinking of Charlotte on the ranch, riding, her love of horses. Her affection for the barn cat. One day they went to see the horses, and the cat had clearly been in a fight and its eye was a mess. Her mother quickly picked up the cat, brought it inside, and cleaned the wound. The cat lost sight in the eye but survived without any infection and seemed eternally grateful. For however strict and rule-bound she was, Charlotte didn't tolerate neglect.

Meghan is thinking of Charlotte and the drinking. When did it begin? Was it just a simple thing, a social tool that got out of hand? When did it turn into a problem? Did she ever try to stop drinking before? Why now? Was it really because John McCain lost? Meghan doesn't have a sense of what's behind it. Her parents do a good job of keeping everything hidden.

Meghan is thinking about the meeting, about the stories she heard, about her emotions that she's finding hard to locate. She can't be angry with Charlotte; how can you be angry with someone who is suffering? She can't be angry with Charlotte because it will just make things worse; it will drive Charlotte away when she needs to pull Charlotte close and treat her as an injured bird. If it seems heroic that she's not thinking about herself, it's not; it's easier to focus on what she can do for others.

When Meghan comes in from the pool, she asks her father, "Did you call yet?"

"No."

"Are you going to?"

"Yes."

"What's taking so long?"

"I don't know."

"You blew up my life. Mom needed to do it for her survival and you need to do this for me." Her bathing suit is dripping onto the terrazzo floor. The drops land with a soft splash.

"I'm aware."

He excuses himself and goes into his office. It was his bad behavior. Irene was young, warm, generous. In the end he couldn't do any of the things that a man should do: make the situation right, marry her. She was a religious girl—she wasn't going to have an abortion, so the next best thing was to bring the baby into his life. He told his lawyer to arrange it. He told Charlotte that he'd heard through the grapevine of a young woman in a bad situation. He didn't mention that the situation was of his own making. He left out the key detail, but Charlotte found out. The day they went to sign the papers, it became clear, and Charlotte, to her credit, didn't flinch. She could have said no. She could have backed out of the deal; instead, she became steely quiet and signed on the dotted line.

At the time he admired her for her "strength." That's how he expressed it to Tony all those years ago. "The woman has extraordinary strength." In retrospect, he's not sure that was the right word.

He pulls the index card out of his back pocket and dials. The phone rings four times—a machine answers. He immediately hangs up and hopes they don't have caller ID.

"No answer," he tells Meghan. "I'll try again in a little while."

"What does she look like? Do you have any pictures?" Meghan asks. The Big Guy seems so shocked by the question that you'd think she was talking about pornography.

"No," he says. It never occurred to him that he would have a picture of her. He has a file on her somewhere. He distinctly remembers it as something he didn't keep in the vault—a manila folder marked Irene with a copy of the birth certificate. The birth certificate doesn't have his name on it; they talked about that ahead of time. There are records confirming that money was sent to Irene and there's a letter from the lawyer. He made every effort to keep things as clean as possible, transactional. When he thinks about it now, he wonders if the word transactional might be a synonym for asshole. When he was seeing her, he often sent flowers. He would call the florist and tell the woman what the card should say. He gave her some gifts, a nice pearl bracelet and a few other things. He was grateful for her, but the relationship wasn't as long or momentous as you might think. It wasn't a courtship; it wasn't a love affair; it was grief counseling.

"What color are her eyes?"

"Brown, I think." He pauses. "She had a nice smile; she worked for the dentist. Her hair was like yours, full and wavy."

"More details, please," Meghan says.

"She was pretty and very nice." Everything he says sounds bland, generic. Why doesn't he have more to say?

"Try calling again," Meghan says about an hour later.

"Right." He gets up to leave the room.

"You can't do it in front of me?"

"No, I can't."

"I don't trust you," Meghan says.

"Too bad." He walks away. He's clearly uncomfortable as well.

"Are you really calling her?"

"Of course I'm calling her. Who else would I be calling?"

"What are you going to say?"

"No idea. I'll have to improvise."

This time he remembers to block his caller ID. The phone rings twice before a young voice answers. When he asks for Irene, the voice shouts, "Mom, it's for you."

"Hello?"

What does he say? "You know what they say about Christmas surprises . . ."

"May I ask who's calling?"

"Oh, sorry, it's me," he says. Does she even recognize his voice? He could have had Godzich call first, but there are some things you have to do for yourself. "It's me. Your old friend. I'm sorry to intrude but . . ."

She makes an audible sound of surprise, distress.

"I didn't mean to scare you," he says. "It's been a long time."

"Yes," she says. "Very. Oh, wow." He can hear her moving around, her hand over the receiver. "Carolina, watch your brother." He hears doors opening and her going into another room.

"I wasn't expecting to hear from you," she says. "You okay?"

"I'm fine."

"You're not sick? I've had a few of those lately, a friend with breast cancer . . ." She babbles on for a bit then stops.

"I'm sorry," he says. "I'm fine. Healthy as a horse." He laughs.

"It's not funny."

"Of course it's not."

There's a pause.

"I'm calling about the girl." He pauses. "The cat's out of the bag and we need to talk." Another long pause. "Charlotte told Meghan that she's not her natural child. Meghan has questions; she wants to meet you. She's a lovely kid, first-rate, smart, beautiful, good at school, never a day of trouble. We're very proud of her. She's a senior in high school now."

"I don't know if I can."

He says nothing. Sometimes it's better to say nothing.

"Of all the days to call," she says.

"It wasn't my first choice. She's on school break."

"We're leaving in the morning for Disney World."

"Nice," he says. "The Magic Kingdom. When are you back?"

"New Year's Eve."

"I think you'll like her."

There's another long silence.

"New Year's Day?" he says.

"I'll meet you in the morning. My husband sleeps late."

"We knew this moment would come."

She says nothing. She is busy packing bags for Christmas at Disney World.

"I'm sorry it's awkward," he says.

He could have not called. He could have hemmed and hawed and stalled for time. He could have just given her number to Meghan and left her to do it herself.

"Thank you for calling," she says. And she means it.

When he opens the door, Meghan is sitting on the floor. "New Year's Day. We'll meet her then."

"Was she excited?"

"Very," he says, hoping that in this instance excited can stand in for shocked and caught off guard.

"The way you pitched me sounds like I'm for sale—good-natured, never gave you a day of trouble."

"What?"

"I was listening at the door. The words you used sounded like a sales pitch. Are you trying to give me back to her?" Meghan starts to cry.

"Sweetie, that's not what I was saying. I just wanted her to know how proud we are and how much we love you. We're not selling you or giving you back; I'm just trying to take care of things, doing the best I can."

"It's gross," Meghan says.

He hugs her. Her damp swimsuit presses against him, leaving an outline of a crying girl on the old man.

"She's going to Disney World tomorrow," he says. "That's why it has to wait."

"We've been to Disney World. Remember how much Mom hated everything except the scariest roller coaster?"

"Yes," he says. "Between you and me, I never understood that—but some things are best left a mystery."

There is a long pause.

"Mom is coming home."

"Is she staying?"

"Yes, she'll be with us overnight; that's all she can do for now. And Tony is coming this afternoon. Should we go out for dinner? Melvyn's? Steak Diane and onion rings?"

Meghan shakes her head. "I'll make dinner. I just want to be home with everyone. And later we can go to church."

"Okay. We'll go to Midnight Mass. I'm sure there's a church out here somewhere. Meanwhile, I'm going to take your mother into town." Every time he says it—the word mother—he feels uncomfortable. Is that the right word, mother? Is he supposed to call her Charlotte now? He can't do it. As far as he is concerned, she is Mother. "We have some errands to run. Last-minute stuff."

"I'll go with you," Meghan says. "You can drop me at the grocery store."

She starts a list: chicken, carrots, potatoes, biscuits, pie. She's evidently spent too much time in the South.

Wednesday, December 24, 2008
Palm Springs, California
2:20 p.m.

Charlotte arrives just after lunch in a surprisingly good mood. He has no idea why and doesn't want to question it. Neither he nor Meghan mentions the phone call or the New Year's Day plan.

"Shall we?" Charlotte says, indicating that she's keen to get to the dealership. She's got a twinkle in her eye that he's not seen in years.

"Yes," he says. "They're expecting us."

The Big Guy can't remember the last time he was at a car dealership—maybe twenty years ago? As soon as they are through the doors, a salesman descends like a vulture. "Is there something I can help you with?" The Big Guy pulls an index card from his back pocket; "Ask for Keith," it says. When he says Keith's name, he's saved from the first vulture by another more sophisticated vulture.

"I've been expecting you," Keith says, shaking the Big Guy's hand as if they already had a done deal.

"Thank god." There's nothing the Big Guy likes less than to walk into a place and have to make himself known. He likes people to be waiting for him: doctor, dentist, accountant, whoever. He can't bear the stress of standing there like an idiot. It occurs to him that maybe not everyone feels like an idiot, but he does. He always thinks that if he was a movie star they'd recognize him, but just being wealthy is not enough. That's why some wealthy people show it off, like an indicator system—notice me, pay attention, see how many thousands of dollars I am wearing in watches, belts, shoes, purses. He finds that kind of display to be grotesque. He's old-school. For men like the Big Guy, wealth is protection; it quells the anxiety of not having enough and the fear of not being in control.

Whatever else is happening, he doesn't want to find himself in the showroom of a Palm Springs car dealer with a giant Sucker sign on his forehead while an old-school used-car salesman, gunning for a bigger end-of-year bonus, tries to sell him a piece of shit that's been sitting on the floor for six months.

"Your assistant mentioned that you're interested in two cars in particular. We also have a few others that you might not have seen. Do you want to take a look or do you just want to focus on the two?"

"What else have you got?" Charlotte asks. "I'm always curious."

He takes her to a large computer monitor and clicks through some pictures.

"We need it today," Charlotte says. "Wrapped and ready. It's a gift."

"I understand," Keith says. "I've done as much of the paperwork as possible in advance. Your assistant, Mr. Godsend, was very helpful."

Keith doesn't realize that he's botched the pronunciation of Godzich. Neither the Big Guy nor Charlotte says anything—but the Big Guy sees a thin smile cross Charlotte's lips.

"Do we want to drive them?" the Big Guy asks. "I thought that was the point."

"They're both ready to go," Keith says.

"Up to you," Charlotte says.

"We'll drive them," the Big Guy says.

"They're convertibles so I've got the tops down. It's a bit chilly but you can put the heat on," Keith says.

"Perfect," Charlotte says. "I brought a scarf."

They get into the red 220SE first and the Big Guy pulls herky-jerky out of the parking lot. They drive around Rancho Mirage. He's tempted to circle around Betty Ford and tell Charlotte how many times he drove by while she was there, how he called her on Thanksgiving but they wouldn't put the call through. He's tempted to tell her everything but worries she'll take it the wrong way—not as evidence that he cares deeply about her but as proof of his inability to understand that she has needs of her own and that he couldn't even give her the space to go to rehab without him.

As they drive around, he feels a kind of excitement building. They take the red 220SE in and take out the cream-colored 190SL. It's a beautiful machine, classic, elegant, inspiring. As they're tooling around the area, there's an unexpected and disconcerting energy between them. He's loath to name it for fear that this would be going too far, although the words lust and exhilaration occur to him. He pushes those away and settles on enchantment or charm and optimism. The December desert breeze is skipping through the car; the heater is blowing clouds of hot air while the radio plays classic tunes. The sensation is like a meteorological phenomenon, a unique weather front of cold over hot. If he was to go out on a limb, he would say that it's like they're young again and on an adventure.

"I'm not sure it's my job to remind you," the Big Guy says. "But in case you forgot, I will. I hope that you know that you can have whatever you want; you don't need permission. I mean it quite literally, whatever you want, whatever you need."

"It's a fiction," she says, tightening her scarf. "Not possible."

"Why not?"

"I'd need a time machine."

There's a silence.

"What I need is a new life," she says. "A life I've made for myself."

Then another long silence.

"All I can do now is start from here. That's what I learned in rehab. There is no going back."

"That's all any of us can do," he says. "From here forward."

They drive a little longer.

"What do you think you'll choose?" he asks. She looks at him blankly. "Which one is for you?" She still seems discombobulated, as though the question were too big, as though it carries the weight of the world. "Cars," he says. "I'm talking about cars. Which one do you like best?"

"Oh," she says, relieved.

There's another long silence.

"We have been through a lot," he says.

"We have."

"We will always have that."

"What?"

"The lot."

Back at the dealership, they defer to Keith when it comes to deciding which car to get. Keith says that despite the red being the "zingier" of the two, the cream is a better car and will hold more value over time.

"I'm all for value over time," the Big Guy says, searching for a punch line. The road test has been an emotional roller coaster.

"I'm going to have the mechanic give it a good going-over," Keith says. "How about we deliver it to you at the end of the day?"

"Done," the Big Guy says. "Godzich will give you any additional information you need." He scrawls his name on the dotted line. "It's a hell of a Christmas present," he says to Charlotte. "I hope this Trixie is a good friend."

"Terrie," Charlotte says. "And thank you. It means a lot to me. A vote of confidence."

They pick Meghan up at the supermarket; she's standing outside with bags and bags of food. On the way home, they stop at the health food store. Charlotte wants to introduce them to a date shake that she discovered in rehab.

"We went on field trips," Charlotte tells them. "We tried all the date shakes. This one was my favorite—they use crystallized dates."

The Big Guy can't remember the last time Charlotte wanted to consume anything other than vodka. He sucks on his straw. "It's like a milkshake."

"Yes," Charlotte says. "Only it's vegan. This one is all about the dates, which are a good source of potassium."

"I bet we could make them at home too," Meghan says.

"For me," Charlotte says, "it's all about getting out."

In the afternoon, the house is filled with holiday music and the rich woodsy scent of the Rigaud candle. Meghan is holed up in the kitchen preparing her feast. Tony arrives in the late afternoon, and he and Charlotte immediately go out to the pool.

If one didn't know any better, one might think all was as it should be, as it always has been. There is a lightness to the mood; is it relief or delusion? Can one drop a bomb of the magnitude they did yesterday and carry on as if nothing has changed? Does the Christmas spirit trump all else?

The Big Guy can't help but wonder if maybe he's too literal-minded, too much like a Labrador. That's what Charlotte used to call him—her dog.

With all the others taken care of, the Big Guy retreats to his office and starts making plans. He's on the phone with Godzich about flying to DC on the twenty-sixth and needing hotel arrangements for him and Meghan; he'll keep her close until she goes back to school just after the new year. There are some invitations to deal with, dinners in advance of the inauguration, meetings that have been requested.

And he has a few plans of his own that need to be put into motion.

The holiday scent expands to include the delicious hints of the Christmas dinner to come: roasting chicken, bread baking. He goes into the kitchen to take a look. "It's impressive. How do you know how to do all this?"

"I cheated," Meghan says. "I bought almost everything already cooked. I'm just assembling."

"Call it what you will. To me, it looks like you know what you're doing."

"We cook a lot in the dorm, mostly baking. The old dorm head, Miss McCutcheon, felt it was her duty to teach us how to prepare simple meals; she said the tradition dated back to the idea of girls' schools as finishing schools, which prepare young women for the demands of marriage. 'A roast chicken is the most basic; it's humble, yet classic. You can serve a well-cooked chicken to your husband or your husband's boss. It's not up-pity like a roast and can't be construed as sucking up. Garlic. Garlic under the skin and lemon in the cavity.'"

"Sounds like you picked up a thing or two."

"Yes," she said. "You know it's only in recent years that they have higher-level math for us. Used to be the girls all took a course in business math, which was code for balancing the family checkbook. But now we go through calculus and trigonometry. I can't tell if they think we might become mathematicians or just need to help our children with their homework."

"I don't suppose that's what you want."

"To be a mathematician? Definitely not. I want to do something sub-stantial."

"Like what?"

"I'm not sure, maybe be a colonel."

A colonel. That wipes him off his feet. An audible crack and sputtering sound pop out. He pretends he's coughing on an almond. "It's quite a big job. A lot of responsibility."

"I'm not afraid of responsibility," she says.

"Have there been any women colonels?"

"I don't know. But there will be. I don't want to just be someone's wife. No offense, but I can't think of anything worse."

"Yeah," he says. "It seems to be a problem."

Charlotte and Tony are in the pool playing catch with some kind of inflatable beach ball that someone must have left at the house or that blew across the golf course from another house. It's got the logo of a local real estate venture; did they do an air drop of beach balls?

He doesn't think he's ever seen Charlotte playing like that; she's jump-ing up and down in the water, throwing the ball back and forth.

He raps his knuckles on the glass. "Are you stoned?"

She hears the sound, looks over, and shrugs. Can she even hear him through the glass?

He goes back to his office and a little while later looks out and sees Charlotte and Tony sitting on the lounge chairs under multiple heavy towels, unmistakably passing a joint back and forth.

He nearly rips the handle off the sliding glass door as he whips it open. "You cannot do that. That cannot happen here. I don't want to get a letter from the homeowners' association informing me that you've been seen smoking dope just off the ninth hole. Take it somewhere else."

"Can we come inside?" Charlotte asks.

"Go in the garage."

"It's cold in the garage and there's no light," she says, as though she's explored the idea.

Charlotte and Tony get out of the chairs and come inside. The Big Guy looks at Charlotte in disbelief as if to say, I thought we were having a nice day.

"I'm sorry," she says. "This is too much for me. It's very difficult for me to stay present."

"Fine. But you can't do that in full view of the rest of the world. Go down in my war room if you must."

They roll their eyes at him.

"Really," he says to Tony. "Are you a pothead too?"

"I was doing it to be companionable," Tony whispers.

"Are you going to say that you didn't inhale?"

"Sometimes, in order to get people to open up, you have to give a little something."

The Big Guy shakes his head and goes back into the kitchen.

"What was that all about?" Meghan asks.

"I wish I knew."

"Did Mom and Tony just go somewhere to get high?"

He doesn't say anything.

"I guess it's just us," she says. "Do I put this in my diary?"

Again he says nothing.

There's a shout from the war room.

"What exactly goes on down here?" Charlotte calls out. "It looks like you had some kind of party where you were the only guest."

"I had a big battle on Thanksgiving and I don't want the cleaning lady messing it up."

"What's the orange stuff?" Tony wants to know.

"Jell-O," he says, "masquerading as Agent Orange."

"Well, there are mouse turds in the Jell-O."

"Maybe they're not mouse turds," the Big Guy says. "Maybe they're unexploded ordnance or hand grenades. Don't mess up my scenes."

"It's not exactly historically accurate," Tony says.

"Open to interpretation," the Big Guy says. "But it's my idea of fun."

While Charlotte and Tony are in the basement, the Big Guy sits in the kitchen with Meghan.

"You're very tolerant of them," Meghan says.

"What choice do I have?"

"You could just say no pot smoking in my house. That wouldn't be unreasonable."

"It's your mother's house too."

"She just got out of rehab. She's actually not even really out; she's in a halfway house. I'm sure they have rules."

"There's one thing I've learned over many, many years."

"What?"

"Sometimes it's better to do less. When you're a person who has a lot of power, unless you have a very specific and profound point to make, it's better to steer the ship with a light touch. Persons in power don't realize how much weight their voices carry."

"Be more specific."

"Today isn't the moment for me to assert my will, my rules, or my desires over your mother or Tony. We should just be glad we're all together. You are home; your mom is home; and Tony is here." The Big Guy looks off into the distance. "I hope this isn't telling tales out of school—I'm going to tell you something to illustrate that many people you know and admire have had lives that are more complex and challenging than you might realize."

"Okay," Meghan says.

"Has Tony ever talked to you about his family?"

"Maybe a little bit about his grandfather's farm down South and how he liked to spend summers there."

"Tony's father was a drinker, very measured and buttoned-up until he got drunk. Then all bets were off. He used to beat the crap out of Tony and call him a sissy. It was a pretty shitty childhood. One time, while they were all visiting the grandparents' farm for the holidays, Tony's father drove his car right through his parents' house in a drunken rage. He had a 1955 burgundy-colored Chrysler Imperial, and as he came down the driveway, he just gunned it, stepped down on the gas, and went barreling into the house right through the kitchen, then he claimed the brakes had failed. As Tony used to tell it: 'Luckily, the good china was already on the table and the turkey was cooked.' Tony's grandmother, a true ole Southern girl, tried to make things seem okay. It's a Southern habit to try to make shit smell like roses if one can. When her son climbed out of the wreckage, she reportedly said, 'Why, thank you. You did for me in one minute what I couldn't do for myself in forty years. I always wanted a new kitchen.' Tony's father could do no wrong in his mother's eyes and maybe that was part of the problem. 'He tried to kill us and you're thanking him,' young Tony reportedly said. 'Always a prankster,' his grandmother said. 'If he wanted to kill us, he would have driven through the back. He knows we're never far from the back of the house.' The accident did, however, leave a nasty wound and a scar on Mrs. Washington's leg."

"Who was Mrs. Washington?"

"Their housekeeper."

"Did she quit working for them?"

"The police and the insurance adjuster came out to the house—after supper, because they didn't want to disturb anyone. Tony sulked all through dinner and refused to have pie until the doctor was called to attend to Mrs. Washington's leg."

"But did she quit? That counts as abuse."

"She was taken care of, as they say. Good insurance. Tony's grandmother got the kitchen she always wanted, and everyone else just shook their heads in disbelief. What I'm trying to tell you is that Tony is a complex person who has taught himself to keep what is most valuable to him hidden and to adjust, to pivot as needed, in order to get by."

"That's certainly one version of it," Tony says, coming into the kitchen. "After the holiday drive-through, as we called it, my mother didn't leave me alone with him. She was frightened for my well-being. My father liked to say, 'Give me a weekend with the boy and I'll make him a man.' That's when Mother and I started planning my escape to boarding school, which wasn't exactly cushy, but there were times at home that I thought he might accidentally on purpose kill me."

"I'm sorry," Meghan says. "That sounds awful."

"It wasn't all bad, because the first person I met at school was your dad. And look at me now." They all laugh.

"Chicken smells good," Charlotte says.

"It's almost ready."

Wednesday, December 24, 2008
Palm Springs, California
4:30 p.m.

The sun sinks behind the San Jacinto Mountains and the house grows dark. Tony turns on the Christmas tree lights and cranks up the music, and they all dance. Anyone looking in through the large glass windows would see a beautiful winter paradise with a middle-aged woman twirling her daughter with her hand, and an old fart and his dandy best friend doing the same. Then they change partners, and Charlotte and the Big Guy do a strange kind of tango while Tony and Meghan dance. They switch again, and it's the Big Guy and his daughter, and he is prouder of her tonight than he has ever been. She has risen to the occasion, proving herself to be an incredible young woman. As they are dancing, he tears up, wishing he could have offered her better and more. He wishes he could rewrite history, but absent that power, he is all the more determined to create a new history, a new road forward. He commits to hauling the past, as if it were Santa's enormous Christmas bag, through the mud, the snow, the rain, the shit, and the hell that's before them so he can deposit it and her firmly in the future before he dies.

"How stoned are you?" he asks Charlotte.

"Very," she says. "It's nice. You might want to try it."

"I'd like to, but not today. Someone needs to remain on deck."

"You're the night watchman."

"I'm the dog," he says.

"Did Mom always love to dance?" Meghan asks her father.

"I'm not sure. But she can really cut the rug."

As they're about to sit down to supper, the doorbell rings, scaring the crap out of everyone.

"Is it the car?" Charlotte asks.

"What car?" Meghan wants to know. "Did you get me a car?"

The Big Guy peeks outside before opening the door. "It's not the car; it's FedEx. My heart is pounding; I could just see the headlines: 'Desert Drug Den Discovered at Prominent Republican Donor Vacation Home.'"

He opens the door and signs for the package. "From our friend in Winnetka, of all places."

"Open it," Tony says.

"I don't know," the Big Guy says, laughing. "I'm a little bit afraid, still not sure how well that meeting went." He rips the box open. It's a bottle of murky liquid that looks like swamp water sealed with wax and resting in a clear plastic vitrine as if it were a little coffin of Christmas cheer. A handwritten note is attached: "Special Edition Holiday Ball Water— Sativa with clove and cinnamon."

"I guess I can't have any," Charlotte says.

"No, you cannot," Meghan says, and it comes out sounding very strict.

They sit down to dinner. Meghan has created a feast worthy of a photo shoot. Not only did she pull off something truly spectacular, but she made it look effortless.

"I wondered what those things were," the Big Guy says, twirling his reindeer antler napkin ring.

"I made them myself," Meghan says. "Out of things I found around the house."

"It's a beautiful table and a beautiful meal. Look at you. Look at all you did," Tony says.

Meghan blushes.

"This is so good," Charlotte says. "It may be the best chicken I ever had. I will say this, while I was in rehab and now at the sober house, I try not to be a snob, but the food is bad. Godawful, really."

"In what way?" Meghan asks.

"It's not made for humans to eat. The ingredients come out of giant industrial jars marked Heavy Mayonnaise or Extra Thick and so on. My friend told me that industrial food is allowed to have more insects and foreign debris per jar than the food we buy."

"Is that really true?" Meghan asks.

"That's what she says. And she should know. She's been through rehab a number of times and even briefly went to prison once."

"Wow," Meghan says.

"Do you want to know what it was really like?" Charlotte asks.

"Yes," Meghan says.

"I don't know that this kind of talk is right for a child," the Big Guy says.

"I want to hear."

"Thank you," Charlotte says, bowing toward Meghan. "Well, I didn't even remember arriving there. For days I had no idea where I was; I thought I was still on my cleanse and that something had happened and they'd moved me to a local hospital where the people were nice but a bit touchy-feely. I kept waking up thinking there was someone else in my room. At first, I thought it was a private-duty nurse, then one night I woke up thinking it was a man who meant me harm. And I screamed—or I thought I did. One time I thought it was someone like a candy striper who was offering me apple juice. Then I came to know this figure as someone who would dance around the room naked except for white nylon underwear. In the middle of the night, arms over her head, she danced while listening to a Sony Walkman with big padded headphones. Like this." Charlotte gets up and demonstrates. "She pumped the air over her head; her body lean, tan, not shaped in a traditional female form. Her granny underwear went halfway up her body, and her small low breasts with deep-brown nipples were slightly swaying along to the music."

"It's too much," the Big Guy says. "Stop."

"Keep going," Meghan says.

"Every night the woman would dance around the room, her feet softly sweeping the linoleum floor, dancing like she'd once taken a ballroom dancing class, dancing like she had a beat of her own. It looked like she was all alone at a disco party for the deaf—because of the headphones—or like she was in some kind of 1960s experimental film or an avant-garde show. No noise except for her bare feet gliding over the linoleum floor. All of it was a little like being stuck in a dream state or a hallucination. As I started to be able to keep track of time, I saw that she was just one person. She was the midnight dancer in the dark, and in the daylight, she was a man in a plaid flannel shirt, worn jeans, and cowboy boots. I would see her go outside and smoke in the area where cigarettes were allowed. For the longest time I didn't know exactly who or what she was. I thought she worked there and that her job was to clean the rooms with a giant floor duster. Then we got into a fight."

"What kind of a fight?" Meghan wants to know.

"One night I woke up and she was standing there, and I said, 'This is my room.' 'I don't think so,' she said. 'I'm quite sure that wherever I am my husband paid for me to have a private room,' I said, and she laughed like that was big-time funny. 'In the world of drunks and drug addicts, there are no private rooms,' she said. I didn't speak to her for days. Finally, she said, 'Aren't you ever going to talk to me? We have something in common.' 'Like what?' 'A problem.' 'I don't see that there's a problem,' I said. 'Don't shut me down,' the woman said. 'Well, I've been married for twenty-five years; I'm good at not seeing things. How do you think I ended up here?' 'So, why don't you fill me in?' she said. We got to talking and it turned out that we did have any number of things in common."

While Charlotte tells her story, the Big Guy eats biscuits. He eats the biscuits so intensely it's as if he were trying to suffocate himself or silence Charlotte by stuffing himself. Bite after bite, he's pushing bread into his craw while she's talking. Meanwhile, as she's telling the story, Charlotte is picking at the chicken carcass. By the time she's finished, the bird has been plucked clean and the meat divided into two piles on the cutting board, light and dark.

"You could make soup out of the bones," Charlotte suggests.

"We're leaving soon," Meghan says.

"Where are we going?" Charlotte asks.

"Church, then Washington," Meghan and the Big Guy say simultaneously.

"I'm exhausted," Charlotte says. "Maybe bed."

"Church," Meghan insists.

"What time is it now?"

"Nine thirty," Tony says, getting up from the table and starting to clear the dishes. "I ate too much."

"I definitely can't stay up for Midnight Mass," Charlotte says.

"Let's go to the early show," Meghan says. "That one has better songs and the children's pageant."

As they're leaving the house, Keith from the car dealership is in the driveway trying to stealthily attach a massive red ribbon to the top of the new car.

"Did you get me a car?" Meghan asks.

"No," Charlotte says.

"Do you need a car?" the Big Guy asks.

Meghan shrugs. "In the future I'll need a car."

"Well, this is a car from the past," Charlotte says. "And it's for a friend of mine. When it's your time, we'll get you a car for the future."

That seems to appease Meghan.

They pass several churches. Our Lady of Solitude. The Living Water Church of the Desert. They don't know what to do, so the Big Guy drives around for a bit.

"What a strange, strange place," Tony says. "A beige sandy world punctuated with mounds of fluorescently green grass, outdoor candy canes, indoor ice sculptures, and—"

"Let's just go to whichever one comes up next," Meghan says.

"Amen," Charlotte says.

As they drive, they debate what's behind any and all the decorations they pass, including an enormous crèche with figures so tall they look as though they might have been carved from telephone poles.

Charlotte tells a story that none of them have heard before about being in a Christmas pageant as a young girl. "The Christmas play was called 'A Living Crèche' and I actually had to pick up the baby Jesus, who was not a doll but a real, warm, wet, wiggling four-month-old. It was terrifying. He was asleep in the wooden cradle until suddenly he wasn't. He was bleating, then full-throatedly wailing, and I didn't know if I was supposed to break character and pick him up even though it was earlier than the moment in the script. I looked to the choir director for a cue and got nothing. Then to the audience; all I could see were their expectant faces beaming back at me; they thought it was all too adorable. When I finally did pick him up, he was entirely soaked through with pee and I thought it was disgusting and I had to carry him just so—all the way down the main aisle and around the choirboys and the sheep. When we got backstage to the dressing area, Jesus's mother took him from me and whipped off his diaper—it may have been the first penis I ever saw—then after she changed him, she pulled out her tit and fed him. I'd never seen that either. Most traumatic Christmas ever." She laughs.

The Big Guy pulls into the parking lot of the Desert Oasis Chapel, a large tan building with the words "If anyone is thirsty, let him come to Me and drink," from John 7:37, written in foot-high Gideon Plexus font on the outside.

"I will give to the one who thirsts from the spring of the water of life without cost," Tony says, as they're walking into the building.

"What's that?"

"Another part of what's written on the outside," Charlotte says.

"Revelation 21:6," Tony says.

Meghan smiles.

Church is amazing. "Awesome" is the expression Meghan would use.

She is with her mother, father, and godfather, and they have their hymnals open and are holding white candles in little wax-catcher paper cups that look like ice cream cones. "Gloria in excelsis Deo! . . . And Heaven and nature sing . . . Repeat the sounding joy. Repeat the sounding joy."

Repeat the sounding joy. Is that even possible?

Early in the morning on the day after Christmas, Charlotte is picked up by someone from the sober house. Startled by the beeping horn, Charlotte hurriedly gathers her things. Before exiting, she slips into the room where Meghan is sleeping.

Charlotte brushes Meghan's hair off her face. "It was lovely to be with you," she whispers. "But I have to go back to my cage."

"Love you," Meghan mumbles. "Merry Christmas. You sing good."

And as she is falling back to sleep, Meghan wonders if Charlotte has to go back to her cage because she is safe there or because others are safe from Charlotte when she's there.

Her father wakes her at nine a.m. "Time to get the show on the road. Did Mom give you a kiss goodbye? She left very early."

"Yes," Meghan says.

"Fine thing," the Big Guy says.

Meghan packs her bags and her Christmas loot and a car takes her and Tony and her father to the airport. Leaving Palm Springs, she feels as though she were being escorted out of her childhood. Her father and Tony walk on either side of her, like security guards or fence posts. In the airport store, she looks for something to buy—a memento, a placeholder, a bookmark, a keeper of information. She finds a notebook embossed with the slogan of Palm Springs, "Give In to the Desert," and a cactus-shaped pencil.

As someone who is always thinking about what just happened, living her life in the rearview mirror, Meghan knows that her life will never be the same. While it may be true that every second is new, what happened to her family is a shock. She knows and then she forgets. Then she knows again. Each time she knows comes with a little jolt, a pang of deception and discovery.

Neither Tony nor her father is an airplane talker. They carry files for review, highlighters in different colors, and reading glasses of assorted magnifications. "Variations of fatigue," Tony calls his collection. "The first pair is a little tired, the second is deeply tired, and the third, exhausted and basically blind."

"I'll try 'a little tired,'" she says, and Tony hands the glasses to her. She tries reading a newspaper. The letters are nauseatingly blurry. "Not for me," she says, handing them back.

"They will be one day," he says. "It happens to everyone. You think it won't happen to you, but then you wake up on your fortieth birthday and the cards that come in the mail are a little harder to read."

"The only move is forward," she writes in her new notebook. She makes a chart of what she expects of herself: resilience, fortitude, homework done on time. "Mom has a good voice," Meghan writes. "She used to sing in a choir." She skips halfway down the page. "Turns out Mom is not really my mom. What does that mean, 'not really'? Dad says that despite not biologically being my mom, she is my mom. Not really. Not real. Real lie." Anxious about what she has written, she crosses out the whole paragraph.

I am not who I thought I am/was/am/would be. Where does that leave me?

Like a fugue, an extended hallucination, the fog of lost identity is a milky primal swirl of confusion and contradiction that settles in the center of her lungs. She breathes around it, breathes through it, but it remains, marking her like a scar.

Fibrosis—the thickening of connective tissue, usually as the result of an injury.

And because there are moments of disbelief, she writes—"Did this actually happen?"

Friday, December 26, 2008
The Hay-Adams Hotel
Washington, DC
11:45 p.m.

In Washington they drop Tony at his house and go to their hotel. When Meghan was younger, her parents had an apartment in the Watergate overlooking the Potomac River. She remembers getting dressed there for a party, her mother in a yellow silk dress, sleeveless, cut straight like a tube. Charlotte had short hair and was wearing something on top of her head, maybe jewelry or a tiara. She had high gloves to her elbows that matched the dress. A woman in a pink uniform came to babysit and brought Meghan a pink helium balloon. Meghan remembers playing balloon games with the babysitter after her parents left, and that the next morning, when she woke up, the balloon was on the floor by her bed. She cried because it wouldn't stay up in the air without the woman in the pink uniform. Until now, that was her idea of trauma. Meghan thinks it's weird how specific and vague a memory can be at the same time.

She is in a fancy hotel wishing she could return to school. She feels a sense of urgency; until she gets back to school, all of life is suspended, and if she doesn't go back soon, Meghan feels she won't be able to go back and that she'll never go to college and her life will not continue. Why? Because she doesn't know who or what to continue as—her sense of self is gone.

"Can I see my birth certificate?" she asks her father.

"I don't have it with me, but I can get it for you."

"Thank you."

He calls Godzich, who promises to fax a copy the next morning.

Saturday, December 27, 2008
The Hay–Adams Hotel
Washington, DC
9:30 a.m.

"It's a fake," Meghan says, when her father shows her birth certificate to her.

"No, it's not," he says. "This is a faxed photocopy. Godzich has the real one in a safe in the office. You can see that it is embossed with the seal from Washington, DC. You were born here just like it says."

"Anyone can make one of these. And it doesn't have her name."

"That's right."

"So it's a fake."

"No," he says. "When someone is adopted, they issue a new birth certificate."

"You said I wasn't adopted, that you were my father." Her voice escalates.

"I am your father, but Mom had to adopt you. When that happens, they make a new birth certificate and put away the old one."

"Where do they put the old one?"

"The state puts it under seal."

"Washington, DC, is not a state," she says.

"Whatever place you're born in puts it away and it can be released only by a judge under extraordinary circumstances."

"Does lying to someone count as extraordinary?"

"That's the way they do it," he says. "The idea was to protect the woman."

"What woman?"

"The woman who gave birth and the woman who adopted the baby."

"From what?"

"People finding out."

"So it's all like an accident that you have to cover up?"

He doesn't say anything.

"Why didn't she have an abortion?"

A long pause.

"She's Catholic."

"You would have liked it if she had an abortion?"

"That's not what I said." He's starting to get angry.

"You didn't say that you didn't want her to have an abortion. You didn't say you wanted me more than anything. You said she's Catholic. Catholicism doesn't allow abortions."

"I wanted you more than anything," he says. "But the choice was hers. I don't think a man should tell a woman what she should or shouldn't do."

"How forward thinking of you," Meghan says.

"Don't talk like that."

"You tell me I am or am not your child, and when I question you, you give me a look like you want to hit me." She pauses. "Did you ever hit Mom?"

"No. Of course not."

A moment passes.

"If a man shouldn't tell a woman what to do with her body, does that mean you're pro-abortion?"

"In what way?" he asks.

"Politically," she says.

"I support a woman's right to choose. I'm not sure that makes me pro-abortion."

The doorbell rings. They stop talking.

"Did you order something?" he asks her.

She shakes her head no.

The bell rings again, followed by a hard knock on the door.

The Big Guy walks down the hallway to the door. "Yes," he says through the door.

"Mr. Hitchens, it's Chris from the front desk, would you mind opening the door?"

The Big Guy looks through the peephole. Two men are standing in the hall.

He slides the chain off and opens the door.

"Would you mind stepping out for a moment?" Chris asks.

"What is this about?" the Big Guy asks.

"Dad?"

"May I have a word?" Chris says.

The Big Guy steps out into the hall and the other man slips into the room. Now Meghan is crying.

"I'm Eugene," the other man says. "From hotel security. Someone called and said they heard shouting."

Meghan looks embarrassed.

"Are you in danger?" Eugene asks. "Do you need help? Is the man you are with hurting you or keeping you here against your will?"

"No," she says, shaking her head. "No, no, no. He's my father. We were arguing about colleges." She sucks in her sniffles. "He wants me to go to a small girls' school like Bryn Mawr or Mount Holyoke and I want something different."

Eugene looks relieved. "The tears," he says.

She nods.

The Big Guy comes back into the room looking distressed. Nothing like this has ever happened to him. "My bad. The fact that it got as heated as it did tells me one thing." He looks straight at Meghan. "We are very much alike— the two of us, peas in a pod." He begins to tear up himself. "It is your life, your future. And it should be whatever you dream up for yourself, not my version of what should happen." He turns to the two men, pulling out his money clip. "I had no idea anyone could hear us." He peels off some cash.

When the two men leave, Meghan and the Big Guy are silent.

"Never in my life," he says.

"Did you mean what you said?" she asks.

"About what?"

"That my future should be what I want it to be."

"Yes," he says. "Of course."

"I've led a very sheltered life," she says.

"We tried to protect you."

"From the truth?"

"From life. From the pain."

Another pause.

"That was our first fight," she says.

"Was it?"

"My friends talk about fighting with their parents, but I never knew how."

"I'm sorry," he says.

"For what?"

"All of it."

Long pause.

"Will you buy me a car? A car like the one that was delivered on Christmas Eve for Mom's friend."

"No."

"Why not?"

"Because you are a child and children don't need vintage cars."

"Okay," she says.

Another long pause.

"Do you need a car?" he asks, concerned that he had dropped the ball, that he had failed to provide something.

"No. I don't even know how to drive."

He is clearly upset. "I'm going to take a walk. Will you be here when I return?"

"Yes," she says. "I have homework."

"Fine thing." He goes into the bathroom and returns with face washed and hair combed. "I'll be back shortly."

About twenty minutes later, the doorbell rings. Meghan is hesitant to answer. She goes to the door and looks through the peephole. There's a man with a rolling cart. He rings again while she is watching.

"Who's there?" she asks through the door.

"Room service," the man says.

"I didn't order anything."

"It was ordered for you. You can call the front desk if you have questions."

"I'm not supposed to open the door. Sorry."

"No problem. I can leave it here. Just call room service when you are done and we'll pick up the tray."

The man takes something out of an insulated box under the tablecloth and sets it down on the floor, a plate with a silver cover. She watches him wheel the cart down the hall. When he's almost out of view, she opens the door and picks up the plate. It's cold.

She brings it into the room, sets it down on the desk, and lifts the lid— voilà.

A banana split.

The doorbell rings again. She goes back. "Sorry to bother you. I forgot that there's a card that goes with it." The man slides the card under the door.

"Thank you," she says, opening the door. "Can I trouble you for a spoon?"

While eating the banana split, Meghan reads the card.

Dear Daughter, I hope you will accept my apology. I am not good at fighting and probably worse at making up. I am enormously proud of you—a senior in high school! Voting for the first time! You have been a source of great joy and inspiration to me from the day you were born—don't ever question it—and don't ever forget it.

Love—Dad

PS: When you learn to drive, I will buy you a car.

"I want to go to the zoo," Meghan says when the Big Guy returns. He is sweaty even though it's December.

"Now?"

She nods.

"Okay, well, I'll call downstairs and see if there's anyone who can take you."

"I want you to take me," she says.

"I haven't been to the zoo in years."

"Exactly," she says. "When I was little, we used to go to the zoo."

"Indeed we did. All right then, the zoo it is."

"WHAT IS YOUR FAVORITE ANIMAL?" she asks, as they are walking the pathways of the National Zoo.

"Elephant," he says. "You?"

"Lion. And panda."

They walk and talk.

"It's a good place," he says. "Good of you to think of it."

"We used to come here a lot."

He nods. "I used to do business with a man who lived in the building next door." He points it out. "The Kennedy-Warren. Lots of folks used to live there, including LBJ and Lady Bird when they first came to Washington. And a plethora of admirals and generals—including Edwin Watson. He was FDR's right-hand man—died on the boat coming back from the Yalta Conference in 1945."

"You are obsessed with history," she says.

"I am. I love it. Nothing better, the best stories, the most profound events."

"I like it too. But I've been noticing that a lot gets left out of history. They only put it in later when they have to."

He doesn't say anything.

"Is there something you wish you'd done, like something you wanted to be when you were growing up that you didn't do?"

"Yeah," he says, sounding a bit resentful. "The truth is, I would have liked to do something really big."

"Like what?"

"Invent the atomic bomb," he says.

"Really?" she asks. "That's kind of weird."

"It ended the war. And there hasn't been another world war since," he says, as though that proves the point.

"A lot of people died."

"There is a human cost to everything."

"If that's true, you'd think people would change, that they'd learn from it and behave differently," she says.

"Never going to happen. People want power. No one in power just gives it up."

They walk.

"If you couldn't invent the atomic bomb, if that wasn't an option, what would you pick?" Meghan asks.

"Chips. I'd have my own computer chip operation. The future is in chips. And a bank—I'd take a piece of a bank. This year the market was crazy, nose-dived in March. People blame it on deregulation in the financial sector. Most people don't realize that big money is like a liquid poured back and forth from one glass to another—the trick is that you don't want to lose any while it's being poured. What you'd like is that as it's poured it gains a little bit right there in midair. I like to think of that as atmospheric condensation, which adds weight to the pour—like cash out of thin air."

"Does that really happen, money out of thin air?"

"I like to think it can happen," he says. "I usually don't talk about these kinds of things with you because I assume women find them boring."

"Not sure you know it, but you're always insulting women."

"I just think it's a different set of interests. If you want to know how the world works, don't take English classes. Study history or, better yet, economics. All the secrets are in economics. Follow the money. Does that ring a bell?"

"No."

"It's what Deep Throat said to Bob Woodward when he was trying to figure out exactly what Nixon did—follow the money. Money leaves a trail. Something that I'm working on these days is trying to reduce my 'footprint.' Going forward, I'm making a concerted effort to lessen my trail. And if I get it right—one day, poof, I might actually evaporate."

"That's not funny."

"I wasn't kidding."

"Don't evaporate," she says. "I need you."

They walk a while longer.

"Do you think Mom will ever come back?"

"Yes," the Big Guy says definitively. "It never occurred to me that she might not."

"She's free now," Meghan says. "Cat's out of the bag and I'm supposedly going off to college. Maybe she wants a life of her own."

"Alone?"

Meghan shrugs.

"She'll come home. Like I said, follow the money."

"If she doesn't want to come home, you have to let her go," Meghan says. "And you need to give her money—it's like reparations."

"Yeah, I'm not sure that's how the world really works," he says. "Maybe you want to be a divorce lawyer when you grow up."

Sunday, December 28, 2008
The White House
Washington, DC
11:00 a.m.

After breakfast, they go to the White House. It's a little different from a routine visit to a family member at work. They show photo identification and pass through a metal scanner before Tony meets them at the reception booth.

"I always worry that they'll say my name isn't on the list," the Big Guy confesses.

"Your name will always be on the list," Tony says. "But this one will be brief; he's only here for a few hours."

"I'm not looking for a lovefest," the Big Guy says.

The hallways are filled with moving cartons. A few staffers are quietly packing up their offices.

Tony knocks on the office door before pushing it open.

"The place is starting to look like a turkey carcass that's been had at," President Bush says, as they come into the Oval Office.

"You've been on my mind," the Big Guy says, putting out his hand.

"Yeah, I'm looking forward to getting outta town; good to see you," the president says, taking the Big Guy's hand in both of his.

The president looks at Meghan, who is suddenly shy. "I don't mean to get in your business, but did Santa bring everything that was on your list?" he asks with a sparkle in his eye.

Meghan doesn't know what to say.

"My girls make very detailed lists; they include sizes, colors, and the names of stores where their dreams can be fulfilled. Sometimes Laura and

I would surprise them. I always think a puppy is a perfect gift for any occasion, but it turns out that not everyone shares my views on that."

"I'd love a puppy," Meghan says, as though it were a possibility.

President Bush makes like he's looking around to see if there's a spare one to be had, opening and closing desk drawers. He gives the impression of being a kid in a candy shop. "Fresh out of puppies," he says. "But we do have pens. Would you like a pen?" He hands her two. "One for you to keep and the other to negotiate with."

The Big Guy laughs.

"And you know what else I've got?" The president digs around in the drawer and pulls out several boxes of White House M&M's. They are cigarette-size boxes with the presidential seal. "We have these on the plane. Air Force One. Used to be they gave out cigarettes, but Nancy Reagan stopped that. Ron had jars of jelly beans, but honestly, how many people want jelly beans?" He hands Meghan six boxes of M&M's. "That should be enough for an international trade deal."

Everyone laughs.

"Thank you," Meghan says, and curtsies. She has no idea why; she just does.

"But seriously," Bush says to the Big Guy. "I want to thank you for your support over the years. It meant a lot to me personally." There's a pause. "You wanna know what I'm looking forward to next?"

"Of course," the Big Guy says.

"Hobbies," Bush says. "When you're president, there is no time for hobbies; you can ride a bike, go for a run, or play golf with the bigwigs, but you don't get to do anything that's just for yourself."

"Interesting," the Big Guy says.

"Painting," Bush says. "I haven't told anyone yet, but that's what I'm gonna do."

"House painting?" the Big Guy asks, sounding a little worried.

"Picture painting," Bush says, reassuring him. "Do you know how many shades of blue there are?"

A long silence passes between them.

"I better get back to it." President Bush pats the Big Guy on the shoulder. "Thanks for stopping by," he says, giving Meghan a wink. "I was up at Camp David with the family, but I had that itch to come in and get a few things done." He pauses. "The truth is, I just wanted to be by myself in the Oval Office for an hour or two before it's all over."

They move toward the door.

"And you I'll see later," Bush says, pointing at Tony.

"We promised each other one last game at the bowling alley," Tony says, as they're walking down the hall.

"I love that man," the Big Guy says to Meghan when they're back out on Sixteenth Street.

"Really?" Meghan says, shaking the M&M's. "I thought you didn't like him so much; you didn't think he was a great leader."

"Feelings change," the Big Guy says. "It's a hard job, especially for someone like him, but he did okay in the end; he's all right."

"Don't you think it's weird," Meghan says, "how that one building is a cross between an office where people work, a historic monument, and a house where a family actually lives. I mean, when you're in there, it's kind of hard to believe that that's the place that runs the whole country. Did you see the carpet?"

"It's not about the carpet," the Big Guy says. "They'll get new carpet. The White House is the seat of our government. The president is the leader of the free world and inspires democracy all over the globe."

"But seriously, do you think that if everyone in America saw how it really works they'd still be as intimidated?"

"Intimidated? What about impressed?" the Big Guy says. "It's not about the building, which is, by the way, deeply historic; it's about ideas and a way of life. One day your generation will be in charge. Tony and I and our friends are desperately trying to make sure it's all still there for you when you're ready."

"Is it in danger?" Meghan asks.

There is a long pause.

"You saw what happened in Phoenix," the Big Guy says. "Grown men and women in tears. Yes, Meghan, it is in danger."

Another pause.

"In other parts of the country people were crying for a different reason," Meghan says.

"History takes the long view."

When they get back to the hotel, Chris from the front desk pulls them aside. "I'm sorry about yesterday."

"What about yesterday?" the Big Guy asks.

"Intruding on you. Hotels are a place people come expecting privacy. But at the moment we have some extra people with us."

"What kind of 'extra people'?" the Big Guy asks.

"Secret Service," Chris whispers. "Next week the Obamas are coming and they're getting prepared."

The Big Guy nods.

"I'm not supposed to say anything, but your suite is one of the ones they'll be using, so it's being 'monitored.' Anyway, I'd like to make it up to you."

"And move us to an 'unmonitored' room?"

"I'm afraid I don't have anything available, but I was thinking I could arrange for you to have dinner."

"We're fine," the Big Guy says. "Thank you."

The Big Guy and Meghan walk to the elevator. "That's rich, isn't it?" he says. "Our room is being monitored. I wonder if that means it's bugged."

"It just means that the two men in suits staying in the room next door aren't a couple."

"Are there men in suits next door?"

Meghan nods yes. "Does that mean I'm sleeping in the bed that the incoming president will be sleeping in?"

"No," the Big Guy says. "I'm sleeping in the bed of the future president and you are in the children's room or the mother-in-law's room. It's my understanding that she goes everywhere with them; for me, that would have been a deal breaker."

"Would the mother-in-law be right next door to the president?"

"Probably not if the marriage is to survive. Most likely you're in the girls' room. Ironic, isn't it? I tried to get Godzich to extend my stay, but they had no rooms available. Once you go back to school, I'm going to be bunking at my club for a while."

"I wonder if they'll have presidential M&M's on their pillows at night?" Meghan asks.

The Big Guy shrugs. "Some things remain a mystery."

Monday, December 29, 2008
The Hay–Adams Hotel
Washington, DC
11:30 a.m.

In the morning, the Big Guy has meetings, so he arranges for someone to take Meghan shopping at a local mall. Meghan bows out of the shopping trip and calls the taxi company. She asks if Mr. Tooth can pick her up and take her to school. She wants to see Ranger.

Mr. Tooth picks her up at the hotel. "Lady Girl, I took the call because I wanted to be sure you're okay. I don't think you can go on campus if you want to graduate with honors and without being charged with trespassing. School is closed."

"I miss Ranger."

"I'm sure you do."

"If we can't go to school, can we go to the Tomb of the Unknown Soldier?" It was the first thing that popped into her head; she had no idea why except that she thought it might mean something to Mr. Tooth given that he's a veteran.

"What did you do for the holiday?" she asks.

"Me? Not a heck of a lot. I don't remember if I told you, but I live with my sister and her family. They have a really nice place, almost like a farm, and I have a little apartment attached to the house."

"The mother-in-law suite?"

He laughs. "That's what they call it, or called it until I moved in. Were you with your folks?" he asks.

"Yep," she says. "But something happened."

He glances at her in the rearview mirror.

"My mother drinks," Meghan says. "That's not the surprise. Remember when I didn't go home for Thanksgiving? Well, that was because she went to rehab. But she came home for Christmas because there was something she needed to tell me—part of the reason why she drinks."

Mr. Tooth makes a noise as if to say, Uh-huh or Tell me more.

"It turns out that my mother is not my mother. My father is my father but my mother was a dental hygienist." She takes a deep breath. "Turns out the idea of a perfect family is like the idea of the American dream—it's all a fantasy, a story we tell ourselves so we can feel good."

"Lady Girl, that sounds rough."

"There's more," she says.

Meanwhile, Mr. Tooth has missed the turn for Arlington National Cemetery and is going around in circles.

"They had a kid before me—and it died."

"That's truly sad," Mr. Tooth says, going around the circle twice before he can exit gracefully.

"I wonder if my mother really tried hard, if she really took care of it; she's not what you'd call warm."

"You could assume she did her best, most mothers do. Did they say what was wrong with the baby?"

"They didn't tell me the exact diagnosis. 'Never had a chance,' my father said. The way he told it, my mother wouldn't give up and insisted they take the baby and try everything. He said it tore them apart and that's why he started seeing the dental hygienist."

"People take comfort where they can find it," Mr. Tooth says, finally getting on the right road.

"If I hadn't already written my college essays, I wouldn't be able to now. I've lost all sense of who I am."

"Well, you could tell this story."

"And you know my godfather—Tony."

"The guy who works at the White House?"

"Turns out he's gay and no one ever told me. I've known him my whole life. You'd think someone would have told me. It's like all this stuff is just falling out of everyone and all I want to do is push it back in."

"I'm not sure you're looking for advice," Mr. Tooth says. "But I'd say, don't resist. The energy that it takes to try to stuff something back into the box is enormous. Let it out; give it air. If you make space for it, it lightens up and goes from being like a stone tied around your leg to floating like a balloon. If you can give it space, you'll become less attached; the more you cling—the worse it gets."

"And on New Year's Day I'm supposed to go meet my biological mother," Meghan says. "We're going to meet her in the morning because her husband sleeps late. I assume that means she's not going to wake him early and say, 'Happy New Year, and by the way, I'm just going to pop out and meet my former lover and my former child.'" She stops. "Honestly, I don't know what to think about anything anymore."

"Yes, you do," Mr. Tooth says.

She shakes her head.

"My bet is that you're afraid of what you're already thinking." He catches her eye in the rearview mirror. "It's easier to believe what others want us to believe, to go with the flow. But it's important to think for yourself. Not everyone can do it. Most people are following along. Personally, I find that scary. But you're not that person. Don't resist who you are. If anything, all that you've told me in the last few months makes the case for you to step into a new, bigger pair of shoes—this is your life, Lady Girl."

"I feel so alone. Like I don't belong to anyone anymore."

"You belong."

"I don't."

"You belong to yourself. As a young woman, that needs to be your strongest allegiance. God, self, and country. Those are my three." He shows her his tattoo, Pro Deo et Patria—For God and Country.

"How do you know all this?"

"Just because I drive a cab doesn't mean I'm a dummy. I read all the time. And Pro Deo et Patria happens to be the motto of my old high school, Archbishop Carroll." A moment of silence passes. "It's my job," he says. "I drive all kinds of people; I have to be able to talk to them. Having an opinion is part of being a citizen. Like I was saying, you can just be a follower or you can make up your own mind. Take the lead." He pauses. "When you think of meeting this woman—is there something you want from her?"

"I don't know. I guess I wonder if she ever thought about me? If she every regretted giving me away?"

"Will you ask her?"

Meghan shrugs. "I don't know. It seems kind of personal. Am I supposed to leave my old family and now be part of her family? I don't think my mother wants me anymore, and I bet this woman has a life of her own and wasn't expecting me to just show up out of the blue."

Mr. Tooth sighs. "Invent yourself—make your own history. You're not tied to what your parents said or did. A lot of people blame others for what happens to them, but mostly it wasn't done on purpose or with malice. It happened. That's how I think of it. Shit happens. Don't use it as a weapon against yourself. Shit happens. The end. I didn't set out to become a toothless cabdriver, but—shit happens." Mr. Tooth is in the parking lot at Arlington National Cemetery. He pauses the meter. "Are you going to go in?" he asks.

"I'd go if you wanted to go."

"No, Lady Girl, unfortunately I can't go with you. I can't leave the car."

"Not a problem. I don't really want to go in; I just wanted to talk to you."

He smiles. In the rearview mirror, she can see where all his teeth are missing. He drives her back to the hotel. When he pulls up out front and stops the meter, she meets his glance in the mirror, that's how they look at each other—always in the rearview mirror.

"Any advice?" she asks him. "Parting words?"

"Yeah," Mr. Tooth says. "Don't be afraid of anyone. I heard the singer Lou Reed say it once in an interview. Never be afraid of anyone."

"Who is Lou Reed?"

Mr. Tooth hums a little bit of "Walk on the Wild Side."

"Oh yeah. I heard that one in a commercial for a motorcycle."

"Honda Scooters." Mr. Tooth sings the chorus again. "Listen, Lady Girl, I was serious when I said that shit happens and that you have to find your own way forward. It was nice of you to invite me to see the tomb with you—but there's something you never noticed . . ."

"Like what?"

"I've got no legs."

Meghan leans over and looks in the front seat and sees that Mr. Tooth is wearing a plaid shirt and jeans, but the legs of his jeans are empty. His steering wheel has special hand controls.

"Lost them in the war?" she asks.

"Nope," he says. "Got hit by a bus; never saw it coming."

Wednesday, December 31, 2008
The Hay–Adams Hotel
Washington, DC
3:00 a.m.

Alone. He hasn't been without Charlotte on New Year's Eve in twenty-five years. Grief catches him off guard.

No one has died; he keeps reminding himself of that fact, but there has been a rupture, a rift, a schism, a fissure, a breach that is of his own making. Estrangement. Disloyal. Unfaithful. Adultery. Lamentation. Tribulation. Sorrow. Heartache.

Awake at three a.m., he reaches for the datebook that he carries with him everywhere. "Unfathomable," he writes on December 31, 2008.

He looks back through the year.

January 21: An alarm, a signal. Subprime. A word that people should have paid more attention to. The stock market plunged. A headline he clipped from *The New York Times* is pasted on the next page: "Stocks Plunge Worldwide on Fears of a U.S. Recession."

March 19: Gamma ray burst. GRB 080319B—the brightest event EVER in the universe. Another signal. These are explosions in distant galaxies, electromagnetic events.

April 21: London—Bionic eyes are implanted into two patients—eyesight to the blind!

May 12: Sichuan, China, a 7.9 earthquake—the most people killed in a single event in China since the 1931 flood along the Yangtze River.

May 25: Charlotte's birthday. He's scrawled, "Charlotte! On Mars." What it means is that it's her birthday and he shouldn't forget—and that

NASA's unmanned *Phoenix* spacecraft is the first to land in the northern polar region of Mars.

September 20: Terrorist attack, Marriott Hotel in Islamabad, Pakistan—he used to own a piece of Marriott.

November 3: Meghan flies home.

November 4: Election Day! Fucked.

So it goes, notations, felt-tip pen scribbles of history, what catches his eye, what links him to the rest of the world.

Four a.m. on the day before New Year's Day. He is trying to distract himself but can't. He has only once in his life felt such heartache.

Only Charlotte was with him that time. Instead of the death of their child binding them, they became like magnetic poles—broken souls repelling each other.

Charlotte turned to drinking and he turned to Irene. In retrospect, he wishes Charlotte had turned to someone else. But maybe men are less comforting than a Manhattan—or a martini, a cosmopolitan, a gimlet, a Vesper, a White Lady, gin, a gin fizz, a Sazerac, a daiquiri, a Bloody Mary, a mai tai, or the Last Word—gin, green Chartreuse, maraschino liqueur, and lime juice. Or vodka, vodka, vodka.

He didn't stop her. In the beginning, desperate for her to feel better, he encouraged her. He drank all of the above right alongside her, but it didn't matter; his companionship was not equal to her grief.

When Meghan was little, they moved to a beautiful house in Connecticut with a long banister that he made a show of sliding down a few times a year. Charlotte said his "mounting the rail" reminded her of a character in John Cheever's story "O Youth and Beauty!"—a man obsessed with his lost youth who in the end is shot dead by his wife. That's the part that stuck with him; he reminds Charlotte of a man whose wife "got him in midair."

They also had an apartment in the city. The Big Guy felt it was incumbent on him to get Charlotte back into the world. "This baby will be fine," he insisted. He took Charlotte into town sometimes for days in a row while a nanny stayed with Meghan. He thought it was good for Charlotte to be distracted, to do the things they used to do, to have a drink or two and let it go. It was almost a dare to prove that she could let down her guard, not be vigilant, and that Meghan would survive. He didn't realize that it also impeded Charlotte's attachment—a problem that was already complex.

Meghan charmed Charlotte but it wasn't easy. Charlotte was scared of her and angry. They didn't spend time together until Meghan was about eight months old. Charlotte broke her ankle in a riding accident and was stuck at home. With the two of them sharing the same nanny-nurse, Charlotte began to notice Meghan.

Charlotte would call him at the office to say, "She smiled at me. She sat up all by herself. She crawled over and pulled at my skirt." Meghan at eight months, nine months, ten months was doing things that the other baby had never done.

He wakes up too early on the morning of New Year's Eve and his first thought is to get on a plane and go home. He wants to call Charlotte in Palm Springs and tell her to come back to the house. He needs his life to return to normal.

He calls Tony. "I need a plan."

Tony says nothing.

"Can you hear me? I need a plan."

"The Plan," Tony says slowly.

"No. I need a plan for tonight. I'm going nuts here, climbing the walls. It's New Year's Eve; Charlotte is gone, and I've got Meghan with me and zippo to do."

There is a pause.

"Where are you?" the Big Guy asks.

"Camp David," Tony says.

"No privacy?"

"Correct. Let me make a few calls and get back to you," Tony says. "I'm sure we can find something suitable."

The Big Guy goes into the living room; Meghan is already up and drinking leftover hot chocolate from the day before.

"You got mail," she says, pointing to a large envelope that someone has slipped under the door.

It's from Chris, the hotel manager. "You turned me down for dinner, you don't partake of breakfast, but will you and your daughter be our guests tonight for a 1920s dance party? We'll be doing the Lindy Hop till dawn. All-you-can-eat buffet, endless champagne, and a special dessert cart that you can roll back to your room."

"It sounds horrible," the Big Guy says.

"I like the idea of the dessert cart we can bring back to the room," Meghan says. "I love dessert carts, so many choices: éclairs, napoleons, fresh whipped cream, pudding, strawberry shortcake, profiteroles, a principessa."

"I don't know that one—the principessa."

"Yes, you do; the last one we had was marzipan and lemon custard. Every country has a princess cake."

The Big Guy laughs. "Are we feeding you enough?"

"I'm not hungry," she says, "I'm anxious. When I'm anxious, I dream of sweets."

"We're gonna do something. Tony is on it. He'll find us a party for tonight."

They've been at the hotel for five nights and have done it all: shopping, ice-skating (he watched; she skated), museums (the East Wing and the Smithsonian), the National Archives, the Kennedy Center, *The Nutcracker* (they both slept).

At this point they are killing time, and with eighteen hours to spare on the 2008 clock, they've come up dry.

"Back to the zoo? I do all my best thinking between the zebras and the elephants."

"Not the zoo," Meghan says. "Mount Vernon."

"Have we not been there?"

"Never."

When Meghan was younger, every weekend they went to some kind of historical place: battlefields, Victorian houses, village greens, rivers, bridges, anyplace where something had happened. It was fun and no one seemed to notice that neither the Big Guy nor Charlotte had any idea of what you were supposed to do with a child on a weekend, but the one thing that none of them could bear was staying home.

They go to Mount Vernon.

"Who knew George Washington was the father of the American mule, a cross between a male donkey and a female horse?"

"I didn't know that," Meghan says.

"Reminds me of some couples we know," the Big Guy says.

"Not funny. Who knew Washington had smallpox and recovered?"

"I never knew that," the Big Guy says. "Did you know he surrendered only once? It was at the Battle of the Great Meadows."

"Didn't know that."

This is a game they used to play.

"George Washington had slaves," Meghan says.

"They all had slaves."

"That doesn't make it okay."

"He was the only founding father whose will specified that upon his death his slaves should be freed," the Big Guy says.

"Upon death is too late."

"Who knew that in 1787 Washington paid eighteen shillings to hire a camel to entertain his Christmas guests?"

"I didn't know that," Meghan says.

A docent interrupts. "Now every year a camel comes to visit us during the holidays. He just went back to his farm yesterday. George Washington loved animals."

"I knew that," both the Big Guy and Meghan say, stepping away from the docent.

"George Washington was America's first spymaster," the Big Guy whispers.

"I didn't know that."

"He used disinformation, false documents, dead drops, and multiple sources."

"I have no idea what you're talking about," Meghan says.

"They call it black arts or tradecraft," the Big Guy says.

Meghan nods. "Did you know he loved the theatre?"

"I didn't know that."

"It's possible that I love history as much as you do."

"The apple doesn't fall far from the tree," the Big Guy says. "I just want you to know that since the election I have committed myself to doing everything I can to preserve and protect the America that our founding fathers risked life and limb to build. I want to be sure it is there for you when you are ready."

Meghan nods. "I know. And you know that the thing about the cherry tree and the axe isn't true—that's not what happened."

"I knew that," the Big Guy says.

"It's occurred to me that while preservation is important, like taping off a crime scene, accepting that America is an evolving narrative is also important. The contemporary version of what the founders were doing when they broke from England would look different today."

"If I was to dig into what you're saying, I might call you a revolutionary," the Big Guy says.

"You might," she says. "Perhaps one should ask—is a revolutionary the same as a patriot?"

They continue their tour. "His Highness, the president of the United States, or protector of the rights of the same," Meghan says. "When they elected him president, they didn't even know what to call him."

"England was already on its third King George when Washington was elected."

"I didn't know that."

"What was the most important thing Washington did?"

Meghan shrugs.

"He stepped down after two terms. He was the first president, and he established that a president should serve only two terms of four years. If he had died in office, it might have given the impression that a president should serve for life. We have another word for that—a king. What did America not want to be? A kingdom. In the end, that may prove to be the most substantial contribution. He wasn't an original thinker, not like Franklin or Jefferson or Hamilton, but he knew how to do things. The smartest guy isn't always the best leader."

"First in war, first in peace, first in the hearts of his countrymen. I like that," Meghan says. "It's from a eulogy. Someday I want to be first."

Back at the hotel, Tony has left word that they are invited to a party at nine p.m. in Chevy Chase.

They have a snack, high tea in honor of Charlotte, who always loved high tea. That was something Meghan and Charlotte would do in whatever city they were in; they would have high tea.

"It's like a dessert cart," the Big Guy says. "Only on three tiers." He takes apart a watercress sandwich. "Weeds. Why do women eat weeds?"

"I feel like we're cheating on her being here and going to meet the lady tomorrow," Meghan says.

"It's okay. She's busy dealing with her stuff right now and we have things to do; it'll all come together in the end."

They rest until eight and there's a quick debate about skipping the whole thing and going to bed early. The one thing that they are not talking about is the elephant in the room. The elephant that announces itself when the Big Guy receives a hurried call confirming their meeting tomorrow at nine a.m. in Northern Virginia.

"Was that her?"

"Yes."

"Did she ask about me?"

"She didn't ask anything. She just told me where to meet her."

"Do you think she's curious?"

"How could she not be?"

"Do you think she's nervous?"

"I'm sure."

"I'm totally nervous," Meghan says.

The front desk rings to say the car is waiting. They ride to Chevy Chase in silence. The Big Guy is afraid to ask what she's thinking and she's afraid to tell the Big Guy how scared she feels.

Before they arrive at the party, the Big Guy gives Meghan the "skinny" about whose house they're going to and what to expect.

"He is William Nelson; she is Eunice Early. The Nelsons and the Earlys are both old Southern families. The two of them have known each other since they were children, but it's not a first marriage. That's the thing; they each grew up and both of them married someone else; then they found themselves in Washington about ten years ago. Strangely enough, they were both widowed and each had two children; he had two girls and she had two boys, and the rest, as they say, is history. I bet the crowd will be a little bit like Tony's Thanksgiving dinner, a mix of media types, lobbyists, and I wouldn't be surprised if there's a Supreme Court judge or two, several live nearby, as do a couple of well-known satirists. That's what every New Year's Eve party needs—a good comedian." He is doing with Meghan what he always does with Charlotte, giving her the lowdown before they arrive. "And I bet the food will be good."

"I feel sick," Meghan says.

"Too many desserts?"

"Tomorrow," Meghan says. "What if I can't do it?"

"You can do it. Just say hello. That's all you have to do."

"What a pleasure," Eunice Early Nelson says. "Come in, come in. The girls have gone elsewhere, but the boys are in the basement playing something they call beer pong. I have no idea how it works. I just hope that none of them vomit on the shag. I'm always having to get the shag rehabilitated."

Bill Nelson finds them in the front living room. "It's amazing," he says. "I don't know how she does it every year all by herself. She starts on the twenty-sixth and works around the clock. Tomorrow she won't be out of bed until suppertime, and even then it won't be pretty. Every year she swears she can't do it again. 'I quit,' she'll say. 'Next year we're going to order Chinese and people will have to live with it. I can't kill myself over a ham.'"

"That's not exactly true," Eunice says, swooping in. "Every year I say never again, but tonight I'll quit at one a.m. I'll go to bed and he can do the rest."

"Caviar and eggs for the stragglers," Bill says. "What can I get you folks to drink?"

"Scotch," the Big Guy says.

"And for you?" Bill asks Meghan.

"Just water."

The large house is classic old Chevy Chase; fireplaces abound and flames lick logs that look like they're glowing in multicolor. Crown molding everywhere. Family photos in silver frames on every surface, piles of books. The place looks lived in—it looks like home.

The Big Guy is jealous. This is the life he always wanted, entertaining with ease, a wife who likes food, comradery, music, noise. He eats a couple of olives, sees no place to put the pits, so he slides them on top of one of Bob Woodward's books on the shelf. "That's for you," he mutters with pleasure. "I leave you the pits."

He drinks. And has another. Soon he's not drunk but needs to sit down. He lands on the sofa next to a decidedly senior citizen.

"Fancy seeing you here."

"Pardon?"

"I knew your father."

"I don't think so," the Big Guy says.

"I'm sure I did," the old man says. "Everyone here, I knew their fathers at one time or another; that's just how this works. What did you say your name was?"

"Hitchens," the Big Guy says. "And yours?"

"I didn't say mine. But you seem nice enough, so I'll tell you. Richardson. Dick Richardson."

"Pleased to meet you."

"Rings a bell, right? Secretary of defense," he says. "Not currently, but for a good forty years I was in one position or another. I went back and forth across Pennsylvania Avenue putting out fires, managing dimwits, trying to keep the ship from going down."

"Rings a bell," the Big Guy says, signaling to a waiter that he'd like another scotch. "Do you want something?" he asks the old man. "A drink? Ham on a biscuit, black-eyed peas? They're a good luck charm."

"I want nothing," the old man says. "I can't dance, can't play golf; I'm two feet from the edge looking out at all of you who think you know what's happening. And you know what I see?"

"What do you see?"

"Nothing," he says. "Just blindness and constipation."

"They make some fiber supplements for that."

"Political constipation, you idiot. You know what worries me?" He pauses for effect. "Horseshoes."

"My daughter has a horse; I'm sure they have a—what do you call a footman for a horse? A farrier."

"Teardrops, tendrils, U-shaped, V-shaped, recession and recovery. It's all a load of bull. Keep your eye on the horseshoe. I'm telling you something real: the far sides, the extremes, are closer to each other than any of us are to the center." He pauses to catch his breath. "It used to be we danced around the edges and met in the middle; now they're repulsed by the middle. It's soft white bread. You can't even swallow it, no way to get it down, you choke on it."

The waiter hands the Big Guy a fresh drink.

"I'm telling you that our balls are in the water; our balls are going under, and it's not about who is on the right or who's on the left, but the fact that we are history. Old white men. We're done. Finis."

The old man moves to get up off the sofa. As he pulls himself up, he farts in the Big Guy's face.

"Apologies," the old man says. "With great age comes wind."

"We are history," the Big Guy repeats. "Ass written on the wind."

The basement smells like boys—sweat and beer. Meghan does one loop around the room and goes back up the stairs. Mark Eisner is in the sunroom stabbing cheese cubes with a toothpick.

He smiles when he sees her. "An unexpected treat," he says.

"Last time I saw you, we both had towels around our heads," Meghan says. "How do you know the Early-Nelsons?"

"Old friends of the family. I didn't know you were in DC."

Since Phoenix, they've exchanged a few emails, and despite the decades of difference in age, they would call themselves friends.

"Do you have a life?" Meghan asks. "Seriously, you never say anything about a girlfriend or a wife or even an ex."

"That's a rather aggressive question."

"Is it? I would think that someone like you would have more of a life." As soon as she says it, she realizes it sounds exactly like something her mother would say. She can hear the words coming out of Charlotte's mouth and feel the sting with which they land. "You're right. I'm sorry."

"You want to know the truth?" Eisner asks.

"'Tis the season."

"I'm infertile. Genetic mutation. An extra X chromosome and I've got small balls."

Meghan pauses, trying to make sense of what Eisner has just said. "That must be hard. I mean difficult."

An awkward silence passes between them.

"I'm sorry," she says.

"Thanks," Eisner says, knocking back what's left of his drink. "Who are you here with?"

"My dad," Meghan says, nodding toward the Big Guy.

"He's your dad?" he asks, cloaking his surprise.

"Yeah. It's a long story."

"At the moment I've got nothing but time and an empty glass." He knocks the ice cubes around in his glass. "Two hours till the ball drops. You want to take a walk around the block?"

They walk up and down the wide streets of Chevy Chase, Eisner chewing on what it might mean to the Big Guy that he knows Meghan. Music wafts out of various houses, swing from one, heavy metal from another.

Small balls. It's not like Meghan has seen a lot of balls, but in this case, she keeps thinking of the tiny red rubber ball that one plays jacks with and the pale pink version attached to a long elastic string that you whack with a wooden paddle. Small balls.

"When I was a kid, we lived just over there. The big draw was the club." Eisner points to a country club hidden behind an ivy-covered stone wall. "My mother hated to cook, hated to clean, hated to entertain. She was an anthropologist from a very fancy family. All she wanted to do was write and be left alone. As often as she could, she would dispatch my brother and me to the club. 'Go to the pool, go play tennis, go have lunch; I hear they make a nice cheeseburger. Maybe your father can take you to the club for dinner. Maybe you and your friends can organize a tournament.'"

Then he stops and turns to Meghan. This is the moment where a creepy older guy might try to kiss her or something, but instead he says, "Full disclosure. I know your father."

Meghan laughs. "Everyone knows my father. Did he ever tell you that when he was a kid he thought his father owned the local country club? He thought he was a big shot until he discovered that they were just members like everyone else."

"No. I never heard that one."

"What do they say, 'fake it till you make it'?"

Eisner laughs. "It just made me nervous; you're his kid."

"That's the least of it," she says. All of her tumult leaks out: the story about the baby, the mistress, Charlotte's drinking, what's going to happen tomorrow morning.

"Wow," Eisner says. "That's a lot from November until now."

"Yeah. Half the time I'm not sure what's real or what I'm imagining."

"Carl Sagan, a very popular astronomer in the 1970s, used to say, 'Somewhere, something incredible is waiting to be known.'"

"How will I know when I know it?" Meghan asks.

"That's the question for all of us. Right now you're in a very specific moment. It's called liminal space. You're in the ambiguous or disoriented phase, also known as the middle of a rite of passage. Part of that is just growing up, but it also has to do with what you found out. Now you're transforming, incorporating that information into your identity. It can be scary, like free-falling."

"Exactly," she says, with a newfound appreciation for Eisner. "How do you know that?"

He laughs. "My mother. Liminal was a favorite word of hers, 'from the Latin *limin.*' You've left something behind and are not yet into what comes next. I don't know if there's any comfort in the fact that this is how all of Washington feels from the first Tuesday in November until the twentieth of January. A cycle of suspension. It's why they're all so clingy. They cling to one another because at a certain point familiar faces are all they have. It doesn't matter what side they're on as long as they're recognizable."

They go back up the steps to the Early-Nelson house. Eisner finds the Big Guy in the small office just off the kitchen.

"I don't quite know what to say," Eisner says.

"Is my fly undone?" the Big Guy asks.

"I know your daughter."

"Know her?"

"I met her in Phoenix; we spent time together talking about termites. She sent me her essay for history class, the one about the election, 'Waking Up from the Dream: Or My Father's Nightmare.'"

"I have no idea what you're saying. You talked about wood eaters and my dreams?"

Eisner shakes his head.

"Let me ask you something. Do you want to marry her?"

Eisner laughs.

"What's so funny?"

"Me," Eisner says. "I'm the funny one. And no, I don't want to marry her."

"Then it's not a problem," the Big Guy says. "We all know people."

"Thanks. I would have pictured your daughter as a girl in a twinset, with pearls and a tortoiseshell hair band, but she's a very cool kid."

"What's wrong with pearls?" the Big Guy asks.

In the living room the Early-Nelsons are making a toast even though there's still an hour on the clock. The Big Guy and Eisner join the crowd.

"We stand on the threshold," Bill says.

"Between this year and next," Eunice says. "Between past and future."

"Between George Bush and Barack Obama," he says. There are a few hisses in the room. "She gave me that line because she knew some of you might have something to say."

"We come together on this night to enjoy the company of good friends, to celebrate what has been won," she says. "And mourn all that was lost."

"A lot of money was lost this year," Bill says.

"Eat, drink, be merry, and let's dance!" Eunice says, and the music swells; first it's Sam Cooke's "A Change Is Gonna Come," then about thirty seconds in, it changes to Katy Perry's "Hot n Cold." The adults start to dance.

Meghan finds her father and shouts above the music, "Can we go back to the hotel?"

"Now, before midnight?"

"Yes," she says. "I'm tired. And I hate this part."

"Sure, okay." He looks around for Eisner, but he's vanished.

"Do we need to say goodbye?" Meghan asks, nodding toward the Early-Nelsons, who are "cutting the rug" more suggestively than anyone their age should do.

"French exit," the Big Guy says.

Mark Eisner is on the front porch, tuned to music coming from a house down the street. He's singing along. "I'm your captain, yeah, yeah, yeah, yeah."

"Happy New Year, Eisner," the Big Guy says, waving goodbye.

"My favorite song from high school," Eisner says, gesturing at the music in the air.

"Sounds like your crowd is over there," the Big Guy says.

"Doubtful," Eisner says. "That's Dick Helms's house, the former director of the CIA. He used to scare the crap out of me when I was a kid. My crowd is right here." He drops to his knees and feigns playing air guitar. "I'm your captain, yeah, yeah, yeah, yeah."

"You're like a big kid," Meghan says, shaking her head.

"Good luck with your essay," Eisner calls to Meghan. "Happy to give it a read if you need any help."

"What's this one about?" the Big Guy asks.

"How war is won," Meghan says, as they get into the car.

Meghan is in bed and asleep before midnight.

The Big Guy, still in his party clothes, makes himself another drink and is sitting on his bed waiting for the ball to drop. He's startled when his cell phone rings.

"You out on the town?"

"Home now," he says. "We went over to the Early-Nelsons for a little while."

"That must have been special," Charlotte says.

"It was nice. They asked after you."

"I wanted to wish you Happy New Year."

"I would have called you but I didn't want to break the rules."

There's a pause, silence.

"Are you okay?" he asks.

"I think so," she says.

"It's not the new year out there yet."

"It will be soon," she says.

There is another pause.

"Is there something else?" he asks.

"Maybe."

"Do you want to tell me?"

"I'm not sure."

"Give it a try," he says, speaking softly.

"I let her do me," Charlotte says.

There is silence.

"It wasn't my idea—but I didn't stop her."

"I'm not sure what you're saying."

"Terrie," she says. "I let her . . ."

"Let her what?"

"Lick me."

"Sex?" A hot rush runs through the Big Guy—shame, excitement, nuclear confusion.

"Like a cat," Charlotte says.

"That woman is your lover?"

"I'm not sure I would call her that."

"Did you do it more than once?" he asks.

"Yes."

"Did you do it to her?"

"God no."

"Were you drunk at the time?"

"No."

"And now? Are you drunk or stoned now?"

"I'm not," she says. "I had to stop with the pot. It was making me eat too much and I started having uncomfortable thoughts about Meghan."

"What kind of thoughts about Meghan?"

"I don't know if I was awake or dreaming, but I kept thinking that because she was upset with us she joined the military, and she became a commanding officer, but I was never clear if it was really the military or some rogue extremist organization. Whatever it was, I kept having the dream over and over. I want her to know I love her. Even though she isn't mine, she is mine. Do you know what I mean?" She pauses. "I worry that she is disappointed in me. I wasn't a very good mother." Charlotte sniffles.

"I don't know what to say. Did you like it? Was it exciting?" The Big Guy pauses. "Forget it. Don't answer. I don't want to know. For now, I'm going to pretend you didn't tell me that she ate you like a cat."

"You can't pretend," she says. "You have to know. That's the new rule; that's how we got into this situation."

"Are you going to keep doing it?"

"I don't know," she says, slightly annoyed, as though that was irrelevant.

"Are you telling me because you really want me to know or because you feel guilty about my buying a car for your lesbian lover under false pretenses?"

Charlotte is quiet.

"All right then," he says. "Well, now you've told me. Do what you will. And frankly, I don't really think that's sex. I mean there's nothing a woman can do that's like what a man does. It's entirely different." There is another pause. "Am I now expected to confess my infidelities?"

"No."

"It's not like there were many. But I will tell you that once, years ago at the athletic club in New York, I was getting a rubdown and the masseur inserted his pointer finger into my anus."

"Really?" she says. "And you never told me?"

"I was embarrassed."

"Did you like it?"

"I didn't not like it," he says. "I don't think any of us are as simple as polite society would like us to be."

"Voilà."

"Voilà."

"Happy New Year," Charlotte says.

"Same to you."

"Where's Meghan?" she asks.

"Fast asleep," he says. "I've been trying to keep her busy. We went to the zoo."

"That's nice. You always loved the zoo."

"And we went over to the White House and said goodbye. G.W. was very nice to her."

"He should be for all the money you gave him."

A moment passes.

He rinses his mouth with what is left in his glass, scotch, neat, 63.5 percent alcohol as compared to Listerine's 26.9 percent.

"When does Meghan go back to school?"

"A couple of days." He's talking quietly because he doesn't want to wake her.

"Then what?"

"We go from there."

"Sounds good."

"We build it again, from the ground up."

"What are you doing now?" Charlotte asks. Her voice is soft, almost seductive.

"I'm getting undressed," he says. "I can wear the costume for only so many hours." He sits down on the bed and takes off his socks. "And you?"

"Just wishing you Happy New Year," she says. "Be in touch." She hangs up.

Licked her like a cat. He lies back and gives the member a little tug. Nothing good comes of it; he's not sure why, could be anything, alcohol, age, or the weight of history.

Our balls are in the water; our balls are going under. Mayday. Mayday. He hears Dick Richardson's voice echoing in his head. The signal is seven short blasts of the whistle followed by one long one.

The captain goes down with the ship, the Big Guy reminds himself.

Thursday, January 1, 2009
Alexandria, Virginia
8:40 a.m.

"What should I wear?" Meghan asks her father. He looks at her blankly. "Who do I go as?"

"You go as yourself."

"Which one?"

"Casual," the Big Guy says. "The real one."

Meghan wants her biological mother to like her, to think she's a nice young woman. She puts on a skirt, dark tights, and loafers. Except for the fact that the skirt isn't plaid, she looks like she's ready to play field hockey.

"Perfect," her father says. "You look perfect."

He is well-groomed in a yellow shirt and his favorite houndstooth blazer. "Tie or no tie?" he asks, holding the tie against his neck.

"No tie. The tie makes it look like a business meeting."

They take the elevator down to the lobby. The room that the night before was decorated for New Year's Eve in black and gold balloons, a 1920s speakeasy like the Stork Club or Cotton Club, has righted itself. There are no puddles of champagne on the floor, no remnants of confetti or noisemakers. The tables are set with white cloths—carafes of fresh-squeezed orange juice are resting in buckets of ice; tiered trays of croissants and pastries are at the ready. Meghan inhales—and remembers that she's hungry; they never ate dinner last night.

The ride to the meeting place is silent, the air suffused with feeling but no language. It reminds her of when they went to a great-uncle's funeral a few years ago; the man had killed himself without warning.

"Are you nervous?" the Big Guy asks.

"Yes."

"Me too. I haven't seen her in a very long time."

"What do you know about her?"

"She had a mother and a father."

"Everyone has a mother and a father."

"And some siblings."

Another pause.

"Does Mom know we're doing this?"

"No."

"Do you expect this woman to be my family now? Like I'll go celebrate holidays with her?"

"What?"

"Are you handing me off to her, like getting rid of me?"

"Are you out of your mind? Of course I'm not getting rid of you. I'm just trying to help you—us—navigate. I don't expect you to do anything except put out your hand and say hello."

There's a pause.

"Do you not want to meet her?" he asks.

"I want to meet her," Meghan says. "It's just all so strange."

"Indeed."

When they get to where they're going, he has the driver let them out far from the door to the restaurant.

He gets out of the car. He's wearing his camel hair coat. His slicked-back gray hair is over his collar—he needs a trim. His body inside the coat is thick, stiff, like an old bear's.

Meghan thinks of them going to vote. It's been only two months ago, but the Big Guy seems smaller. He's occupying space differently, as if he's trying not to be seen.

They get to the door and he pulls on the handle; it's locked. A flush of panic washes over him; whatever is going to happen, he doesn't want it to happen in the parking lot.

"You okay?" Meghan asks.

"Yeah," he says, knocking hard on the wooden door. There is a sound, some fiddling with keys, the lock, then the door opens.

"Happy New Year," the waitress says, holding the door open for them. "First customers of 2009. Coffee is on the house."

"Thank you," the Big Guy says.

"Sit wherever you like."

They take a booth across the room. He sits facing the door.

The waitress brings menus and the coffee.

"Tea for me," Meghan says. "If you have it."

"Sure do."

"What was the name of George Washington's horse?" Meghan asks.

"Chestnut?"

"Blueskin," Meghan says. "He was one of Washington's two main horses. And he was half Arabian, sired by a stallion known as Ranger."

"I didn't know that," the Big Guy says.

"Isn't it amazing? Washington had a connection to Ranger, sort of."

"What was the other horse called?" he asks.

"Nelson," she says. "He was chestnut color, so you're only a little wrong."

"Half right. That doesn't get me very far."

They sit nervously attending to their drinks. The Big Guy pretends to read the menu. Then he looks up, does one of those fast-flash check-yourself things, stands, and goes toward the front of the restaurant.

Meghan waits in the booth. Her back is to the door; she's not sure what to do. At a certain point, she stands up and turns around. As the woman approaches, she puts out her hand. "I'm Meghan."

"I'm Irene."

"I know."

There is a moment of awkwardness about who should sit where.

The Big Guy sits and Meghan slides in next to him in the booth.

"You are so beautiful," Irene says.

"Thank you."

The waitress comes by. "Can I get you something, coffee, tea, hair of the dog?"

The Big Guy chuckles. "I'm the dog."

"What grade are you in?" Irene asks.

"I'm a senior in high school, applying to colleges if you can believe that."

"Do you know what you want to be?"

"No idea. Maybe something in the government."

"I wanted to be a doctor and deliver babies."

"That would have been wonderful," Meghan says.

Irene shrugs. "I went to school for two years, but then I had to work. You're lucky. You'll go to a good school and have opportunity."

"Thank you," the Big Guy says, but the women aren't looking at him.

"Do you study Spanish in school?" Irene asks.

"French," Meghan says. "I picked French because Thomas Jefferson went to France, and when I was thirteen, I was obsessed with Thomas Jefferson. He was my hero until I learned more about him, and then I left him for Eleanor Roosevelt."

There is a long pause.

"It's super uncomfortable," Meghan says. "He had children with Sally Hemings; I wrote a paper about it. When we went to Monticello, the guide talked about it but in a hush-hush way like he wanted us to know and not know at the same time."

They are quiet.

"History is complicated," the Big Guy says.

Irene nods. "There are different kinds of knowing. My mother is half Spanish and half Colombian, and my father is white. They live in Florida near my two brothers. I never told any of them I was pregnant. My parents are religious. I am religious as well. Or I like to think I am."

seven. He is a handful. If anyone tries to tell you that boys and girls are the same, they've never had children or been to a playground."

The Big Guy comes back to the table. "Would you like me to take a picture of the two of you?"

"Sure," Meghan says. There is a moment of awkwardness about whose phone to use. "Use mine," Meghan says quickly. She hands her father the phone and shows him what button to press. Meghan sits next to Irene in the booth. They sit side by side, not touching, as if they were strangers. Her father takes the photo and shows it to them.

"Maybe one more," Irene says. In the next photo, she puts her arm around Meghan's shoulders. It wasn't obvious in the moment, but the camera catches all. In the second photo, Meghan's shoulders are raised—like hackles.

"I better get back to the house," Irene says, standing. "But I'm very glad to have met you. Thank you."

They stand. Meghan doesn't know if she should say anything about wanting to see Irene again sometime or about meeting the rest of her family. Is this it? Or will there be more? It feels like there's no space for that.

"Will you stay in touch?" Meghan asks.

There is hesitation. Meghan begins to cry.

"I'll try," Irene says. "It's not about you; it's me. My husband doesn't know I had a baby. Is it okay if I hug you?" Not waiting for an answer, she wraps her arms around Meghan.

"I love you," Irene tells Meghan. "I have always loved you. And I know you know that. Here"—she taps Meghan's chest—"in your heart. That's where you keep me—in your heart."

Then she is gone.

The Big Guy pays the bill and they leave. The black car pulls across the parking lot and picks them up at the curb.

"She's a very nice lady, right? Normal person." He pauses for a minute.

"Yep," Meghan says. "She even put sugar in her coffee despite being a dental hygienist."

"That's funny," he says. "I never thought about that."

"Two packets."

"Do you feel better now, having met her?" he asks.

The car silently glides down the ramp from one roadway onto another; there is the ka-thunk, ka-thunk of the tires over the seams in the pavement that reminds her of the sound of the truck tires rolling over the cattle guards at the ranch. She is thinking back to November, the bison at the fence, their enormous shiny eyeballs, which apparently don't work well—they compensate with a strong sense of smell and good hearing. She thinks of Ranger and how well he senses things. How he knows what's going on all around him. She remembers reading that horses see everything magnified fifty times. She feels like whatever just happened rests inside her—magnified fifty times.

"How could you do that to Mom?" Meghan asks.

The Big Guy doesn't say anything for a minute. "Maybe when you're older you'll understand."

"You cheated on your wife and you lied to everyone, to Mom, to me, and probably to that woman—Irene. I know you; you need to think of yourself as a good person; that's important to you. I bet you told her that you were going to leave your wife."

There is a pause.

"We've never had a relationship where you berate me," he says. "I don't want to start now. And worse, you sound shrill. Don't forget that I'm the adult and you're the child."

"That's just another way of keeping me down; either it's because I'm a girl or because I'm a child. You wanted me to be strong, fierce, and go after the things that mattered—except when it's about you."

"Correct." He pauses. "I'm not saying you're wrong. I'm saying I can't handle it. I have my own sentiments about all of this."

"Now I have to worry about your feelings? I thought I was the child. Children don't worry about their parents' feelings. Now I'm supposed to take care of you because that's what women do and because Mom's not talking to you either?"

"Is there some way I can fix this?"

"No," Meghan says. "It's not something you can throw money at. That's what you do; you buy things, you pay people to take care of things."

"I am not a perfect person, I accept that. I know what my flaws are, but I do mean well; I want the best for you and your mother."

"Which mother?"

"My wife, your mother. Can you accept that we waited until we thought you were old enough to understand?"

"That's a lie," Meghan says. "You wanted to wait forever. You only told me because Mom, Charlotte, your wife, forced you to. It would have been difficult for you to tell me years ago because you would have had to deal with your own problems. The person this protected most was you. You're not the person you claim to be."

"I can understand that it looks that way from where you sit," he says.

The biggest thing about meeting her birth mother is how anticlimactic it was. Irene is nice, normal, and has made a life for herself that doesn't involve Meghan or the Big Guy. That's good—she's free.

"If I was being honest, I feel ill in an indescribable way—demented. Who am I? Who do I belong to? My entire identity is a false narrative. I'm fake. That makes me unreal."

"I don't see it that way," the Big Guy says. "The way I see it, now there are no secrets."

"It's as though an atomic bomb went off inside me." Meghan looks at her father. "Your bomb, the one you wished you'd invented. Well, it turns out you did—it's me."

Friday, January 2, 2009
The Hay-Adams Hotel
Washington, DC
2:45 a.m.

The maker of the bomb.

What does it mean to accept responsibility? Is it something he can do? It is difficult to look in the mirror and see oneself not as one wishes one was—but as one is.

How does one live with what they see? The fallout of one's life, one's decisions, habits, and assumptions, the things that have been taken for granted, power, money, privilege, and—dare he say it?—the color of his skin. That's what's got him and the Forever Men so upset. They woke up and discovered they were not on top anymore. It's a rude awakening after hundreds of years and they're taking it hard. It's not just that Obama won, it's as though the founding fathers were assassinated. The truths they held self-evident have become a moving target. If he was to say that they were gaslit by history, he wouldn't be taking responsibility, he would be side-stepping his role in history.

The Big Guy can't sleep.

What if you thought you were a good guy? What if you needed to believe that with all your heart, and yet you woke up, and for the first time you knew that you are an asshole?

There is a lingering sense of disbelief.

You know you're an asshole and yet you want to find a way around it.

You know it's true, and still there is some ember deep within that won't allow you to admit it. That ember is linked to how you see yourself as a man.

I am a man, you tell yourself. I am a flawed man but I am not an asshole.

I am compelled to reject the idea that I am an asshole because if I concede, if I surrender to this knowledge—there is a problem; I still have to live with myself.

And I cannot live with myself as an asshole.

I have no respect for assholes and therefore would have no respect for myself.

I cannot live like that.

It is the middle of the night and he is talking to himself.

He's traveling through time, the time of his life.

How can this wrong be made right?

The Big Guy is up late, thinking about Charlotte. He loves her deeply; that is now clearer to him than to her.

He makes a list of what he knows about Terrie, the cat, Charlotte's lover. He writes down what Charlotte told him about her family, about her addiction, about her motorcycle. He's trying to think of Terrie's last name—he remembers it sounding familiar, a newspaper name like Hearst or Getty but one tier down.

He thinks about Charlotte getting him to buy the car for her lover and he loves her for it. The only way for him not to lose Charlotte is to embrace Charlotte (and Terrie) and whatever comes next. It strikes him as ironic that he can find a way to take back control of the country but not his marriage.

He is grateful that Charlotte cracked and got help, and that they all survived. The truth came out; there has to be some good in that.

There has to be a way back and a way out—both at the same time.

He is thinking of Charlotte at the ranch, Charlotte and her horses. They ended up with the ranch not just for tax reasons but because Charlotte was sick of the sycophants in Washington and she felt claustrophobic in New York and the same but different in Connecticut, where she said it was like being inside a glass bottle and everyone knew everything about them. She didn't want to go to luncheons with other ladies; she didn't want to sit on boards or give money to libraries, hospitals, or breast cancer research. She wanted to be free and left alone. That was the one thing she wanted, the one thing she had never had.

And Meghan—his creation. She is the bomb. She is the thing that blew it all up.

Friday, January 2, 2009
The Hay–Adams Hotel
Washington, DC
6:20 a.m.

The Big Guy wakes her up early.

"Sleeping," Meghan says, her eyes still closed.

"Time to get up."

"Too early."

He jiggles her shoulder. "Up we get, Magpie," he says, using a nickname from long ago.

"Are you okay?" she asks, eyes cracking open.

"Fine. Just getting an early start."

He hands her a cup of hot cocoa. "Room service comes in twenty minutes if you order it at six a.m., but at three p.m., it takes hours." He pauses. "Put your clothes on, wear something warm."

"Where are we going?"

"It's a surprise. And no, I didn't buy you a car."

It's still dark when they climb into the back of the car waiting downstairs. They drive past the White House, make a right on Fifteenth Street and another onto Independence Avenue. The streets are empty. When they get to the intersection of Independence Avenue and Home Front Drive, the car slows down. It pulls up behind a parked truck and trailer with the hazard lights blinking.

"Put on your flashers," the Big Guy instructs the driver. "The last thing I want to do is take it up the ass at seven in the morning." The driver pushes the red triangle on the dashboard and the hazards go on.

"You know what's in the trailer?" the Big Guy asks.

Meghan has no idea what's happening.

"Your horse," he says. "Repairing the damage I've done. Earning your trust is going to take a long time, but for now I thought you could use a ride on your horse."

"Is it legal?" she asks.

The thought hadn't occurred to him. "I have no idea. Who is going to stop a woman on a horse?"

"Did you ask Godzich?"

"No," he says. It never occurred to him.

"But you never do anything without asking Godzich."

"I sincerely hope that's not true."

Meghan shrugs. "If I get arrested, you better get me out of jail."

"You have my word."

"It would be pretty funny—what did you do over Christmas? Oh, I found out I'm not who I thought I was. Then I got arrested for riding a horse through the streets of Washington, DC, like I owned the place."

Mr. Kelly, the groom from Meghan's school, backs Ranger out of the trailer.

"You have no idea how much I missed you," Meghan says, kissing Ranger on the nose.

"I didn't bring him here for you to make out. Hop on," the Big Guy says.

"All the girls kiss the horses," Mr. Kelly says, handing Meghan her riding gear and pulling a makeshift curtain over the back of the trailer so she can change.

Meghan returns kitted out. She adjusts Ranger's cinch, pulling everything a little tighter, then throws the reins over Ranger's head, puts her foot in the stirrup, and sits on the saddle.

With a kick of her heel, Ranger steps over the curb onto the grass. She is gentle with the horse, walking him, warming him up, careful to keep her own desire in check until he is ready.

"I put a tracker on the horse," Mr. Kelly says. "Ever since the incident in the woods, I'm not taking any chances."

"Give me a minute," the Big Guy says, signaling to Mr. Kelly and his driver. He heads off on foot toward the Lincoln Memorial. The sun is just coming up.

As he walks, he is thinking about Lincoln, the first Republican president, creating the party out of fragments and chaos. As a young man, the Big Guy loved Lincoln, but his father thought Lincoln was a dope. He remembers it distinctly, "a dope." When his father said that he felt like crying, he may actually have cried, but that's not the part the Big Guy wants to remember.

The rising sun casts a warm orange glow on the white marble of Lincoln's statue. There is something melancholy about visiting an old friend who has been lost. He looks up at the great man for more than a moment, then nods as if bidding him adieu and starts walking back to the car. He is thinking of what happened when Lincoln was shot. People took to the streets. What calmed them were Lincoln's own words, "Malice toward none," and the question, What would Lincoln do?

He looks down from the memorial and sees Meghan cantering, then breaking into a full gallop and heading off.

She rides astride.

She is charging down the National Mall, arm raised as if she were leading an army.

She is what has never come before.

She is the revolution.

The sun is on the water; the Washington Monument is before him in reality and in reflection. He walks toward it and spots Meghan doing laps, tight circles around the monument. He thinks of George Washington, Mount Vernon, and the good time he and Meghan had there on Wednesday.

He thinks of Washington's relationship to the British; Washington served in the British Army during the French and Indian War and was annoyed that Virginians were paid less than officers with royal commissions. A disgruntled employee, he resigned, married Martha Dandridge Custis, and the rest is history.

In June 1775 Congress ordered General George Washington to take command of the Continental Army fighting the British in Boston. "Our glorious cause," Washington called it.

He thinks of Washington riding his horse Blueskin. Meghan says that's the one he was most often painted as riding even if it wasn't true because the horse stood out in paintings.

He thinks of Washington in battle; his first battlefield victory wasn't until September 1776, the battle at Harlem Heights. And Washington crossing the Delaware at night in a winter storm, catching the British by surprise. And the second battle at Trenton on January 2, 1777. Two hundred and thirty-two years ago on this very day. He thinks of the sign on the bridge in Trenton, the sign he passed many times taking the train from New York or Connecticut to Washington: "Trenton Makes—the World Takes."

He thinks of Washington and his humility. At the end of his presidency, Washington told his colleagues, "If you wish to speak to me again, it will be under my own Fig and Vine."

The Big Guy gets back in the car and has the driver head in the direction Meghan is riding—toward the Capitol. He calls Meghan on her phone, watching as she slows Ranger to a walk and answers the call.

"Where are you?" she asks.

"I'm right here," he says, rolling down the car window and waving broadly. "Look behind you."

"I see you," she says, turning her head.

"I see you as well and it's magnificent. When you get to the Capitol, make sure you go around back, that's where the good stuff is."

"Like what?"

"The Library of Congress and the Supreme Court. That's where you want to end up, the Supreme Court; I'll meet you there."

This is it, the beginning.

He had a jeweler in Palm Springs make enamel buttons, one-and-a-half-inch rounds, like heads of state or members of Congress wear so they can identify one another as being "in the club." He has them in individual black-velvet boxes. He gave the jeweler the idea for a symbol combining the rune for abundance with the scales of justice, the Rod of Asclepius for medicine, and the good old-fashioned dollar sign.

He arrives early. Chez François has been his special place in Washington for more than thirty years.

As soon as he's in the door, he feels restored, in part because the air is perfused with the scent of freshly baked bread.

"Hello, old friend," the maître d' says. "Jacques is not here today, but he asked me to give you this." He hands the Big Guy a wrapped box the size of a football.

"I thought he stopped making them," the Big Guy says.

"We just didn't know where to send yours. I will say that this year's is excellent."

"The famed holiday fruitcake. There's a fellow I know at the Pentagon who has ten years' worth in his freezer."

"We hear rumors." The maître d' leads the Big Guy to the table in the far corner. "That's a nice tie pin. Very European. I've not seen one like that before."

"You have a good eye. It's a fifteen-karat gold collar bar."

"I didn't know there was such a thing as fifteen-karat gold."

"Smart man. It was discontinued in 1932. The pin belonged to my grandfather. He believed a man wasn't dressed if he wasn't pinned."

"And so, today it's a special occasion? Big business? Bachelor party?"

"Lunch with the boys; I had to come up with something to keep myself sane." The Big Guy carefully puts one of the black-velvet boxes at each man's place, not on the plate but on the right just above the knife and below the wineglass.

"I like to believe I know what some men think, but I suppose one never really knows," the maître d' says. "I would have imagined you'd be unhappy today, but you seem in the mood for a party."

"If my French were better I would explain, but the short version is, I am unhappy but I am doing something about it and that makes me happy—I am a man of action."

The maître d' shrugs. "I stay out of politics, that is the secret to my success."

The Big Guy laughs. "Oh yeah, how's that been working out?"

"Beautifully. Do you know how many times I've been asked to make a Baked Alaska in the shape of a submarine?" The maître d' laughs. "The good news for me is that this is not my country, so I do not have to choose—you are all my friends."

Before more can be said, Bo comes in with Kissick on his heels. "The judge is behind us; he's paying his driver. Between us, I'll say it now, I don't like jewelry on men, but see what you think."

The judge comes through the door, pausing to make sure all eyes are on him. He's sporting the requisite Texas hat and a bolo tie with an enormous chunk of turquoise mounted in silver.

"Glad you could make the trip, Douglas," the Big Guy says to the judge.

"Happy to be here," the judge says. "On days like today, one is comforted by the presence of fellow travelers. It's been shit so far. The pregame has been on since six a.m.; it doesn't stop, and of course I can't help but watch. It was a relief to leave the hotel."

"Is that your good luck charm?" Bo asks, nodding toward the turquoise.

"Something like that," the judge says.

"Nice hat," the Big Guy says, giving the judge a pat on the back. "It's a real tall one."

"This one is beaver and ermine from Resistol, one of my favorite companies. I'm a loyal man, sold my piece of the shop back in the 1960s when LBJ thought that cowboy hats were a diplomatic gesture. I was pleased when Reagan reclaimed the mantle, but I was out of the business by then. That said, I still like to wear 'em. And they are weatherproof. Y'all make fun of us for how we complain about the heat, but at least we have heat. What you have here is slush and misery, a swamp that turns into a slippery mess for four months of the year."

"Ain't it the truth." The Big Guy has always prided himself on his ability to get along with everybody.

Twitch Metzger shows up from Chicago rail thin, wearing high pants cinched with a narrow belt, a shirt buttoned to the top, no tie, and wing tips. He's six foot three, and the outfit comes off like a costume, somewhere between salesman, preacher, and circus act.

Bo puts out his hand to shake. "Glad to see you."

The Big Guy turns his attention to the judge. "I want to thank you again for the invitation to come visit; I'm sorry I wasn't able to be with you in Fort Worth."

"Don't give it another thought. I so enjoyed our impromptu Thanksgiving and wanted to return the favor."

"Much appreciated. I've been dealing with a few things that couldn't be avoided."

"My wife's a drunk too," the judge says. "God love her, but she's a drunk. She won't admit it though. My trick: smart locks. I don't let her out of the house after six p.m. Hell yes, it puts a crimp in our social life but you do what you have to. Everything out of her mouth after seven p.m. is a foul play."

The Big Guy is caught off guard; it hadn't occurred to him that (a) people knew Charlotte had a drinking problem, and (b) they talked about it behind his back.

"My wife finally realized it had become a problem and is doing better now," the Big Guy says. "With any luck, yours will come to the same realization."

"I just wanted you to know we share a sinking ship."

"I feel bad for these women," the Big Guy says. "If they'd done something with their lives, maybe this wouldn't have happened. For the smart ones, wife and mother aren't exactly the careers they had planned on. In retrospect, we should have encouraged them more."

The judge nods. "Smart as whips. That's part of the problem. Just like Martha Mitchell, heard it all and no one wanted to believe her."

"I knew her and John back when they had a house at the Apawamis Club in Westchester. They had a little girl, Martha Jr., and they called her Marty," Kissick says. "The woman was driven crazy by everyone trying to shut her up. I like to think things have changed at least a little bit."

Eisner arrives sweating despite the fact that it's January. His pants are clipped to his legs. "I rode my bike," he says, putting his helmet on his seat. "Be right back—going to wash my hands."

"Please tell me his bike is a Harley, not a Schwinn Sting-Ray with a banana seat," Bo says.

The Big Guy shakes his head. "I hope to god he rode his bike because that's what he likes to do, not because he can't afford a car."

"He's got a car," Kissick says. "I've been in it and it's got a bike rack."

"Does he think he's saving the world by riding his bike?" Bo asks.

"If anything, he's saving himself. It's part exercise, part mental health," Kissick says.

"Between us," Bo whispers to Kissick, "I keep our scrivener in my back pocket as a suicide bomber in case we need to buy a vowel or an action figure. No one is going to stop a white man in Dockers from entering any building in America."

"What makes you think he'd offer himself up like that?"

"He's got no one in his life and he would die a hero. And if he wasn't inclined, I'm pretty sure I could make him want to die, if you know what I mean . . ."

"You're the scariest man I've ever met," Kissick says. "Terrifying."

"I take that as a compliment," Bo says.

The Big Guy taps his glass to bring them to attention. "Before we get too far, I just want to thank you for your effort and your willingness to embark upon this endeavor. We come from different places and different experiences, but I take great comfort in knowing that we share a common goal."

"It certainly was a pain in the ass getting out here. Who picked this place?" the judge wants to know.

"I did," the Big Guy says.

"It's far from everything," the judge says.

"I used to come here with my parents," Eisner says, taking his seat at the table.

"Back in the day, when the restaurant was downtown, I used to see Bob Haldeman there with Ehrlichman. You know what I loved about Haldeman?" Metzger says.

"I can't wait to hear this," Bo says.

"He was an ad man, worked at J. Walter Thompson for a long time. I met him with my dad when I was a kid. He was an advance man for Ike's reelection and my dad really liked Ike."

Bo laughs. "I remember the button . . . I Like Ike."

"Pete Peterson came up with that at Market Facts. But it was Irving Berlin who wrote the song for the 1952 campaign," Metzger says.

"The same Pete Peterson who ran Lehman and then started Blackstone?" the judge asks.

"The same," Metzger says.

"You boys are forgetting that Ike was drafted to run for president, the only time in US history that a private citizen was delivered to the Oval Office like that," Bo says.

The General enters. "Apologies for my tardiness. I was scouting the perimeter, spotted something of interest." He sets his Steiner binoculars on the table. "Spotted a red-breasted merganser not far from the front door."

"Is that the enemy?" Kissick asks.

"It's a duck," Bo says.

"Correct," the General says. "And I am pretty sure I spotted a saw-whet owl."

"Hmm," they all say, having no idea what that might mean.

"The saw-whet is a very secretive animal, but I am damn near positive. I'm gonna take that as a good sign."

"Has anyone looked at the menu?" Eisner asks.

"I was waiting for the doctor to arrive," the Big Guy says.

"Are we getting one course or two?" Kissick wants to know.

"Whatever you feel like," the Big Guy says.

"Sharing or every man for himself?"

"Kissick, just pick what you want. You don't need to interview everyone," the General says. "Trust yourself. You can do it."

"Two courses," the Big Guy says.

"Does someone want to remind me where our beloved is?" Bo asks.

"Charlotte?" the Big Guy asks.

"Tony," Kissick says.

"He's working," the Big Guy says.

"At the White House?" Bo asks.

The Big Guy nods.

"Is he packing for Bush or unpacking for Obama?" Bo asks.

"He's doing his job," the Big Guy says tersely.

"What's with the ring boxes?" Bo asks. "We getting engaged?"

"The boxes are my gift to you," the Big Guy says. "We'll open them at dessert when we have our little naming ceremony."

"Remind me, what is it Jews do when they mourn?" the judge asks.

"They rend their clothes, tear them in anger and shame. It's a Bible thing—not just Jews," Kissick says.

"Whatever it is, it happened to me this morning. I rended my ass pocket on a rough wooden hanger and no one at the Four Seasons could stitch me up in time." He lifts his suit jacket and flashes his substantial ass. "My shorts are showing."

"There's a word for that," Metzger says.

"Pornography," the Big Guy says.

"For when everything goes wrong," Metzger says.

"Recount?" Bo offers.

"Resistentialism: the spiteful behavior of inanimate objects, usually electronics, but it can be applied to anything if there are enough causative elements," Metzger explains.

"I might just get two appetizers; I'm trying to watch my weight," Kissick says. "I doubt any of you are aware, but we accountants get a paunch—a donut of fat that's very unhealthy."

"Don't show me your donut," the Big Guy says.

"I can't get rid of it. It's the job, sitting at a desk all day. I maintain that accountants digest things differently."

"Apologies, apologies," Dr. Frode says, arriving at the table. "Traffic." Frode's beard has grown substantially since they last saw him. It's so long that he has it divided into several sections with rubber bands and there's sort of a bun or bulb at the end.

"Maybe it's a disguise?" Eisner whispers.

"It's certainly not sanitary," Kissick says.

"It must have some kind of special meaning," the Big Guy suggests.

"Skegg," Frode says. "That's what the beard is called. All Norse gods have them except one."

"Which one is that?" Bo asks.

"Loki. If you read the *Codex Regius*, it becomes clearer. Personally, I enjoy the Njáls saga more—a blood feud, family honor, a tale rife with omens, dreams, and the struggle against one's fate. When I'm not in the lab splitting atoms or tracking hot zones and bioterrorist activities, I like a bit of escapism."

"Who doesn't?" the Big Guy says.

Bo checks his watch, a vintage Rolex Submariner. "T-minus fifteen on the Mall." He shoves a white corded earbud into his left ear and fiddles with something inside his jacket pocket.

"You missed the debate. One course or two?" the judge recaps.

"Two courses," the Big Guy says.

"There's a lot of duck on the menu," the judge says.

"They have a Baked Alaska," Kissick says.

"You're looking at dessert already?" the Big Guy asks.

"I like to back into my decisions," Kissick says.

"You just said you were watching what you eat."

"Is Baked Alaska fattening?"

"More sugar than fat," the doctor says.

"What about wine?" Kissick asks.

"There's a Gevrey-Chambertin pinot," the Big Guy says. "I've had it before, nicely textured, grippy with soft, firm tannins . . ."

"You're not fucking this wine, you're drinking it," Bo says. "I hate when you boys start a pissing game with the wine. I'm the man who grows grapes; let's go American with Shafer Hillside Select. Judge, do you care to weigh in on the decision?"

"Nope."

The Big Guy leans over and asks Eisner, "Have you talked to Meghan lately?"

"Yes."

"Been quite a time," the Big Guy says, testing the waters to see if Eisner knows what the family has been going through.

Eisner nods. "We chatted about liminal identity on New Year's Eve."

"Fine thing," the Big Guy says. He has no idea what liminal identity might be.

"We talk mostly in pictures." Eisner pulls out his phone and shows the Big Guy a photo he's not seen before: Charlotte riding in the new car, top down, waving at the camera—smiling.

The Big Guy chuckles—a self-defense mechanism. He's glad that Charlotte and Meghan are in touch but feels left out. He looks again. Charlotte looks relaxed—satisfied. He assumes Terrie took the photo.

"Did Meghan tell you about riding her horse down on the Mall?"

"She did." Eisner shows the Big Guy another picture: Meghan on Ranger, the US Capitol in the background, and a message—"January 2, 2009. Off to a good start."

"Let's hope it stays that way; 2008 was pretty crappy. We had a rough patch just after the new year; she said her sense of self had been shattered. When I took her back to school, she asked for 'space to process things.' Both she and Charlotte are 'processing.' But I assume you already know that?" The Big Guy looks at Eisner, who nods tentatively. "It's okay. I'm glad she talks to someone."

"Can we please order?" Kissick asks, as he flags the waiter. "Does Dover sole have a season?"

"At this time of year, ours comes from Alaska," the waiter says.

"I'll have the sole," Kissick says. "Can they prepare it without butter?"

"No butter at all?" the waiter asks.

"Olive oil if necessary," Kissick says.

"I'll have the bouillabaisse," the judge says.

"Make that two," the General says.

"Any allergies?" the waiter asks.

The General pulls his EpiPen from the side pocket of his tactical pants and puts it on the table. "We're good," he tells the waiter.

"Chateaubriand," the Big Guy says.

"Same," Metzger says.

"The last couple of months have been informative," the Big Guy says to Eisner. "I kept saying that the election was a wake-up call, but it wasn't just about McCain losing and the failure of the Republican Party. It was bigger; I'd drifted into some strange old-fart coma and lost sight of everything. I didn't see that Charlotte and Meghan were struggling. For years I thought I was taking care of Charlotte, but it turns out that she was trapped, she couldn't see past me to clear sky. I was living in my own world, built on the Ping-Pong table in my basement. Not only was I not seeing them for who they are, I was actively denying them their own story. It was all about me, my need to protect myself. What an ass I am."

"It's happening," Bo says, cutting into the conversation. "John Paul Stevens is giving the oath to Biden."

The doctor orders cooked vegetables.

"If you are vegetarian," the waiter suggests, "the chef can prepare something else. He uses some mushrooms, maybe some leeks, whatever he has back there that is good."

"Excellent," Frode says. "If you don't mind, I'll just go into the kitchen and talk with him myself." He gets up and heads toward the kitchen. The waiter, stumped, folds Frode's napkin and puts it back in place.

Bo mutters something under his breath, not entirely clear, but akin to, "If the doctor was any weirder, he'd be wearing an aluminum-foil cap."

"For all you know, next year he'll be making millions selling foil caps," Kissick whispers to Bo.

"Everybody and their mother is down there: Jimmy Carter, GHW, Clinton, even Hillary, not as the loser but as a former first lady; that's gotta sting," Bo says.

Kissick tunes in to the fact that there is a white cord running from Bo's ear into his jacket pocket. "Are you listening to something?"

Bo makes a face is if to say, Duh. "I've got it live on my Zenith Royal, same one I've been listening to ball games on for more than a quarter century. I like things that can be relied upon."

Kissick smiles. "I love you and I hate you. What station?"

"WTOP."

"I spoke to W," the judge says to the Big Guy. "He mentioned that he saw you, that you came by to help say goodbye to the place. Between us, I'm pretty damn sure he's the last Bush who's gonna be in the White House for the foreseeable future—I really can't see Jeb on Pennsylvania Avenue."

"Jeb is a nice guy," the Big Guy says.

"My point exactly," the judge says.

"Roberts is giving the oath," Bo says. "They're off schedule by five minutes."

"Is it like an execution? There's a schedule?" Kissick asks.

"It's an event," Bo says. "With a timeline."

"Maybe the doctor ordered vegetables because he keeps kosher. Maybe he's a Jew," the judge says to Kissick.

"He's not Jewish," Kissick says. "He's Asatru. It's a Nordic religion of peace and tolerance—like Unitarian."

"You'd be surprised who's a Jew," the judge says.

"He just took the fucking oath of office and he used his middle name—Hussein," Bo says. "Holy fuck."

The sound of applause leaks out of the kitchen. "I don't suppose that has to do with the doctor," Eisner says.

"Barack Hussein Obama, who'd a thunk it." The Big Guy shakes his head.

Frode returns to the table with a plate that looks like a painter's palette. "Samples of the sauces." He dips his finger into one and tastes it. "I'm a terrible cook but I enjoy dabbling."

The Big Guy is focused on Eisner. "Did you hear anything from her today? Are they watching live from the Academy?"

"She's there with Tony," Eisner says.

"She's where?"

"There. At the inauguration."

"Really?"

Eisner pulls up a photo on his phone: a selfie of Meghan high up on the steps of the Capitol and another looking out toward the Washington Monument. The crowd is in the tens of thousands, maybe hundreds of thousands.

"Sweet land of liberty," the Big Guy says, shaking his head in awe. "You never know where you're gonna end up."

"'When you come out of the storm, you won't be the same person who walked in. That's what this storm's all about.' Murakami from *Kafka on the Shore*," Eisner says.

"Throw me to the wolves and I will return leading the pack," the Big Guy says.

"Something like that," Eisner says.

Bo is busy listening to the US Marine Band. He presses the earbud deeper into his ear.

The waiter is hovering, waiting to pour the wine. The first pour is into Bo's glass. He swirls the wine around the glass a few times before tasting it.

"It's tight," Bo says to the waiter.

"That's how I like it," the judge says. "Tight when I start, then over the course of the meal, it should open up."

Bo shrugs. "Go ahead and pour, and open a second bottle if you would, thanks."

The waiter starts to pour each man a glass, but the General covers his. "Bring me a ginger ale. This is a sober occasion in my world. A lot of people think someone might take a shot at him. Even if they miss—it would be a problem."

"Like pulling the pin out of a grenade," Bo says, looking at Eisner.

"Every time you say something like that, you look at me; it's creepy," Eisner says.

The Big Guy shakes his head. There's only so much he can take in at once. "Let me see those photos again," he says to Eisner.

Eisner shows the Big Guy the stream of photos from Meghan this morning.

"I didn't want to violate Meghan's trust, but I thought you should know," Eisner says.

"Good man," the Big Guy says. "I'll tell you a secret, history is not fixed. It's fluid. That's what we're seeing right now."

"Speaking of the swearing-in, I heard Robert Gates is the designated survivor," the judge says.

"Odd choice," Kissick says.

"Isn't it?" the judge says. "Both parties keep a list of options, and then they give out the role as a prize, a parting gift."

"Tony told me that Obama calls Gates Yoda," the Big Guy says.

"At the moment, Yoda is deep inside the mountain talking to himself," Eisner says.

"Is that something we should be talking about, Tony and Obama? Is it going to be a problem?" Kissick wants to know.

"It's not a problem," the Big Guy says. "Tony's cards are close to his chest."

"Closeted," Bo says. "That might be the better word for Tony's cards."

"I know him better than anyone, including my wife, and I trust him with my life. He is working for the Office of the President, not for Obama personally. Having someone in-house is good for us."

The food arrives at the table, delivered by three waiters with the maître d' hovering.

"Anyone want to say a prayer?" the Big Guy asks.

"Yeah," Kissick says. "I hope to hell we get out of this alive."

"You wanna be more specific about what *this* is?" the judge asks.

"The next four years."

They raise their wineglasses. "To life!" the Big Guy says.

After a few minutes of lip-smacking oohs and aahs and pass the salt, the doctor asks for more sauce. He may only eat vegetables but he likes to drown everything in sauce. There is more talk about medicine. "Ask me anything, just not about your old knobby knees," Frode says.

"How conceivable is it that someone would launch an attack on the food supply?" Kissick asks.

"More than conceivable," the doctor says. "We're constantly evaluating foodborne illnesses from *E. coli* to staph bacteria, salmonella, and hepatitis A. Other diseases, too: dengue fever, cholera, meningitis, bubonic plague, and enterovirus D68—that's one to keep an eye on, first isolated in California in 1962. It's rare but on my radar."

"A man after my own heart," the General says.

"What does the D68 do?" Kissick asks.

"It's paralytic in nature," the doctor says.

"I'm eating," Bo says. "Can't a man enjoy his lunch?"

"My father had polio," the judge says. "He wore a metal brace on his left leg. That's how the family came to Texas; it was supposed to cure him. I guess it did. He lived—but with a limp."

"The stuff we're talking about is only part of the picture," the doctor says. "Places that were frozen long ago will melt; things that have been dormant will come back to life. The permafrost isn't so permanent; animals that died of diseases, their bodies frozen, will reanimate."

"Are you talking about dinosaurs?" Kissick asks.

"Not dinosaurs, but maybe reindeer. In the early twentieth century, more than a million reindeer died from anthrax."

"I thought reindeer were made-up," Eisner says.

"Anthrax is one, but there are worse; take for example 1918—"

"That's when my father was born," the judge says.

"In 1918 flu wasn't even a reportable disease, but in October 1918, 195,000 people in the United States died in one month. It was a world-wide pandemic, first reported in Kansas. It came in two waves; the first wave was mild compared to the second."

"You're making my skin crawl," Kissick says.

"I'll take it further. That flu was of avian origin."

"Meaning?" Kissick asks.

"It came from birds and mutated to infect humans," the doctor says. "Avian also means migrates. Kansas is on a bird migration route. I'd say that three-quarters of emerging infectious diseases are of animal origin. A couple of years ago some NASA scientists revived bacteria that had been in a frozen pond for 32,000 years. Your wine there is, what, about five years old. Imagine something 32,000 years old; last year they got a bacterium that was eight million years old and another that was 100,000 years old. And that's just the tip of the iceberg." He laughs at his own joke. "Like it or not, there's shit on the horizon. The question is, what will be weaponized? We've got freezers full of security-sensitive microbes and toxins." The doctor pauses, considering what he's about to say. "Something to think about is how you realize a goal . . ." He doesn't so much finish the sentence as drift off, leaving the word goal to linger.

"What kind of a goal?" Kissick asks.

The doctor pauses before speaking. "We've figured out how to keep people alive for a long time, how to manage illnesses. We can't take care of everyone. There are a lot of people just sucking the systems dry."

"The question is, what do you want the outcome to be?" Bo says. "Why is that not clear to all of you?"

"It's pretty clear," Metzger says.

"Is it?" Kissick asks. "We can't go around killing people."

"Why not? Give me one goddamned reason why not," Bo says.

"Because we're civilized," Kissick says.

"Fine," Bo says. "I was just curious about what you were going to say. I bet you don't realize that sometimes I say things to be provocative."

"The things you say can be taken as reflections of your truths," Kissick says. "Something to keep in mind."

Kissick turns to the doctor. "Killing people, am I right? That's the subtext of what you're talking about. Euthanasia, assassination, or, to use another word, genocide."

"I didn't say that," the doctor says. "Management of the herd is a talent. There are times one needs to make decisions to ensure adequate resources or control the spread of disease."

"In a crisis, there's a hierarchy to who gets care," the General says.

"It goes to those most likely to survive," Eisner says.

"Or to those who can foot the bill, let's be real," the judge says. "Folks with cash go to the front of the line."

Bo interrupts, repeating the words he's hearing in his earbud. "'What is demanded, then, is a return to these truths. What is required of us now is a new era of responsibility.'"

"Have you been listening the whole time?" Kissick asks.

"To them or to you?" Bo asks.

"Them?" the judge asks.

"Yes," Bo says. "It would be wrong for us not to be listening."

"I feel it's my obligation as a man of the . . ." the General says, revealing that he has the other half of Bo's headset in his ear.

"Cloth?" the judge suggests, still focused on his ripped pants.

"Armed services," the General says.

"Are you armed?" Kissick asks anxiously. It never occurred to him that the General could be armed.

"I would be lying if I denied it," the General says. "I've always got something on me. I'm sure you know about the Law Enforcement Officers Safety Act, which allows us to carry while off duty."

"What exactly is it that you do in the military?" Kissick asks.

"I can't answer that, but it is considered a skill set that goes beyond the average citizen."

"Special powers?" Eisner asks.

"More like a heightened awareness of where the dangers lie," the General says.

"An attorney friend of mine and I talk about this kind of thing all the time," the doctor offers.

"Who do you talk to?" the judge wants to know.

"And what do you talk about? It sounds to me like you're in the netherworld between the right to die and the right to bear arms," Metzger says.

"We talk about the limits of the law, of authority, and our frustration. We are very frustrated."

"Who is your friend?"

"Bill Barr. He and my wife are in a Bible study group together."

"You live in McLean?" Bo asks.

"Bethesda," the doctor says. "Bill is in McLean. I like to be close to the office."

"I know Barr," Bo says. "I always thought he was kind of a dick."

The doctor shrugs. "Sometimes it's hard to have friends when you're smart and powerful."

"Some of the dickiest guys I know are very smart," Bo says. "So, are you telling us that you and Barr talk about weaponizing viruses and bacteria?"

"No," the doctor says. "We talk about how we see the world. The view from on high."

"Did you tell me that you like to hunt?" Kissick asks.

"Yes," the doctor says.

"So you're not eating vegetables because you're opposed to eating meat?"

"Correct," the doctor says.

"How can you be a doctor, whose job is to save lives, and also be a hunter?" Kissick wants to know.

The doctor looks at Kissick as though he were a moron. "Animals are not human. If I kill it, I eat it."

"One of these days you'll have to come see me down in Texas and I'll take you to my club, the International Order of St. Hubertus. We love to hunt."

The doctor doesn't acknowledge the judge's invite; he just keeps talking. "The US food supply is dirty; this can't be breaking news to you. I don't eat beef or pork, and the chicken is shot up with antibiotics and hormones. At my own home, I eat meat. I have my own suppliers, local farms."

The judge repeats his invitation. "Let me know when is good for you and I'll have you down. We don't encourage outside visits but you'd fit in well."

The doctor looks at the judge and grunts like a wild boar.

"I don't want to take you away from the brilliance of talking about foodborne bacteriological weapons while we're eating, but down there on the Mall, things are moving quickly and we have some things to get done today," the Big Guy says.

"How can a physician talk about culling the herd?" Kissick asks. "That's what I'm hearing. Am I right?"

"It's really a public health issue or one for the ethicists," the doctor says.

"I suggest we stay focused," the Big Guy says. "What brings us here today is that the jig is up. If we don't press start, the things we value most will become unrecoverable. Stepping into the unknown requires courage. That's what Tony was trying to tell us in Palm Springs."

Bo shakes his head. "Tony was trying to come out of the closet. He wanted to tell us that his boyfriend is a Black trauma surgeon."

"Did he tell you that?" Eisner asks.

"He was trying to tell us but we didn't give him the space," Bo says.

"I'm sure that's what someone is saying right now on the Capitol steps," the judge says.

"Actually," Bo says, "that moment has passed, along with Aretha Franklin singing 'My Country 'Tis of Thee,' a poem, and the benediction. Now the US Navy Band is playing 'The Star-Spangled Banner.'"

"Thank you for the update," the Big Guy says.

The sound of applause leaks through Bo's earbud.

"Tell me your volume is all the way up," the judge says.

"It's not. However, many millions of people are down there today; they're celebrating."

Tuesday, January 20, 2009
Washington, DC
The United States Capitol
11:30 a.m.

They have been out in the cold for hours. "It's not for the faint of heart," Tony says.

"Nothing is," Meghan says.

Along the way, there have been checkpoints: metal detectors, sniffing dogs, the flashing of the laminated IDs they are wearing on lanyards around their necks and the small pins on the outside of their overcoats.

"It has a chip in it," Tony says, tapping the pin. "They know who is wearing it and where the pin is."

"Do you know who they are?" she asks.

"Secret Service, FBI, and then some."

Tony's credentials give them a good vantage point and, more important, access to a bathroom in the Capitol building, which Tony jokes is really where the power rests.

"It's all about who gets to pee where and which seats get blankets on account of the twenty-eight-degree temperature."

The charge in the air, and standing witness to history, keeps them going despite the bone-chilling cold. It's not where Meghan expected to be, and yet here she is.

As people make their way to their seats, there is a lot of waving hello, fist bumps, and salutes as if people were tipping their hats.

"It's amazing, isn't it?" Tony says.

"Remember how I said voting seemed rinky-dink. This is the exact opposite."

"Indeed," Tony says. "But it is the power of what happens at the polls that gets us to this moment."

"How many inaugurations have you been to?"

Tony laughs. "Are you trying to make me feel old? This is my sixth. My seating has improved noticeably over the years."

Ten days ago, Tony called Meghan and asked if she wanted to join him. "Do you need a note for school?"

"I'm eighteen," she said. "I am an adult, and besides, the headmistress owes me. Shouldn't be a problem." They didn't discuss whether or not to ask her parents for permission.

"Why didn't William want to join you?"

"They scheduled a case for today that's complex and the surgical team didn't think it should be delayed."

"Did he tell the patient, 'Man, you're lucky because I was supposed to be at the Capitol today'?"

"The patient is a woman and I doubt he said anything. Look," Tony says, nodding toward the main platform. "See that guy making faces? That's Mr. Confident, Rahm Emanuel, Obama's chief of staff. I don't like him. Too big a personality for the job."

"Are we going to talk about the elephant in the room?" Meghan asks.

"That we're Republicans at a Democratic inauguration?" Tony says jokingly. "Or that I haven't seen you since you met Irene?"

"Did you ever meet her?"

"No. I didn't know about her until it became a problem."

"You mean until she got pregnant."

Tony nods.

"It's all very weird, like I'm falling through space, splintered. I can't talk to Mom or Dad about it because they clearly have their own feelings about the whole thing. It's like I'm in a thousand pieces. I'm Humpty Dumpty on the floor and have to reassemble myself from scratch by asking not just who I am but who do I want to be."

In the background, a military band plays brassy celebratory tunes.

"Can we talk about the other elephant?" Meghan asks. "About why you didn't tell me that you were gay?"

"Of all the times I imagined how we might have this conversation, there was never this version," Tony says, gesturing to all that is going on around them.

Meghan looks at him. She's not going to let him off the hook.

"One doesn't talk to children about sex," Tony says. "End of story."

"It's not about sex, it's about love."

"That's a very modern idea. Spoken with the naivete of youth, for which I adore you. But no."

"It's also about honesty."

"Sweetie, being gay was a crime in Washington, DC, until 1993. People went to jail for it, lost their families; careers were ruined; people were killed."

"That's crazy."

"Crazy and true. During the Lavender Scare in the 1950s and 1960s, men and women were interrogated and asked, 'Do you identify as homosexual?' The son of Lester Hunt, a Democratic senator from Wyoming, was arrested for soliciting sex. And the Republicans decided to make a thing of it. They tried to get Hunt to resign from the Senate, which would have given the Republicans the majority."

"That's not cool," Meghan says. "What's that saying about the sins of the father being visited upon the sons?"

"This was the 'sin,' if you even want to call it that, of the son being used as blackmail against the father. You know what happened?"

"No idea."

"Senator Lester Hunt shot himself in the head in his office right in that building behind us with a rifle he brought from home."

"That's awful."

"Stewart McKinney, a Republican congressman from Connecticut, died of AIDS in 1987 while in office. And so did Freddie Mercury, Mr. We Will We Will Rock You, and Rock Hudson and the guy who played the father in the TV show *The Brady Bunch* and tens of thousands of others."

"That's all really bad," Meghan says. "But not telling me also meant that despite knowing you all my life I never really knew you." She starts to tear up. "There's a difference between secret and private."

"Some things are generational."

Meghan shakes her head. "Secrets cause damage. Look at my mother."

Tony says nothing. He adores Charlotte.

"Have you seen this?" Meghan shows Tony a photo of Charlotte and Terrie. "She's hiking in Zion with her new girlfriend."

Tony is surprised. "You think they're girlfriends?"

Meghan shrugs. "Something's putting that smile on her face." She shows Tony a text from Charlotte: "New Year's PS—One thing I've learned along the way, keep your eyes on the horizon. Don't focus on what you think others want you to be, focus on who you want to become."

"That's very sweet," Tony says.

"It's sweet. But it doesn't sound like her—too normal."

They both laugh.

"And speaking of something that doesn't make sense." Meghan pauses. "How can you be gay and be a Republican?"

"Rest assured, you're not the first to ask. One shouldn't speak in generalizations, but we all live with contradictions of one kind or another."

In the background, speeches are being given.

"The fact that Rick Warren is giving the invocation is one of them," Tony says.

"How did you meet William?"

Tony pauses for a moment. "In a bar downtown. About ten years ago."

"Are you going to get married one day?"

Tony scoffs. "Doubtful."

"Why not?"

"I don't know. It just seems unlikely."

"Because you don't want to?"

"I don't even know why." He pauses. "You might think because I'm gay that I'm automatically radical, but as you know, I am quite old-fashioned, like a colonial old lady."

"Knitting by the fire with wool you spun yourself?"

"Doing crossword puzzles with a magnifying glass. Take a peek over there."

"John McCain. He showed up."

"They all show up."

"It must be hard for him."

"Feelings are not easy for the majority of the people up there. They don't stop long enough to have emotional lives."

Meghan makes a sad face. "What keeps them going?"

"Power," Tony says. "Proximity to power. When I first met Obama, he asked me, 'What do your people want?' I thought he meant Republicans. I must have looked confused because then he tapped his hand on his heart. And I knew that he knew I was gay and was asking me what gay people wanted from him. 'My people are your people, sir,' I said, and he smiled. 'It's true,' I said. 'We are all the same people.'"

"That is so not Republican of you."

"I'll tell you something I've never discussed with anyone."

"Okay." Meghan waits.

"The AIDS epidemic changed me. I saw men I'd known for years crusted with sores and wasting away. Their families refused to visit, refused to claim their bodies, refused to bury them. It was a side of human behavior that intellectually I knew was possible, but not humanly. It broke me. And I know it will happen again. It won't be the same thing, but something will turn American against American."

Meghan nods. "When I asked Dad about the common man, he said he never wanted to be the common man because the common man was a poor son of a bitch."

Tony laughs. "That's what he said?"

Meghan nods. "That and more."

"Economic status is one thing, but the struggles of different communities for recognition and equal rights need to be shared struggles. Progress isn't made in isolation."

"Now I'm worried," Meghan says. "You have devoted your life to furthering the conservative values of the Republican Party but on the inside, you're like what? A socialist?"

"No."

"Why are you involved in whatever it is my father is doing?"

"Do you know what your father is doing?"

"Not exactly. I know he is piling up money, building a 'war chest.' I hear him talking to people. Preserve and protect, those are the key words."

"I share your father's deep love for this country and concern about its future."

Meghan is all ears.

"Your dad and his friends call me a liberal."

"A chameleon," Meghan says. "Who changes with the temperature."

"Your father says that?"

"No, not Dad, but one of his friends. I don't remember his name."

"There are those who demand attention and others who do not need to be known," Tony says. "Perhaps it is safer to go unseen. Long ago I taught myself not to need the approval of others—that is the key to my success. Your father wants to reclaim his vision of America, to go back in time. What he doesn't accept is that we can't stop the clock. So the question is, with his set of values and point of view, where does one locate the future? I am watching, waiting for the moment to reveal itself."

"Like a superhero with a cape?" Meghan teases.

"Or a man with a mind of his own."

"But seriously, what are you doing in Washington? Who is the real Tony Armstrong?"

"This is where I belong, but when I was younger, I did think it would be fun to work at Buckingham Palace."

"Funny."

"Delusions of grandeur," Tony says. "By the time I was out of college, I had a job here and a mentor who told me, 'Kid, go where the action is. It doesn't matter what you believe or don't believe; put yourself in the action; that's how you start and the rest will figure itself out.' It was good advice. I've always been an outsider. I do my work with a sense of remove that gives me a long view of most situations. In DC there is a public view and a private view, and they are very different. I never wanted to run for office. To have a public life, you have to be charming and made of steel. People know everything about you and use what they know against you. But behind the scenes, if you have the ear of those in power, they take your call. Well, I find that very satisfying. Despite it being news to you, I've always known that I was—"

"Swiss," Meghan says.

"What?"

"My father used to say you were Swiss."

Tony cracks up. "Not Swiss. Swish. That's how they used to say someone was gay. He's swish. I love your dad. He was always so serious. His idea of a good time was going to visit battlefields. But he was real and so straight that my being gay meant nothing to him. 'I cannot imagine wanting to be in relation to another man's—'"

Meghan holds up her hand to stop him. "I don't need to hear more."

They pause. The crowd is silent as Chief Justice John Roberts swears Obama in on Abraham Lincoln's Bible. If ever air could be filled with import and dreams, it is at this moment. The crowd applauds and the band begins to play "The Star-Spangled Banner."

"The thing you have to remember," Tony says, "is that the world evolves: society, culture, what is normal, what is expected. All over the world people have had to fight for their rights and those fights aren't over. Personal experience changes people. Most white men are oblivious to discrimination because it doesn't happen to them. A lot of the people who are here today didn't expect to see a Black president in their lifetimes. Look around . . ."

A man walking by stops and shakes Tony's hand. "Are you here for outgoing or incoming?"

"I am simply present," Tony says.

"Ever the middleman," the guy says.

Meghan gives Tony a quizzical look. "Don't you have to take a stand? Is being present enough?"

"Bearing witness is a role. Working to shape and tell the story, writing yourself and 'your people' into history—that's the important thing."

"OMG," Meghan says. "I see Miley Cyrus and Demi Lovato."

"I'm assuming Miley Cyrus is not Cyrus Vance's granddaughter?"

Meghan doesn't get the joke.

"The thing William is going to be mad about is missing Yo-Yo Ma."

"Generational," Meghan says. "I have no idea what you're talking about. What is a Yo-Yo Ma?"

A little while later, Tony tugs on Meghan's coat. "Let's go."

"It's not over," Meghan says.

"Exactly." Tony leads Meghan through the crowd into the Capitol, down a hallway and then another, then down some stairs. The building is warm compared to the air outside. The sounds of the events outside are dampened.

"Where are we going?" Meghan asks.

"When the ceremony is over, President Obama will escort former President Bush to the helicopter and we will be there to say goodbye. We have time for a bathroom break if you need one."

"Thank you," Meghan says.

Tony and Meghan make their way through the Capitol to an area that is for the most part empty except for the Secret Service and military honor guards. In the background, they hear the whine of the helicopter's rotors outside.

"It's called Marine One when the president is on board and Executive One when the outgoing president is on board."

They wait silently. There is the echo of feet, almost like the sound of a horse's hooves; a procession approaches, the Obamas and the Bushes surrounded by a phalanx of Secret Service agents. Meghan sees Tony and the former president exchange a nod. The whine of the helicopter engine outside becomes louder. She starts to cry.

"Why are you crying?"

"I don't know," she says. "It's a lot. The Bushes are leaving. I really liked them. We had a good time at the White House."

Tony nods. "We'll have a good time again. I promise."

A few minutes later, as the Secret Service agents are ushering the Obamas through the building, the new president sees Tony and stops.

President Obama puts out his hand and pats Tony's shoulder. "How we doing so far?"

"Beautiful," Tony says. "If I might introduce my goddaughter, Meghan."

Meghan extends her hand. "Congratulations, Mr. President."

"Thank you," Obama says, shaking her hand. "Glad to have you with us."

It's not where she expected to be, and yet the experience brings the last two months full circle, an induction, an immersion, an evolution.

"That is crazy," Meghan says. "I just shook the president's hand like ten minutes after he was made president."

Tony smiles. "It's addictive; I will tell you that."

"Obama is a Lincoln man, sworn in on Lincoln's Bible," Meghan says. "My father is a Washington man. Did you know that when Washington was elected they didn't know what to call him? During the war, they called him General or Your Excellency. One official suggested Your Most Benign Highness. A senator suggested His Elected Highness. Someone else offered Your Majesty the President. And then Vice President Adams suggested His Highness, the President of the United States, and Protector of the Rights of the Same."

"Quite a mouthful," Tony says.

"After more debate, things settled down and Washington became the first president of the United States."

"Good story."

"Another interesting fact," Meghan says, as they make their way down more stairs and through the tunnels of the Capitol. "Washington was originally a British soldier. He fought for the British during the French and Indian War."

"I knew that," Tony says.

"He became disaffected when he didn't receive a royal commission and it became clear that England valued the Virginia militia less than British soldiers. So after he was demoted, he resigned. He was what they'd call a disgruntled employee."

"I didn't know that."

"It's like what you were talking about earlier, a personal experience or relationship to the issue. Washington was disappointed by how he'd been treated by the British Army, so as anti-British sentiment began to grow after the French and Indian War, his own disappointment in England's response to a decade of the colonies asking for representation in Parliament and an end to repressive taxation made it increasingly clear that things would not be peacefully resolved. There was the Stamp Act, then the Boston Tea Party, then Concord—"

"The shot heard round the world," Tony says.

"Exactly. Washington, the former British soldier, became the first commander in chief of the Continental Army. The takeaway is that sometimes in order to be an agent of change one must recant, volte-face, leaving behind what one formerly held to be true, whether that is one's politics or one's family."

The Big Guy is holding Eisner's phone, scrolling through the photos as they come in. "What a world we live in. It's like having your own reporter right there in the mix—eyes on the prize. That is really something. Despite all the drama, I'm optimistic about Meghan—and Charlotte too. Meghan is a smart and resilient young woman who knows history better than I do. As we went through this episode—for lack of a better word—I saw in her a new depth that I was never really sure was there. Substance. One never knows what kind of impact you're having on your kids, and given that my role modeling was less than ideal—maybe a little too self-involved—it's impressive. She is forging her own path. For her, history is not yet written."

Eisner nods. "Indeed, it is just the beginning. I gotta say that makes me happy and also a little jealous."

"Let us not be distracted," Kissick says. "We have secured office space at 1700 K Street. We are now also an LLC—or several LLCs. We are a 527 organization known as the Forever Athletic Association. The FAA."

"That's our name?" Bo asks. "It sounds just like the Federal Aviation Administration."

"Intentional misdirection," Metzger says.

"I wanted a benign moniker for now," Kissick says. "I have also dealt with the questions around banking. All set there."

"Strong work," the Big Guy says. "I'm thinking I'll get an apartment in town so I am closer to the epicenter and Meghan. Also, we need code names. I've taken Raymond Chandler for myself."

Bo laughs. "And what am I? Pinot noir?"

"If you like," the Big Guy says.

"I don't like," Bo says. "Call me Zenith."

"I'll stick with Colonel Mustard," the General says.

"Frode," Kissick says. "I have you down as Boner or Disco Queen."

"I'm not going to ask where those came from," Frode says. "I'll be Hot Waste. That's what we call radioactive debris."

"Fine," the Big Guy says. "You're Hot Waste. Tony is Myrna Loy, his choice."

"I might have wanted to be Myrna Loy," Metzger says. "She is from Chicago, after all."

"You know what the Secret Service calls Cindy McCain? Parasol. And Reagan was Rawhide," the General says.

The Big Guy looks at Metzger. "For you, I have Flak Jacket, Twizzler, or T. Rex."

"I'll go with the theropod," Metzger says. "Rex means king in Latin. I was always a fan of the band." He sings from "Bang a Gong," pounding the bass beat on the table.

"T. Rex it is," the Big Guy says. "And Eisner, the youngest among us, is Crayola. It's fitting. The crayon debuted in 1958 on *Captain Kangaroo*. The name comes from the French word for chalk."

"Fits perfectly," Bo says.

"Did I leave anyone out?" the Big Guy asks.

They point to Kissick.

"Apologies. You, my friend, are either Hijinks or Pawnbroker."

"Hijinks," Kissick says. "Now if I might get back into the substance of the matter."

The General clears his throat. "Before you go in too deep, Kissick, may I take just a minute?"

"I yield the floor."

"I'll keep it short. As I said to the Big Guy months ago, I want to assure you that times like this have been on our radar for many years. We have known that a decision day would come. It was never an 'if come' but a 'will come.' I have spoken with those above and we appreciate your investment in our preparedness. The kinship between us is real, and we will work with you to ensure that we are all on the same page and speaking the same language. Since the end of WW2, we have been placing high-ranking officers, foot soldiers, citizens, and surrogates not unlike yourselves in areas that include our military, banks, communication and transportation facilities, and other essential operations. We have charts of who is in charge and who gets the little white cards that get you deep into Raven Rock. I just want you to know we are signed on and good to go."

The Big Guy is tearing up. "Thank you, General, I am so moved."

Bo winks. "I knew you would deliver."

"I am only a surrogate," the General says. "I am a vessel, a carrier of these directives. That is what we must all remember—we are all citizen soldiers of one sort or another."

"Beautiful," the judge says. "Please tell your people we are ever grateful and they can count on us for continued support."

"About those little white cards, they're real?" Kissick asks.

"Indeed," the General says, pulling out his card and flashing it in Kissick's direction. It's plain white, thick, with something that looks like a lump in the middle.

"It looks like what you use to get crumbs off the table," Kissick says.

The General shrugs. "It's the 'get out of the nuclear war with your ass still attached' card. There are five thousand of these on the East Coast and equal amounts on the West Coast."

"Who gets them?" Kissick wants to know.

"Those deemed essential."

"Put my name on the list," the Big Guy says.

The General laughs. "I'll see what I can do. The Supreme Court justices have them—but just for themselves, no wives."

"Not a problem as far as I'm concerned," the judge says. "Being without the wife."

Bo goes into his earbud recitation drone again. "Now it's the replay. 'Hope over fear, unity of purpose over conflict.'"

The judge says, "He's not wrong when he says, 'Starting today, we must pick ourselves up, dust ourselves off, and begin again the work of remaking America.' We are looking at opposite sides of the same coin. Maybe there is comfort in knowing we are seeing the same thing. We are more awake than we've ever been."

"But when the question is asked—What is our dream?—you can be sure that the answer will be different," Kissick says. "We may live in the same country, but we are not dreaming the same dream."

"Are you using the word dream on purpose?" Metzger wants to know. "Do you mean dream in the Martin Luther King sense of the word?"

"That sounds like a question my wife would ask," the judge says. "She is a real Texas lady, lets you know what she thinks in that traditional Southern way. You think she's saying something nice, but she's really taking you down a notch. It's a skill. You just don't want to talk to her after six p.m. She'll fillet you; she can debone a man faster than a fishmonger."

"I was asking so I might understand you a little better," Metzger says.

"He's down there today in a goddamned wheelchair," Bo says.

"Who?" Kissick asks.

"Dick Cheney, the man the Big Guy has a man crush on. Even Franklin Roosevelt didn't let himself be seen in public in a wheelchair. Apparently, Dick hurt his back moving boxes the other day."

"Happens to the best of us; nothing ball cutting about that," the judge says.

"How aggressive are we going to be?" the doctor asks. "Once this thing gets going, will we even know we're at war?"

"Oh, Jesus, you're calling it a war?" Kissick asks.

"What do you want to call it, a coup?" Bo asks.

"Some people would say it's treason," the judge suggests.

"Some people would be wrong," the Big Guy says. "Extraordinary measures. If we don't keep the US of A on track we are less secure as a country, less prosperous and less impactful around the world. We must remain an economic and political superpower. Let us be clear—we are protecting and preserving democracy. It's a load of bull to pretend we have never asserted ourselves to maintain democracy and another load to claim that life is fair. Life is inherently not fair. Democracy is not fair. Factories don't ask workers what time they'd like to come in, banks don't ask customers how much interest they want. Not every opinion is equal. That shouldn't come as a shock."

"'A new birth of freedom,' it's from the Gettysburg Address," Bo says. "The good news for us is that this country has seen some weird shit. When they see more, it's all gonna seem normal. That's the trick, to make what we want look like the new normal."

"This is the quiet phase of a campaign that will return America to its roots and rekindle the dream that our forefathers had for a country where hard work pays off, where home and family are valued," Kissick says.

"Nice," Metzger says. "I'd hire you."

"What are the chances of Obama getting reelected?" the judge wants to know.

"If this election proved anything, it's that we don't have the control we thought we did," the Big Guy says. "There's always something to see when you're looking back. But looking forward, one must have a vision of one's own ability to conceptualize the future."

"'I love you back.' That's what Obama keeps saying." Bo pauses and stabs at his food. "Trust me, there are people who already know if Obama will go two terms."

"That's who I want to be in business with, the people who know," the judge says.

"Some of it will depend on how things unfold," the Big Guy says. "I'm not convinced that Obama's going to get any traction in the House and Senate."

"I was at dinner last week with the Turtle, among others, and can confirm that they're going to cockblock him at every opportunity," the judge says. "The man looks like an owl; you know he had polio when he was just two years old. He's charmless and as dull as dishwater but he commands. If you saw him anywhere else in the world, you'd think he was someone's cranky grandpa. But in DC, McConnell is a dangerous man, perhaps the most dangerous man because he cares about only one thing—power."

"Are we going to tell people that he's not from here?" Metzger wants to know.

"What does that mean?" Kissick asks.

"Africa," the judge says.

"Let's just say he wasn't born in the United States. Hawaii wasn't always in the United States; it was a latecomer," Metzger says. "And he's a Muslim."

"Is he?" Kissick asks.

"He identifies as Christian," the doctor says.

"His middle name is Hussein and people want to believe that he's not one of us. They don't want to say they're racists. This gives them an out. He's not American. He's a threat to our way of life," Metzger says, pouring himself another glass of wine.

"How so?" Kissick asks.

"Like a socialist," the judge says. "In Texas we don't like socialists."

"You know that's all made-up stuff," Metzger says. "Guys like me, we sit in our basements and make up shit that we think sounds plausible. Obama is no more or less American than the rest of us. Oh yeah, and Hillary Clinton's a lesbian."

"Everyone knows that's true," Bo says.

"Is it?" Kissick asks.

Bo jumps in. "Ted Kennedy had some kind of medical crisis and they just carried him out. They were eating seafood stew and something they called a 'brace of birds,' which sounds like roadkill. It's a lot, gentlemen. Even for the most stalwart of us, it's a lot." Bo looks at the men. "Between now and our moment, there will be multiple events, forces we can't yet anticipate that are not yet on the horizon. That's why we have these conversations, that's why we have to train. We have to train ourselves for what we know from history, from what the time we live in tells us, and for what our deepest and darkest imaginings of our future might be."

"Is this the earbud talking or is it you?" Kissick asks.

"It's me," Bo says. "I'm talking to you in my voice, not the earbud voice." He closes his eyes, retracing his words. "Those who wish us ill are evildoers; their minds are darker than most of you can imagine, so if you tell yourself whatever it is can never happen, I will tell you that not only can it happen, it likely already has happened and has been dealt with so as to keep it out of sight—"

"Should I be happy about that? Shit happens? Is it better for me to be left in the dark?" Kissick asks.

"Ninety-nine point nine percent of people can't handle the truth. They panic. They go apeshit. There's nothing subtle about it," Bo says.

"Another good reason that we keep ninety-nine point nine percent of people out of the loop," the doctor says.

"I'm going to keep bringing you back to what I've prepared," Kissick says. "This is a long-term plan to return America to itself. And we'll need talking points that are clear and concise." Kissick looks away from Bo and over at Metzger.

"I'm a salesman, not a novelist; I work in the short form," Metzger says. "Punchy phrases, haiku. 'McCain is ailin', chooses hockey mom Palin. You betcha, we're pucked!' That's a real one from a woman named Chaunce Windle of South Bend, Indiana; I read it and it lodged in my head."

"Our communications people will have a portfolio of outlets, radio, newspapers, and TV," Kissick says. "You can still party down under with Foxy Rupert, but the real news will be on platforms yet to be born."

"Exactly," Metzger says. "What twenty years ago sounded like science fiction is here now."

"What I want to know is what we're actually going to see. How will we evaluate our effectiveness, what are our guideposts, indicators of success?" the judge asks.

"Thank you for that," Kissick says. "Picking up where I left off, the rollout features a period of economic, social, and political unrest as well as destabilization and the naturally occurring failure of poorly maintained transportation and communication systems. Under the guise of protection, we will see the erosion of civil liberties and the rise of rogue non-politicians."

"I didn't know you had it in you," Bo says to Kissick. "I like it. I like it a lot."

"A couple of footnotes," Metzger throws in. "You may recall the New Right grew rapidly in the 1970s, now it's the tired Old Right. We're going to have to reinvigorate them as well as tap into a growing resistance— survivalists, iconoclasts, people who are living off the grid, conspiracy theorists, and unaffiliated others. We're going to bring them in and carry them forward."

"We will be the gathering place, the watering hole for the lone wolves." Kissick throws his head back and howls. "Sorry, I'm a little drunk. I really never drink."

"The more invisible we are, the more powerful. We do not connect the dots until we throw the switch, then the world will be awed by our power," the judge says.

"Invisible to all but one another," Bo says. "Security is important."

"Listen up, I'm giving you an actual tip," Metzger says. "Not just some hot air. Pay attention. Two words that are game changers."

"Game changers?" Bo asks.

Metzger starts again as though he were playing charades. He holds up two fingers. "Two words," he says, then pauses. "Big Data."

"Ah," Kissick says. "Exactly."

"Big Data," Metzger repeats. "There's stuff happening that you'll never see, a kind of modern mind control. You won't see it or feel it, but it is already dividing this country into the thinnest of pathological slices. Big Data," Metzger repeats again. "Right there, I just handed you the whole thing. We are on the cusp of extinction, about to become invisible. In this 'new' world, there are ways of communicating that are more effective than television ads and scented magazine blow-ins. The computer provides an experience so personalized that it will know what kind of shoes you're going to buy before you even know you need new shoes. It will know what you are going to eat for breakfast tomorrow before you finish lunch today. Supercomputers will collect, parse, and sell perversely specific information about you. You will be delivered news, information, food, clothing, and sex based on that data. That data will get smarter and soon you will be fed only what you have signaled you like to eat. And you won't know the difference. You will see only what you want to see and think that it is the whole picture. Nothing will indicate that there is another side to the story, an opposing opinion. You will think that what you are reading is true. You will think that you feel better, think that things are looking good, lining up, because you never see anything beyond your own reflection." He pauses and finishes his wine. "More important, and this is why I am telling you, you must force yourself to become more aware. You might think you are making a decision, changing the television channel of your own free will, but there is no free will. You will think you are in control, but everywhere you go, Big Data will be there before you. It's going to happen; it is already happening, and you have no idea of the size and scale and neither does anyone else save a few Silicon Valley unitards. By the time people catch on, the world will be so thick with propaganda that when China sends you a birthday card to your home address you're gonna think it came from your mama. When you call your mama and thank her, she's going to say, you're welcome, sonny, and think she actually sent it to you."

"I just came in my pants," Bo says.

"You farted," Kissick says. "I can smell it."

"Well, it felt good," Bo says.

Eisner flashes the Big Guy a pic from Meghan. Multiple pairs of feet, well-polished shoes on a marble floor. "She's trying to be discreet."

Bo grunts and jams his earbud deeper into his ear. "Now they are marching down Pennsylvania Avenue, two hundred and fifty horses, a mariachi band, and all the rest."

"It's scary stuff," the Big Guy says.

"I'm gonna add a little icing to the cake," the doctor says. "Memory. No one can hold a thought in their head. There is no memory, no context, and no history; and you wanna know why?"

"I do," the Big Guy says.

"Antidepressants. Ten percent of the population takes them, mostly women, and one of the side effects is that this affects memory. Millions more are hooked on opioids; the boys who make those pills are pulling in billions. And the black market is just as big. It's a public health epidemic. The herd is culling itself."

"While you're busy creaming in your jeans, they're in the White House setting up their voice mail and ordering stationery. Gentlemen, we need to get to work," the judge says. "It's been lovely, but I can't sit any longer. I've got to move."

"What you will see is domestic disturbance, chaos, a feeling of un-safety," Kissick says.

"Unsafety is not a word," Metzger corrects him.

"Imminent danger." The General scowls at Metzger.

"There will be outbreaks, which at first seem distant, but because they are reported on the news and posted on the internet, they will provoke others to take to the streets. There will be public 'punishments' like when the Pilgrims put men in the stockades; only this time the rap on the knuckles will be more like a knock on the head, a choke hold that knocks the breath out of someone. They will call it murder and take to the streets. There will be looting. It will move closer to home. It will instill fear. Fear itself is a good control; it makes people feel vulnerable and exposes tender spots. What starts somewhere on the West Coast will catch fire and spread to the middle of America, Phoenix, Chicago, Minneapolis. Then it will come closer to home and we will tap into that fear. There will be a roll-back of freedoms, the withering of local law enforcement, violence as spectacle with disregard for constitutional rights. As this begins to unfold, we won't know that this is what we dreamed of. It will look like chaos, like it can spin out of control; to be successful, we have to get to that edge. In the chaos there will be an opening, an opportunity," Kissick says. "It will look like a natural occurrence, a call for security, a return to our core values. That's our sweet spot. What we are launching is a slow-moving wave that will sweep across the country largely unnoticed until the American people have been decimated economically, physically, and spiritually. People will be ordered to stay home, not to congregate. It will be difficult to reach consensus about anything; no one will know what is fact and what is fiction."

"Between the plague and the toxic waste and the decentralization of the government, America will be a dead zone. People will start growing their own food supply because of shortages and contamination, and we will return to a barter system. Many will be unemployed and have no money," Frode says.

"Due to the failure of the poorly maintained roads, you won't be able to cross the bridge to go to grandma's house," Bo says.

"It will look like the world is going to hell," the General says. "Like we are in the grip of a behemoth, a monster that is physical and psychological. There will be ringing in the American ear—tinnitus, an alarm that cannot be turned off, a bell that cannot be silenced, a tintinnabulation that echoes across the country."

"Our economy will divide into those who have more and those who have nothing. On the world stage, the view of America will be cloudy. Our allies will be looking for that shining city on the hill, and they will see ravages of wildfires, catastrophic floods, illness, and death. It will look terrifying but not entirely unfamiliar, as much of what will happen will not be unique to America. A global iteration of this unrest is baked into the plan," Kissick says.

"How are you going to cause all these things that I'd call acts of God?" the judge wants to know.

"That's the easy part; we're already on target, thanks to climate change," Bo says.

"People around the world will become more tribal; borders will open and close like poorly played accordions, and mass confusion will result. The median citizenry will retreat and divide by money, race, religion, and sexual preferences. Fracture is part of the plan," Kissick says. "Out of chaos comes opportunity, and nostalgia for the America they once knew and loved."

"The great American experiment, in pieces on the floor," Metzger says.

"What was it Will Rogers said about democracy . . ." Bo pauses. "There was never one that didn't commit suicide."

"We're not here to self-destruct," the Big Guy says. "In fact, the opposite. We are here to protect and preserve."

"As we say in my field, sometimes you have to rebreak a bone to set it right. That's what we're doing," Frode says. "We are breaking the back of America to set it straight."

"I am proud to be with you," the judge says.

"Just don't let them call it the Last Stand of the White Man," Bo says.

"God help me if that's what it is, but it's a catchy title; you should use it for your memoir," the judge says.

"The United States Semiquincentennial is in 2026," the Big Guy says.

"The what?" Bo asks.

"The two hundred and fiftieth anniversary of the signing of the Declaration of Independence," Kissick says.

"Let that be our touchstone," the Big Guy says.

"That is eighteen years from now. You said the rollout would be in twelve to fifteen years," Eisner says. "I'll be old by then."

"Everybody gets old, Crayola; it can't be avoided."

"Some of us will be gone by then," the judge says.

"Everything takes longer than you think," the Big Guy says. "The plan needs time to mature."

"I just never thought I'd be that old," Eisner says. "I'll be fully AARP by then."

"My youngest graduates college that year," Kissick says.

"Meghan will be thirty-six in 2026," the Big Guy says.

"It's nice how you've got your lives all planned out," Bo says. "It's unfortunate that sometimes life is not so neat, plans change."

"July 4, 2026," the General says. "Consider it a date."

"Out of chaos—opportunity. When the moment comes, it will feel essential, urgent. It will be clear that America needs to reclaim its identity," Bo says.

The waiter brings a beautiful and enormous Baked Alaska with an enormous sparkling candle to the table and sets it down in front of the General. The waiter douses the dish with cognac and sets it on fire.

"When I was in the kitchen, I told them it was your birthday," Frode whispers to the General.

Between the sparks from the volcanic candle and the fire on the meringue, the whole thing looks like the Revolutionary War on a plate.

The men's faces are aglow with fire and a kind of giddy high.

"All the boys like the big candle," the maître d' says, coming over to the table. "I wanted to do something special. I am so happy to have you here."

"Merci beaucoup," the General says.

As sparks fly in all directions, one of the waiters rushes across the room with a dish of vanilla ice cream in hand and dumps the ice cream over the sparkler, which sputters to a stop. Everyone laughs.

"Not funny," the waiter says. "You could accidentally burn the house down."

"It is funny," the General says, serving Baked Alaska to the table. "It is very fucking funny."

"One final piece of business for today," the Big Guy says. "Gentlemen, open your boxes." The men each fumble to open the black-velvet boxes. There are oohs and aahs. Kissick pricks his finger with his.

"You're gonna have a long night's sleep now, princess," Bo says to him.

"You're doing it again," Kissick says. "Scaring me. Why? Why do you have to do that?"

"Because it's so easy," Bo says.

"These are pins made to reflect who we are and where our hearts lie."

"Why are there two more than needed?" Kissick asks.

"Good boy, always counting things," the Big Guy says. "The remaining ones are for Tony and a player yet to be named."

The men all nod.

"There's something else," the Big Guy says.

"Of course there is, like a secret handshake," the judge says. He's standing now behind his chair, doing calf stretches.

"I need to tell you a couple of things."

"I'm listening."

"There comes a point where there is no going back. There is no return after lunch today. We might know one another in passing, but we won't be having Thanksgiving together. We won't be making late-night calls; we won't be searching things on the internet; we will be leaving no mark. We'll have a way of contacting one another—that will be set up in the next couple of weeks, a contact, like a man on the surface," the Big Guy says.

"I want to get your addresses, permanent and any vacation homes, car VIN numbers, all of it," Bo says.

"For what?" the judge asks.

"For me," Bo says. "My belated Christmas gift to you is going to be secure communications and training."

"That concludes our meeting. I'm not sure when I will see any of you next. I assume that you're not hitting any of the balls this evening," the Big Guy says.

"The only balls I'll be in touch with are my own," Bo says. "But I will be at the prayer service on February fourth."

"As will I," the judge says.

"Me too," the doctor says.

"Wouldn't miss it," the General says.

"Are we pressing go?" the judge asks. "Is this the launch?"

"Affirmative," Bo says.

"We are good to go," the General says.

"Let's get it going," Metzger says. "Set the drinking bird in motion."

"Are we ready?" Eisner asks. "This is the formal observation of the beginning; we have ignition."

"We are ready," the General says.

"Green light go," Kissick says.

"Seal of approval," the General says.

"Authorization," the doctor adds.

"See you in Philadelphia in 2026," the Big Guy says. No matter what, he is going to have the last word.

"We have liftoff," Eisner says, as the men stand and raise their glasses.

"The Forever Men."

The Big Guy and Kissick are the last to leave.

"It went very well. Button pushed. Green light go," Kissick says, as the two men haggle over the tip.

"There are times when it is not worth being dryfisted," the Big Guy tells Kissick.

"And there are times when doing more than what is required draws undue attention," Kissick says, taking fifty bucks off the table.

"Narrow-souled," the Big Guy says. "No matter what good fortune comes your way, you remain a clusterfisted chincherd."

Kissick shrugs. "I am what I am. So, best-case scenario, how do you think this whole thing ends?" Kissick asks the Big Guy as they're walking out of the restaurant.

"My daughter will be the president of the United States. I am the maker and she is the bomb."

"That's not what I thought you were going to say."

"If I was predictable, it would be boring."

JACK

'Honest, uncompromising, and savagely funny'
Madison Smartt Bell

'A moving novel, and a very refreshing one. Jack is such an
engaging, attractive human being, it's a pleasure to believe in him'
David Foster Wallace

A. M. Homes's debut introduced the world to one of the freshest,
brightest voices in contemporary fiction. Sweet and sharp, *Jack* is a work
of great charm and insight from an extraordinary writer.

'The engaging, doggedly funny Jack is likeable from the first paragraph,
a good kid caught in circumstances too much for him. And in the
particulars of those circumstances, A. M. Homes touches upon
something unique' *New York Times*

'Homes's cool, controlled prose and knowing humour, coupled with
a knack for telling a good story, have earned her a legion of readers.
Tragi-comic, touching, superbly written *Jack* is yet another gem' *Uncut*

Also by A. M. Homes and available from Granta Books
www.granta.com

THE SAFETY OF OBJECTS

'American dreams for fitful, sleepless, suburban nights' *Scotsman*

'Homes couldn't be more deliciously named: she kicks over the doll's house and gives suburbanity a good shake. *The Safety of Objects* shows her defining her territory and her mastery of the deadpan perverse'
Daily Telegraph

A. M. Homes's first collection of short stories established her as one of the most provocative and daring writers of her generation. Putting an uncanny spin on the American dream, these stories are simultaneously strange and hilarious, outrageous and utterly real.

'Awesomely well written, in the sense of arousing fear and wonder in the reader . . . Here are all the things that even today, even in our frank outspoken times, we don't talk about. We think of them punishingly in sleepless nights' Ruth Rendell

'Wonderfully skewed stories . . . sharp, funny, and playful' *LA Times*

IN A COUNTRY OF MOTHERS

'Fiercely witty, frenetically paced, and seriously engaged . . . irresistible'
Madison Smartt Bell

'Very few writers push the envelope with such style and confidence'
Mark Haddon

When Jody's life stars unravelling she books an appointment with Claire – a prominent psychotherapist with secrets of her own. As the relationship between Jody and Claire deepens, the boundaries between patient and friend, love and compulsion, start to blur, and the two women find themselves drawn into a dangerous proximity.

'A. M. Homes is a very dangerous writer. This country of mothers is not one you easily enter, but it is also one you do not easily leave' *Washington Post*

'Exhilaratingly perverse' *New York Times*

Also by A. M. Homes and available from Granta Books
www.granta.com

THE END OF ALICE

'This is everything fiction should be – wrenching, disturbing and emotive' *Independent*

From the confines of his cell, a convicted paedophile receives letters from a sweet-seeming college student who has decided to seduce a boy in her neighbourhood.

Not for the faint-hearted, *The End of Alice* caused a major controversy on publication. Today it considered a classic of late 20th-century literature, a macabre and thrilling look at desire and its terrible consequences.

'Beware, gentle reader, the soothing aspects of life as we know it are about to be profoundly disturbed . . . With all the cunning and control of a brilliant lover, Homes takes us places we dare not go alone'
Los Angeles Times

'Homes instructs us about ourselves and shows us what we are blighted with, and cringe from, our compulsions, repressions, longings and glimpses of madness' Ruth Rendell

Also by A. M. Homes and available from Granta Books
www.granta.com

MUSIC FOR TORCHING

'Brilliant . . . I found myself rapt from beginning to end' *New York Times*

Paul and Elaine have two boys and a beautiful home, yet they find themselves thoroughly, inexplicably stuck. Obsessed with 'making things good again', they spin the domestic terrors of family life into a frenzy that soon careers out of control.

'Homes doesn't so much critique suburban American life as shoot it, stab it, chuck it in the boot of her car and drive it into a lake' *The Times*

'The prose is all ice; at any moment it will give way beneath your feet'
Ali Smith, *TLS*

'A sly, fast-paced and darkly comic novel about a suburban marriage that's going to hell, fast' *Wall Street Journal*

'Excellent' *Observer*

Also by A. M. Homes and available from Granta Books
www.granta.com

THINGS YOU SHOULD KNOW

'Funny and glinting and masterful, light as air, strange as a dream. Monstrous as truth; the real and classic thing' Ali Smith, *Guardian*

'The best collection of short stories I read this year . . . profound weirdness, unorthodox sex-acts, wonderful prose and the sense that you are being taken for a stout walk along the frontier of modern fiction' Mark Haddon, *Scotsman*

'This prose has teeth . . . You cannot shake a Homes story off your mind, you cannot rid yourself of the creeping unease it brings to your bedside table' Zadie Smith

'Homes's stories make you laugh out loud then finally break your heart. That's why she has and deserves her A-list status' *Observer*

'Insanely good' Dave Eggers

THIS BOOK WILL SAVE YOUR LIFE

'Very funny and engaging . . . it's packed with unexpected pleasures'
Guardian

Trading stocks and shares out of his beautiful LA home, Richard Novak
sees no one except his trainer, housekeeper and nutritionist, who delivers
regular supplies of macrobiotic low carb food. He is so out of touch with
his feelings that his life has slowed almost to a standstill. Following an attack
of inexplicable and excruciating pain that lands him in the emergency
room, Richard befriends Anhil, a doughnut shop owner. His solitary
routine broken, and his diet sabotaged by sugary baked goods, Richard's
dramatic emotional thaw begins . . .

'I think this brave story of a lost man's reconnection with the world
could become a generational touchstone, like *Catch-22* or *The Catcher in
the Rye* . . . And hey, maybe it will save somebody's life' Stephen King

'Consistently imaginative and very funny . . . Homes is excellent
on the inner workings of men' *Time Out*

'This book is a gentle, entertaining antidote to the over-achievements of
much of modern life . . . it shifts your perspective on life in the
most darkly entertaining way' *Observer*

'While Richard Novak has virtually nothing going for him, Homes
proves, with this stylish, compassionate tale of transformation, that she
has everything going for her' *Esquire*

THE MISTRESS'S DAUGHTER

'A compelling, devastating and furiously good book written with an honesty few of us would risk' Zadie Smith

'Gripping, salty, unnervingly good . . . a searing story packed with questions of identity' *Daily Telegraph*

On the day that she was born in 1961, A. M. Homes was given up for adoption. Her birth parents were a twenty-two-year-old woman and an older, married man. Thirty-one years later, out of the blue, they tracked her down. *The Mistress's Daughter* is a riveting account of what happened next.

'A fascinating, immensely moving story from a truly outstanding writer' *Elle*

'Utterly compelling . . . resonates for all of us who wonder how much of us is inherited, how much learned' *Evening Standard*

'Never less than gripping . . . this book is a fine thing' *Guardian*

'Hilarious, brutally heartfelt and uncompromising' *Independent*

'A. M. Homes's new memoir is a gripping tale of identity and family ties . . . beautifully structured and tautly written' *Harpers Bazaar*

'An electrifying memoir . . . Ruthlessly exact and unadorned, it is an endlessly generous, intelligent and compassionate account of one person's biological rage for the truth' *Irish Times*

Also by A. M. Homes and available from Granta Books
www.granta.com

DAYS OF AWE

'This prose has teeth. You cannot shake a Homes story off your mind'
Zadie Smith

'Ingenious' *New Statesman*

'Superb' *Daily Telegraph*

In tales that explore our attachments to each other, Homes peers beneath the surface of what it means to be a family and into our marriages and our secret histories. In these stories, a man is nominated for president while doing his weekly grocery shop with his family; old friends rediscover themselves and one another at a conference on genocide; a Los Angeles family, obsessed with surfaces, lives in fear of what lives below. *Days of Awe* is a visionary, fearless and outrageously funny work from a master storyteller.

'A distinctive black humour abounds. . . "Handle with care" is the warning that springs to mind' *Independent*

'Breathtakingly accurate satire and laser-cut portraits of American life from a seriously heavyweight author whose snapshots remain etched on the retinas' *Evening Standard*

'A satiric, surreal take on contemporary America. With her trademark acerbic wit, Homes dissects the psychodramas of her characters. . . Funny, outrageous, reflective and shot through with unexpected tenderness' Joanne Hayden, 'Best Books of the Year', *Irish Independent*

MAY WE BE FORGIVEN

WINNER OF THE WOMEN'S PRIZE FOR FICTION

'This is the great American novel for our time' Jeanette Winterson,
'Books of the Year', *Guardian*

Harry has always envied his younger brother George – a high-flying TV executive with two kids, a beautiful home and a covetable wife – but Harry also knows that George is a dangerous man with a murderous temper. When an adulterous kiss at Thanksgiving prompts a chain of unexpected events, George finally loses control, and the result is an act so shocking that the brothers are hurled into entirely new lives, ones in which they must both seek absolution.

'Wonderful, wild, heartbreaking, hilarious and astonishing . . . A piercing, perceptive and deeply funny novel about the nature of life, family and love' *Independent on Sunday*

'Homes's sharp, detailed prose teems with gloriously free, un-airbrushed life' *Telegraph*

'Horribly funny and unexpectedly uplifting . . . Sensational' *Daily Mail*

'The narrative intensity of Jonathan Franzen's *The Corrections* and the emotional punch of Siri Hustvedt's *What I Loved* . . . It's the best thing I've read this year' *Observer*

AN INSTANT PLAYSCRIPT

A YEARNING

RUTH CARTER

ADAPTED FROM YERMA
BY FEDERICO GARCÍA LORCA

London
NICK HERN BOOKS

TAMASHA PLAYS

An Instant Playscript

A Yearning, adapted from *Yerma* by Federico García Lorca, first published in Great Britain in 1999 as a paperback original by Nick Hern Books Limited, 14 Larden Road, London W3 7ST

Published jointly by Nick Hern Books and Tamasha Theatre Company

A Yearning copyright © 1999
Ruth Carter

Typeset by Country Setting, Kingsdown, Kent CT14 8ES
Printed and bound in Great Britain

ISBN 1 85459 450 8

A CIP catalogue record for this book is available from the British Library

SUPPORTED BY
THE NATIONAL LOTTERY
THROUGH
THE ARTS COUNCIL
OF ENGLAND

*Funded by an Arts for Everyone grant
from the National Lottery through
the Arts Council of England*